ACADEMY OF MODERN MAGIC COMPLETE COLLECTION

MAGGIE ALABASTER

DIGITAL MAGIC

1

———————————

"This is it," I said.

Some people think when you get told you've been admitted to a magical academy, an owl drops off a letter to your door. Or maybe a giant tracks you down to inform you of some latent magic ability.

Of course, that only happens in fiction. In reality, they tell you by text message.

"Well, what are you waiting for? Read it." That was my best friend, Jess, her eager brown eyes a stark contrast to her bleached blonde hair.

"What if I don't get in anywhere?" I asked. My heart raced so hard I was sure the whole coffee shop heard it. I tapped on my phone screen with my fingernail.

"You won't know if you don't look," she reasoned. "If you don't, I'm going to look for you." She made to grab the device from me.

I moved it out of her reach. "Hey, no you won't!" She would do it too, but I needed to see for myself first. "Fine, I'll look."

I waited another minute or two, took a deep breath and tapped the home button. The screen lit up. I selected "messages" and opened the text.

It read:

Ms Peyton Jane Chapel,

We are delighted to inform you of your acceptance to the Academy of Modern Magic.

Semester 1 commences on March 13.

Regards,

AMM administration.

My heart sank.

"You didn't get in?" Jess asked. "I'm so sorry. At least you can come to school with me."

I showed her my phone.

"Oh." She frowned. "Is that bad?"

"Well—"

I had wanted to attend the University of Arcana, or even the College of Advanced Magical Education. The Academy of Modern Magic was a fine school, but the others had offered education in all things paranormal for over five hundred years. In the paranormal community, as with most things in the world, prestige was everything.

Unlike the rest of the world, you can't apply to a magical tertiary institution. They choose the witch, wizard or shifter and their decision is final. Take it or leave it.

"Leaving it," meant going to a human university and learning ordinary subjects.

"It's not my first choice," I admitted. I put my phone down on the table and picked up my tea for a sip.

"But it's still a paranormal university." I didn't miss the note of envy in her tone. It jerked me out of my self-pity. In spite of being born into a magical family, Jess hadn't inherited a drop of ability. Nor was she a shifter. As paranormals went, she was normal.

"I'm sorry, I shouldn't be an ungrateful ass," I said.

"Yes, at least be a *grateful* ass," she replied.

I snorted a laugh. "I haven't decided to go yet. I could still study accounting."

"Pfft." She waved a hand and almost smacked her enormous costume jewellery ring on the table. "You would be bored out of your fucking mind. You're going to accept, you know you are. You're the daughter of the great Lucinda Knight-Chapel."

"All the more reason *not* to go," I grumbled. My mother was a prodigy. The first witch to graduate from the University of Arcana at the tender age of fifteen. Having grown up amidst adults who admired and feared her, she had never wanted, nor related to, her only child. I was an apology to my father for her always being so busy and rarely spending two consecutive nights under the same roof.

Jess shook her head and grinned.

"What?" I asked.

"I can't imagine you as an accountant, but if you go that way, can you do my taxes?"

"Fuck off," I said. I swatted her on the arm, then forced myself to be serious, at least for a while. "You really think I should accept, don't you?" I asked. This was the rest of my life we were talking about. My future in the human world, or the paranormal one. If I chose the human world, I would have to hide my ability to use magic. That would make tax time so much more tedious.

Jess put a hand over mine. "Peyton, I would have loved to go to university with you. We could have skipped lectures and gotten blind drunk together, talked about the guys and girls we screwed, and all that stuff. The truth is, I don't have your ability."

She raised a finger before I could respond. "I'm okay with that, I swear. I've had to deal with it for eighteen years. For a long time I wished I'd inherited my parent's magic, but it is what it is. Meanwhile, you have skills. You should learn how to use them."

She sat back and smiled. "We can always hang out on the weekends, right?"

My lips moved for a moment, but the words were hard to say. "AMA is in Sydney. It's too far to come back here to Melbourne for a weekend." I sighed with regret. "There's always text and video chat." We would probably see each other more than we did now.

"See, there you go." She nodded and picked up her coffee. "We'll be tired of each other in no time."

I laughed. "I'll never be tired of you." I would miss her terribly.

"What you going to tell Lex?" she asked.

I shrugged with one shoulder. I hadn't even thought about him until now. "I'll just tell him I'm going away to study. It's not like we're committed anyway." We were friends, fuck buddies, but that was all. He had made it clear he didn't want more and neither did I.

Jess nodded. "Imagine the hot paras you'll meet at AMA." She licked her lips. "Save one or two for me."

I was about to answer when a shadow moved past the corner of my eye. I turned to look, but nothing was there.

"What's wrong?" she asked.

I frowned and shook my head. "I thought I saw something scurry past. It was probably just an animal. I guess it moved too quickly for me to catch it."

She raised her eyebrows. "I didn't see anything." She leaned over the edge of the table. "It was probably a bird on the lookout for crumbs."

"It seemed bigger than a bird," I said slowly, then shook my head. "Maybe I imagined it. All this talk of going away has me on edge." In spite of that, I scanned the area. All I saw was people drinking their coffee and talking or staring at their phones. Nothing strange or out of place. Certainly no cats or dogs. Not even any children.

"It could be what you're drinking," Jess commented. "What self-respecting witch isn't addicted to coffee?"

I snorted at that. "Me. The stuff is terrible. Give me a good cup of tea any day." I picked up mine and sipped, but wrinkled my nose because it was too cool.

"See?" she said, "coffee still tastes good cold." She downed the rest of hers in a gulp.

"It still doesn't." I put down my mug at the same time a shadow passed on the other side of us. "Tell me you saw it that time?" I stood so fast my chair scraped on the floor underneath it.

Jess looked up at me, then down at the ground. "I didn't see anything. Maybe it's a," she lowered her voice, "magical thing."

I sat down with a plop and almost missed the chair. "It's possible," I whispered. Because whispering and looking around me wasn't suspicious behaviour *at all*.

I shook my head and sat up, as if I hadn't just been acting strangely. "I'm sure it's nothing to worry about," I said firmly.

A woman at the next table over gave me a funny look. I smiled back and did my best to seem like an innocent undergraduate on her summer vacation. Which I was... sort of.

She gave me a side-eye and looked away.

Jess choked back a laugh. "Smooth, Peyton, very smooth," she told me.

I rolled my eyes. "I try," I said. I pushed my dark hair back off my face and gave her a wry smile. "So, we were talking about hot university students?"

"Way to change the subject," she said approvingly. "You'll have to give me all the details."

"All of them?" I asked.

"Every. Juicy. One." She gave me a sly smile. "Come on, you know I'd do the same for you."

I barked a laugh, a little louder than I had intended. "No, you wouldn't. Please don't start now. I love you to bits, but I'm happy for your juicy details to remain private."

"As long as they stay juicy." She stuck her finger in her mouth and made a loud sucking noise.

I made a face. "It's like listening to my sister's sex life."

She pulled her finger out noisily. "You don't have a sister."

"Just you," I said warmly.

"Awww." She tilted her head. "I prefer you to any of mine." As the youngest of eight, Jess was lucky she wasn't the only one who couldn't do magic. Her two oldest brothers had no ability either. By the time her parents had her, they were accustomed to a mixed paranormal and non-paranormal household.

"For one thing," she added, "you're not as noisy as they are. Well, most of the time." She winked at me.

"When am I ever as noisy as seven other people?" I asked. I held up a finger before she could answer. "Never mind, I can guess. That was one time."

She grinned. "Sure it was. I bet you scream like that every time."

"I—" The table rattled and interrupted my train of thought. "You felt that this time, didn't you?"

Her face paled. "I think everyone did."

The table rattled harder. Patrons leapt from their chairs and hurried toward the door.

The ground shifted underneath me when I stood. I put out my arm to keep my balance and grabbed my phone before it slid off onto the ground.

"We should get outside." Jess handed me my bag and swung hers onto her back.

"We're perfectly safe," I told her.

She gave me a meaningful look and headed toward the door.

I sighed and followed. She was right, of course. I could save us from a falling building with my magic, but not without people seeing it. What was the point of having magic if you couldn't save the people you care about? That didn't mean I wasn't ready if I needed to be. I wouldn't let us die to hide what I was. No one would believe magic was involved anyway, if I was careful.

As I stepped out into the sunlight, a shadow scuttled past me. At least as tall as me, and as wide, it flashed by before I made out what it was. I knew I hadn't imagined it this time; it made a breeze with its passing. The cool air would have been relief from this hot day, had it not given me chills up and down my spine.

The wind was followed closely by a snort, which I suspected only I heard. It sounded male, but I couldn't be sure. If it was and I caught him, he'd get a kick in the nuts for this. Fucking around with normals, and causing earthquakes made us paranormals look bad. Or it would if the normals knew we existed in their midst.

Jess was apparently oblivious to his passing. She had her phone out and was filming the tables still rattling inside the cafe, and the sign which swung back and forth outside the hamburger place next door. A car alarm went off nearby. She turned her phone toward it.

If any of the cafe's customers saw or heard anything but the earth tremor, they gave no sign. They huddled together in small groups, held each other and talked in low, frantic voices.

The ground stopped shaking after a minute or two, but my heart raced for much longer after that.

2

The Academy of Modern Magic building looked like most of those on the street. Grey stone, wide windows, a glass doorway. The root of a stunted tree cracked the sidewalk in front of it.

A sign on the wall beside the door read, "Academy of Modern Technology." If you google, you'll find a whole website listing classes which aren't held here, and no way to apply. All the links redirect to a school for normals. I know, because Jess and I looked before I left home.

I headed up the front steps and through the glass door. I half expected it to look like something out of a movie—moving staircases and weird creatures lurking here and there.

Instead, I stood in a normal-looking foyer, with signs for self-defence, protective magic, shifter training and toilets. As for weird creatures, well I saw a few of those. I assumed they were shifters. To the untrained eye, they seemed like nothing more than ordinary cats, dogs and a bird or two. To someone who had grown up knowing paranormals existed, they looked like animals, but the way they stopped to look at me suggested they were something more.

"Dyson Gill," a voice shouted, "it's rude to shift in the middle of the corridor. Put some clothes on!"

I followed the trail of giggles to a guy who stood in the corridor leading to shifter training. He was naked except for the unapologetic grin on his face. He had dark hair, shaggy on the front, and abs which made my ovaries sit up and take notice. I couldn't resist letting my eyes wander a little lower to peek at his cock.

Yep, that sent my ovaries into a happy dance all of their own.

I forced my eyes up until he met my gaze. Oh shit, he'd caught me looking. Oops. My face turned red.

His grin widened until another guy stepped up to give him a poke on the shoulder. He winked at me before he turned away.

"Hey, sorry Kane." Dyson didn't sounds sorry at all. "Just trying to keep everyone entertained."

His friend—I assumed—had a redder face than I did.

"Yeah, yeah, just put that thing away, okay?" Kane waved at him.

Dyson wiggled his brows, but then shifted. Where a guy had stood, was now a shaggy dog of some kind. Gods only knew what breed he might have been.

"I'm sorry about him." Kane spoke to me before I realised he knew I was watching. "My brother was always the exhibitionist of the family."

"Oh, he's your brother," I said. In spite of the fading red in his face, I supposed there was a resemblance. They both had the same squarish jaw and blue eyes. That was where it ended though.

"Twins," Kane said wearily. "Not identical."

Dyson stuck his tongue out and panted.

"Are you a shifter too?" I asked without thinking. Some paranormals liked to keep what they were a secret. Fair enough, since normals might hunt and kill us if they knew. It never hurt to be careful.

"Yeah." Kane's face reddened again. He stuck out his hand. "Kane Gill."

"Peyton Chapel." I shook his hand.

He did a double take. "Chapel? As in—"

I sighed. "Yes, my mother is Lucinda Knight-Chapel."

He looked confused. "No, I was wondering if you're related to the footballer."

I gave him a blank look. What I knew about football would fit on a grain of rice. With room left over.

"Gavin Chapel," Kane said. His face lit up. "He's brilliant."

"Um, okay." I shrugged.

Kane's face fell. "Yeah, well, it doesn't matter." He eyed my suitcase. "You're new here?"

Dyson panted, but it sounded a lot like a laugh.

"Yes," I replied ruefully. "I'm not sure which way to go."

"Oh." Kane brightened again. "I can show you. Um, if you like."

I was starting to realise blushing was his thing. His face went pink again. I found it strangely endearing. I wasn't inexperienced in dealing with guys, but they didn't usually go red around me. They were usually—well—more like Dyson. Outgoing, obnoxious and sexy. Kane's shyness was adorable. And yes, he was sexy in his own way.

"That would be nice, thank you." I grabbed the handle of my suitcase and gestured for him to lead on.

He licked his lips and said, "Dyson, you should probably go and get some clothes on."

Dyson shook his head and walked at Kane's heels instead.

Yep, obnoxious. I sure can pick it. All right, standing naked in a corridor full of people was probably a giveaway. I have nothing against body confidence, don't get me wrong. The gods know I'd like more of it myself, but walking around in the nude for attention, that was something else. Bold. Very bold. Admirable even. Poor Kane. I didn't envy him being shy and awkward with a brother like that.

"Have you been assigned a room?" Kane asked.

I pulled out my phone and checked the information package I'd received a couple of days ago. That was just after the conversation in which my mother had looked disapproving that I was coming here, while my father looked proud. Given that was their standard responses to everything I'd ever done, I put it out of my mind.

"I'm on the third level," I replied, "room 68." So close to sixty-nine.

The way his eyes were wide, I guessed he too was thinking about mutual blow jobs. I knew how big Dyson was, but was Kane as big? Bigger maybe?

"Ah, we can take the elevator up, unless you prefer the stairs," Kane said. "Um, some witches prefer to levitate their cases."

I licked my lips and cleared my throat. "The lift is fine. I'm not a huge fan of stairs." Wow, I sounded lazy as fuck. Thanks mouth, for shooting off before my brain could catch up.

"Me either." Kane led the way to a bank of elevators. "The stairs are often packed with shifters practicing their running or flying. They can get...dangerous."

"I suppose it's safer for them than being outside," I said. "People would notice a bunch of animals running around."

"Yeah, I guess so." He didn't meet my eyes. Instead he pressed the upward arrow and stared at the screen which showed the elevator was on the fourth floor.

I looked down to Dyson, who stood with his tongue hanging out, the picture of canine innocence.

"Do shifters often walk around in their animal form?" I addressed the question to them both.

Kane answered. "Not usually. Dyson probably made a bet with someone that he'd appear naked in front of the new arrivals."

"Ah." I nodded. "Does he bet often?" I eyed the shaggy shifter. He wagged his tail at me.

Before Kane could answer, the door slid open. He gestured us inside. The door closed behind us.

Dyson shifted and leaned against the elevator wall, arms crossed over his chest. My eye drank in his naked glory before I managed to look away.

He chuckled. "I only bet when I know I can win. I figured Kane here would forget, so I thought I'd invite you to the welcoming party tonight."

"Party?" I echoed like a dork. Well hells, how was I supposed to think straight when I stood in a small elevator with two hot guys, one of them naked and with a semi-hard cock? I was only human. Well, witch.

"Yes," Kane was looking anywhere but at his brother. "In the common room for level two." He glanced sideways at his brother. "You know there are cameras in here, right?"

Dyson grinned a panty-melting smile. "It's only skin, Kaney-boy."

"That doesn't mean I want to see it," Kane said uncomfortably.

His brother smirked, then turned his attention back to me. "I'll shift after you agree to come."

I swear he pronounced it cum. "Um, sure, sounds like fun."

"Great." Dyson returned to his shaggy form just before the door opened again. He trotted out ahead of us.

"I'm sorry about him," Kane muttered. "He's…"

"I'm sure he's harmless." I patted Kane's arm and felt the muscle under his shirt. He must work out.

"Mostly," Kane said.

We walked in silence until we reached room 68. Dyson padded to the room beside it and wagged his tail.

Message received, loud, clear and wet.

The door to 68 had no keyhole. I gave them a questioning look.

"You need to enter the code on your phone," Kane explained. "It'll punch the numbers in for you. Everything here works on magic from a phone or tablet." He sighed. "It's the new way of doing things, so normals don't notice."

I blinked in surprise. "We use modern technology as a conduit for magic?"

He seemed impressed I'd grasped the concept so easily. "Exactly. Some people here prefer to use tattoos and transfer their magic that way, so it's an adjustment for them." He gave me a questioning look, which I ignored. If he wanted to know if I had any ink, he'd have to find out for himself.

"So no learning to blast magic out my palms?" I asked.

"Not here, no. Trust me, your devices will do everything you need, and with normals none the wiser. Well, more or less."

"Right." Even the most clueless normal would notice if I knocked them backward, off their feet, whether I used a smartphone or my fingertips. Still, for subtle magic, this could be interesting.

I checked the info package for the room code—no, it wasn't triple six or six-nine-six-nine—and punched it in. The door clicked and Kane pushed it open.

The room was small, just two beds under the window, desks on either side and drawers and a place to hang clothes beside those.

"Looks like your roommate isn't here yet," Kane held the door so I could wheel in my suitcase.

I wrinkled my nose. I had never had to share a room. I didn't really want to do it now.

I put my things on one bed and Dyson jumped up on the other. He shifted and smiled.

"I'll share with you. We could just push the bed together and snuggle."

"Dyson!" Kane groaned and pushed the hair back off his face.

"What?" Dyson asked. He gave his brother an innocent look. "All right, you can watch."

Kane turned red and his pants tented. So that's how it was, huh? Kane got off on watching. I couldn't blame him. I was tempted to jump Dyson and let Kane watch. Then join in.

The idea made my mouth go dry. "So, um. Party later tonight?"

"Right." Dyson lay back, hands behind his head and looked very jumpable. "We'll see you there. Dress casual. Or not at all." He winked.

Now I went red.

Dyson stood and sauntered to the door. "I'll see you there then." He shifted and trotted out the door.

"I'm—" Kane started.

"Don't say you're sorry about him," I said quickly. "I doubt he's... uh...easy to contain."

Kane sighed. "He really isn't. Sometimes I wonder if maybe..."

"Maybe what?" I prompted.

"Maybe he's adopted," Kane finished. "Or I am. Then I remember we look alike."

I patted his arm again. "I feel your pain. Sometimes I wonder if I'm really related to my mother. She's an overachiever and I'm—" I sucked in a breath. "I'm not."

Kane licked his lips, took my hand and squeezed it. "Families are complicated."

"That they are," I agreed. "I'll see you at the party tonight then?"

An adorable grin lit up his face. "I wouldn't miss it."

"Great." I waited.

He looked confused, then realised he was still holding my hand. His face turned that shade I was starting to get used to. He let my hand go and stepped toward the door.

"Later."

"Yes, later," I agreed.

He hesitated on the threshold, then stepped out and let the door close behind him. With any luck, my roommate would be as nice.

3

"I'M ARIANA. You better not snore." A woman around my own age stood in the doorway, phone in one hand, handle of her suitcase in the other.

I looked up at her from where I sat on my bed. "Peyton. I don't know, I'm usually asleep at the time."

She frowned at me for a moment, pursed her lips, then burst out laughing. "I'm sorry, I guess I did sound like a bit of a dick. I had this whole speech prepared and it all went right out of my head the moment I opened the door."

She rubbed her forehead and tucked a strand of blonde hair behind her ear.

I raised an eyebrow at her. "You prepared a speech?"

She smiled awkwardly and tucked her phone into her pocket. "I tend to overthink things. If I don't I—well—make a dick of myself. Only, I did anyway." She sighed.

I snorted and held out my hand. "Welcome to the club. And don't worry, I'm not that easily offended."

She dragged her suitcase behind her and shook my hand. "Witch or shifter?" She clapped a hand over her mouth as soon as the words left her mouth. "I'm sorry, I know it's rude to ask. See what I mean?

My mouth gets me into a world of trouble." She stepped back and flopped down on her bed. Right where Dyson's naked ass had been only an hour or so earlier.

I shrugged. "It's probably a normal question to ask here. I mean, we're all one or the other. Usually."

"Usually," she asked.

I shrugged but didn't elaborate. "I'm a witch," I said for clarification.

"Oh, me too! I'm so glad we're both witches." Her eyes widened. "I mean, nothing against shifters, but..." She cupped a hand around the side of her mouth, as if there was anyone to hear, and in a whisper added, "I've never met one."

"Oh." I thought about that for a moment. "Are you sure? I mean you wouldn't know, right?"

"Well, damn." She stared at me. "I suppose not," she agreed. "Okay, I'm not *aware* of having met one. Have you?"

I tried hard not to think about Dyson and his cock. I failed.

"Er, um." I licked my lips. "I've met a couple of them since I arrived. They seem—nice."

"Thank the gods." She exhaled softly. "I'm sorry. I've never really had much to do with magic. I knew I could do some strange things, but until I got my text, it didn't really click, you know? I mean, who the hells assumes it's magic?"

I cocked my head. "Witches and wizards?"

She laughed. "Apart from them I mean. Normal people don't think magic is real."

"Some people do," I told her. Let's face it, people believe in all sorts of things, some more peculiar than others. Magic was certainly not the weirdest of them.

"I suppose that's true," she admitted. "But if they knew it was, they'd probably freak out."

"Same if they knew shifters were real." I thought back to that shadow I'd seen when I'd had lunch with Jess. I hadn't ruled out the presence of a shifter of some kind. If someone else had seen it... Then again, considering how rarely we had earthquakes in Australia and that hadn't rattled people—no pun intended—maybe they wouldn't care about a shifter.

Her eyes widened. "I might have freaked out a little when I found out. I mean, we have cats." She lowered her voice to a whisper. "Fuck, what if one of them was a shifter? I used to get undressed in front of them and… everything."

I suspected "everything" might involve vibrators or a sexual partner. Very awkward in front of a cat, I would imagine.

I swallowed hard. "Unless you fed them human food, they probably wouldn't stick around," I pointed out. I'm sure cat food was delicious—if you're a cat.

Her expression brightened. "I hadn't thought of that. You're right. Also I watched them all get born, so unless a shifter is kidnapping cats and taking their place, then it's probably not likely."

"Probably not," I agreed. Although, I'm sure there were shifty shifters out there. Speaking of shifters—

"Apparently there's a party on tonight, if you wanna go." I kept my tone light. No pressure. Besides, I was trying to hide how excited I was about it.

Ariana had other ideas. She let out a squeal which bordered on painful. "Shit yeah, I'd love to go! I've never been to a party with paranormals before!"

I winced. "You might want to just think of them—us—as people, not paranormals." It was hard enough to be different without being treated that way by those we had the most in common with.

Her mouth formed an O. "Right. I'm sorry. This is all so new and overwhelming." She brushed her hair off her face.

I smiled. "You're right, it is. I've been a part of the paranormal world since I was born, but I've never been to university before. And I've never formally studied magic. See, we're both new to this."

She sagged with relief. "Thank goodness for that. I was worried I'd get stuck in a room with someone who thought I was a clueless twat. Or worse."

"What's worse than a clueless twat?" I asked.

She thought for a moment. "A clueless twat who puts pineapple on pizza?"

I snorted a laugh. "I like pineapple on pizza."

She wrinkled her nose. "Heathen."

I stuck out my tongue at her. "Just don't tell me you like anchovies on yours."

"Well…" She looked toward the ceiling, but a smile played on the corners of her mouth.

I cleared my throat and declared, "I'm told I snore."

She put a hand to her mouth in mock dismay. "Oh no! Me too."

I laughed. "You can't complain if I do then."

"Oh, I still will," she said. "Or I'll do to you what I did to my sisters and tickle the heck out of you."

"Only if you want to be turned into a toad," I said dryly. I hated to be tickled.

She gasped. "You can do that? Can I do that?" She stared at her hand as if expecting it to unleash something terrible on the world.

"No," I said firmly. "Unless you're really a frog shifter." I gave her a shifty-eyed look.

"Shit, I don't think I am," she replied. "I mean, I would know if I could turn into a frog, wouldn't I?"

"Probably. You would have scared the crap out of yourself and your family by now. Unless, they're paranormals too?" They wouldn't be the first to keep vital information from their children in the hope they wouldn't possess any magic ability.

"No. Yes," she replied.

"I could be wrong, but I think it has to be one or the other of those," I remarked.

"It is, sort of," she replied. "My parents aren't paranormal, but my aunt Chrissy is a witch. She was always the bad egg of the family because of it."

I frowned. "So your parents knew and ostracised her?" It could have been worse, they could have burnt her at the stake.

"My mother knew. She's her sister." Ariana sighed deeply. "I don't think my father knew why they didn't talk, they just didn't."

"So..." I ventured carefully, "how does she feel about you coming here? Your mother, I mean?"

Ariana pulled a face. "She... she doesn't know. She thinks I'm studying nursing."

Well shit, the girl has some balls, I had to give it to her. "I don't think you'll be learning to take temperatures or giving out medication here."

"I know," she said wryly. "I'm hoping I can work in the magical community. Maybe teach here some day, or work with paranormal children. It seemed easier to say nursing."

I nodded. Those both sounded like noble careers to me. "I have no idea what I want to do." I didn't want to follow in my mother's foot- steps and work to keep knowledge of the existence of paranormals contained.

Every so often, normals would find out and all hells would break loose. She had to make sure the situation didn't get worse. Or so my father said. He always avoided the question of how she did this. For all I know, she had them killed. Or did it herself. I had no desire to either find out or kill people.

"You have lots of time to decide," she said enthusiastically. "You can try a bunch of different things and see what you like."

My mind pictured me trying Kane and Dyson and my mouth went dry. "What happens if I like them all?" I asked, my voice higher than usual.

Her mouth moved, but no answer came out. Finally, she said, "Maybe you can find a way to do them all?"

I choked on air and started to cough.

"Oh shit, are you okay?" Ariana leapt up from her bed and sat beside me. She started to pat me on the back and handed me a water bottle from the table beside my bed.

I nodded my thanks, opened the bottle and took a swig. Then another. I wished it was vodka but it helped me catch my breath.

"I'm fine," I said faintly. "Thank you."

"You're welcome." She slid away a little. "You seem worried about choosing what you want to do with the rest of your life."

"A little bit." I told her about my mother in as few words as I could.

She listened attentively and nodded. "Apparently we both have mother issues," she said wryly. "Maybe they could get together some time, have coffee and talk about how disappointed they are in us."

"Until your mother finds out mine is a witch," I said. "Then things would get ugly."

"Very true," she said sadly. "Maybe some day people—I mean normals—and paranormals can live together and not keep secrets about what they are."

"There will always be people—normal and paranormal—who keep secrets." I capped the water bottle and placed it back on the table.

She gave me a funny little smile. "That's true too. Well, you never know I suppose."

"You never do," I agreed. "In the meantime, we have a party to get ready for."

"Ohhh, yes!" She grinned. "Will you help me to choose what to wear?"

"Of course. I think it's probably just casual though." Plus she would probably look good in anything. She was adorable and seemed genuinely sweet.

"Even casual, we should look our best, right?" She gave me a hopeful look.

To be honest, I'd never been particularly interested in fashion or makeup, but it might be nice to make an effort for a change.

"Right." I had a feeling this was going to end with her making me look pretty, rather than me helping her choose an outfit.

"Great." She jumped to her feet. "Let's start with your hair."

"My hair?" I patted my head.

"Yes, you'd look amazing with it straightened. Maybe with a little colour here and there." She opened her suitcase and started to pull things out.

Colour? Well, what could go wrong?

4

"I'M SO SORRY," Ariana said for the hundredth time. "It was supposed to be a streak of blonde. I thought it would look cute."

I looked at the streak of green in my hair and tried to smile. "It *does* look cute," I said awkwardly. "It'll fade or grow out eventually anyway." I hoped. She had done it by magic, so it was anyone's guess what might happen.

"I'm sure it will," she said uncertainly.

"Maybe we should wait until we've taken some magic classes to try any more spells we found on the internet." I pulled back my hair and tied it in a ponytail. The green wasn't so obvious that way. Or so I told myself. Hey, my hair was green, I needed to console myself somehow.

"That's probably a good idea. I had no idea it would work like that." She leaned toward the mirror and smeared lipstick onto her lips. "Do you want some?"

I held up my hand. "Black lipstick isn't really my thing." I was surprised it was hers.

"I've never worn it before," she admitted. "But I figured I should try to look more badass."

That would explain the yellow dress with huge purple flowers and the ballet flats she wore.

"I have a way to go," she added.

"Hey, I think you look badass enough," I told her. "Besides, badass is a state of mind, not what you wear." Look at me, for example. I wore a pair of jeans with holes in the knees—torn, not designer holes—and a plain red t-shirt. I didn't even register on the badass-o-meter on the outside. On the inside, on the other hand, I rated much higher. Maybe…half a point or so.

I tugged down the front of my t-shirt to expose a little cleavage. That upped my rating by at least a quarter of a point. Woo-hoo, three quarters of a point. Only a bajillion to go before I'm an actual badass.

"Ready?" she asked.

"Absolutely." The idea of seeing the brothers again made my heart do a somersault, triple backflip with an added cartwheel. It may or may not have landed on its feet. Knowing my luck, it had landed flat on its face and is now trending on the heart version of YouTube under the subject of "embarrassing but hilarious falls."

I grabbed my phone and shoved it into my back pocket. As far as I could tell, we couldn't get back into our room without one. How did shifters get into theirs then? Most couldn't do magic apart from shifting. Maybe they had ordinary old keys.

"Second floor common room," I said to myself.

"That's probably second floor and follow the noise," Ariana said with a laugh.

"Probably." I laughed too and headed toward the stairs with a few others who seemed to be headed in the same direction.

A couple of them glanced at me and smiled, but most looked as nervous as I felt. They must have placed all the first years on the third floor.

The minute we stepped out on the second, Ariana's suggestion to follow the noise seemed like an understatement. Music pounded down the corridor which was lined with students drinking, talking and making out. We had to push through to get to the common room.

That was packed already. Lights had been strung up around the room and flashed with no particular rhythm.

"You came!" Kane appear in front of me, wearing jeans, a worn t-shirt and a huge grin. My eyes bulged at the way his muscles seemed to be struggling to stay inside the fabric of his shirt.

"Here." He pressed a drink into my hand. "It's only beer," he shouted over the music.

"That's okay, I like beer," I shouted back. "This is Ariana."

He glanced at her, raised a finger and disappeared into the crowd. He returned a moment later with two more cups. He handed one to Ariana and toasted us with his.

I grinned and sipped. It wasn't very good beer, but at least it was cold.

"You need to think bigger, brother." Dyson appeared through the mass of people wearing a shirt so tight I could make out his lickable abs. In one hand he held four shot glasses. In the other he held a bottle of tequila.

Kane scowled. "I was getting to that."

"Sure you were," Dyson said. "Come on, let's step outside and get some air before piñata time."

"Piñata?" Ariana squealed. "I love piñatas!"

"Well, we better be back in time for it then." Dyson ushered us toward the door and out into the corridor.

We walked until we reached a spot where we could all sit and not have to yell to be heard. Dyson handed us each a glass and poured into them one by one.

"Shall we make a toast?" he asked.

I glanced at Kane, who looked annoyed at being overshadowed by his brother. "Maybe Kane should make it."

"Sure, why not." Dyson shrugged. "What'll we drink to, brother?"

Kane licked his lips and glanced at me. "To new friends?"

Dyson shrugged. "Good enough I suppose. And to having a good time tonight." He gave me a wink and downed his tequila.

I threw mine back and grimaced. I had drunk it before, but never by itself. It was probably an acquired taste. I felt buzzed almost immediately.

"Not bad," Dyson said. He locked his eyes on me and said, "It would be better licked off nice and slowly."

If I blushed, Kane turned twice as red. He looked as though he'd had the same thought, or at least he was thinking it now. He swallowed visibly. "Yeah, what he said," he muttered.

"I third that," Ariana agreed.

I could barely look at her, but when I did, she was looking at me with the same expression the guys had.

Oh my gods—yes, paranormals often believe in many—I might die right now. I wasn't used to being the centre of attention, especially like this. I felt as if my whole body caught alight.

I was saved from having to answer by a chant which echoed up and down the corridor.

"Piñata, piñata, piñata!"

"Come on, we don't want to miss this." Dyson tucked the bottle under his arm, grabbed my hand and pulled me to my feet.

Instead of heading back into the common room, he tugged me down the stairs to the lowest level and out a set of doors to a large courtyard. In the middle, two students were hanging a huge piñata from a pole. The piñata was shaped like a raven with a party hat at an angle on his head.

"Paranormal party planners are the best," Dyson said. He gave my hand a squeeze, apparently oblivious to the fact him holding it was making my knees weak.

"Who's first?" someone called out.

A slender woman with dark skin and hair stepped toward and took the stick she was offered. She closed her eyes, took a swing and missed.

The crowd cheered. Apparently whether or not she hit it didn't matter to those gathered.

She shrugged and handed to the stick to a tall, burly man with a hipster beard and man bun.

He swung and hit, but hardly made a dent in the piñata.

"Wouldn't it be easier to use magic?" Ariana asked.

"Of course it would," Kane agreed. "That's the point. It's more fun to take things slowly." He glanced at me again and blushed.

"Life is too short, brother." Dyson handed him the bottle and stepped forward to take the stick. He ran his hands up and down it suggestively.

The crowd wolf-whistled.

He gave me a wink and swaggered toward the piñata. With a flourish, he swung. The stick only caught the edge of the raven's tail and sent it into a spin.

Kane laughed. "Good try, *brother*."

Dyson bowed, then handed the stick to Kane. "Let's see if you can nail it first then."

Kane blushed.

So did I.

Kane's swing caught the raven's party hat and knocked it sideways, but not quite off.

Dyson clapped. "You did better than me. Nice work." He seemed sincere.

"Thanks," Kane muttered. He handed the stick to Ariana.

Almost skipping, she stepped closer to the hanging raven and waited for a few moments before she closed her eyes and swung. The stick connected with a thunk that sent the raven flying so hard I was sure it would snap the rope that tied it to the pole. It swung back and did a wild dance before it slowed to a regular swing.

The crowd cheered.

"Your turn." Ariana handed me the stick. Oh gods, I was going to miss and make a massive dick of myself, wasn't I? Oh well, what was new?

I swallowed hard and tried to ignore my racing heart. I focused on the raven and followed the rate it moved before I closed my eyes. I raised the stick and swung. When the stick connected to the piñata, it sent a jolt all the way down my arms. I winced.

Like before, the raven flew wildly, but the rope and the piñata held.

I shrugged and handed the stick over to the next person.

"Magic really would be easier," I remarked.

It took five more people before the raven burst open and sent its contents pouring down to the ground. I blinked in surprise, then snorted a laugh.

"Lube?" I asked.

"Of course," Dyson grinned. "This is a party!"

Scattered all over the ground were hundreds of tiny tubes of lubricant. Everyone hurried forward to grab them up and fill their pockets.

Dyson deliberately picked up one close to him, winked at me and pushed it into the back of his jeans.

I swallowed hard. My mind started to wander, imagining how and where he'd use that on me. His warm, slippery fingers, covered in a layer of cool lube…

"Thank the gods my dress has pockets!" Ariana's voice brought me back to the present with a jolt.

I snagged a couple of tubes, but that was all. I wasn't going to risk getting crushed by a bunch of paranormals just for lube. I tucked mine into my pocket and stepped back.

Out of the corner of my eye, I noticed someone watching me. I turned my head to look.

He had dark hair, cut shorter on the sides and longer on the top, and honey-coloured skin. Every stitch of his clothing was black. Every item fit so well it looked like a second skin. Maybe he was really a ninja or something. One of his eyebrows twitched, but that was all the movement from his entire face or body. If I hadn't seen that, I might think he was a statue. One good-looking enough to make me wet from a distance.

In spite of all of that, I frowned. Part of me felt as though I'd seen him before. The rest of me was sure I would have noticed if I had.

His eyes narrowed slightly.

I offered him a smile. It probably looked more like a grimace.

His expression unchanged, he turned away and disappeared into the crowds. Not hard when it was dark and most of the people there wore black. Still, there was something different in the way he did it.

"That was weird," I muttered.

"What was?" Ariana asked. She cocked her head at me.

"I… Nothing." I shook my head. The guy had probably been staring at my green streak. I touched my hair and grimaced.

"Okay, if you're sure." She looked worried.

"I am," I said firmly. "Let's go back upstairs, I feel like dancing."

It was Kane who took my hand this time and led me back up toward the common room. I glanced back several times but saw no sign of the strange guy. No doubt I would see him around at some point. I half hoped that would be the case, if only to ask why he had been staring and how he knew me. For some reason I couldn't put my finger on, I was sure he did.

"For those of you new to magic, it does not involve the use of sticks." The lecturer—"call me Madame Luc"—looked about a hundred years old and spoke in a thick accent, but her eyes were bright. She scanned the room slowly. Her gaze settled on each one of us, for a few seconds at least. Her eyes swished over me and she frowned slightly before moving on.

We all laughed nervously.

"Sticks, Madame Luc?" a student called out. She had dark hair, dark skin and wide eyes.

"She means magic wands," said another, a young man with a shaved head. "Right, Madame?"

"Oui," Madame Luc replied. "That is correct." She rolled her rs. "For those of you who are not new to magic, in my class, you will not be learning how to use your hands." She gestured dismissively. "Oh, I know some will know how to use magic already, maybe better than me."

The class laughed again.

"But non! No. You will unlearn what you already know!" Her eyes narrowed as if we might challenge her.

"How do we unlearn?" someone muttered.

If Madame Luc heard, she ignored them. Instead she said, "Get out your devices."

Most of us had finished high school the year before. There, we were told to put our devices away during class, and not to touch them. This was a refreshing change.

"Some of you will already have been practicing with your devices." Madame pointed toward the green streak in my hair.

My face heated.

Ariana raised her hand slowly. "That was me, Madame, I did that."

Madame Luc stepped over to the table we were sharing and looked down her long nose at Ariana.

"Do you suppose you're in trouble for that? Maybe you will get expelled for trying spells without permission?"

Ariana shrank back in her chair. "I… I don't know, Madame, I didn't think." She looked as though she was about to cry.

"You are not in school anymore," Madame declared loudly. "Did your magic harm anyone?"

Ariana glanced at me. "I don't think so, Madame."

I shrugged and shook my head. "I'm fine," I replied. "It'll grow out."

"There you are," Madame replied. "The rules are the same here as the laws of any country. No killing, maiming, and so forth. However, I recommend against using untried spells you find on the internet. They are like—how do you say this? Using google to be your doctor."

Ariana nodded. "Of course, Madame. I'm sorry." She glanced toward me, her expression somewhere between relieved and mortified. I didn't blame her, Madame Luc was a formidable witch.

"Open your browser," Madame said. "Not the normal browser, but Conjurer. Make sure you have version thirteen. Version twelve was—gah!" She threw up a hand. "Always with the glitches and crashing. Thank the gods they released the update recently. If you don't have that version, download it now. The academy internet is secure."

I had to search my settings to be sure I had the right browser. Oops, version eleven. I sighed. It would take the better part of an hour to download the latest one. I pressed the button and waited. Three second later, my phone pinged.

Update complete.

Holy fucking dancing goats, the net must be fast here.

"Woah," a guy said from the table beside ours. I presumed he'd found the same thing.

"Um, Madame," a student in the back said tentatively. "What if your device doesn't support the latest version?" I turned to see a guy with brown hair and a face full of freckles.

Madame Luc walked to a set of drawers beside her desk, opened it and pulled out the latest smart phone, still in a box. "Here. You come and get this."

"Well, if I'd known *that* was an option," the young man with the shaved head muttered.

A few people murmured their agreement, but as the student hurried forward, his face red, wearing what was obviously old jeans and shirt, I couldn't begrudge him a new phone.

"What is your name?" Madame asked him.

"Hamish Small," he said, speaking to his chest. He wasn't little though. He was tall, with broad shoulders.

"Monsieur Small," Madame Luc handed the phone to him with a flourish, "if you need assistance with anything here, you ask. While it is true that some of us bite, we can also help with your basic needs."

Hamish accepted the phone and nodded. "I understand. Thank you, Madame." He walked back to his table and sat.

"What was that about?" Ariana whispered.

I shrugged. "The paranormal community takes care of its own." Well, some of the time anyway. I'd be lying if I said there wasn't conflict, but when push came to shove, a free phone wasn't a big deal, nor were some new clothes.

"Now your browser is ready, yes?" Madame asked. "Open to para-normal.magic.ama.edu.au and type in "levitation." Then wait."

I did as I was asked and looked over to Ariana. She looked excited, but nervous. I got that. I was feeling the same thing. Sure, I had been around magic all my life, but that didn't mean I didn't have things to learn. I had never, for example, levitated anything.

"Your phone will ask what you want to levitate." Madame moved around the room, placing a small, wooden block in front of each of us. "In that field, you must ask it to lift this block."

I frowned. "What wording, specifically?" I asked.

"That is for you to work out," she replied.

I exchanged glances with Ariana.

"Is this how you usually do things?" she whispered loudly.

"No, I've never done this before," I admitted.

Her mouth formed an O. "How hard can it be?"

"Right," I said lightly. Magic was usually reasonably straightforward. We drew it from the world around us, specifically nature or things made from natural materials, including metal. It was easier to use if I was surrounded by trees, but a phone needed an internet connection. I had no idea how powerful magic might be when used via a device, apart from unlocking bedroom doors.

"All right, let's see." I spelled out, "lift block," and pressed the enter button. I watched the block expectantly but nothing happened.

"I guess it's not that then," Ariana said. "I'm going to try, "lift wooden block," and see if that works."

I nodded and watched her block. Nothing.

"Oops!" The student with the shaved head floated off his chair and toward the ceiling. "Don't try just "lift" and nothing else." He looked nervously upward, but a smile tugged at the corners of his mouth.

"Indeed, do not," Madame agreed. "At least, until you have better control over your magic. It's not your phone which is making things happen, it is you, *via* your phone."

There was a clue in there, I was sure of it. I thought for a moment, then put in the same words. This time, I focused on the block and pressed "enter". The block wobbled, but it lifted off the table a centimetre or two.

"Good!" Madame clapped her hands. "There, you see who is in charge here? You, not your technology. Now, do it for longer."

I tried, but I couldn't get the box to lift any higher. Ariana, on the other hand, made hers rise halfway to the ceiling. Just about everyone else in the class, including Hamish, did better than I did, but at least I wasn't a total failure. My block *had* levitated first. And I hadn't made myself fly around the room. Bonus.

I was about to put my phone away when it pinged and a notification popped up. When I clicked on it, my phone went black.

"What the hells?" I frowned at my screen, then tapped at it.

"What's wrong?" Ariana asked.

"I think my phone just died, or got hacked, or something." I was becoming annoyed now. I could replace my phone and everything was backed up to the ubiquitous cloud, but it would take time to do it.

"Oh, that's—"

She cut off her words when my phone flickered back to life as if nothing had happened.

"That was strange." I checked my notifications but there was no sign of the one I had clicked on, not even amongst the ones I'd deleted. "Just a glitch, I suppose." Maybe version thirteen of Conjurer wasn't as smooth as Madame Luc had hoped.

"I guess so. Tech is weird sometimes," Ariana agreed.

"I will send your homework to your devices," Madame declared.

Everyone groaned. "Homework? On the first day?" someone called out.

"Homework at university?" moaned someone else.

Madame Luc smiled. "Oui. We do things a little differently at the academy, especially since you're starting with some basic skills."

Another notification appeared on my phone. I looked carefully this time before I clicked, but it was just from Madame Luc, as she'd said.

"Homework, week 1, lift a small object with your device." I read out loud. "I can do that." I had been planning to practice that anyway.

"Easy peasy," Ariana enthused. "Maybe I'll even try something a bit heavier. Like—you."

I snorted. "You are not going to levitate me."

She pouted. "Oh come on, it could be fun."

"Great," I smiled, "then try it on someone else. Dyson might enjoy it. Or Kane." I pictured Kane, his face bright red, floating above the ground. Dyson—well, I pictured him naked and my face went hot.

Ariana gave me a sly smile. "I'm sure they'd like it if you tried them."

I swallowed. "Um, anyway…it looks like the class is finished." Anything to change the subject. Thinking about the guys was one thing, talking about them was another.

Ariana laughed softly. "Saved by the bell, hmmm?"

"Exactly," I said lightly. Of course, there weren't literally class bells here, but close enough. "And it's time for lunch. I'm starving." I swung my bag onto my back and headed for the door.

"Me too." She fell into step beside me. "I thought learning magic might be hard, but it's fun."

"You say that now," I told her. "Just wait until Madame Luc throws something harder at us."

"I assume you mean that figuratively?" Ariana asked.

"To be honest with you, I don't know," I admitted. "When it comes to magic, just about anything is possible." Including something or someone getting into my phone and doing the gods only knew what. I'd have to go through the settings and beef up my security, if that was even possible. If magic was involved, then changing the settings wouldn't do a thing. Well, except to make me feel better.

"Are you trying to scare me?" she asked. She didn't look even slightly scared, to be honest. She looked…excited.

"Would I do that?" I asked.

She grinned. "Probably not. Come on, we should hurry if we don't want to wait in line behind everyone else."

I nodded and walked faster to keep pace with her, but at the back of my mind was a niggling doubt that maybe we really should be scared. The problem was, I didn't know what we should be scared of, or what we should keep an eye out for. I would just have to keep an eye out for anything. That totally narrowed it down. Not.

I sighed to myself and hoped the dining room had pizza. I could use a slice. Or several.

6

"SOME PEOPLE THINK combat training is a waste of time."

Lincoln Nash wasn't much older than I was, maybe mid-twenties at the most. Some of the students were probably older than him, but none had the hardened look he wore in his eyes. Whatever he'd seen or done in the past hung heavily on him. At least, I assumed that was the case. It was possible he was just a natural born asshole.

"Yes," he continued, "you can use magic, or teeth, beak or claw, but sometimes those aren't available to you. Even when they are, you need to use them to the best advantage. There are people out there who want you dead." His gaze scanned the silent class of wide-eyed first years.

"Over the next three years, you'll learn the basics of self-defence, both paranormal and otherwise. We'll start with the otherwise first. Next year you'll start on using your particular abilities and in third year you'll be honing them. By the end of that, you should be capable of surviving a test that would make the Hunger Games look like a party."

I glanced toward Ariana. Her lips were parted and she was blinking rapidly. For someone who had only recently learnt of her powers, this must be a lot to take in.

"Mr Nash," someone called out. "Do you mean that literally? Is there…a test of some kind?"

"First of all, don't call me Mr Nash. Sir is fine." The lecturer looked across the room and finally settled on the person who had asked the question—a student with short, spiky rainbow hair. "What's your name?"

"Carter. The correct pronoun is they. In case anyone was wondering." Carter shrugged.

Nash nodded. "Very well then, Carter. There wasn't going to be such a test, but there is now." His expression was completely deadpan.

A few students chuckled uneasily, while others groaned.

Carter laughed. "Good one, Mr, I mean, sir. You had everyone going for a minute there."

Nash shot Carter a look and their smile faded.

Without clarifying whether or not he was joking, Nash looked away. "Right then class, pair up and spread out."

Before I could move, Nash had grabbed my arm and pulled me aside from the group. I wasn't prepared for the jolt of lighting that passed through my arm and went straight to my groin. He frowned at me as though I had done something. Apparently he'd felt it too. He licked his lips and looked away.

Ariana looked stricken for a moment before she stepped over to pair up with Carter.

"Face your partner," Nash ordered. "You're going to try to flip each other. No shifting, no magic or there will be consequences."

I waited to hear what those were, but apparently that was all the information he was going to give for now.

"Now watch."

Before I could respond, I found myself on my back. Nash straddled my hips and pinned my hands to either side of my head.

Well hello there.

I swallowed hard.

"If I was armed, or shifted into an animal with big teeth, you would be dead right now," he told me. "Or worse."

I laughed awkwardly. "Lucky you're harmless then."

He quirked one eyebrow and the corners of his mouth tugged upward a fraction. "Never make that assumption." He climbed off me and held out his hand.

Thank the gods I didn't have a cock, or my pants would have a pretty little tent for the whole class to see. I grasped his hand and let him pull me up, but I watched for a sign he might use the opportunity to flip me. Yeah, I'd seen that move in movies plenty of times, and wasn't born yesterday.

When he made the move, I was ready. I let him pull me forward a step, then I tugged him, popped out my hip toward his groin and flipped him over my shoulder. He landed on the practice mat with a grunt.

A titter of laugher—yes, that's a thing, look it up—passed through the class. For a moment I though Nash might be angry. Instead, he looked impressed.

"You've learnt this before." He got to his feet, his hands close to his body.

I shrugged. "My parents insisted I learn to take care of myself."

He nodded. "Good, but there's still room for improvement. Maybe you should try to join the academy team. We meet on Friday after last class. No guarantees though, we only take the best."

I blinked. "Me? I…" would be wet as hells the whole time I was around him, but there were worse things in this world. "I suppose I could." Who was I kidding, he'd waved a challenge in front of me like a rag to a bull. I suspected he knew that too. There was nothing most paranormals liked more than a challenge, especially me.

He nodded. "Good. Let's try again. Everyone stop and watch—" He cocked his head at me.

"Peyton," I supplied.

"Right. Watch us and learn." He licked his lips in a predatory way that made my heart race. He was dangerous, I had zero doubts about that, but I would learn a lot from him. About self-defence, get your mind out of the gutter. Or leave it there, because that was where mine was.

~

"Ugh, everything hurts," Ariana groaned. "Carter seems nice, but they had me on my back more often than not. It's not fair to pair me up with someone stronger than me."

I frowned at her across the lunch table. I hurt too, but I didn't mind it too much. I hadn't done serious exercise in a while and it showed. I really did need to remedy that.

"If anyone tries to attack you, chances are they'll be bigger and stronger than you," I pointed out. "Or a shifter. What will you do then, stop and tell them, "My, what big teeth you have?" Because I don't think the big bad wolf is going to take the time to answer."

Ariana grinned. "I suppose not." She rolled her shoulders. "Can you teach me what you did to Nash?"

I hesitated. "I suppose so, but I'm not a black belt or anything."

She stopped mid-roll. "You're better than I am. Or anyone else in the class. You might even be better than Nash."

"I doubt that," I replied, "but thank you. Maybe we can practice before Friday. I'd hate to get there and be laughed out of the team before I even join."

"You won't," she said with more confidence than I felt. "You're amazing."

"Thank you." Dyson plopped a tray down beside mine and slipped into a seat. "I do try." He grinned.

Ariana rolled her eyes. "I wasn't talking about you, silly."

"Silly?" He put a hand to his chest in mock offence. "I'm hurt you would say such a thing."

"She's just being honest." Kane flopped down beside Ariana.

"Wow, kick a guy when he's down, why don't you?" Dyson told him.

"With pleasure." Kane bit into his burger and smiled.

"Speaking of pleasure." Dyson's eyes slid to me. "Would you like to go out tonight?"

Kane almost choked on his burger. Ariana patted his back as he coughed.

"What's up, brother? Disappointed I beat you to it?" Dyson asked him.

"I…" Kane blushed. "I was going to ask, I just…"

"Just…" Dyson prompted. "Just what?"

Kane mumbled something.

I cleared my throat. "Does anyone want my answer?"

"I do." Ariana looked curious.

I didn't know what to say to her, so I turned to Dyson. "I would love to." Then to Kane, "Maybe we could make plans for another night?"

He nodded while still trying to catch his breath properly.

"There, see, that was easy." I sat back in my chair. Two dates, no strings. It seemed simple enough to me. At least simple as dating could ever be. If either of them thought they'd tie me down, they were mistaken. Better they know that now, before anything got too far.

"Excellent," Dyson looked pleased with himself. "After our date, you'll forget all about my brother." He shot me a wink which burned a path right down to my belly and set it alight.

"Dream on," Kane said. "I'm not that easy to forget. After our date, all you'll say is, "Dyson who?" You'll see." That last was directed at his brother.

"Perhaps you should see a vet," Dyson suggested, "you appear to be suffering from delusions." He grinned slyly.

"Fuck off," Kane growled.

I glance at Ariana and we rolled our eyes at them both.

"Men," she muttered.

"Amen to that," I replied.

Something moved past me, close enough to touch my arm lightly and send shivers down my spine.

"Who did that?" I asked.

Ariana frowned. "Who did what?"

I put my fingers to my arm. "Someone brushed past me."

"There's no one there." She glanced around, confused. "At least, I didn't see anyone."

"I didn't either," Kane said.

"Neither did I," Dyson said, "but witches and wizards can hide behind a bubble of magic."

"Yeah, I guess that was what it was," I said uncertainly. It was probably some dumbass trying to play a trick on me. It wouldn't be the first time a paranormal pranked another. "That reminds me, there was a weird guy at the party."

"Only one?" Dyson asked jokingly.

I snorted. "Okay, several, but one in particular." I told them about the starey guy who had disappeared into the crowds.

"I can think of a few people who fit that description," Dyson said slowly. "In case you hadn't noticed, paranormal academies are havens for weirdos."

"Like you." Kane smirked at him.

Dyson shrugged. "Guilty as charged. You're no less strange than I am though. You might even be more so."

Kane stuck his tongue out at him. "Am not."

Dyson sniffed. "Apparently you're more childish."

Kane laughed. "I'm not that either."

"Anyway," I drew the word out. "This guy could be any number of guys here. I have a feeling I know him from somewhere, but I don't remember having seen him. I'll know him if I see him again though."

"You might have another admirer," Ariana suggested.

"That would be odd, for sure," I said. "I'm used to having none."

"You?" Dyson said in disbelief. "That would be like saying Kane isn't a virgin."

Kane blushed and muttered something which sounded like, "What would you know?"

"Oh, I know plenty. I even know which are your favourite videos on Porn Hustle. You like the—"

Kane flushed even more red than I'd seen him. "All right, all right, no one needs to know that."

"Oh, I don't know, these two might be curious." Dyson gestured toward Ariana and I.

I *was* curious. While I was no fan of porn made just for men to enjoy, I'd watched my share of it. What I didn't want, was for Dyson to embarrass his poor brother any further.

"Not especially," I said lightly. "I think that's a personal thing between a guy and his electronic devices."

"Exactly," Kane muttered.

"I agree," Ariana said. Her own cheeks were an adorable shade of pink. I guess she partook as well. She'd get no judgement about that from me, that was for sure. In fact, after all this talk and my class with Nash, I might need to find some time alone with my own electronic devices. Yes, plural. You know one is my dildo, okay? I know it's not technically electronic, but you get the idea.

Dyson huffed. "Fine, I won't share his. Personally I like the ones where the guys goes down on the girl for ages and ages." As he spoke, he locked his eyes on mine. I had no doubt of his meaning. I better wash down there extra well before our date tonight. Just in case.

7

"JEANS OR A DRESS?" I stood in front of the mirror and frowned. In one hand I held a red, low-cut tank top. In the other, I held a short, black dress. I held one in front of me, then the other.

"You'd look gorgeous in either of them." Ariana didn't even glance up at her phone when she spoke.

I lowered both. "Are you all right? I can stay here if you need me to."

She glanced up for a moment. "No, it's fine. Go and have fun." She looked back toward her phone.

I lay the clothes on my bed and sat beside her on hers. "Do you want to talk about it?"

She turned off her phone and put it aside. "I'm okay, really." Her eyes begged me to leave it alone.

I gave her a long look. "I won't push, but if you want someone to listen, I'm here. Any time, okay? I mean, we're friends, right?"

"Right." She licked her lips and looked away.

I hesitated for a moment, then rose and grabbed the tank top and some jeans. Casual would probably be the better way to go. I slipped into the small bathroom we shared between the two of us, took a quick shower and changed.

When I stepped back into the room, she was gone.

I sighed and did my hair into a ponytail before I threw on a hint of makeup. I had only known Ariana for a handful of days, but I didn't want to think she was upset with me. It occurred to me maybe she liked Dyson or Kane and I could have kicked myself for not asking. When I saw her next, I would get that out of her. In the meantime, I would go and enjoy myself.

I tucked my phone into my pocket and slipped out to meet Dyson at the front the door to the academy.

His eyes lit up when he saw me and he licked his lips.

"Hey, sexy," he said by way of greeting.

"Hey," I replied. "You're not looking bad yourself." Not bad? He wore black jeans and a dark grey t-shirt which hugged his body in a way that made me want to tear his clothes off and fuck him right there against the wall. Hard and fast and…

Instead, I smiled. "Where are we going?"

He offered me his hand and led me out the door. "I thought we could go to somewhere beside the harbour. I know a place."

I knew a few places too, but most you had to book twelve to eighteen months in advance. Needless to say, I'd never *been* to any of these places.

"Don't believe me?" he asked teasingly. "Don't worry, I know all the best places to *eat*."

I blushed a little. "I'm sure you do. Just like I'm sure you know just the right way to play with your food."

He grinned. "I absolutely do. I'm happy to demonstrate. But after we have dinner. We might need our strength."

I swallowed. "Yes, we might just."

He led me over to an ancient VW and opened the passenger side door.

"Is this roadworthy?" I asked. The rust around the front and back of the car didn't exactly fill me with confidence.

"Of course it is," he replied easily. "Failing that, you could always ride on my back."

I eyed him and slipped into the car seat. I doubted his dog form was big enough to support my weight for more than a short time. At least he hadn't made any silly jokes about riding around on broomsticks. I couldn't think of anything worse than flying around with a stick up my butt crack. Magic didn't enable me to fly anyway, so that point was moot.

He chuckled and walked around to the driver's side. To my surprise, the car started the first time.

"My dad is a mechanic," he explained. "The rust is *just* this side of legal, but the rest of the car is fine. Trust me."

"You know the only people who say trust me are people I shouldn't trust, right?" I asked dryly.

He grinned and put his foot down. The car jolted forward, but then headed along the road at not much more than a crawl.

I burst out laughing.

"What? You expected a Maserati under the hood?" he asked.

That made me laugh harder. "Not exactly, but..."

"I know, I know." The smile never left his face. "You know what they say about guys with fast cars and small dicks. Well, you've seen my dick, so you know why my car is slow."

I considered that for a moment. "You know, I find I can't argue with that." And now my mouth was dry, thinking about his cock and what it would feel like under my fingers.

"I mean, I don't want to brag or anything."

I shook my head. "Maybe we should change the subject." As fascinating as his dick was.

"Good idea. I love my cock, but I'd like to hear more about you."

I shrugged. "I'm pretty boring. What do you want to know?"

"Everything," he replied.

"That's not very specific," I remarked. "You might need to narrow it down, just a little bit."

"Okay, let's start with where you were born. Did you always know you were a witch? Have you met a dog shifter before?"

"That's a lot of questions. Which do you want me to answer first?"

"Start at the beginning?" he suggested.

"Fine." I leaned back into the car seat. "I was born in Melbourne. I guess I've always known, because I don't remember a time when I didn't. My parents are both paranormals—witch and wizard—so I was raised in the community with other paranormals. My earliest memory is of my father cleaning up a bowl of stew off the floor after I blasted it there."

Dyson gave a snort of amusement. "You were a bit of a brat?" he asked.

"Of course not," I replied, "I just really didn't like fish stew."

"Oh, that's unfortunate."

I glanced over to him. "Why is that? Are we going to a fish stew restaurant?

"Well..." He drew the word out. "Actually no, I'm allergic to seafood."

"That's a relief," I replied.

"And chocolate," he added.

"Really? That sucks." Although, it did mean I didn't have to share.

"Dog shifter," he said. "Apparently that also means I can't have stuff dogs can't."

"Oh, that sucks. So no wine either?"

"Nothing with grapes," he agreed. "Luckily beer and spirits are okay though. And doin' it doggy style."

I groaned. "I should have guessed you'd go there."

"Too predictable?" he asked.

"Just a little." I held my fingers slightly apart. "That leaves me with the last question. I've met a few shifters—usually friends of my parents—whose shifter form I don't know. They could have been dogs. Or birds. Or—anything."

"Insects?" he suggested. "I knew a guy who could turn into a scorpion. Nasty piece of work, he was. Him and his brothers."

"Scorpions are known for their aggression," I pointed out.

"These guys lived up to it, and then some. Still, they could have been mosquitoes or something really nasty."

I wrinkled my nose. "They'd get squashed if they came near me."

He chuckled. "Me too."

"So—have you always known you were a shifter?" I asked.

"Kind of." We stopped at a set of traffic lights and he looked over at me. "My parents are both shifters, from a long line of shifters, so they figured Kane and I would be too. They just didn't know what we'd shift into. I think they were hoping we'd be wolves, or something like that. Bears, maybe."

"They weren't happy with a big, ole shaggy dog?" I asked lightly.

"Since they're both wolves, not really. I had a dorky uncle Bob who's a dog. He's the clown of the family. Or was until I came along. I suppose they didn't want me to end up like him."

The light changed and we moved again.

"How did he end up?" I asked, hoping he didn't mind me asking.

"He's a funeral director," Dyson replied.

I blinked in surprise. "I didn't expect that. Why is that so bad?"

"It isn't, but my parents expected me to do something useful, like join the military. The academy has a recruitment program that leads directly into a paranormal unit of whatever armed forces the student prefers."

My mouth popped open. "There's a unit of witches and wizards?"

"And shifters," he said with a nod. "Depending on their performance, they can then go into a regular unit."

I shook my head, my mind blown a little. "I had no idea they knowingly let paranormals join the armed forces."

"It's a little known fact," he said, "but think about it. Do you believe World War two was won using only conventional weapons?"

"Are you saying the atomic bomb was actually magic?" My stomach turned at the idea of magic being used in that way.

"I don't know," he admitted, "but there was a whole female unit called the Night Witches. Do you think that was a coincidence?"

"I suppose not," I agreed. "So what do you want to do when you grow up?"

He hesitated. "I want to be a kindergarten teacher. Where better to mould youngsters into open-minded adults?"

Where indeed. "That's great. The world needs more awesome teachers."

"Awww, you think I'm awesome?" he asked. "If I was my brother I'd be blushing by now.

I laughed. "I knew the academy had an education degree, but how is it different to a normal university?"

"We're taught to look for paranormals and quietly teach them to use their abilities," he explained. "And liaise with their parents. It's a big adjustment for some of them, especially those who had no idea what they were."

"I imagine it would be a shock." I thought about Ariana and what she must have felt when she'd found out.

"Exactly. Kane, being a massive geek, is studying science. He wants to know how paranormals came about and why normals can't do the things we can."

"Oh, that sounds interesting." I had often wondered the same thing myself. Could normals become paranormal, or the other way around? The idea was oddly compelling, but not something I wanted to devote my life to exploring.

"You really think so?"

We must have reached our destination because he drew up to the side of the road and parked the car.

"I really do." I unclicked my seatbelt and opened the door. At least they had an idea of what they wanted to do. I had none. Not even a little bit. Well, except to enjoy myself tonight.

"Just between us," he offered me his arm, "don't ask him about it, unless you want to hear science stuff for hours."

I accepted his arm. "I'll bear that in mind." Although it sounded interesting to me. "It's fantastic you both have things you're passionate about."

"Something we're definitely not lacking in is passion." He gave me a wink which made my heart flip. My palms were suddenly sweaty.

"I'm sure you're not." The burst of heat in my stomach travelled through my entire body and almost made my toes curl. Part of me wanted to drag him into the back seat of his car and find out.

But first, food.

8

"How did you find this place?" I asked. The food was so good, if I ate another bite, they'd have to roll me out the door. I was pretty sure everyone here was a paranormal of some kind. It was nothing I could point to specifically, just a vibe. A hint of magic in the air, perhaps.

"I know a guy who knows a guy," Dyson replied. "Actually guy who knows a girl who knows a guy who… You get the idea."

I laughed softly and downed the last of my wine. "I get it. Don't tell me, you're really shifter royalty of some kind."

He cocked his head. "Is there such a thing? Maybe there should be. Can I just declare myself king or something?"

I pretended to think seriously about it for a moment. "I think you have to invade something first. Besides, isn't Kane the older brother? That might make him king first."

Dyson clicked his fingers. "Damn, that's a big flaw in the plan. Never fear though, I can think about an invasion and plot to over-throw my brother at the same time."

I snorted. "Should I start calling you Your Majesty?"

He waved a hand in dismissal. "Nah, but you can bend the knee any time." The look he gave me made my pulse race and sent blood throbbing through my lower body and between my legs.

"I'll bear that in mind," I said as coolly as I could, which wasn't very cool because my voice broke on the last word. Stupid voice. I swallowed and smiled sweetly, as if nothing had happened.

He gave me a knowing smile in return. "I'll pay for dinner."

"No." I sat up straight. "I will. I mean, I'll pay for mine."

"Independent girl, I like that." He nodded approvingly and pulled out his phone.

We had both had ours in our pockets until now. A guy who didn't stare at his screen all night was a refreshing find.

We rose and tapped our phones on the machine at the front of the restaurant. Modern technology, it was like its own kind of magic.

"It's almost too easy, isn't it?" he said as we walked out into the autumn night air. "Tap, pay, forget."

"You sound like my father," I teased.

He tucked his arm into mine. "Either your father is very hip, or you're implying I sound like an old fart."

I leaned into Dyson. "I wouldn't rule out either of those things," I teased.

He chuckled. "Do you feel like a walk beside the harbour?"

No. I feel like dragging you into a dark alley, tearing off all of your clothes and licking my way up to your...

"Sure. It's a nice night out."

The sky was clear, although the city lights all but obscured the stars. The air held a hint of late summer, even though it was April. Winter never fell too hard here, but the weather would cool soon enough to dress warmly against it in a month or two.

We made small talk as we walked toward the foreshore. As always, the bustle of people and sound of restaurants echoed across the water. Sydney, like all big cities, never slept. Still, we managed to find a bench away from anyone and, if not in darkness, at least it was darker here than in other places.

"This is more like it," Dyson said as he pulled me to him. "Nothing against crowds, but sometimes it's nice to be alone." His mouth was so close he breathed warm air on my cheek and neck.

I shivered. "It is," I agreed. "What do you normally do when you're alone?" The question was so stupid I could have kicked myself for asking it.

He laughed softly and leaned in to nibble my neck. It sent a burst of heat between my thighs.

"Usually I sleep, or fantasise about beautiful women, like you," he murmured.

My face heated. "You think I'm beautiful?"

He sat back and looked at me in surprise. "Of course I do, you're gorgeous. In fact, there's nothing hotter than a woman who doesn't realise how gorgeous she is."

Before I could respond, he pressed his mouth to mine, firm, but with promise. His tongue slid across my lips. I opened my mouth to let him probe inside.

His hand went to my hip. I wanted to beg him to touch me all over, but his hand stayed there until he pulled back.

His face was flushed, but he smiled. "I should get you back before you turn back into a pumpkin."

The way his jeans tented in the front suggested he felt what I felt. The fact he was willing to step back and wait was both endearing and infuriating. My body was on fire and I wanted to be doused. On the other hand, there was no rush. It wouldn't hurt to get to know each other first.

Ok, it might hurt, but I'd live.

I nodded and let him pull me to my feet. "For the record, that's not what happened in that fairytale."

He shrugged. "I've always thought it was more plausible than wearing a shoe made of glass. Wouldn't it snap when she put her weight on it?"

"Probably," I agreed.

He laced his fingers in mine and we walked slowly back to toward the car.

Before we got more than a few dozen footsteps, something rushed past me.

I froze.

Dyson stopped and turned back to me. "What is it? Is something wrong?"

"You didn't feel that?" I scanned around in front of me and listened.

"I feel a lot of things right now," he said jokingly, "you might need to be more specific."

I huffed a laugh. "It felt like something brushed past my leg."

He frowned. "I didn't—"

Something whizzed around both of us, fast enough to whip up a breeze. It paused and for a split second I caught sight of—

"That couldn't possibly be—"

"I think it is."

Then it was gone as fast as it had come. I waited for a long time, but if it came back, it concealed itself better. After maybe five minutes I almost was sure it was gone. Only then did I sag slightly.

"Either I'm losing my mind, or that was a gargoyle," I said.

"If you're losing your mind, then so am I," Dyson agreed. "I've heard about some…weird shifters, but I've never seen one before."

"You think that was a shifter?" I asked.

He shrugged. "What else? Gargoyles aren't usually a thing, unless they're carved out of stone."

"Gargoyle shifters aren't usually a thing either," I said softly. I frowned. "Wait, what do you mean you've heard of some weird shifters before?"

"Just that," he replied. "Most shifters are animals of some kind. Occasionally they're animals which are now extinct, but… I've heard some can shift into creatures that never existed."

"Like gargoyles."

"Exactly. And—believe it or not—dragons." He ran a hand over his hair and looked troubled.

"Dragons?" I echoed. "How?"

"I'm not sure. A combination of magic and the ability to shift. But —not, because they don't exist."

I had already guessed magic was involved in some way. I hadn't seen the gargoyle because they had been inside a bubble of magic. The ability to make oneself invisible was a basic skill for most witches and wizards, although it was often the bane of their parents. Luckily sound escaped the bubble, so giggles helped to locate wayward young paranormals.

The gargoyle had dropped their bubble for long enough to show us what he was, if not who. The question was why? Well, that was one of the questions anyway. I asked Dyson another, "Why the hells is a gargoyle following me around?"

He raised his hand in a shrug. "Because he thinks you're cute too?"

I rolled my eyes slightly. "What makes you think they're a he?"

"Just a vibe I got," Dyson replied easily.

"Oh, for a moment there I assumed gargoyles could only be male." I quirked an eyebrow at him.

"Non-existent creatures, just like regular paranormals, can do or be whatever they want," he said easily. "They won't get any judgment from me."

"Me either."

He nodded. "I had a feeling you wouldn't. You don't seem the type to go around judging people."

"My life is complicated enough," I replied. "Is it true that trans shifters can shift into the sex they feel best represents them?"

He swung our hands between us and started to walk again. "It is. A trans woman shifter can become a lioness. Cool, huh?"

"Very," I agreed. "I guess magic gets it better than the outside anatomy does."

"Magic is as clever as fuck," Dyson agreed. "Smarter than me, even."

I laughed. "You're so modest."

"Not in the slightest," he said unapologetically. "Why try to hide it when you're good looking, talented, clever..."

I shook my head at him. On anyone else, his brash nature might be annoying. On him, it fit like a tailored suit and expensive shoes. Or board shorts and bare feet.

"Seriously though, should I be worried if a shifter slash witch or wizard is following me?" The question was mostly rhetorical. Given my mother was a powerful witch, she had enemies. There was always a chance that sooner or later she'd piss someone off enough that they'd come after me. If that's what this was, the sooner we got back to the academy, the better.

"I think between us we can take care of any magic slash animal they throw at us," Dyson replied. "I heard about your skill in self-defence. Maybe you could give me some pointers some time."

"I'd be happy to," I said, although I don't know what I could teach a guy who could shift into an animal which could rip a person's throat out if he wanted to. I guess he might not always be in a position where he could shift. It never hurt to be too careful.

Without giving him any warning, I had one arm twisted behind his back and the other pressed to the wall beside him. He was taller than me, tall enough that my eyes were level with his chin. His mouth opened in surprise.

"Lesson number one, always be on guard against attacks," I told him.

"Um, I'll bear that in mind." He leaned down to kiss me but winced at the pressure on his arm.

"Oops, sorry." I let him go and took a step back.

He rubbed his arm lightly. "Remind me not to piss you off."

I smiled wryly. "I really didn't mean to hurt you."

"If anyone asks, I'll say I fell over my own two feet." He took my hand again.

"Rather than say a woman got the better of you?" I asked, a little more touchy than I intended.

"Absolutely not!" he replied immediately. "Rather than admit I was caught off guard. I have a reputation to uphold, after all."

"Oh, you do?" I asked.

"Of course. Who ever heard of a dog being caught unawares?"

I had no answer for that. "Why is Kane so shy about saying what he can shift into? Is it really that bad?"

"That depends what you call bad," Dyson said. "I'm not telling you though. That would violate the bro code."

"Bro code?" I laughed.

"Yes. Even though we fight, and he thinks I'm a dick, there's still things I wouldn't do. Lines I wouldn't cross."

"Dating the same woman is all right?" I asked tentatively. Plenty of guys wouldn't be okay with it.

"As long as everyone is consenting, then anything goes," he replied.

I nodded. "So tell me, is walking around naked in the corridors something you do often?"

He threw back his head and laughed. "Not usually, but I made a bet. I couldn't very well lose, could I now?"

"I guess not." It's not the kind of bet I would make made, but each to their own. "What would you have lost if you had?"

"Ah now, that would be telling." He tapped his nose with his finger.

"Don't tell me, bro code?" I asked.

"Something like that," he agreed.

We reached the car and he opened my door before walking around to the driver's side.

I stopped with my hand on the door and looked around. I had that feeling again—that someone was watching. Could it be the gargoyle shifter? How did a gargoyle shifter even exist? I would say something about it all was off, but the whole thing gave me the chills. Whatever I did, I would have to watch my back.

I slid into the seat and closed the door firmly behind me. The clunk it made was satisfying. They just don't make cars like they used to.

I resisted the urge to lock it. If the gargoyle wanted me dead, I probably would be. Showing himself to us was a warning, I was sure of it.

What I didn't know was why.

9

"PEYTON, can I talk to you after practice?" Nash's expression was as intense as ever, but there was something more today. Something I couldn't quite read.

Curious, I nodded, "Sure, sir." I was slick with sweat after a rigorous training session, but I felt good. Since joining the academy's combat team, I was more fit than I had ever been. Nash rarely smiled and pushed us all to the edge of our limits, but he kept us on our toes. We all bitched and complained about aching muscles and all the hard work, but by the end of a session, I knew he'd wrung more out of me than I'd known I'd had. By the end of the first month at the academy, I'd even dropped a dress size.

I'd spent much of that month keeping an eye out for the gargoyle, or some other mythical creature, but saw nothing out of the ordinary. After a few weeks, I started to forget about it. Maybe whatever it was about wasn't going to happen after all.

I grabbed a towel and wiped my face. What I needed right now was a cold shower. Being around Nash, Dyson and Kane, but with nothing happening with any guy, I was getting antsy. Sharing a room made it all the more perilous. A girl could only have so many "extra long" showers before it became obvious as to what I was doing in there. Not that I was ashamed of masturbating, but I would always feel uncomfortable doing it when Ariana was sitting in the next room listening to the water flow.

I flopped down onto the mat and stretched while everyone filtered out of the training room. It wouldn't do to have sore muscles tomorrow. Saturday was party night, when a bunch of us would head to the city and drink and dance until the sun came up. Waddling to the train with stiff muscles would be embarrassing, to say the least.

Finally, Nash sat beside me and wiped his face with his own towel. "You're doing well," he said simply.

"Thanks." Gods, he might not be the friendliest guy, and he was a teacher, but damn, having him sit so close made my heart race.

He nodded. "I was wondering if you wanted to do some extra training? One on one?"

I almost choked on my pent up lust. *One on one? Oh hells yeah.*

"Um," I squeaked. For real, I squeaked. "I, uh—" Have lost the ability to be articulate. *Fuck.*

"You don't have to," he said, a slight frown on his brow. "I just thought—you could be amazing?"

"I'm not already?" The stupid words left my lips before I could stop them.

He smiled—actually smiled—although it was faint. "As a matter of fact, you are, but there's always room for improvement."

I blushed. "Yeah, that's true. The bit about improvement, I mean. I've learnt a lot from you already but I'm sure I can learn more." Some of it might actually be related to hand to hand combat.

"That goes both ways." His expression gave away nothing. "You're never too old to learn."

I snorted softly. "You're not old at all."

He ran a hand over his head. "No, I suppose not. Sometimes it feels like—" He shook his head. "It doesn't matter."

"No, it does." I put a hand on his arm. "If you want to talk about it, I'm a good listener."

He licked his lips. "Let's just say it's been a long road to get here. I won't bore you with the details."

"I bet they aren't boring," I assured him.

He thought about that for a moment. "No, you're right, they're not, but there's a lot I'm not proud of."

"No one's perfect." I lowered my hand to the mat. "Not even me."

"Are you sure about that?" The corners of his eyes crinkled.

"Are you teasing me?" I asked.

"Maybe just a bit," he admitted. "Why, does it seem like the stick is so far up my ass I can't make a little joke?"

"Well—" I hedged.

He sighed. "Like I said, there's a lot I'm not proud of."

"Did you kill anyone?" I intended it as a joke, but the laughter died before it left my throat. His face was like a stone wall, except the sides of his mouth, which were pulled back so hard I thought he might snap.

The blood drained from my face. "You did?" I should probably get up now, run away and never look back.

"To be clear," he said, his voice as tight as his expression, "I only did it because they would have killed me first if I hadn't. And some friends —well, allies—also."

I licked my lips. "Is that why you're here? Because of what happened?"

"In a manner of speaking, yes," he replied. "To keep them safe, to keep myself safe and to teach paranormals like you to do the same." His eyes searched my face as though he was looking for something behind my eyes.

"I understand," I said softly. "Sometimes life makes us do things we don't want to do. People get hurt, or worse. As long as you don't go around looking for trouble…"

"At times, trouble finds us," he said, "but if I could have avoided taking a life, I would have."

I nodded. "I believe you."

For some reason, he looked relieved. He nodded. "Good. You're the first person I've told." His expression turned anxious. "You have to swear not to breathe a word to anyone."

"I swear. Who would I tell anyway?" I asked lightly.

He raised an eyebrow at me. Okay, he was right, I had a few friends I could blab to, but I wouldn't.

"I mean it, I won't tell anyone," I assured him. I held up a finger. "I pinky swear."

He looked taken aback but hooked his finger around mine and we shook.

The next thing I knew, he'd pulled me to him and mashed his lips against mine. I was so shocked I couldn't breathe for a moment. Then I was kissing him back. My tongue tangled with his and my arms wound around his neck.

My heart racing, I lay back and pulled him down with me, so he lay over me, his mouth on mine.

If he was surprised by this turn of events, he gave no sign. He didn't even pause. Instead, he took my hands, pinned them above my head and straddled my body. I wound my legs around his hips and ground myself against his growing erection.

He groaned. He kept one hand on my wrists and the other ran down my sides to cup my ass. By the time he slid it around to rub at the front of my leggings, I was all but panting. I rubbed myself against his hand, wanting more, needing more.

He pulled at the front of my leggings and slipped his hand inside and under my panties.

"Oh, gods," I whispered. "Please..."

"Please, what?" He ran the tips of his fingers around the top of my legs, over my ass, everywhere but where I needed him.

"Please touch me," I begged.

"Hmmm," he mused. He pulled his hand out of my panties and for a moment I thought he'd step away. Instead, he pulled at the top of my leggings, tugged them halfway down my legs. I kicked them the rest of the way off. My panties followed. "Tell me what you need," he whispered.

"I need your hand on my clit," I said, my mouth dry. Not surprising, I think all the moisture in my body was now between my legs.

"What's the magic word?" He ran his fingers over my thighs again.

"Please." If he didn't hurry, I was going to scream. Maybe that was what he wanted. He obviously liked it when I begged.

His tongue traced my lower lip. "I like being called sir in class, but I think out of class, it might be appropriate too, especially now."

I was going to come without his help at this rate. "Please, sir."

I gasped as he plunged his fingers into me. With urgency and not a bit of gentleness, he rammed them in and out of me. I bucked against his hand and bit my lip from screaming in ecstasy. This was *exactly* what I needed right now.

Just before I came, he pulled his hand away. "Not just yet." He grabbed up my discarded leggings and used them to tie my wrists to each other. I had never been tied up or dominated like this before. I was beyond turned on.

I watched him move down my body, bit by bit. Slowly he pushed up my tank top and claimed a nipple with his mouth. He sucked for a few moments, then bit down on my tender skin. I cried out and my eyes watered, but I was no less aroused. An intense look on his face, he did the same with my other nipple.

"Please, sir," I panted. "I need to come."

He raised an eyebrow at me, then scooted down lower. He parted my legs and dove in, face first, his tongue lapping at my folds and clit.

"Mmmm, gods," I breathed. "Yes." The pressure built again. He looked up at me, eyes on mine while he licked and sucked at my tender, swollen bud. I bucked against his mouth. Gods, it felt so damned good. I didn't care that he was my teacher, my coach, or that anyone might walk in on us. All I knew was the feel of his hot mouth.

I couldn't contain the cry when I finally came, heat washing over me and carrying me away for long, slow, intense minute.

I wasn't even down when he pulled away and wiped his face. He crawled up to untie my hands and toss me my panties and leggings.

"Sir?" I frowned at him. "You don't want to...fuck me?"

He swallowed audibly. I could tell by the erection tenting his pants that he did.

"Of course I want to," he said, his voice strained. "I can't... I shouldn't have... you deserve better than an asshole like me."

Before I could even respond, he'd jumped up, grabbed his towel and stormed out of the training room.

"Was it something I said?" I muttered to myself. I watched the door in case he changed his mind, but it stayed shut while I quickly pulled on my clothes and wrapped my towel around my neck. My body throbbed where he'd touched me. Some of the lust was satisfied, but not all of it, not by a long way. I wanted to have his cock inside me, to feel…

I shook my head. Man or woman, no meant no and he'd been very clear in that. If anything like this happened again, well, we'd see. For all I knew, he'd avoid me now. I hoped that wasn't the case. Just thinking about the things he'd done to me made my pulse race. He'd given me a little taste, but I wanted more, much more.

I sat on a bench to pull on my socks and shoes and thought about the things he'd said. Lust wasn't a normal reaction to being told someone had killed someone else, even for me. The logical response was to be repulsed, but I had meant it when I said I believed him. He didn't seem the kind to take a life for no good reason. I knew normals sometimes put paranormals in a position where we had no choice but to fight back. I'd heard this from my mother all my life. To hear it from someone else and have it be so raw, was something else. I suspected whatever had happened, it hadn't happened long ago.

I teased my lower lip with my teeth. Did I really want to know what had happened? Part of me knew it was none of my business. The rest of me knew I'd look into it. If nothing else, I wanted to know if it had anything to do with the strange things I had seen. Although I had no reason to assume they were connected, I had a feeling they were.

I tied my laces into precise bows and rose. If he hadn't come back by now, I suppose he wasn't going to.

I sighed to myself. I was going to need another "extra-long" shower, even after that orgasm. "Damn it," I said to myself. "And damn you, sir."

I turned off the light and closed the door behind me. This would definitely complicate things, but I didn't care. His tongue was amazing.

I O

ARIANA GAVE me a worried look over her coffee cup. "Are you sure you're all right?" she asked. She had been watching me with that expression for a couple of days now. I'd given her short answers whenever she spoke to me. Not rude—at least I hoped not—but as brief as I could get away with. Mostly my thoughts were occupied with Nash and the way he'd fled the room in such a hurry.

Him and study. I wasn't going to let my education suffer for the sake of a guy.

I ran a hand over my hair and sighed. "I'm sorry, I just—" How did I even begin to explain what had happened? Should I try? While there weren't any laws against screwing teachers, the academy might not look favourably on Nash for what we'd done. Sure, I was a consenting adult, but he was the one who could fail me if he wanted to. To say he'd held all the power wouldn't be an exaggeration. It was a turn on that made me wet to think about, but it wasn't wrong. The fact I'd surrendered to him so fully...

And there went my mind, imagining me tied to his bed while he licked me from my... I cleared my throat. I probably shouldn't be thinking of him like that. Still, he was hot and I didn't regret anything. Not yet anyway.

I glanced around the busy dining hall, then I told her, without going into too much detail, what had happened.

She gaped at me. "You and—wow!" To my relief, she seemed impressed. I hadn't been sure she wouldn't go straight to the school board and tell on us. "Dyson, Kane and now him. I don't know how you do it. Guys just..." She mimed swooning.

I smiled, but it turned in a grimace. "Complicate the hells out of my life?" I suggested.

"That too," she grinned. "Isn't that what they're for? Although," she sighed, "the only one who has shown any interest in me is Hamish."

Now it was my turn to gape. "Oh? When did that happen?" Had I really been so caught up in my own drama I hadn't noticed what was going on with her? She was—well, my best friend here at the academy. I missed Jess though, now more than ever. She would have known what to do. No, she would have told me to chase all of the guys and to be sure to sleep with them as often as possible. I might not chase, but I was *trying* to do the latter. Well, as much as I could without throwing myself at them.

"Yesterday," Ariana replied. "He almost fell over my foot, then he asked me out for dinner."

"And?" I prompted. "Are you going?"

"I..." She looked down at the table. "I thought about it. He seems nice and all, but he's not really my type."

"Oh." I nodded. "What is your type?"

She glanced back up, but before she could respond, Kane appeared beside our table. He stopped and stood with his hands in front of him. He toyed with his fingers, an obvious sign of nerves.

"Hey, Peyton, I was wondering if... um. Sorry, am I interrupting something?" His face turned adorably pink.

"Yes," I said.

At the same time, Ariana said, "No."

"Uh..." He stood looking awkward and licked his lips. "Maybe I should come back later." He took a step back.

"No, stay. It's fine, really," Ariana said. She swallowed the last of her coffee and rose. "I should get going anyway, I have an essay to write."

She wrinkled her pretty nose. "The history of magic is interesting, but I wish I could use magic to write essays." She shook her head and hurried away.

"I'm sorry, I didn't mean to interrupt," Kane said. He settled into the chair beside mine.

I shrugged. "It's okay, I can catch up with her later. Did you want something?"

"Yes," he replied immediately. "I mean, I—" He swallowed, but I didn't miss the hungry look he gave me. "I wanted to ask you something."

My pulse raced. Maybe the pretend voice of Jess in my head was right, I should jump into things more. "Yes," I replied firmly.

"Yes?" he echoed. "But you don't know what I'm going to ask."

"Are you asking me out? If so, then yes. If it's something else then I've probably just made a fool of myself." I laughed awkwardly.

"Oh, I was." He tapped his fingers nervously on the tabletop. "I—really, you will?"

"Of course, I've been waiting for you to ask. If you hadn't, I would have done it." Maybe. If I ever worked up the courage.

His blush deepened. He really was too stinkin' cute for his own good. "Great."

"Yeah. Um, so, did you have a date and time in mind?" I cocked my head at him.

"Oh, yes. Tonight. I have two tickets to a band. It's nothing big, just a pub band. I just thought…"

"That sounds perfect," I assured him. "I love live music."

"Me too." He grinned. "I'll pick you up from your room at eight."

"I'll put it in my phone." As if I would possibly forget.

I pulled it out of my pocket and turned on the screen. I brought up the calendar app and pressed on today's date.

The screen went black.

"Fuck, not again." I tapped at the screen. Where I touched, something appeared. I peered at it closer. "What the hells?"

"What is it?" Kane asked.

"I don't know. It looks like there's something in my phone." I lowered it so he could look. In place of the screen, or just blackness, vague shapes moved across the glass.

"What the… I've never seen anything like that before." He pressed a finger on the screen. The shapes surged toward his finger. He pulled it back and they dispersed. "That's fucking weird."

"You're telling me." I told him about the first time this had happened. "It wasn't quite like this though. I—" The screen went black and then flickered back to the normal, white screen of my calendar.

I placed the phone down on the table and watched it for a while, but nothing else abnormal seemed to happen.

"Is there any chance my phone is haunted?" I swallowed.

"I think that would only happen if ghosts were real," he replied.

"I wouldn't assume they aren't," I said uneasily. "I mean, we exist and apparently gargoyles and dragons too. The gods only knows what else might."

"That's true, I suppose." Dyson must have told him about the gargoyle. Or had I, while drinking one night? I couldn't remember. Either way, he knew. "Why haunt a phone though?"

"Why not haunt a phone?" I tapped the details of our date into the calendar and pressed "save." "They might be able to surf the net and watch porn."

Kane laughed softly. "I suppose they might."

I eyed him sideways. "Is that what you would do?" I asked teasingly.

"Um, I might." His throat bobbed. "Or stalk my brother on social media. If I die any time soon, it's probably going to be his fault somehow."

He gave me such a wry look, I burst out laughing.

"He is a lot to handle," I agreed. Not that it was a bad thing, in any way. Okay, maybe in a twin, but not in a guy friend-slash-whatever we were.

Kane sighed. "I know he doesn't mean to be. He's just…outgoing."

"Right." Without thinking, I leaned over and pressed my lips lightly to his. It was nothing like the heated kiss with Dyson or the unbridled lust with Nash. This kiss was sweet and soft. Kane tasted of some kind of spices I couldn't identify.

I sat back and licked my lips.

Kane looked stunned.

"I'm sorry, I shouldn't have assumed," I said softly. "I didn't think."

"No, it's all right," he said quickly. "I liked it."

"Really?" Thank the gods for that.

"Really." He raised a trembling hand to my cheek and ran a finger over it. Slowly, so slowly, he sat forward and kissed me, a little more firmly this time.

I decided it was cinnamon he tasted like. Maybe some nutmeg thrown in there. He tasted better than a pie. I could have gobbled him down, then and there. Instead, I pulled back and smiled.

"That was nice," I told him.

He smiled. "It was nice for me too." He looked as though he had more to say, but he said nothing. He took my hand in his and kissed the centre of my palm. For such a sweet gesture, it sent a jolt of heat right to my core.

If I was Jess, I might drag him under the table and screw him then and there. I wasn't though, and phones had cameras. If there was anything I knew about this place it was that everyone had a phone, even the shifters.

I swallowed and forced pure thoughts into my dirty mind. One or two managed to stick. My mind objected to too much cleanliness. Life was too short for that.

"I should go and get ready for our date then," I said once my head was clear enough for me to risk speaking.

"Me too," he agreed. He looked like a man who had stumbled onto a pile of good luck and didn't know what to do with it. Gods, I hoped I didn't disappoint him.

He glanced down at my phone and frowned. "You should probably take that to Madame Luc. Just in case there's something strange going on with it. It might just be a software glitch."

"It's possible," I agreed. "Or one of the social media platforms is using some new tech to stalk its users." If that was the case, all their users would be in an uproar. Then they'd go back to using it as though nothing had happened. People were, if nothing else, good at denying the existence of a problem until it impacted them directly. Even then...

"Yeah." He touched my screen with a fingertip, but it did nothing but turn on the screen and ask for my passcode. "It seems fine now."

I grinned.

"What?" he asked.

"I was just wondering if your brother would pretend to be sucked into the phone, just for shits and giggles."

Kane smiled wryly. "That's exactly something he would do," he agreed. "Maybe I should have. He keeps telling me to lighten up."

I cocked my head at him. "I like you just how you are." And I liked Dyson and even Nash. When did things get so messy?

"I like you how you are too," he replied. He rose and offered me his hand. "Just think about what I said about Madame Luc."

"I will," I agreed. I had some time before our date. Maybe I would speak to her first, if only to put both of our minds at rest.

"Really? I mean, good." He nodded vigorously.

"Really," I assured him. I guessed Dyson brushed him off whenever he made any suggestions like that. Poor guy, it must suck being a twin at times. Or being a sibling of any kind. Twins didn't necessarily have the monopoly of being jerks to each other.

I tucked my phone into my pocket, but to be honest it made me feel uneasy. If it was haunted, then I had a ghost near my ass. If it wasn't, then I had something else weird near my ass. Call me crazy, but I kinda liked my butt. It was one of my better features. I preferred it un-haunted or possessed by phone demons or social media software.

"See you in a couple of hours." He gave me a quick kiss on the cheek and slipped away.

I smiled and headed in the opposite direction.

11

I KNOCKED on the open office door and peeked inside. "Madame Luc?"

"Oui?" She looked up from behind her desk and tucked some hair behind her ear. "Yes, come in. Uh, Peyton Chapel, am I correct?"

"Yes, Madame," I replied. "That's right." I stepped into the doorway. "I'm sorry to bother you, but I think I have a problem with my phone. I was hoping you could help."

Her office was tiny. I could probably have touched the opposite walls with my fingertips. All it contained was a small desk, a computer and a filing cabinet. No books; not one.

Welcome to the digital age.

"Yes, yes." She held out her hand. "What is the problem?"

I handed her my phone and told her what I'd seen. "It's done it twice that I know of, but it's never done it before."

She raised the phone until it almost touched her nose. She tilted it this way and that, then lowered it and touched the screen. It turned on as normal. She held the phone toward me so I could enter the passcode, then looked through the settings. She frowned as she pressed and swiped and pressed again.

"Could it be a glitch?" I asked. "Or a virus?" I tucked my hands into my pockets. The idea someone might have done this on purpose made me want to grind my teeth.

"Possibly," she replied. She frowned at the phone in a way that didn't fill me with confidence. "Devices can behave in peculiar ways. Sometimes we find out why, sometimes we don't." She glanced up at me, then back as something loaded.

"Right. Maybe it won't happen again." I shrugged. "Or I should get a new one."

"Perhaps." She turned the phone off and handed it back. "I can see nothing wrong. No strange settings or apps. Your storage capacity looks normal for what you have on there. You might want to delete some photographs though. You may find it works faster with more memory available."

I grimaced. I was probably attached to all four thousand of the photos I had on there.

Maybe.

Okay, I could stand to get rid of three or four of them. Maybe five.

"What do I do if it happens again?" I asked.

"See if you can take a screenshot, or have a friend record it." She leaned back in her chair. It groaned in such a way I thought it might break and send her crashing into the wall behind her. Fortunately, it held. You'd think an academy which could give out phones could afford decent chairs. Priorities.

"In the meantime," she continued, "I wouldn't worry too much. It should be fine." She started to nod, but something in her expression made me wonder if she was being completely honest with me.

"All right, thank you." I backed up into the corridor just as she closed the door.

I caught the words, "You are welcome," before she closed it completely. I stared at the door for a moment before I turned away and almost ran into the guy who had stared at me at the party.

Close up, he was even better looking than he was at a distance, but his expression was stony.

"Um, sorry," I muttered.

"Look where you're going, and you don't have to be." His voice was as cold as the look in his eyes. Like he was at the party, he was dressed from head to toe in black. Everything fit him perfectly, which was to say a little too tight, so his biceps bulged out of his short sleeves. I'd bet his jeans hugged his ass, but I couldn't very well check from here.

I opened my mouth to offer some sort of explanation, but his tone rubbed me the wrong way.

Instead, I retorted, "You should take your own advice. You could hurt someone if you run into them."

He curled his lip at me. "*Please*, I'm not that clumsy." The accusation that I was, hung in the air between us like the invisible but toxic fog that comes after taco Tuesday.

I swear, if he could have shot lasers out of his eyes, he would have. I'd be incinerated on the spot. Nothing left but a pile of ashes. Smoking hot ashes, but still... Unfortunately for him, I could have used magic to knock him on his ass. Fortunately for him, I didn't want to get in trouble for doing it.

"Whatever," I snapped. "Are you going to move out of the way? You're taking up half the corridor." Yeah, that was an exaggeration, but I didn't care. He pissed me off and I wanted to be away from him, but in a way that didn't look like I was intimidated.

He laughed, but it was a bitter sound, not one of humour. "You could move out of *my* way."

"For fuck's sake," I growled. "What are you, a four year-old?"

"I was thinking the same thing about you," he replied coolly. "Are you old enough to be here?"

"No, I'm a fucking prodigy." I planted a hand on my hip and squared my shoulders back. "I'm really twelve."

He mimed my posture. "You certainly act like it."

I dropped my fist. "How the hells would you know how I act? You've just met me."

He shrugged with one shoulder. "I've seen you around."

"Yeah, at the party the other week. Why were you staring at me?" I narrowed my eyes at him.

He hesitated. "I was looking *past* you." He was a crap liar.

"Bullshit." I smirked. "You were looking straight at me."

He averted his eyes from mine. "I've never seen anyone with green hair before."

There was more, I could tell, but I wasn't going to get it from him. To be honest, I wasn't bothered to try. Who cared why he was looking at me? He was obviously an asshole. One I'd given enough time to already.

"Yeah, well, get used to it." So far, it hadn't grown out, even at the roots. I should have asked Madame Luc about it. I made a mental note to do that later. I really did prefer I not have a streak of emerald hair for the rest of my life.

"It doesn't sound like you have gotten used to it." Now he sounded amused, but totally at my expense.

Fucker.

"That's none of your business." I put a hand on my hair and shoved past him.

He laughed—*laughed*—at me. I watched him out of the corner of my eye, his face only a hand's width from mine, before I put him behind me.

I rounded on him. "Has anyone told you you're a jerk?"

He grinned, but there was nothing warm about it. "Frequently. It's kinda my thing."

"Obviously," I snapped.

He crossed his arms over his chest. He looked muscular under his black t-shirt, but only if I was looking. Which I wasn't. Much. Okay, a bit. But not too much, since he was an asshole. "Yeah. What's your excuse?" he asked.

I smiled sweetly. "I'm perfectly nice, unless you rub me the wrong way."

He leaned in closer to me. His breath caressed my cheek. He smiled of musk, and strangely, pizza. A tasty combination on anyone else. Okay, on him too, but I didn't want to dine at this table.

He spoke in a whisper. "I think you prefer to be rubbed the *right* way."

I pushed him back with my fingertips. "Of course I do, but I'm particular about who does the rubbing. Assholes need not apply."

Although, where did that leave things with Nash? He claimed to be one himself. He certainly acted like it sometimes. He was different though, I decided, because I knew there was a good guy under there somewhere. This guy—he seemed like jerk, through and through. And through.

"You don't know what you're missing," he told me. "There's nothing more fun than an angry fuck."

"You've got the angry part down pat." My gaze scanned him up and down. "I'll pass on the fuck though. You don't seem like you know how to satisfy a lover." That was a flat-out lie. He looked like a guy who knew exactly what he was doing. I had to bite my tongue to keep from licking my lips.

He snorted. "Right back at you."

I smiled, flipped him off and said, "Fuck you."

"You wish."

"Not a chance." Why was I still standing there talking to this guy anyway? "What's your name?"

He appeared surprised by the question. "Matt. Why?"

"Because it's more satisfying to say your name when I tell you to get lost." I cleared my throat dramatically. "Fuck off, Matt. See, much better."

He rolled his eyes. "You wish, *Peyton*."

Now I was the surprised one. "How do you know my name?"

He looked smug. "I made a point of learning who to avoid."

My mouth dropped open. He really was a whole new level of dick. "And yet, you can't get out of my way in a corridor."

"That wasn't my fault," he said.

I started to retort but closed my mouth and shook my head. "I've wasted enough time on this conversation." More than enough. I should be in the shower right now.

"Funny, I was thinking the same thing," he remarked.

"That you've wasted my time?" I asked. "At least we agree on that."

He rolled his eyes and opened his mouth, but I turned away before he could speak.

With hurried steps, I headed away, toward my room. I muttered to myself as I went. It got me a few stares of confusion or amusement, but I ignored them. It was what I did when I was particularly annoyed. This—Matt—had me at a whole new level of irritated. I'd met all kinds of people in the past, and the gods knows we can't like everyone, but this was different. If I didn't know better, I would think he had gone out of his way to be objectionable. Like—he'd followed me and lurked around in the corridor so he could almost run into me and insult me.

Of course, this whole line of thinking was totally insane. Who would bother to do such a thing to another person? Oh yeah, stalkers. But aren't stalkers usually crazed admirers? Apart from suggesting we sleep together *because* we didn't like each other—and I'm pretty sure he was joking about that—he obviously didn't like me at all. We all have those people we take an instant dislike to, right? I know I have met a few. That could be all this was. Something still niggled at the back of my mind though, something I couldn't put a finger on.

I chewed my lip and pulled out my phone to unlock my door. I thought back to the gargoyle and the warning I assumed they'd been trying to give me. Could they be warning against Matt? If they had, I got the message loud and clear. Stay away from the guy. If that was what the gargoyle had tried to tell me, they could have sent a text.

"Stay away from hot, but toxic guys who only wear black," I muttered. That was pretty good advice, right there. I made a note to follow it from now on. That didn't stop me from thinking about him when I got into the shower and wondering what his body looked like under his clothes.

I rinsed the idea away with my shampoo and followed it down the drain with my eyes. I would focus instead, on my date with Kane. That, I was looking forward to.

I smiled and got a mouthful of shampoo. While I spat and rinsed, I made another note—keep your mouth shut in the shower.

Also good advice. See, I could be wise, once in a while.

1 2

I WAS STILL FUMING when Kane knocked on the door. Ariana must have ducked in and out while I was in the shower. Some of her stuff had been moved around, but only a hint of the perfume she preferred remained.

I took a deep breath before I turned the knob and opened the door. Naturally, that set off a coughing fit. My mouth still tasted of shampoo. I must have swallowed some of it. At least my insides would be squeaky clean.

Kane stepped inside and patted my back while I doubled over, my hand over my mouth.

"Are you all right?" He grabbed my water bottle from the table beside my bed and handed it to me.

I took a gulp, then another, and managed to nod. "Yes, I'm fine, thank you. I just like to choke on air from time to time."

He chuckled but looked as though he wasn't sure if he was supposed to do that or not.

I gave him a watery smile and placed my bottle back on the table. At least now I had forgotten about Matt. Oops, now he was in my head again. I shoved the thought of him away and smiled brightly.

"You look very handsome." He really did. The faded jeans with holes in the knees and fitted, blue t-shirt made me almost drool on the floor. I say "almost" because I turned away to grab my bag and wiped the side of my mouth so he couldn't see. Classy, that was me.

When I turned back. His face was pink, but he smiled broadly. "You're looking amazing yourself."

"Thanks," I mumbled. My skirt hung to just above my knees and my t-shirt was low cut to show a hint of cleavage. Not too much, I didn't want to look desperate. Be quiet, I wasn't *that* bad. Yet.

I'd put my hair up in a ponytail, taken it out and put it back up at least a dozen times since I dried it. It was currently down, so I guessed that's how I'd be wearing it tonight. Just in case, I grabbed a hair tie and slid it down my wrist.

"Okay, I'm ready," I said.

"Great." He gave me a look like he'd prefer to peel off all my clothes slowly and lick honey off my... He cleared his throat. "I guess we should go then."

"Yes, we should."

We stood and gazed at each other for a while longer. Finally, I stepped toward the door and opened it. "After you."

His eyes widened. "I'm sorry, I think that should have been my line."

I smiled and shrugged with one shoulder. "I'm an independent girl, I can open a door." I waved him out ahead of me and closed it behind us.

"All right, but let me get the next one," he said.

"If you insist."

He did insist, apparently. He opened every door between us and the pub, or he would have, but there was only the front one leading out of the academy and the one which led into the pub. The latter was already open.

We flashed our licences to the bored bouncer who only glanced at Kane's. He didn't even look at mine. I wasn't sure if I should be insulted or not.

"Would you like a drink?" Kane shouted over the throbbing music.

"Sure!" I shouted back. I grabbed his hand and led him toward the bar to order our drinks. Beer for him, bourbon and cola for me.

He yelled something I couldn't hear. I gave him a confused look and shrugged. He tried again. Once again, I shook my head.

"I can't hear you!" I yelled.

"What?" He looked exasperated, took my hand and led me to a door at the back of the pub, which opened onto the beer garden. "I said the band is out here."

"Oh. Gotcha." At the side of the garden—really just an outdoor space with tables—a wooden platform was covered in speakers, drums and various other band-related stuff. A couple of guys and a girl were occupied settings things up and testing instruments and sound.

"Let's sit."

I followed Kane to a table at the back of the garden, furthest from the band.

"I'm pretty sure we'll hear them from here." He slid onto a bench and moved over to make room for me.

"I'm pretty sure we'd hear them at the academy," I said with a grin.

He chuckled. "Probably."

I nestled in a little too close and he casually slung an arm over my shoulders.

"This is, um, nice," I said. His fingers were a hair from my breast.

"It is. I'm glad I got some time alone with you. Well, sort of." He waved a hand at the crowds which had started to flood in and fill the tables. Before long, it was standing room only and the band started up.

They played a few classic pub anthems and we sang along and grooved to the music. Every so often, Kane's hand would touch my nipple and send a jolt of heat though me. After a while, I forgot to listen to the band and was focusing on him instead. I suspected he was completely oblivious until he did it again and blushed. This wasn't just a casual brush past this time though. He rubbed the tips of his fingers over my sensitive peak.

Dear gods. I bit back a moan and wriggled so my ass was pressed against his groin. His erection grew until it was poking into me.

It was dark in this part of the garden and everyone but us was focused on the band. No one saw him slip his hand inside my shirt and under my bra. He caught my nipple between his thumb and forefinger and rolled it gently.

I let out a ragged breath and wriggled against him again. He pulled his hand out of my shirt and moved it down under the table.

No way, he wasn't going to…

He touched my thigh, then moved his hand over between my legs.

I swallowed and looked around to make sure no one was paying any attention to us. They weren't. I parted my legs and let his fingers dive down between them.

He rubbed against the front of my skirt, lightly at first, then more insistently.

"If you keep that up, I'm going to—" I panted.

"I want you to," He said in my ear.

Oh. My. Gods.

I licked my lips but didn't object when he tugged my skirt up a little more. He slipped a hand underneath and rubbed against the front of my panties.

I was so aroused by now I barely cared if anyone was watching. Still, I glanced around to double check. Nope, all eyes were on the band, or the other people at their tables.

With a ragged breath of his own, Kane worked my panties aside and touched my heated core.

I bit back a moan. I wanted to buck against him when he worked my clit, but I dare not do more than rock slightly.

"Come for me," he said in my ear.

And I thought he was the shy, quiet one. Well, you know what they say about them—they're usually the most outrageous.

I bit my lip. My head swum and stars danced above my head. He worked me a little harder, a little faster.

"Mmmm," I moaned. "I… I…" I came against his hand. My breath came out my nose in soft little pants. Pleasure washed over me, making the blood pound in my ears louder than the music.

I finally came down from my high and sagged again him.

"Good girl." He pulled his hand back out and tugged my skirt back into place.

I fixed my shirt while I caught my breath. "Should we finish this somewhere private?"

"Unless you want to stay and watch the band play," he said. His erection still pressed into my back, but he didn't sound as though he was in a rush.

I swivelled around to face him. "You really got off on that, didn't you?"

He smiled awkwardly. "Making you feel good? Yes."

"I mean, with all of these people here." I jerked my head toward them.

He licked his lips. "If they wouldn't kick us out, I'd strip down naked and take you on the table top."

His words aroused me all over again. I wasn't sure I could be that daring, but the idea of all those people watching us…

Oh gods.

"Is it the people or the thrill that we might get caught?" I asked.

He considered for a moment. "Both. I'm usually the one who doesn't get noticed." He grimaced at that. Of course he wasn't, Dyson was the one who paraded around naked. Apparently it ran in the family, but Kane hadn't acted on it yet. That I knew of.

"That would get you noticed all right." I could just imagine the kind of porn he preferred; groups and public places. At least we could do the latter. "I think I saw an alley on the other side of the pub."

A smile lit his face. "You'd be game?"

"Let's find out." I rose and offered him my hand.

He took it and we hurried out the rear entrance, past another bored bouncer. This one gave me a look which suggested maybe he had seen Kane with his hands up my skirt. My face heated, but I gave him a smile as we walked by.

The alley was pitch dark but joined the back of the pub to the busy street. I could have made a bubble of magic around us to hide us, but I didn't want to. Anyone could walk through at any moment. That made it all the more exciting.

No sooner had we stepped into the shadows that Kane's hands went up my shirt to caress my breasts and tease my nipples. He pulled down one side and my bra cup with it and leaned in to run his tongue over my hard peak.

I undid his jeans and tugged them down just enough to free his erection. Just as I suspected, his cock was big, like Dyson's, and rock hard. I ran my hand up and down his warm length. He moaned and grabbed on to my waist.

"I don't want to come in your hands," he said breathlessly.

I didn't want that either, I wanted to have him inside me. Now.

He lifted the front of my skirt and tugged down my panties. They fell to my feet and I kicked them off.

He turned me so my back was to the wall and put a hand under my leg to bring it up to his waist. I guided the tip of his cock to my opening and moved my hand out of the way.

He groaned and pressed himself into me. We both let out a moan then and stood like that for a full minute. Then he began to move, thrusting in and out of me with a careful rhythm. With every thrust, he hit me inside and out and drove me toward another orgasm.

"You feel so good," he breathed.

"So do you."

With his spare hand, he kneaded my breast, massaging my nipple and driving me closer and closer to the edge.

With all the noise coming from inside the pub, no one could hear me, so I didn't hold back little moans and sighs as I reached the edge of the precipice. I lifted my chin and cried out as another wave washed over me, filling my body with pounding, heated sensation.

Kane followed me a moment later, thrusting harder and harder into me, before he gripped my breast and let out a series of grunts.

Finally, he relaxed his posture and leaned his forehead on mine as we caught our breath.

A cough made me jump and I looked up as a couple of people

walked past. I had no doubt they'd gotten a good look at my exposed breast.

Oops.

They walked on by without stopping, but they both looked back a few times. Part of me wished they'd seen more.

Kane pulled out of me, dropped my leg and pulled up his jeans. He gave me a long look, as though he wanted to drink me in. "I've never met anyone like you," he whispered. He kissed me lightly on the mouth. "I'll walk you home," he said softly

I tugged my shirt back into place. Maybe I should feel weird about this, but I didn't. Not even a little bit.

13

"Today, we are working on something more complicated." Madame Luc declared.

After a couple of months at the academy, we had all mastered the art of moving things with our phones. The guy with the shaved head—Mustafa—learned how not to lift himself by accident. That was fortunate since his nose would have ended up mush eventually.

We had also learnt how to knock each other back. Hamish's arm had healed after being broken when he was thrown into a wall a bit too hard. As witches and wizards, we learnt how to blast people back to protect ourselves. Now we had to learn how to hold back, to control the exact amount of magic we used. Learning restraint, it turns out, is much harder than learning to use magic in the first place.

"On your phones, go to the usual website and click on lesson seven." The lecturer paced in front of the room. She seemed agitated today. Every lesson had become progressively more difficult, but we'd eventually managed them all, if not mastered them. What was so different about seven that looked like she walked on pins and needles.

I glanced at Ariana and we both shrugged and clicked on the lesson.

"Oh," I said softly.

"You will see," Madame Luc said, "that you have options. Due to the space in this room, we will work one at a time. Everyone push your tables to the back of the room."

We did as instructed and stood milling about. Everyone looked as nervous as I felt.

"You," Madame pointed at Mustafa. "You go first."

"Um." He rubbed at his nose. His hair had grown out a little and now stood in spikes on his head. "Okay." He stood apart from us, scrunched up his face and clicked on his phone.

A shape appeared in the open space to the side of the room. It writhed and danced like it was obscured by flames and smoke.

Mustafa's face creased in a deeper frown.

The shape coalesced a little more, into—of all things—a goat. The goat bleated but looked out of focus. It took a few steps forward and latched onto the jacket of one of the students, Violette Ying.

"Hey, it's real!" she squealed as the goat took a chunk out of the garment and started to chew it.

The class cracked up laughing, including Violette. That was until she inspected the damage more carefully. "Hey, that was a new jacket, you stupid fucking animal."

"Tut-tut, language, mademoiselle," Luc scolded. She couldn't punish her for swearing, since this was university, but that didn't mean she liked us doing it.

"Sorry Madame," Violette said, "but it was expensive."

The goat finished chewing and lunged at Violette for more just before it disappeared entirely.

"Why did you choose the goat?" Violette asked, glaring daggers at Mustafa.

"I dunno," he replied, "I thought it'd be fun."

She grunted and muttered something about, "Fucking goats, ruined a perfectly good…"

"Mademoiselle Ariana," Madame Luc waved in her direction. "You try. See if you can get yours to appear more strongly. And maybe no goats, eh?"

Ariana grinned. "I'll try." She tilted her phone so I couldn't see her screen, then clicked on it, a sly smile on her face.

"What did you—shit!" Mustafa ducked as he was swooped by a bird which appeared as if out of nowhere. "Bloody hell, Ariana." He threw himself under the nearest table and hid.

The magpie—a black and white bird famous for swooping during their breeding season—was more in focus than the goat but disappeared after only a minute and one swoop.

"I'm sorry!" Ariana exclaimed. "I thought it might perch and sing. I quite like the oodle-oodle sound they make."

"Yeah." Mustafa crawled out from under the table and seemed to be pulling together what dignity he had left. I felt sorry for him, but it had been funny. At least a little bit.

"Try to keep it for longer next time," Madame said. "Although the magpie may be efficient in distracting an attacker for long enough for you to run."

"Madame," I said, "my father has a tattoo on his arm. Wouldn't that be quicker than using a phone?"

"Oui," she replied, "but it's much more obvious. To use a device means you may not be detected as the one doing the magic. However, it is wise to have a—how do you say—backup plan."

I nodded. "I see, thank you."

"You are welcome. You may go next."

I wrinkled my nose. I should have seen that coming. Lucky I had already chosen my creature out of the long list of those I could try to conjure up. My finger hovered over it, while I drew magic from around me. A tiny bit came from the silver Celtic-style ring I wore on my right hand. Although it would replenish, I preferred not to suck it all out at once. I drew more from the wood in the tables. The magic from them was weak and sad from being so compressed when made and covered in gum ever since. The metal in the legs held more magic, so I took some from there too. What I really needed was a good tree, or a cow. Believe it or not, cows actually contain a lot of magic. Being animals and eating grass, they were the epitome of nature. Why do you think milk is so good for you, not to mention a good burger?

I concentrated my magic on my phone and pressed the screen.

There, in front of me, a dark shape formed. After a moment, it came into sharper focus.

"It's a gargoyle," Violette said in surprise. Or was it awe? Maybe both.

The gargoyle turned toward her and bared what looked like sharp, pointy teeth.

"Crap!" She dove under the table when it took a step toward her. It lunged and took a chunk out of the table above her head. She screamed. "Peyton, get rid of it!"

"I don't know how!" I replied. I frowned at it, willing it away, but it turned toward me instead.

"Oh shit." I backed away a few steps, but my back hit the wall. "Madame, what do I do?"

"You need to wait it out," she replied, much more calmly than I felt.

The gargoyle turned and started toward her, its gait a slow, deliberate lope.

"Can it kill people?" Mustafa asked from under the table. When had he gone back underneath? It didn't matter, it was probably a smart move.

"Oui," Madame replied. "It's created by magic, but it's very much real." She even looked calm. How did she manage that? "The question is, how long will it last, and how would you fight such a creature?"

That was two questions, but I don't think anyone cared just now.

"Run like hells?" Mustafa suggested.

The gargoyle turned toward him and slashed at the table with long claws. It left five deep gouges in the tabletop.

"Stop talking," Hamish suggested. "It keeps going after people when they—eek!" He dove under the table beside Violette.

We all fell silent. The gargoyle paused and looked around slowly. It seemed to take us all in, one by one. Perhaps it was trying to decide who the tastiest one of us was. Evidently, it decided on Ariana. It moved toward her.

She let out a squeak.

"I don't think not talking is working," I remarked.

The creature glanced toward me but continued to stalk Ariana. She sidestepped around the edge of the room, toward the tables. It followed slowly, toying with her.

Her face was white as a sheet now. Her eyes were huge.

I moved behind the gargoyle. It didn't look back, but I sensed it knew I was there. How the hells had I magically created an intelligent creature, I had no idea. That was a question for later, if we survived this.

Ariana backed into a corner and the gargoyle closed in. It licked it lips, or what passed for lips at least. The slurp it made turned my stomach. This motherfucker I had created wanted to eat my best friend for lunch. Or a snack. The gods knew how much gargoyles actually ate.

It raised a claw and reached toward her.

At that moment, something inside me snapped. Digital magic be damned, I needed the old-fashioned kind. I drew a little from each of my classmates and threw it at the gargoyle. The blast knocked it sideways, off its feet and into the wall. It grunted as it slammed into cold, hard brick.

There, that'll show you—shit.

The gargoyle rose to its feet and shook like a dog after a bath. If the dog was pissed off enough to take your head off, that was. Hey, some dogs really, really hate being bathed.

It bared its teeth and started toward me like it was on a mission. It didn't just want to eat me, it wanted to grind my bones into dust and lap up every last drop of my blood. Not necessarily in that order. I saw that in its eyes, and more.

"Hey." I gave it a wave. "What's up?"

The gargoyle paused and cocked its head in confusion.

"Nice weather we're having," I said. "Well, if you like winter that is. It a bit cold out there, to be honest."

The gargoyle hissed.

"Yeah, a lot of people feel that way about winter," I agreed. "Personally, don't mind it."

The gargoyle growled.

I swallowed. I didn't know if it understood me, but I kept on talking, trying to distract it. "Aren't gargoyles supposed to be protectors? Why are you attacking us? Shouldn't you be defending us?" From what, I didn't know, maybe the goat or the magpie.

The gargoyle's growl deepened.

"That's what I thought."

It lunged and I threw myself to one side. I hit the floor hard and threw my arm up over my face. I screwed my eyes closed tight and waited.

Nothing happened.

I cracked open one eye, then the other. The gargoyle was gone.

"Well, that was different." I tried to stand, but my knees refused to hold my weight, so I stayed the floor and shook for a while.

"That was close." Mustafa looked as if he might spend the rest of the class under the table.

"Oui," Madame replied. "Magical creatures can be hard to control."

"You think?" Violette grunted.

"The situation was always well in hand." Madame's tone was curt. "This room is designed to protect against magic. None can get in or out."

"So, it could have killed us, but not left the room?" I asked.

"Precisely," Madame replied.

"Bloody hells, the liability insurance on this pace must be through the roof," I muttered.

"Oui," she agreed, "but how else are you to learn?"

"Maybe we should have started by creating something harmless?" Ariana said. "Like a turtle."

"Turtles bite," Mustafa said.

"Well… a kitten then," Ariana replied.

"Kittens also bite," Violette said. "And scratch."

"At least they don't try to eat your face," I pointed out.

"Oui, no more gargoyles in the classroom. I will have to contact the site and have them remove that option." Madame sniffed. "All right, who is next?"

14

"Hey, sexy."

After the class with the gargoyle, I was much more cautious of the one I had seen on my date with Dyson. I was jumpy too. So much so that when Dyson appeared at my elbow and spoke suddenly, I jumped almost out of my skin.

I pressed a hand to my chest, over my racing heart. "Dear gods, don't sneak up on a person," I said, once I'd caught my breath.

He grinned. "Sorry."

I narrowed my eyes at him. "You don't look sorry."

His grin just widened as he draped his arm over my shoulder. "I heard you created a monster," he said casually.

"No, I just *met* you," I said sweetly.

He threw back his head and laughed. "I guess I deserved that after scaring you."

"Damn right you did," I told him. Then I sighed. "You're right though." I filled him in on the whole gargoyle thing while we walked through the academy.

He looked thoughtful. "A magically created creature and a shifter are very different animals, generally speaking. Assuming the gargoyle we saw was a shifter, then you'll only be in danger if he wants you harmed."

"And if it was created by magic?" I asked. "Blasting it didn't seem to do much of anything to the one I conjured. It shook it off like I'd shoved it with my hand."

"It wouldn't matter if it was a gargoyle or a unicorn. If it was created to attack you, it will." Dyson shrugged.

"That's reassuring," I said sarcastically. "Except I didn't create it to attack me." I frowned. "Not that I know of, anyway. I'm pretty sure I don't have a death wish."

"Most magical creatures just do what their nature tells them to," he said slowly. "A magical dog will bite, bark or pee on your leg. Same with a shifter, but only if you ask nicely." He grinned.

"Under no circumstances would I ask you to do that," I said dryly.

He pouted. "Shame." His eyes shone, so I knew he was joking. At least, I hoped he was. I didn't want to shame anyone for their kink, but this one wasn't one of mine.

He ran a hand over his hair. "Magically created creatures are usually only aggressive if that's their nature, or if the witch or wizard told them to. Then they'll attack whatever is in front of them."

"I don't recall telling the gargoyle to damage academy property," I said slowly. "Since gargoyles aren't real, as such, then the gods only know what their nature is."

"Aggression is usually part of the existing spell; the tattoo or in this case, the link. I'm not sure why an academic website would have it inbuilt like that. That seems—badly thought out."

I snorted. "Ya think?"

He laughed. "Just a little bit. Still, no harm done. Although, think nice thoughts next time you conjure up any creatures, just in case."

"You think I did it?" If I had imbued the gargoyle with its not-so-charming personality without thinking, I wanted to know about it.

Dyson shrugged "It's possible. Magic isn't an exact science, especially when you're new to using it the way you're learning to here. Although, the gargoyle should have come with a failsafe embedded in the spell to make sure it didn't matter if you had. Or…"

"Or what?" I prompted.

"Or Madame Luc didn't expect any of you to be able to make the spell last for that long. One of my friends, when he took the class last year, could only make a butterfly appear for a matter of moments."

"Butterflies aren't known for living long," I pointed out.

Dyson looked surprised, then burst out laughing. "That's true," he said when he managed to contain himself. "But longer than his, I suspect."

"Did he ever learn to make them last for longer?" I might have to try to make mine last for less time, in case I conjured up something nasty again.

"Not really," Dyson replied. "Last I heard, he managed to make a snail, but someone else stepped on it before anyone could tell."

I wrinkled my nose. "That sounds messy."

"I suppose it would be. Dead magical creatures tend to last longer than alive ones, for some reason, but they're virtually impossible to kill."

"I'll keep that in mind," I said. "If I create a gargoyle, I'll be sure to step on it."

Dyson chuckled. "No offence, but I don't think your feet are big enough."

"I would be offended if you said they were," I told him.

He looked down at my feet and shook his head. "They look perfectly normal to me."

"Thank the gods for that."

We reached my room and stood awkwardly the door for a few moments.

"Um, do you want to come in?" I asked. My heart raced. I liked him, a lot, and his brother too. Even Nash was in the back of my mind constantly. I had imagined how Dyson's hands would feel on me, his tongue, his… Would he be like his brother, or did he prefer to keep things more private? I suspected the latter. He had a more outgoing personality, but Kane was outgoing when it came to sex.

"Uh, thanks, but I should go. I have to, er, study." He held his hands loosely in front of him, like he was hiding a raging hard-on.

"Are you sure?" I asked. "I wouldn't mind some company."

"I'm sure," he said. "I don't like to rush things." For good measure, he leaned down to press a warm kiss against my lips. He deepened it after a moment. His tongue tickled along my lower lip.

When I opened my mouth to him, he pulled back. "Well, good night."

I dropped my eyes. Yep, that was an erection all right.

"Night. Sleep well."

"Yeah, sweet dreams." He shook his head and seemed to regain hold of himself again. "Don't forget to dream about me. And my dick." He winked and swaggered off down the corridor, leaving me confused and shaking my head.

I opened the door and closed it behind me. Ariana was sitting on her bed, headphones on her ears, grooving to music only she could hear. Just as well Dyson had declined. We would have had to find somewhere else to go anyway.

"Hey." I dropped my bag on my bed.

"What?" Ariana shouted. "Oh, sorry." She pulled off her headphones. "Did you say something?"

"No, just hello." I shrugged and flopped down beside my bag. I told her what Dyson had said about magical creatures.

Her eyes widened. "So in theory I could create an attack unicorn?"

I hesitated. Was that really what she took away from all of this? "I mean... I suppose so," I replied slowly. "Are you likely to want to do that?"

"Make an animal that can stab my enemies with its horn? That sounds pretty awesome to me," she enthused.

I cocked my head. "You have enemies?"

She gave me a lopsided smile. "Well, not exactly, but you never know what might happen in the future. Normals don't always like knowing paranormals exist."

"Right, but I don't want to kill them for it." I would defend myself if I had to. Maybe not with a unicorn. That gave me an idea though.

"We should get tattoos," I declared.

"I thought the idea of being here was..." She held up her phone.

"It is, but in a pinch we still need traditional magic," I said firmly. "You could have a unicorn tattooed onto your arm. Imagine how cute that would be."

She grinned and nodded vigorously. "With a pink mane? Oh no, rainbow!"

I pictured a rainbow unicorn on a killing spree on her behalf and held back a laugh. It was a strange mental image, for sure.

"What would you have?" she asked.

I thought for a moment. As long as the spell was pointed in the right direction, then I should be all right... "Maybe a gargoyle," I said with a shrug. "They are kind of cool, when they're not destroying tables and trying to attack my friends."

Ariana made a face. "Maybe you should get something more benign, like a velociraptor or a bear."

Benign? I raised an eyebrow, but I understood she was being ironic. "Maybe a drop bear," I joked.

The idea that koalas turn into ferocious, carnivorous beasts was pretty funny. From what I gather, some international tourists still thought the myth was true. It's not. Trust me when I tell you, not all animals in Australia are trying to kill you. Unless, of course, a witch or wizard creates a magical attack koala.

I considered that for a moment but shook my head. Best not to perpetuate that rumour, tempting though it was.

Ariana giggled. "A kangaroo would be a formidable protector, with those powerful legs."

"True," I agreed, "but I really like the idea of having a gargoyle."

She nodded. "Okay, all we need is a tattoo artist who can do magic."

I rubbed my earlobe between my thumb and forefinger. "That shouldn't be too hard. Someone here will know where to find one. I'll shoot a message off to Kane."

"Or Dyson," she said. "I would think he'd be more likely to know."

"Yeah," I said slowly. "But things with him are weird."

"Oh." She leaned back against her pillows. "Maybe he's not into you like that."

I sighed. "I guess not, but I thought he was." Why did men have to be so damned mysterious?

I grabbed up my phone and sent a message to Kane. He replied a few moments later with an address nearby and a promise to take us there. That was followed by a photo of a tattoo in the shape of a snake. It was beautifully done, very intricate. It looked as though it might come alive at any moment. It couldn't, since he was a shifter and not a wizard, but it was still stunning.

I turned the phone to show Ariana.

"Unsolicited picture of his snake, hmmm?" she asked jokingly. Her eyes shone with amusement.

I snorted a laugh. "Better that than a dick pic." I liked the *feel* of his cock, but I didn't need a photo of it. Luckily, I suspected Kane wasn't the kind of guy who would send pics like that anyway.

I responded to Kane and put my phone on the table beside my bed. "Looks like we're getting inked."

I wondered if there was a magical hairdresser who could get rid of the green in my hair. I didn't say that out loud though. I knew Ariana had just been trying to help. At least she hadn't made me bald for life. Compared to that, what was a little bit of green?

I sighed again and got up to shower and change into my pyjamas. My dreams would be interesting tonight: gargoyles, drop bears, snakes and Dyson's dick. My subconscious was going to have a field day.

"A least you have someone to send you dick pics." Ariana sighed.

"Be careful what you wish for," I said with a grimace. "There's a whole internet out there full of guys ready to share their cocks with you." And the gods knew what else.

She stuck out her tongue in disgust. "Good point. Never mind then. I think I'll stick to..." She shook her head and didn't finish her sentence.

I gave her a long look, in case she had more to say. She just pulled her headphones back over her ears and went back to grooving silently.

After a while, I stepped into the bathroom and closed the door behind me. There was definitely something going on with her, but I had no idea what. At some point, I hoped she'd open up to me and share. Until then, I would be here for her as much as she would let me.

I slipped under the water and let it rinse the frustration of her, and Dyson down the drain.

1 5

Uh, really?

"I'm supposed to trust you to put ink on my skin?" I stared at the tattoo gun in Matt's hand and grimaced.

"Not at all," he replied coldly. "You're free to go somewhere else if you prefer."

"You two know each other?" Kane looked from one to the other of us.

"Yeah, she almost ran into me because she doesn't look where she's going," Matt said, his eyes still on me.

I gave him a "fuck all the way off," look and said, "I was distracted. He didn't have to be a dick about it."

"She's a real charmer, this one." Matt smirked.

"Um, I could go first," Ariana offered. She held her phone in her hand and shifted from foot to foot. I knew she'd found a picture of the unicorn she wanted and was eager to have it on her skin.

I stepped back. "Be my guest." I waved my arm toward the chair.

She grinned and sat before showing Matt the screenshot she'd taken. If he thought it funny or strange, he gave no sign. Instead, he nodded and got to work.

In the meantime, Kane took my hand and led me over to the other side of the tattoo parlour.

"Are you all right? You seem upset. I know Matt can be a bit abrasive—"

"He's an asshole," I said quietly. "How do I know he won't ink a wombat on me instead?"

Kane tried to bite back a grin but failed. "That would be cute," he said, "but we're all here to watch and make sure you get what you want. Matt is a professional. He wouldn't risk his reputation just to be a dick to you."

I gave Kane a side-eye. "Are you sure about that?"

He looked uncomfortable. "If you hate him that much, we can go somewhere else. I know another place, but they aren't quite as good…" He jerked a thumb toward the door.

"I don't hate him," I said quickly. "I just think he's an ass. But if you trust him—"

"I really do." Kane pushed his sleeve up to reveal the snake he'd shown me the night before. In person, it looked even more impressive. "I only wish I could make it come to life too. It would be epic." He pulled his sleeve back down.

"Hey," I said, keeping my voice low. "You can shift. That's pretty amazing, you know. I can't do that."

I licked my lips and hoped he'd tell me what he could shift into.

He kneaded his hands. "I know, I should be glad for what I have."

"Something like that," I agreed. "How does it go—we always want what we can't have."

"Hey." He stepped closer to me. "Sometimes we want things we *can* have." He leaned in to nibble at my ear.

I writhed a little but didn't push him away. "That's true," I agreed. "But not here, in front of these two."

Kane blushed. "No, of course not, I wasn't thinking…"

He was thinking exactly that, I saw it in his eyes and the way the front of his pants stood to attention.

I smiled knowingly. My blood heated. "We might have to try to find a place."

He swallowed audibly. "Really?"

"Yeah, really." I had no idea where though. I couldn't just google, "public places suitable to have sex in," could I? Is that even a thing?

Go ahead and look, I'll wait.

It said something about parks or forests, didn't it? I filed that away for future thought.

"I like you," I told him. "A lot."

"I like you too," he replied. "You like Dyson too, don't you?"

"I do, but I don't think he feels the same way."

Kane looked perplexed. "I would say—"

He was interrupted by Ariana's squeal. We both jumped.

"Are you all right over there?" I called out and shot daggers at Matt with my eyes.

He ignored me, but she grinned.

"More than all right, it's amazing so far. Come and look." She waved us over as best she could without moving her opposite arm.

Honestly, the last place I wanted to be was closer to Matt, but I moved until I could make out the outline of the unicorn and its face. I had to admit, the detail was extraordinary.

"Did you make that with magic?" I asked.

"A bit of magic has gone into it, yes." Matt's tone was curt. "To make sure she does what she's supposed to. We don't want her to leap off and destroy half a classroom." He looked up and shot me a meaningful look.

Oh good, he knew about that. *Wonderful.*

I grimaced. "Make sure you do it right."

He looked up again, oh so slowly this time. "I always *do it right,*" he said coolly.

The inflection was not lost on me. In fact, my stupid body responded to him in a more unwelcome way. Thank goodness lady boners weren't as obvious as dude boners.

"Mmm, I'm sure," I said, my mouth suddenly dry.

He looked away. "Are you going to let me do it to you next?"

"No way—" I started to say. I caught myself. "Oh, you mean the tattoo."

He snorted. "What else would I mean?"

"Nothing," I muttered. His expression was bland, but I sensed he was laughing on the inside. Would the world judge me badly if I took that tattoo gun and shoved it where the sun don't shine?

"It's very nice, Ariana," I told her.

She gave me a funny look but smiled. "This was a good idea of yours."

I wasn't so sure about that, but I returned her smile and watched as Matt added more detail. A hoof here, rainbow mane there. Before long, the unicorn looked as if it might really leap off her skin and wander around the tattoo parlour.

"You're very talented," I said without thinking.

"No shit," Matt replied without so much as glancing my way. "That's why you're here."

"Are you always so arrogant?" I asked, before Kane took my arm and pulled me back, away from him.

"It might be a good idea to let him concentrate," Kane said. "Otherwise he might make a mistake."

"Never going to happen," Matt said over his shoulder.

I curled my lip in his direction but turned away. "I'm sorry, he just —" I wasn't going to say, "rubs me the wrong way" again. I'd learnt my lesson after the first time. "He annoys me," I said finally.

"So I see." Kane turned me toward the front window and started to massage my shoulders. "He certainly is very sure of himself."

I dropped my chin to my chest and groaned. Gods, that felt good.

"That's one way to put it," I agreed.

"You're so tense," Kane said. He expertly kneaded out a knot or two and pulled my hair aside to kiss the back of my neck. "You don't have to do this, you know."

"I know." The feel of his lips sent heat through my entire body. "I want to."

"That's good, because it's your turn," Matt said.

Ariana smiled and showed off the unicorn which seemed to prance over her skin.

"It's very nice," I said. "I look forward to seeing it come alive some day."

"Are you fucking serious?" Matt snapped. "The only way that unicorn comes to life is if she's in danger. You would wish that on your friend?" He gave me a "what-the-hells-kind-of-friend-are-you?" look and turned away in disgust.

I gaped at him. "I just meant—"

"I don't care what you meant," he said, his tone curt. "Are you getting one done or not?" His eyes held a challenge. He was sure I'd walk away. He'd probably put money on it.

Fuck that.

"Since apparently you're the best, then I might as well." I flopped down in the chair while he gaped at me.

He sucked in a breath and let it out in a hiss. "Fine, what do you want and where do you want me to put it?"

There he went again with the innuendos.

Stick it where it fits, I thought sourly.

I smiled sweetly. "Same place as Ariana and this please." I held up my phone to show him.

His honey skin paled. "I…you…" He swallowed. "You want a gargoyle?"

"No, I want a fluffy bunny with a sweet little cotton tail," I said sarcastically. "Yes, I want a gargoyle. Is there a problem with that?"

"I…y…no. No." He squared his shoulders. "It's fine."

I exchanged confused glances with Kane. If there was some reason gargoyles bothered Matt, he clearly didn't know why either.

Ariana shrugged. "I said the same thing. I mean, the gargoyle she created could have killed us all. That's our Peyton for you, always keeping life interesting."

Our Peyton?

"Yeah well, I'd like to have a gargoyle I can control," I said lightly.

Matt twitched. "As if you'd control a gargoyle," he said derisively.

"Oh? I didn't realise you were an expert." I said.

"I'm not," he replied. "I just heard what happened in Madame Luc's class, that's all."

That was not all, but I wouldn't ask. For one thing, I doubted he'd tell me. For another, I didn't really care. He was probably just behaving this way to piss me off.

I leaned back and pulled up the sleeve on my left arm so he could work.

"You want it just like that picture?" he asked. "Lots of black. Red eyes."

"Horns, wings, big ears," I said. "All of those things." Just like the one I had created and the one Dyson and I had seen on our date.

"Fine."

The tattoo gun stung as it touched my skin, but I forced myself not to flinch. The lower arm might not be the best place for a tattoo, in terms of pain, but I wanted it accessible in case I needed it. For that, a few minutes was worth it.

I gritted my teeth and watched carefully as he worked. Call me a cynic, but I didn't trust that he wouldn't ink a fluffy bunny onto my skin instead. Granted, an attack bunny might be pretty awesome, but I would look a lot less badass.

Bit by bit, a gargoyle started to appear on my skin. First the outline, then the bits in between; eyes, mouth, claws, the insides of his ears. Or was that her ears? Either way, it looked even more impressive than Ariana's or Kane's tattoos.

Every so often, I glanced toward Matt. His eyes were focused on his work, mouth set in a hard line. A bead of sweat formed on his forehead. He must be trying very hard. Was it professional pride, some kind of interest in gargoyles, or because he didn't want to give me an excuse to bitch later? You know I would take it if he gave me one. Oh yes, I would.

"That's amazing," Ariana said breathlessly. She stood on my other side, her eyes wide and intent on my arm.

"It's okay," I said casually.

Matt flinched slightly and a frown crossed his brow. "It's more than all right," he growled.

"I guess it is," I said after a moment. "I'll tell you when you're done."

For a moment I thought he might actually stomp off and refuse to finish. He frowned more deeply and went on working until he sat back and set his tattoo gun down beside him.

"There." His gaze met mine and again they held a challenge.

I leaned down to inspect my tattoo carefully. Eventually, I sat back and nodded. "I like it. Thank you."

After a few seconds, his frown lifted and was replaced with a smug look. "You're welcome. You know where to find me when you want a *bigger* one."

Again with the innuendos.

I smirked. "I'm perfectly satisfied with the one I have." With that I hopped up from the chair and let him interpret that however he liked.

16

"WHAT IS THAT?"

Nash hadn't spoken to me other than to instruct me since our—whatever that was. The fact he did now took me by surprise.

"It's a tattoo," I said coolly. Or at least, cool on the outside. Inside, I was a tumult of burning emotion and lust. In spite of him being aloof for weeks, my knees still turned to mush when he was close.

He snorted. "Obviously. What is it for?"

"What do you think it's for?" I replied, a bit more blunt than I had intended.

"So you can defend yourself," he stated. "Do you have that little faith in your skills?"

For some reason, his words stung.

"I have plenty of faith in myself," I retorted. "It's other people, other paranormals I don't have faith in."

"And?" he prompted.

I hesitated. "And how long it takes to pull out a device and use it."

He nodded. "It's never wise to rely on only one method of self-defence."

I cocked my head at him. "Why the third degree about it then?"

"Is that what you thought that was?" He looked at me through half-lidded eyes.

"What would you call it?" I grabbed up my towel and pulled it around my neck.

"I don't know." He picked up his own towel and started to walk away.

"I don't get you," I said to his back.

He stopped, but didn't look back. "What's to get?"

"Hells if I know," I said in exasperation.

He turned around slowly, his expression guarded. "Maybe there's a reason for that."

"Maybe there is." I stepped closer, moving slowly like I approached a wild animal. "You don't have to tell me, but I'm a good listener." I licked my lips. "I didn't tell anyone about the things you told me the last time."

"Peyton," he said softly. So softly my pulse raced faster. Gods, he was so close now his breath brushed my cheek. "I want you. That's the problem."

"I don't see why that's a problem," I said, my voice higher than usual. "We're both adults."

He swallowed. "I'm your teacher."

"Do you give me preferential treatment?"

"Gods," he said breathlessly, "I want to."

I could have melted on the spot. "Why don't you then?" We were almost eye to eye, nose and to nose. His breath brushed over my lips. I thought for a while he'd kiss me. I half closed my eyes.

"I can't." He stepped back away from me. "It's not just that I'm your teacher. I'm damaged, Peyton. Damaged in ways you couldn't begin to imagine or understand."

I wasn't going to let him walk away that easily. "Why don't you try me?" I pressed my fists to my hips and gave him a challenging look. "You said you took a life. Why?"

"It's complicated." He seemed conflicted, like he wanted to tell me, but was scared of what I'd think of him if he did.

"I have time." I had an assignment to write for my history class, but it could wait.

He opened his mouth, closed it again and shook his head. "It's nothing a student needs to know about." Just like that, he closed up again, tight.

I hesitated, then let out a breath through pursed lips. "All right, but if you change your mind, I'm here for you."

"Yeah." He gripped the ends of his towel in tight, white fists and headed out of the training room.

I watched his perfect ass until he passed through the doorway. I headed for the showers. In spite of having a bathroom upstairs, attached to mine and Ariana's room, I preferred to shower down here after training. It saved me walking through the academy covered in sweat and meant Ariana didn't have to wait until I was done, to take her turn. Or vice versa.

I dragged off my sweats, dropped them on the floor and stepped under the warm flow. Like always, it washed the worst of my cares away, at least for now. Still, in the back of my mind was the lingering wonder about Nash and whatever darkness lurked around his soul. What was it with all these guys and their enigmatic personalities? First there was Dyson and his mixed signals, then there was Matt, who may or may not just be an asshole and last was Nash. Him I got the least of all. Matt, I didn't want to get, to be honest. The others though... They both intrigued me.

Not, I should add, that Kane didn't, but he seemed a lot more straightforward than the rest. Thinking about him and what he wanted to do with me made my mouth dry.

I turned off the water and stepped out to grab a towel. I wrapped it around myself and searched my bag for a pair of clean panties. Before I even found them, I heard footsteps outside the bathroom door.

Had I locked it?

The nob turned.

I started to search for my phone but gave up after a moment. I turned to face the door and held up my arm, ready to call the gargoyle if I needed it.

The door swung inwards. My breath caught in my throat.

"Nash?"

He stopped dead. "I was hoping you'd still be here."

"You changed your mind about talking?" I asked.

"No." He shook his head slowly and licked his lips. He shut the door behind himself and locked it.

Excitement burned through me like wild fire.

He closed the distance between us. He grabbed my shoulders, turned me and all but threw me against the sink. I slammed my palms onto the counter.

He whipped off my towel and threw it to one side.

In the mirror, I watched him undo his jeans and push them down far enough to free his erection. A moment later, he had me bent over the sink and rammed himself into me, hard.

I gasped out loud.

"I told you I want you," he said with a grunt. "You drive me crazy."

I looked toward the mirror. My breasts swung with each thrust. His eyes were closed and his expression was one of pure bliss.

I closed my own eyes and enjoyed the feeling of him pounding into me, touching me deep inside. He reached around to find my clit and rubbed firmly with each thrust. I had already been extremely aroused, so his touch pushed me toward the edge like a raging rapid.

Before I could come, he pulled out of me, turned me around and lifted me onto the sink. He leaned in to lick one of my nipples, then sucked for a few moments before he drew my legs around his hips and slid back into me.

"You feel better than I could have imagined," he said, his voice rough. "And I did imagine this. And so much more."

"Oh?" From this angle, every thrust hit me inside and out. Only a handful more and I would topple over the precipice.

"Mmm," he replied. "Mostly I pictured you tied to my bed and letting me do whatever I want to you."

I moaned with the increased sensation his words sent all the way through me. "You like having power?"

"Oh yeah," he grunted. "I want you to give yourself to me, fully."

I wasn't sure what more I could do for him at this point. "What do you want?" I asked him. "What do you need? Sir."

He moaned. "Don't stop calling me that. When I fuck you, I want you to call me sir." He thrust harder, deeper.

"Yes, sir," I whispered. I was so close to cresting now.

"I want you to do what I tell you," he added.

"Yes, sir," I said again. I reached my peak and fell over the top into a pool of intense and powerful desire.

He pulled out of me and pulled me down from the sink. "Get on your knees," he ordered.

"Yes, sir." My head was still swimming, but I knelt in front of him.

He grabbed a handful of my damp hair and guided my mouth to his cock. "Take me in as deep as you can."

I couldn't respond now, with a mouth full of cock, but I managed a small nod.

"Deeper." He thrust into my mouth, almost to the back of my throat.

I tasted myself on him, but I sucked and ran my tongue over his length and tip.

He grunted and slid himself in and out, past my lips. "Your mouth is incredible," he breathed. He pounded a little faster, hips bucking, breath more and more ragged.

"Gods, Peyton…" He groaned loudly and came, squirting hot cum into my mouth and down my throat.

I swallowed a couple of times and kept sucking until I had milked him dry. Only then did he pull out of me and offered me his hand to get up.

"We probably shouldn't have done that," he said with a hint of regret, "but I don't want to stop. I know I'm not the only guy… you should see guys your own age…"

"I want to do that again too," I said, guessing where he was going with this. "I…" I blushed slightly. "I like when you get all bossy with me." For an independent girl, I actually enjoyed it when he dominated me. I wouldn't want Kane or Dyson to do it, but there was something about Nash that made me want to surrender myself to him, to let him touch me any way he liked.

He looked surprised but smiled. "Great. I'll get bossy more often then." He cupped my breasts and rubbed his palms against my nipples. "When we're apart, you do whatever you like, but when we're together like this, you're all mine." As if to empathise his words, he leaned in to claim my mouth. His tongue pushed past my lips and invaded my mouth with as much force as he'd used with his cock.

He moaned against my mouth, then stepped back. "I could be with you a million times and never tire of you." He pinched my nipples between his thumb and forefinger, until I flinched from the delicious pain.

"Of course, I'm that awesome," I joked.

He smiled. "Yes, you are." A shadow passed across his face and he dropped his hands and stepped back. "Undeniably. And gorgeous."

"I don't know about that, sir," I said with a smile. I resumed my search for clean panties and pulled them on while he watched.

"I do," he said simply. He looked as though he couldn't quite believe what we'd just done.

I wasn't sure I did either. I had screwed a teacher in a bathroom at the academy. That was definately not something I had expected to do when I came here. Did I regret it? Hell no. He was hot and I would do it again. It wasn't as though we were getting married or anything.

I pulled on my bra and he hooked it up for me.

"A guy who knows how bras work," I said, "I'm impressed."

He chuckled. "I usually prefer to take them off, but I'll make an exception in this case. For now."

I smiled and tugged on track pants and a t-shirt. In spite of him being "bossy" this felt comfortable. Not like a teacher and a student, but like a man and a woman, with a genuine connection. Could it become something more? Only time would tell.

"Stay after training tomorrow," he said. "I want to give you extra training so you never need to use that gargoyle of yours."

"Do you have a tattoo?" I asked. I had yet to see one on him, although I had been looking.

"I don't need one," he said. Without explaining, he unlocked the door and stepped out of the room.

17

"IT REALLY IS STARTING to get complicated." I ran the tip of my finger around my tattoo and glanced up at Ariana. She lay stretched out on her bed, on her stomach, her headphones around her neck.

"Maybe you should just decide who you like the best and concentrate on them?" she suggested. She popped something into her mouth before holding the packet out to me.

I peered at the label. "Weed gummies?"

She shrugged. "They help me to relax and ease the pain from typing so much. Try one."

I put a hand up. "No thanks. Another time, maybe."

"All the more for me," she said breezily, but she closed the packet and put it away in the drawer beside her bed.

I sat back against my pillows. "I don't know who I like the best," I admitted. "Kane is adorable. I could see myself falling for him. Dyson is... I don't know what he is, but I want to find out. Nash—" I licked my lips. "He's exciting."

Ariana didn't seem even slightly bothered by the fact he was a teacher. In fact, she had grinned when I'd mentioned him. Evidently, she had a rebellious streak I hadn't known about.

"I'm not saying you have to choose, but if you don't, then your life is only going to get more complicated," she said. "Sooner or later you'll have to pick one of them. If they care about you, the guys you don't choose will get hurt."

I sighed. "I know. I don't want to string anyone along, I just... I mean, we're just messing around right now. Nash said he doesn't care if I'm seeing anyone else."

"How does Kane feel?" she asked.

"He knows I like Dyson too. I haven't said anything to him about Nash." I winced at the idea.

"Then you should do that first," Ariana said firmly. "You don't want him to find out when he walks in on you."

I suspected Kane might enjoy standing back and watching, but I didn't tell her that. I nodded. "You're right, I should. I'm just not sure how I even start that conversation."

"Just be honest." She pulled her headphones off from around her neck and put them aside. "It's not like you guys are officially dating or anything, right? So what's the worst that could happen? He doesn't want to see you anymore."

"He's a shifter and I still don't know what he can change into," I said dryly, "he could be capable of clawing my face off."

Ariana laughed. "This is Kane we're talking about. He's more likely to shift into something which can lick you to death. Besides, you have your gargoyle to protect you. Maybe two." She cocked her head. "You haven't seen the other one again, or the mysterious blur?"

"No." I had been watching for it for weeks now, but I hadn't noticed any more than a stray breeze, which I attributed to winter winds. Just thinking about them made me shiver. I peeled back my covers and slipped underneath them.

"I'm starting to think I was either imagining things, or someone was doing magic and I just happened to see some of it. The gargoyle was obviously from the same website we used in class. I should count myself lucky it didn't attack us."

Ariana nodded slowly. "That makes sense, I suppose. You wouldn't have been the first to use it."

"Exactly." I nodded. I felt better having figured all of that out. Now maybe I could put the sighting out of my mind and focus on more important things, like the guys—I mean, studying.

Even without sleeping with a lecturer, I was doing well. My mother would expect nothing less, naturally. Although I found the history of magic to be somewhat boring, I enjoyed learning about the anatomy of witches, wizards and shifters, loved defence training and even the psychology of paranormals. I still didn't know what I wanted to do when I had finished studying, but I had a lot of interesting options.

"Can I tell you something?" Ariana asked softly.

I glanced over at her. She looked nervous, as though she thought I wouldn't like whatever she had to say.

"Of course," I replied firmly. After all, we were friends and I had spent the last hour telling her about all of my dramas. Listening to her was the least I could do.

"I..." She blushed. "I'm bisexual." She bit her lip and looked worried.

"Oh," I said lightly, "that's great. You like guys and girls, right?"

"Right." She looked relieved. "You don't think I'm, I don't know, a freak or something?"

"Of course not, why would I?" I frowned at the idea that I'd judge her badly for something so natural.

"My parents are a bit funny about things like that," she admitted. "My siblings too. If they knew, they might not speak to me again."

"That's terrible," I blurted out. I slid out from under my warm blankets, sat beside her and took her hand. "I hope they would love you just the same as they do now, but if they don't, well, you have family here." Strange that for all my mother's shortcomings, I didn't think she'd turn her back on me for my sexuality.

Ariana gave me a watery smile. "Really?"

"Absolutely," I said firmly. "You're my best friend here at the academy. I love you like a sister. I'm so glad we ended up roommates, even if you do snore."

She grinned. "I'm glad too. Although, I don't snore as much as you do."

"Do too," I said with a laugh. I drew her in for a quick hug.

"I love you too," she said in my ear, "like a sister. Although..."

I drew back and looked her in the eyes. "Although what?" I asked cautiously.

"If you were my sister, you would have put magic ants in my bed." She giggled.

"I could still do that," I offered. "Let me just get my phone."

"No thank you," she laughed. "It's a very tempting offer though."

I grinned. "All right. If you change your mind, you know where to find me." I stood and retreated back to my own bed. "You know what though?"

"What?" she asked.

"I wouldn't have put ants in your bed."

"No?"

"No. I would have put snakes. I prefer those to ants." I leaned back and pulled the blankets to my chin.

"Oh, so do I," she replied, "but not in my bed."

"I'll bear that in mind." I smiled.

She was silent for a while before she asked, "Reptiles or dicks?"

I snorted in surprise. "I beg your pardon?"

"Reptiles or dicks?" she asked again. "What kind of snakes would you put in my bed?"

"Ohhh." I pushed hair out of my eyes. "Which would you prefer?"

She looked thoughtful. "I guess that depends whether or not a guy was attached and how big the dick was."

"Substantial," I said with a nod. "A substantial cock, or a carpet snake."

"I think I'm going to have to go for the cock, as long as the guy attached is reasonably good looking."

"This is turning into one heck of a Christmas list," I joked. Christmas was half a year away and a hot guy was probably not on my list of obtainable items. At least, not ones I could give away. "Let's see, big cock, hot. Nice, I assume?"

"Definitely nice," she agreed. "I would also accept a hot girl with a strap-on."

I raised my eyebrow at that. "I'll make a note of that. A carpet snake might be easier. Or a dildo."

"I would never say no to a dildo." She lay on her side, facing me.

"A vibrator would be a lot less complicated than a relationship." My mind suddenly conjured up an image of Ariana using one on herself. Running it over her... I swallowed. Wasn't my life confusing enough, without throwing thoughts like that into the mix?

"If vibrators would make coffee, maybe we wouldn't need men," she joked.

I laughed. "They have their uses. Men, I mean."

"Yeah, but it would be great if dildos made coffee." She sighed.

"Yes," I agreed, "yes it would. Some day, maybe."

"Hey." She sat up suddenly. "Can we make coffee with magic?"

I frowned. "It's possible to heat water using magic, but I don't think we could conjure up a fresh cup. It would disappear like the magically created creatures."

"In that case, I'd rather conjure up cake. All the moistness and none of the calories." She lay back again.

"I think it would also have none of the taste of cake. That's probably why I've never heard of anyone doing it."

"It would make a good prank," she remarked. "If pranking was something either of us did."

"It would," I agreed. "Watch out for magic cake crumbs in your bed."

She laughed. "Now I know to wait until they disappear, I won't have to worry."

"Drat," I grumbled jokingly. "Now I'll have to think of something else." I clicked my fingers.

She giggled. "Can I ask you something?"

"Sure." I covered a yawn with my hand. "Fire away. So to speak."

"If you had to choose one guy, *only* one, who would you choose? Don't think too hard." She watched me over the top of her blankets.

I sighed. "I honestly don't know. I feel differently about them all, but I don't feel more for one than the others."

"I guess there's only one thing for it then," she said.

"Get a vibrator?" I suggested.

"Okay, there's only two things," she amended. "They'll have to fight it out in a duel."

I laughed. "To the death?"

"Oh no, nothing so savage," she said quickly. "Maybe just a friendly game of poker, or a joust."

I shook my head and laughed again. "As much fun as it would be to see them joust, I doubt it would end well."

Ariana pouted playfully. "I suppose not. I wonder who would win that though."

I mused for a moment. "Probably Nash. Kane would hold back and… I don't know what Dyson would do."

"Maybe that's your answer," she said. "Nash is the only one who would fight for you."

"Physically fight, yes," I agreed. "But only in a joust. Dyson would win at poker. He gives away nothing about his thoughts. Nash's are all over his face."

"And Kane?"

I tucked my hair behind my ear. What would Kane excel at, apart from making me come in a garden full of people?

"I'm not sure," I said slowly, "herding naked brothers, perhaps?" As skills went, it was certainly an interesting one.

Ariana laughed. "Herding naked men could catch on, as an international sport."

"Indoor sport," I added. "A sunburnt dick would hurt like a bitch."

"Good point." She nodded. "Unless they were covered in sunblock. Just think how they'd all glisten then."

"I can totally imagine that. You should take the idea to the Olympic committee." I nestled into my pillow.

"Being naked at the Olympics is traditional," she said. "We could just go back to that."

"I suspect some of those family first groups might object," I said sleepily. "Won't someone think of the children?"

Ariana exhaled loudly out her nose. "You're right. Scratch that then. I guess you'll have to find something else he's good at."

"I will," I replied. It was possible whatever he shifted into was unique and allowed him to do something the others couldn't. Whatever that was. Wasn't Nash a shifter too? I had no idea what he could become. I would bet it's not a fluffy bunny or a kangaroo. No, nothing cute. Possibly a wolf or a lion.

I fell asleep imagining Nash as a wolf, with a long, nubile tongue.

18

"SO WHAT CAN YOU SHIFT INTO?" I placed my plate and cup on the table and flopped down beside Kane.

He looked at me in surprise, a fork halfway to his mouth. Instead of lowering the utensil, he pushed the ravioli inside and started to chew. I suspected, to avoid having to answer my question.

That was okay, I could wait. I placed my arms on the table and sat patiently until he swallowed.

"Why?" he asked finally.

"Why what? Why do I want to know what you are?" I poked my own fork into my dinner. "Because you won't tell me, but that hasn't stopped me from wondering." In fact, I was more curious now than I was when I met him. What could be so bad that he wouldn't talk about it?

"Is it really that embarrassing?"

His face turned red.

That would be a yes, it was.

"You don't have to tell me, if you really don't want to," I said gently. "I'll contain my curiosity."

"No, I want to tell you," he said after a few moments when I thought he might get up and run. He sagged a little. "I'm a bird."

"Okay," I said slowly, "what kind?"

Kane put down his fork, placed his elbows on the table and propped his head on his hands. "An owl."

I blinked. "That's it?"

He sighed. "I know, it's underwhelming, isn't it?"

"I think it's amazing," I assured him. I was still confused though. "Why don't you want people to know about it?"

His brow creased. "Really? An owl, at a school of magic? Can you imagine how many people would ask me to carry letters for them?"

"Oh." I reached for his hand. "That would be annoying."

"Exactly. Dyson said he was going to write a letter and have me deliver it to everyone." He looked so sad my heart melted a little more.

"I'm sure he was joking," I said gently. "He might be jealous he can't fly." I was. I would love to soar above the trees, to be free on the breeze.

Kane blinked a couple of times. "Do you think so?"

"Definitely. Being a dog is great and all but flying must be something really special." I squeezed his hand and gave him a smile.

"It really is," he enthused. "The world looks different from up there." He glanced toward the ceiling.

"Don't you have shifter training?" I asked before I released his hand and started eating.

He sagged again and averted his eyes. "I do private training. My trainer knows what I am, but he keeps it quiet."

"He?" I asked.

"Yeah, Nash." Kane stuck a fork in a piece of ravioli.

"Ah." My face heated. "So you know him pretty well then?"

Kane shrugged. "Well enough, I suppose. Not enough to know what he can shift into. Why?"

I almost responded by saying, "No reason," but I didn't want to lie. "I..." I swallowed hard. "We have a thing. I don't exactly know what it is or where it'll go, but—"

"A thing?" Kane echoed. He didn't seem to be angry or upset, just surprised.

"Yeah, um." How did I put this? "Sex."

"Ah." He nodded, then cocked his head. "Does this mean you don't want to see me anymore?" Anxiety flashed through his eyes.

"No, I still want to. If you want to?" Now I was the anxious one.

"I do want to," he said quickly. "I like you. A lot. More than a lot." He blushed. "If you want to see other guys too, that's up to you. I hope you choose me in the long run though." I didn't think it was possible, but his blush deepened. He was just so stinking adorable.

I leaned over to kiss his mouth.

His arm went around my neck to draw me in closer and deepen the kiss. He broke off just before I became completely breathless.

"Peyton and Kane, sitting in a tree," he said, smiling at his rendition of the children's rhyme. "K-i-s-s-i-n-g."

"Not unless you can fly us both up there," I pointed out. "Or if it's not too high up."

"I'll bring a ladder," he said with a smile. "As long as I get to kiss you."

"I'm all for keeping my feet on the ground, but I like the kissing part." I leaned in for another.

"Do I have to throw a bucket of water over you both?" Dyson asked. He slipped into the chair opposite his brother.

"Do you have one?" I asked teasingly.

He grinned. "I'm sure I could find one."

I stuck out my tongue at him. Was he jealous? I couldn't see anything in his eyes but humour. He was the kind of guy, I decided, who hid his feelings behind jokes. I liked to laugh as much as the next person, but I wanted to know what was going on with him. He was a closed book, or a closed phone with a complicated passcode.

"There are better ways to make me wet," I told him, trying to get some kind of response.

"I bet there are." His eyes travelled down my body. "Although that kiss looked it would have done that already."

"I..." He wasn't wrong about that.

"I'm going to get another drink," Kane said suddenly. "Do you want anything?"

I waved toward my untouched glass of cola. "No thanks, I'm good for now."

Kane nodded, gave me a meaningful look and hurried away.

"Well, that was subtle," Dyson said sarcastically.

"Oh, you thought so too, huh?" I grimaced. "I think he's suggesting I talk to you about...things."

"Things? I'm always up for a discussion about things. What kind of things? Dicks?" He grinned, but his eyes seemed guarded. "I could go on about mine all day."

I smiled. "I'm sure you could. I mean... What do you *want* to do with it? With me. If anything," I added in a hurry. "I mean..." The words stuck in my throat. A frank conversation had quickly become awkward, especially since he just sat there watching me make a fool of myself.

"Do I want to sleep with you?" he said finally.

"Yes. No." I took a sip of cola to wet my mouth. "We went on a date. We had fun, didn't we? And we've had fun since."

"Ah." He nodded. "Is this about you inviting me into your room and me saying no?"

"Yes." That was exactly what this was about. "Was it something I said or did?"

He licked his lips. "No, not at all. It's nothing like that."

"Then, what is it like?" I asked before I could stop myself.

"This is going to sound strange," he said slowly. "I walk around naked and talk about my dick, but when it comes to relationships, I like to take it slowly."

"Oh." Now I felt silly. I had jumped to all kinds of conclusions, but never to this. "You mean... Just because you're naked, doesn't mean you're asking for it?"

"Pretty much." He gave me a lopsided smile. "Is that weird?"

"No, not at all. Women have been telling men that since forever. I should have realised it goes both ways. I'm sorry." I looked toward my half-empty plate.

"You're forgiven." He put a finger under my chin and turned my face toward him. "I like you, a lot. I'm used to being the jokester.

Talking about my feelings is difficult, but I'll try." He gave me a look of warmth that made my heart skip a beat.

"You're doing great," I said softly. "I like you too."

He lowered his hand and leaned over to kiss me softly on my lips before he sat back. "I'm very likeable." The jokester was back now, but I had seen enough of his tender side to satisfy me.

"Yes, you are." I patted his cheek.

"When you're not being annoying." Kane sat back in his chair and looked from his brother to me and back again.

"When am I ever annoying?" Dyson gave us both a look of pure innocence.

Kane snorted.

I wondered what it would be like to have them naked and sweaty, on either side of me, lips, tongues, hands… I sipped my cola to cover the expression on my face. I probably had lust written all over it.

"You're both wonderful," I said when I could trust myself to talk. "In your own unique ways."

Dyson grinned. "He told you what he could shift into, didn't he?"

"I did," Kane muttered.

"I think it's great," I said firmly. "I was worried it would be a chihuahua or a camel."

Dyson threw back his head and laughed. "I've never heard of a camel shifter."

"Of course you haven't," I said, "who would admit to being one?"

Kane was grinning now. "Maybe that's what Nash is."

I shook my head and laughed. "I can't picture it, somehow. He'd be more likely to be a wolf." I thought back to my dream and licked my lips.

"If he was a wolf, the whole academy would know about it," Kane pointed out. "No one would want to hide it if they were one. Same with lions, tigers and bears."

"Oh my," Dyson added.

"That's true," I agreed. To be honest, I wouldn't rule out the idea that he was the gargoyle, but I didn't say it out loud. I'd sooner accept my assumption that someone had created it and I'd just been in the right place to catch a glimpse.

"So, you and Nash too, huh?" Dyson asked, his tone blunt but his expression still jovial.

"Yeah." I explained the situation to him as I had done with Kane.

Dyson nodded. "Got it. Three guys vying for your heart. May the best paranormal win." He winked at me. "I look forward to that being me."

"Dream on," Kane told him. He shot his brother a scowl.

Dyson responded with a smile.

Kane did have a head start on his brother, but I wouldn't assume anything at this point. For all I knew, it might not work out with any of them. If that was the case, I would be disappointed, but I'd accept it. Love was one of those things in life you couldn't force, no matter how much you might want to.

Wait, did I just say love? I liked these guys, but I wasn't there yet. Some day, maybe. The problem was, I could see myself falling head over heels for all of them. At some point, I would have to decide who I liked the best. I didn't want to think about that day. It might be that by then one or two would have drifted away and gotten involved with other people. It might also be that they didn't and I would have to hurt someone.

Gods, complicated suddenly seemed like one hells of an understatement.

"So, Peyton, would you like to see a movie after dinner?" Kane asked.

"I'd love to," I agreed.

"So, Peyton, would you like to go out with me tomorrow night?" Dyson asked.

"I'd love to do that too," I replied.

"Game on, brother," Dyson grinned.

Kane rolled his eyes. "This isn't a game."

"No, I suppose not." Dyson looked serious for a change. "That doesn't mean I'm not going to walk away with Peyton on my arm at the end of it."

"If you guys are going to fight over me..." I said in warning. "If this comes between you, I'm done. With both of you. I'm not going to create problems between brothers."

"You won't," Dyson assured me. "This is how we usually are."

"It really is," Kane agreed.

I hesitated. "Well, good then." The last thing I wanted was to start a war between them. I sensed their brotherly bond was fragile enough. I refused to be the one who broke it.

19

"WHAT THE FUCK?" I stopped dead in my tracks. I hadn't seen any gargoyles, apart from the one on my arm, for weeks. The site we used in class had removed the option, but Madame Luc hadn't offered any explanation for why it was there in the first place.

I hadn't called up the one on my arm either. To be honest, the idea of doing that scared me. What if it didn't work? What if it did work and the creature turned on me? It might hurt someone else it wasn't supposed to. The list of what might go wrong went on, but those were my top three.

Imagine my surprise then, to see one in front of me on the sidewalk on my way back from a morning run. Spring was in the air today, but only a hint of it. Winter's fingers still gripped the city. Before too long, we'd be bitching about the heat and preparing for Christmas.

Right now though, my attention was on the creature in front of me. Long hind legs, shorter front ones, long, wide ears, horns. It looked just like my tattoo. Or vice versa.

Like a cat, it stepped toward me, red eyes focused firmly on my face.

I raised my hands. "I'm harmless, honest." I swallowed and took a step back.

The gargoyle moved forward, to cover the space between us. He—for some reason I thought that was the right pronoun—bared his teeth at me.

"I don't taste good either," I said. Although given Kane had spent most of the last three movies we'd been to with his face buried between my legs, maybe that wasn't accurate. I wasn't planning to offer the creature a taste of my sex.

The gargoyle snorted softly, as though it found my words amusing. That was weird.

"Wait, you can understand me?" The magically created one had given no sign of having understood a word. It was—for want of a better expression—a mindless killing machine. This was something different.

"You're a shifter, aren't you?" I lowered my arms and crossed them over my chest. I was still somewhat cautious, but no longer scared. I could deal with a shifter if I had to. Maybe. Okay, I *hoped* I could.

The gargoyle cocked its head at me and let out a low growl.

"Nope," I said without flinching. "I'm not buying it. Try again."

He sniffed as though trying harder was beneath him somehow. In spite of that, he snapped at me. His teeth came to within a centimetre of my leg.

I jumped back a little. "Hey, watch it!" I swear to the gods the gargoyle laughed at me. The sound came from the back of his throat and was only slightly less intimidating than his growl.

"You're an asshole, you know that?" I told him.

He licked his muzzle in response.

"Yeah, whatever." I rolled my eyes. "Why are you following me? This is the third time I've seen you. Unless there are two others like you out there."

For some reason, that seemed to infuriate him. He growled again, deeper this time, but I sensed it wasn't directed at me. He was angry at the implications of what I'd said, not because I'd said it.

"You don't like the idea there might be others like you?" I asked. "Why? Do you want to be special or something?"

He raised a clawed foot and waved it at me.

I exhaled. "This would be a lot easier if you shifted and talked to me like an actual person." I squinted at him. "Nash, is that you? I'm not going to be upset that you're a gargoyle, or if you've been following me. Promise."

The gargoyle snorted loudly.

Not Nash. Thank goodness I didn't say anything more provocative.

"Okay, can we clear up one thing," I said. "Have you been following me? Nod for yes."

Nod.

"All right, now we're getting somewhere. Can you tell me why?"

Head shake.

"Am I in danger of some kind?"

Nod.

"Wonderful," I said sarcastically. "From you?"

Head shake.

"That's good to know." I put a finger to my lips. "Is this about my mother?"

The gargoyle disappeared. Don't get me wrong, this is a reasonable response to any mention of my mother. I've wished many times that I could do exactly that. In this case, it was beyond irritating, and it was strange. The creature didn't lope away into the night, it was just…gone.

"I'm well acquainted with the trick of forming a bubble around oneself and becoming invisible," I said dryly. What I had never seen, or heard of, was a shifter with magic. "Come on, drop that thing and let's talk."

Footsteps moved away from me; the scratching of long claws on pavement. The gargoyle was leaving. Although a magic bubble hid a witch or wizard from the eye, it didn't hide sound. Dude was a mani-pedi away from creeping off, but it was enough that I couldn't guess what direction he was heading.

"Wait a minute," I called after it. "Come back tell me what the hells is going on. Please."

Unfortunately, the sun had risen a while ago, and people started to step out of their homes and head to work. Several gave me a funny look as they hurried past. Not as funny as the one they would have given to the gargoyle, but bad enough. Hells, this was Sydney, surely they'd seen worse than a person talking to themselves on an otherwise quiet street?

I shot them a smile and brushed my hair off my face. Whatever was going on, I wasn't going to find out right now. Stupid gargoyle. What was the point of following me and warning me, but not telling me what I should be looking out for? Very helpful. Not.

I shook my head and started back toward the academy at a slow jog. I would get to the bottom of this, one way or another. In fact, I knew just the person to ask.

"How can a gargoyle shifter do magic?" I planted my hands on my hips and gave Nash a direct look. If anyone would have the answers, it would be him. I wasn't leaving until he did.

He closed the door behind me and locked it.

I had been to his room before. The space was clean and tidy, almost too much so. It looked almost un-lived in. I knew that wasn't true, he was just a clean freak. I had seen him straighten out chairs and bedsheets until they were exactly how he wanted them. Nothing was out of place now. I bet even dust didn't dare to venture into here.

I returned my gaze to him and arched an eyebrow.

He sighed and gestured for me to sit on one of the plump armchairs to the side of the room.

"It's a long story," he started.

"I have time," I said.

He sat down in the chair beside mine but perched on the edge as though he couldn't relax while talking about this. Whatever *this* was.

He scratched his head. "They can do magic because they're hybrids."

"Come again?" I asked.

"I'd love to." He looked weary but managed a smile. "I think that will have to wait until after this."

"Damn right," I said. "So what the fuck do you mean by hybrid? I know witches and shifters can breed, but the kids are one or the other."

He nodded. "That's right. Or at least, it was." He blew out a long breath through pursed lips.

When he didn't go on, I waved a hand at him. "It was until what?"

He sat back in the chair and steepled his fingers. "Until Zeta started blending witch and shifter DNA. They created hybrids with what they deemed the ideal mix of magics."

"Wait, back up a bit." I leaned forward and put my hands on my knees. "Zeta? What's that?"

He rubbed the tip of his nose. "They're a government department. More or less top secret. Definitely evil. They're committed to bringing the world under their heel, with the help of their hybrids. They want to kill off the rest of the paranormals."

"Well that sucks," I said dryly. "So wait, they're taking bits of two kinds of paranormals and making a whole new breed?" My mind twisted and turned with that information. How could that even be possible? It seemed like something out of a science fiction book.

"Exactly." Nash nodded.

"And the gargoyle is a hybrid?" A created being, not unlike the one I had had tattooed on my arm. How was that for irony?

"More than likely," he agreed. "Zeta apparently has a twisted sense of humour, because all of their hybrids are creatures from mythology."

"That certainly explains the gargoyle," I agreed. "So there's others out there? Sphinxes? Unicorns?" I thought about the one on Ariana's arm. This was going to blow her mind.

"Possibly, although I haven't met any of those in particular."

"So, how do you know all of this?" I asked.

He cleared his throat. "Because I'm a hybrid."

My mouth dropped open. "Are you a gargoyle too?"

He snorted. "No." He looked away, toward the window. "I'm a dragon."

I blinked and stared at him. "No shit?"

He looked back at me, a faint smile on his lips. "No shit. I can also do magic."

I shook my head to try to clear it. "That's why you don't need a tattoo," I guessed. "Because you're already your own badass protector."

He smiled faintly. "Something like that. I try not to let the dragon loose though. Things don't...end well."

I reached over to put my hand on his. "This—Zeta—they did things to you, didn't they?" I kept my tone gentle. Not only because I cared about him, but because no smart person pisses a dragon off.

He shifted uncomfortably. "I used to work for them. A long time ago, before I knew..." he shook his head. "I helped them to do some terrible things."

"But then you stopped," I said.

He smiled faintly. "Yes. They didn't like it much."

I frowned. "That's why you had to take a life? Did they come after you?"

"Me and some friends," he said, his voice a harsh whisper. His eyes looked haunted. He must be thinking back to that moment.

I chewed at my lip. "It sounds a bit like they deserved it." I knew that was a terrible thing to say, but there were some awful people in the world. Now there was a few less. Maybe I was more like my mother than I'd realised. Ugh, that sucked.

"Just because someone is an evil asshole, doesn't mean they deserve to die," he said without irony.

"I beg to differ," I said dryly, "but it's done now and I won't judge you for it." He wouldn't have done it if he'd had another option, I knew that with everything inside me. "What happened to your friends?"

He shrugged with a shoulder. "They're probably still out there, fighting back. Zeta knew me too well, so I'm here. New identity and all."

"Oh really?" I asked, "what were you before?"

He smiled wryly. "I was a cop."

I nodded. "I can see you doing that. Helping people and all."

He snorted. "Yeah, maybe a little, here and there." He paused before he added, "My name used to be Richard."

I grinned. "Dick?"

He rolled his eyes. "Yeah, I got that from time to time. Now, is it time for you to get some dick?"

I stood and pulled him to his feet. "I think it's past time."

He let my hand go and swept off my shirt before he guided me to the bed and the scarves draped over the end. He tied my wrists firmly and started a long, slow exploration of my body.

2 0

IT WASN'T until much later I realised I hadn't asked Nash why a shifter might be following me. On the other hand, the whole Zeta things was more or less explanatory. They sounded like exactly the kind of people my mother would butt heads with.

Unless…

My breath caught in my throat. If Nash had worked with them, maybe she had too. She had always been vocal about the superiority of paranormals over normal people. To think she would work an organisation Nash described as evil—surely even she wouldn't go that far?

"Hey, is your hearing switched off or your brain?"

I blinked, surprised to see Matt standing in front of me. Outside the academy was a public place, but that didn't explain why he'd talk to me.

"Gargoyle got your tongue?" he asked derisively.

I shook my head slightly. "I beg your pardon?" Had he just said what I thought he'd said? How the hells did he know about that?

"Gargoyle." He pointed toward my arm. "Or have you forgotten you got inked already?"

Oh. Duh. I narrowed my eyes at him. "Fuck off, Matt."

He grinned. "Great comeback." He started to clap slowly, sarcastically.

"Yeah, whatever." I rolled my eyes. "Did you want something?"

"Not particularly." He smirked. "You just looked like you'd seen a ghost."

"Would you care if I had?" I asked.

"I might not like you, but I have some compassion for my fellow paranormals." He leaned against the wall beside us and crossed his arms over his chest.

I tried to ignore how his muscles bulged out of his black t-shirt. Did he ever wear any other colour? "Right." I exhaled through pursed lips. "I'm fine. Thanks for asking."

"Are you sure?" He lowered his chin and looked at me under his brows.

"Yeah." I couldn't exactly confide in him, could I? "I just got some news. I'm trying to process it."

"Bad news?" he asked.

"I'm not sure," I admitted. "It's complicated."

"Do you want to talk about it?" He quirked an eyebrow at me.

"I thought you didn't like me?" I mimicked his expression.

"I don't, but I'm not a complete dick. If someone needs to get something off their chest, I can listen."

"As tempting as that is," and it was, a little bit, "I'm not sure what there is to say. I need to think about things for a while." And I really needed to talk to Kane and Dyson. If anyone would know about hybrids...okay, they might know nothing, but they deserved to know.

He pushed himself off the wall. "Suit yourself. Just do me a favour and be careful, all right? I've heard some strange rumours about something going down in the paranormal world."

Now he had my attention. "What kind of rumours?"

He ran a hand over his hair. "I'm not exactly sure. Just...strange ones."

"Is it about Zeta?" The words were out before I could stop them.

His lips dropped apart. "How do you know about them?" he asked carefully.

"From a friend," I replied as casually as I could. "How do *you* know about them?"

His expression shut down hard. His eyes were like chips of stone. No hint of emotion was visible in their depths.

"If I were you, I'd stay well away from them and don't mention them again," he said coldly.

"And what if I do?" I stood my ground. I wasn't scared of him, nor would I let him intimidate me.

He hesitated for a moment, then with some effort relaxed his pose. "Then it's your funeral, I guess. If you're lucky."

I cocked my head. "What do you mean by that?"

He leaned in until his nose was almost touching mine. "I mean Zeta likes to use paranormals for their own gain. They won't wait around until you give permission for it either."

I tried not to flinch, but I thought back to what Nash had said about the creation of hybrids. Someone had to carry those children and supply the DNA. The only way either of those things would happen would be against my will.

I swallowed and took a step back. I forced a smile as though not completely rattled by all of this. "Why aren't we fighting back?"

"Who says we aren't?" he asked. "Do you think students would be privy to that kind of information?"

"Apparently you are," I said ironically.

He shrugged. "I made it a point to find out, after..." he shook his head. "It doesn't matter. The point is, you're better off to keep your pretty little nose out of all of this."

"Too late," I replied simply. "I'm not letting this go, just because you think I should." Especially if he was going to be so condescending.

"Don't think I'll weep at your funeral," he said.

"I'm surprised you'd even be there," I retorted.

Something flashed across his face, something like regret. It was gone before I could do more than register it. "You're right," he admitted. "I have something more important to do that day."

"You're a real fucking charmer, you know that?" I said sarcastically.

He grinned. "Of course I am. When I like someone."

"For your information, I'm very likeable," I said with a sniff.

"You're fuckable, but that's about it," he said coolly.

"Wow, what a compliment." I snorted. "It would be a cold day in all the hells before I let you go there."

"You seem to be busy enough as it is," he replied. "Do your knees even recognise each other?"

My mouth dropped open. "Did you just try to slut shame me?"

He shrugged one shoulder. "If the hat fits…"

Before I could think, I held out my palm, formed a ball of magic and hurled it at him. It struck him in the middle of his oh-so-chiseled chest and knocked him back off his feet. He landed on his ass with a grunt of pain.

He leapt up with a growl and tossed a ball of magic back at me.

I ducked sideways. It soared past my shoulder and slammed into a tree, sending bark flying in every direction.

"Really?" I asked angrily. "Mine wasn't made to do that much damage."

He shrugged and made another ball of magic. "I wasn't aiming to kill. That time." He drew back his hand, his eyes fixed on mine.

A thrill of fear passed down my spine. Without thinking, I dropped to a crouch and threw myself at his legs. He went down again, hard. The ball of magic went wide. It hit an electrical pole and sent up a shower of sparks.

"You fucking idiot." I rolled off him. "Are you trying to kill us all?" Just in case, I formed another ball of magic.

He stood on unsteady legs. "Not all of us, no."

"Just me?" I watched him carefully for any sign of his next move.

"You threw the first shot," he pointed out.

"Only because you were being an asshole," I retorted.

"I was not, I was just being honest." He stood straight, hands at his sides.

"That's one way to put it. I stand by my assessment of you—you're an asshole."

He grinned. "You're only saying that because you don't know me."

"Thank the gods for that," I said. "You're probably worse than an asshole." I decided he wasn't going to attack me again and let the magic dissipate, but I remained on my guard.

His mouth quirked to the side. "What's worse than that?"

"I don't know and I don't really care." Whatever it was, it could stay away from me.

"Of course you don't, you're too busy messing around in things you shouldn't be, and throwing magic at people who aren't your enemy."

"Says you," I told him. "You're doing a pretty good imitation of an enemy as far as I can see."

He raised his chin and barked a laugh. "If you think that, you must have had a much more sheltered life than I guessed. Compared to some, I'm completely harmless." His eyes shone with amusement and condescension. What a dick. He knew nothing about me, except that I had a tattoo and was involved with Kane. How dare he correctly assume my life had been sheltered up until now?

Rude!

I purpose my lips. "You're referring to Zeta again?" I guessed. "For someone who thinks I should forget about them, you bring them up a lot." I cocked my head in what I hoped was a challenging look.

He blew out a frustrated breath. "I didn't say you should forget. I said you should be careful and not get involved. Or complacent. It's likely they have agents here at the academy. They're probably on the look out for their latest victims."

Part of me wanted to laugh and accuse him of being melodramatic. Instead, a shiver went down my spine. The idea that anyone at the academy would sell us out to an evil government organisation was nothing less than horrifying. Who would do such a thing?

My mouth went dry. How about someone who worked with them? Nash claimed he didn't anymore, but what if that wasn't the truth? What if his desire to dominate me went beyond sex?

"I see it's finally sinking in," Matt said. "Don't trust anyone."

"Including you?" I asked.

"Especially me," he agreed. "You don't know me from the next guy."

"And you're shifty as fuck," I added.

He laughed. "That too. At least I'm hot."

I rolled my eyes. "That's a matter of opinion." If he wasn't such a dick, I would tear his clothes off and screw him silly. Damn it. I didn't want to think that way about him. He was infuriating.

"I can see that opinion on your face." He was so smug I almost sent another ball of magic at him, this time at his head.

I grunted. "You suck at reading people."

"No I don't." He shook his head. "I'm very good at it. In fact—" He stopped and his eyes widened. He came toward me at a run and slammed me down to the ground.

I landed with a thud, the wind knocked out of me. How I didn't hit my head on the concrete and break it open, I didn't know. Still, everything was going to hurt like a bitch later.

What the fuck?

A snapping sound, followed by an angry shriek echoed across the area.

"What the fuck?" I asked when my breath returned.

"Shut up and stay down."

As if I had a choice. His body lay on top of mine, his arms over my head. I was pinned down hard.

Something big soared over the top of us. It turned and headed back.

"Shit. Shit, shit shit. Don't move." Matt buried his face in my shoulder and froze.

I bit back a cry of alarm as a winged creature passed overhead. For a moment, I thought maybe it was a dragon. Then I got a clear look and my heart raced like a drumroll. Great gods above, it couldn't be. Could it?

The phoenix was huge—twice as big as a grown person—and covered from head to toe in bright blue feathers. At the shoulder, they were midnight blue. The shade lightened down the wings, to a brilliant blue at the ends. The phoenix might be pretty if it wasn't obviously hells bent on attacking us. The creature let out a long, low shriek and circled above us. They made a dive and snapped with the enormous beak.

"I think they can see us," I said, my voice high. "Get off me so I can throw some magic at them."

"No," Matt growled. "I'm going to roll off. When I do that, you're going to run. Get inside the academy and close the door."

"I'm not just going to run," I argued.

"Then you'll die," he snapped. "On three. One. Two. Three." He rolled away.

2 1

INSTEAD OF JUMPING up and running, I leapt to my feet and aimed a ball of magic at the phoenix.

When it came over for another pass, I drew back my arm and waited. Just a bit closer, just a bit...

"Peyton, no!"

Matt's shout registered a fraction of a second after I released the ball of magic. Let's face it, I wouldn't have listened to him anyway. Hey, I never said I made the best choices.

The ball struck the phoenix on its face. It shimmered against the blue feathers for a moment, then grew and came back at me twice the size of the one I'd sent.

"Fuck!" I threw up a bubble of magic around me. The ball hit a heartbeat later and sizzled. I gritted my teeth to hold the magic in place. If it gave out, I was done for.

Blood pounded in my ears, raced around my body, a hot torrent of adrenaline. The bubble started to fail.

For the first time since I'd seen the phoenix, I was truly scared.

Matt called out something, but I couldn't make it out. A moment later, there he was, beside me, reinforcing the bubble with his own magic.

I let out a sob of relief as the pressure was shared, then lessened. The ball of magic gradually lost its power. No, Matt was absorbing it into our bubble. Whatever, we'd live to fight another minute or two.

"What part of "get inside" did you not understand?" he growled.

"The part where you don't get to tell me what to do," I retorted.

"And look where that got you," he snapped. "It almost got you killed."

"I was taking care of it." I glanced around. Where was the phoenix anyway, and how the hells had it amplified my magic like that?

"Bullshit. Another second or two and you'd be dead." He too was looking around.

"Yeah, well, thanks. Why is this fucker trying to kill me anyway?"

"Maybe he knows how annoying you are," Matt replied.

"How do you know it's a he?" I decided to ignore the insult, since he had—you know—saved my life.

"Just a guess." He turned in a circle, eyes skyward.

"Do you think he's gone?" I asked. I caught sight of faces peering out the window at us. Yeah, thanks for the help everyone.

"Not a chance. He won't have given up that easily." Matt sounded troubled. "We need to get insi—duck!"

For once I had the sense to listen. I dropped to a crouch as the phoenix made another pass. He opened his beak and scooped up a mouthful of magic as he went.

"What the hells?" I stared.

Matt pulled me to my feet and gave me a shove toward the academy door. "Get inside, *now*."

I staggered toward the threshold and turned. "What are you going to—"

My mouth dropped open as Matt stopped still and shifted. Yes, you guessed it, into a gargoyle. All right, in retrospect I should have figured it out, but I hadn't. Yet there he was, horns and all. His skin—or was that hide—was a glistening black, his eyes orange and red, like flame.

He let out a deep growl.

The phoenix shrieked in response.

I clapped my hands over my ears and stepped back further into the building.

"Peyton, what the hells is going on?"

I turned my head at the sound of Kane's voice. He and Dyson hurried down the corridor toward me. The whole academy administration peered through the door at me. At least three quarters of the students gathered around the windows, all trying to catch a glimpse.

"Just a little phoenix attack," I said as lightly as I could.

Kane put his arms around me and drew me to him.

Dyson looked a little pale. "Phoenix?"

I nodded. "The gargoyle is on our side. I think."

The phoenix screeched and flew at Matt. In the middle of the street, they slammed into each other. The phoenix grabbed a hold of Matt's arm, uh, leg, with his beak. He tugged his head to the side and grazed his beak down the bone of Matt's leg.

Matt let out a scream of pain. He tried to jerk his leg free, but his opponent held tight. His back legs scrabbled fast and hard, to keep him upright. I sensed if he fell, he was dead.

"What do we do?" I asked frantically. "Magic bounces off him."

"I don't think an owl is much of a match for that," Kane said quietly.

"Neither is a dog," Dyson replied. He sighed loudly.

I grabbed out my phone and clicked on the app. "There must be something." I scrolled down the menu of creatures and dismissed them as I went. The magpie was too small. The goat was—well—a goat. Cat, dingo, fox, horse, zebra. Crap, that was it.

I almost threw my phone against the wall in frustration. What good was learning all of this if we were helpless during one attack?

The invader forced Matt down lower and lower. Matt snapped at him and writhed, but he was getting increasingly weaker.

Finally his legs gave out and he fell to the road. His attacker stood over him, wings outspread, legs to either side of him. He let out a shriek of victory that threatened to shred every nerve in my body. His head snaked back and forth, then he opened his beak. I was sure he was about to rip out Matt's throat.

"Fuck this," I growled. I put my phone away and ran out toward the road.

"Peyton, no!" Kane called out behind me.

"Hey, fucker!" I waved my arms in the air. "It's me you want, right? Well, here I am. Come and get me."

The phoenix turned slowly, then stepped off Matt. His gaze was intent on me.

"Good boy," I taunted. "You don't want to kill anyone, right? Well, anyone but me. I don't suppose you can tell me why?"

The phoenix moved toward me, slow and deliberate. He was hunting me.

"I guess not." I shrugged. My hands sweated like crazy and I felt sick. At any moment, the phoenix would lunge and it would be all over for me. Fine, whatever, as long as no one else got hurt.

"You all right, Matt?" I called around the phoenix.

He groaned, shifted back into human form and crawled behind a parked car. In the corner of my eye, I saw Dyson and Kane run out to help him back inside.

"It's just you and me then, fucker," I told the phoenix. "What have you got?" Okay, it was a dumb question, but let's face it, I knew the answer. He was a shifter with magic. Not just magic, but the power to expand and deflect the magic of others. Created, I assume, by Zeta in some kind of laboratory. Just like Matt and Nash. Gods, who else was a hybrid around here?

The phoenix stepped toward me, his beak open, tongue licking the air between us.

"You have disgusting breath," I told him. If he could amplify magic, I wonder...

I pulled back my sleeve to expose my tattoo.

The phoenix's eyes narrowed. Uh-ha, he knew what I was up to. Before he could move away, I flicked my arm and willed my personal gargoyle to come to life. With a rush of air, the magic flew toward the phoenix and hit him on the wing.

A moment later a shape formed on the road between us. The

gargoyle was twice the size of the one I had created in class. Twice the size of Matt. It growled deeply.

The phoenix backed up a few steps.

"Peyton!"

I registered Nash's presence a moment before he rushed out onto the road and stood beside me.

"Are you going to tell me to go inside, sir?" I eyed him in my peripheral vision.

"You seem to have this under control," he said. "Nice work."

"Thank you, sir. It's good to have you out here with me though." I figured there was no safer place to be than shoulder to shoulder with a dragon.

"I wouldn't be anywhere else," he said. "Sorry it took so long though. I didn't know this was happening until Ariana told me."

I frowned. "Ariana, where is she?" I realised I hadn't seen her in any of this.

"Inside," Nash said simply. "Safe. Luckily she knew who to come to."

"How—" The question would have to wait for another time. The gargoyle lunged at the phoenix and raked its claws down a wing. It drew back for another attack, but promptly disappeared. Just as well, it could have inflicted a lot more damage at its present size. As it was, it had done enough.

The phoenix shrieked and tried to flap, but the wing dangled help-lessly. Frantic, it backed up a handful of steps and desperately flapped its other wing. It lifted off the ground half a metre but flopped back down again.

He let out a pitiful creel and tucked his good wing to his back.

"Is that a surrender?" I asked.

"Possibly." Nash sounded troubled. He took a few tentative steps forward, hands out in front of him. "Give it up," he told the phoenix. "It's over now. You can escape here."

The phoenix lowered his head and gave another creel, this one even sadder than the first.

I almost felt sorry for him, but he had tried to kill me.

"Shift," Nash ordered. "Let's see who you really are."

The phoenix's head wove back and forth on his neck. I took that as a no. That was understandable. We paranormals spent our lives trying to hide our secret identities from the world. Even assassin phoenixes. Especially them, probably.

"You can shift alive and answer my questions, or you can do it dead," Nash said. "Frankly, I don't care which." His tone was so cold it made me shiver. He meant every word. I doubted anyone there thought otherwise.

"I'd prefer alive," I said, "then I'd know why this was happening."

Nash glanced over his shoulder at me.

That was all the distraction the phoenix needed. He snapped out his supposedly damaged wing and took flight.

"Shit!" Nash cursed.

For a moment I thought he might shift and give chase. Instead, he turned back and ushered me inside. In a matter of moments, the phoenix was gone.

"What the hells was that?" I asked. "I've never seen magic heal so quickly."

"Hybrid," was all Nash said. "If they came after you, they'll try again. It's unlikely they'll wait too long."

"Why me?" I demanded. "What did I do to Zeta?"

"It's probably not about what you did," Nash replied, "but what you could do for them."

"Which is what?" I asked. "I'm just an ordinary witch."

Nash gave me a long look. "To be honest, I don't know. There's something about you they want and they won't stop until they get it."

"Well that's fucking great," I muttered. "At least they don't want me dead."

His mouth set in a firm line. "Whatever they need, you might wish they had killed you before they take it."

"That's reassuring," I said dryly.

"It isn't meant to be," he said simply. "Get your friends and lovers and meet me in the training room. It's time we all had a little talk."

That sounded ominous. "All right. Sir."

He shot me look that made my blood heat. The adrenaline surge was gone, but it hadn't diminished his ability to arouse me with only a glance. Damn the man, he knew it too.

"Don't take long." He gave my hand a quick squeeze. "I'll be keeping a closer eye on you from now on." He leaned in to whisper in my ear. "Maybe I should just keep you tied up, for your own good."

My knees weak, I hurried off to find Kane and Dyson.

2 2

I FLOPPED down onto the soft training floor between Kane and Dyson. Matt sat opposite me, dressed in clean clothes, apparently healed after almost having a leg chewed off. Ariana sat beside him, her head lowered, hair over part of her face. Nash paced.

I followed him with my eyes.

"Can we start with why Zeta wants me dead?" I said. I had considered asking why the hells Matt was here in the first place, but he had defended me. That was another question I wanted answers for, but it wasn't as important as the one I had asked.

Nash stopped pacing and waved a hand toward Ariana. "I think she can answer that."

I gaped at Ariana, who raised her head and swallowed visibly. Her face was pale. She looked...scared.

"She can?" I asked, confused. I fixed my gaze on her. "You can?"

"Can I just begin by saying I didn't mean to deceive you. I mean, I did, but—" She ran a hand over her hair.

My heart sank. "You're working with them?"

Kane growled and moved as if to rise and throw himself at her.

I put out an arm to hold him back. "Let's hear her out first."

Ariana licked her lips. "I don't work for Zeta, no. I work with—"

She glanced toward Nash. "Factors who are fighting back against them. Your mother..."

"What about her? Is she working with Zeta?" I snapped. I was getting tired of these half answers.

"She used to," Ariana said, her voice small.

I leaned back and looked toward the ceiling to compose myself. "She doesn't now?"

"It's hard to break ties with them," Ariana said slowly.

Nash snorted. "She's right there. Your mother is too high profile to hide." He didn't need to add, "Like I did." The words hung in the air.

"What did she do for them?" I wasn't sure I wanted the answer to that, but I needed to know.

"She..." Ariana chewed her lip. "Zeta was trying to incorporate paranormal DNA with that of normals. To do that, they needed test subjects."

My stomach turned. "Please don't tell me she supplied those test subjects."

Ariana looked away.

"Oh gods." I was going to throw up all over the perfectly good training floor.

Kane put an arm around me, and I leaned into him. Gods knew I was no fan of my mother, but I had no idea she was such a monster. That left so many questions about my own conception and development, but I didn't want to think about that, not yet.

Once my head stopped spinning, the implications hit me like a blow to the face. I don't mean a blow job, I mean the bad kind.

"You knew about this?" I pulled away from Kane and glanced around the room.

"I knew," Ariana said quickly. "I was sent here to keep an eye on you. To keep you safe."

I narrowed my eyes at her. "So, you're not new to magic?"

"That part is true," she said. "My aunt Chrissy works with—I guess you could call them the resistance. She thought I'd be less obvious than someone who is a known shifter." She nodded toward Matt.

"Right." I turned to Matt. "Where do you fit into all of this?"

He shrugged. "Same. I was asked to keep an eye on you. I argued against it, on the grounds you're a spoilt brat, but they insisted."

I snorted. "Gee, thanks."

He smirked. "You're welcome. And don't thank me for saving your ass."

"As I recall, I saved yours too, so we're even," I said dryly.

He shrugged with one shoulder and winced. Apparently his arm still hurt after all.

"What about the rest of you?" I asked. My gaze swung up to Nash, who seemed angry, for some inexplicable reason.

"I knew, but only after we—" he hesitated, "got involved."

Matt shot him a look of surprise, then made a face as if disgusted that anyone might be interested in me.

Yeah, fuck you too, I thought.

"How much after?" I asked.

"After you got that tattoo," Nash said. "I spoke to Matt about it. He told me about your mother and Ariana."

My heart sank deeper. Even if they were trying to protect me, they had kept so many secrets from me, I wasn't sure I could trust them.

"No one thought to ask me what I thought about any of this?" I growled.

"I didn't know anything about it," Kane assured me.

"Neither did I," Dyson said quickly. "You saw what Peyton did out there today? All the rest of us could do was to stand there and watch. She's more badass than we are."

"Exactly," Kane agreed. "She can take care of herself."

"Thank you," I told them both.

"If you think that, you're all fools," Matt said derisively. "That was one phoenix. One attack. What will they send next time? People with guns? An army of dragons?" He jerked his chin toward Nash. "Now they know the academy is here, they'll come after us all. This is now about more than Peyton. Every student here is at risk."

"Then we'll move the academy," Nash said. "It wouldn't be the first time."

I blew a breath out pursed lips. "So them coming after me has revealed the existence of the academy? All because of my mother. Why not go after her? Why kill me?"

"It's unlikely they want to kill you," Nash said. His tone gave me chills.

Oh yeah, that whole making paranormal babies against my will thing, I had forgotten about that.

Matt nodded his agreement. "At best they might hold you until your mother complies with their wishes. At worst, they'll break you until you beg to help them."

"Fuck no," I muttered.

"We're not going to let anything happen to you," Kane assured me.

"Me either," Dyson said. "We can pack up and leave right now if you want to. We can go somewhere far away, where they can't find us."

That was tempting.

I sighed. "If we do that, we'll spend the rest of our lives looking over our shoulders."

"We all do that already," Matt pointed out. "More so now they know we're here. Every minute we delay, gives them time to rally and come after us."

"I should have killed the phoenix when I had the chance." Nash scowled.

"Why didn't you?" Matt turned accusing eyes toward him.

Nash gave him a dark look, but I knew what he was thinking. The lives he had taken haunted him as it was. He didn't want to add to that body count. Not to mention Zeta would find him if he shifted into dragon form. They would know where he'd hidden and come after him, hard.

"It's done now," I said softly. "We need to deal with today and tomorrow."

"Peyton," Ariana started.

"I don't want to hear it," I snapped.

She flinched as if I'd struck her. "I was only trying to—"

I cut her off. "You pretended to be my friend. I cared about you, but you were lying to me the whole time!"

Tears spilled down her cheeks. "I was your friend." She sniffed. "I *am* your friend. Just because I was sent to help, doesn't mean I didn't care."

I shook my head. "You should have told me." I glanced toward Nash. "You too."

His mouth twitched downward. "I told you what I could. I was scared you'd risk yourself if you knew any more." His eyes were full of regret, but I forced myself to look away.

"And you." I jerked my head toward Matt. "That was you that day with Jess."

"Yep," he replied easily. "I thought I'd check you out, see what you're made of."

"That earth shake," I said, "that was you?"

"I might have rocked your world a little bit." He didn't even look slightly sorry for it.

"People could have died," I reminded him.

He rolled his eyes. "Everyone was fine. I know how to be careful."

"Sure you do." I pointed toward his arm. "How's that going?"

He pulled his sleeve up to reveal skin covered in nasty scars. "I'll have a nice reminder of how I tried to save the ass of an ungrateful brat."

I bared my teeth at him. "Who are you—"

"Enough," Nash snapped. "We fucked up. We should have been honest with you, but we don't have time for you to be butt hurt."

I gaped at him. Butt hurt? Because my best friend and my lover had been lying to me? I was more than butt hurt, I was furious, and with good reason. A little voice in the back of my head reminded me they had just been trying to keep me safe, but I was too angry to pay it much attention.

"Everyone go and pack, but lightly. We need to evacuate the building as soon as possible." Nash waved us toward the door.

Kane gripped my hand. "I'll help you."

I regarded him for a moment. "You worked with Nash. He really said nothing about any of this?"

Kane licked his lips. "Uh."

"What the fuck, Kane?" Dyson snapped.

What the fuck indeed.

"It's not like that," Kane protested. "He just suggested I be careful if we go anywhere. And...look out for anyone who might follow us."

"Did you ask why?" Dyson asked.

Kane's mouth worked for a moment. "Not really, no. I agreed to be careful and that was that."

There was more to this, but we didn't have time for that right now.

I pulled my hand from his and stood. "I can pack my own bags. You all worry about yours."

Kane shot me look of pure hurt and got to his feet. "If I'd known, I would have told you."

"You didn't tell me Nash gave you that warning," I said curtly.

"No, but—"

"Then don't say you would have, because you didn't," I snapped. "I can't trust a single one of you."

Dyson raised a finger. "I swear, I knew nothing about any of this."

"I told you about Nash's warning," Kane said softly.

He might as well have reached into my chest and pulled out my beating heart. Hot tears pooled in my eyes and trickled down my cheeks. I put up my hands before anyone could say another word.

"I'm done with all of you." I swallowed to hold back a sob. I felt as though my whole life lay in ruins around my feet, like they'd stomped all over it. "I'm going to pack and when I'm done, I never want to see any of you, ever again."

"You don't mean that," Ariana said. She reached a hand out to me.

"I mean every word," I assured her. At the time I did. Later, when I had calmed down, I might think differently. Right now though, I felt sick and wanted to be away from these people. "Stay the hells away from me."

"Peyton—"

I didn't know who spoke, I had already turned my back and hurried out the door. Once there, I broke into a trot, pushed past other students and ignored the one or two people who asked if I was okay.

It wasn't until I was alone in my room that I broke down into sobs.

How had my perfect little piece of the world come to this? I had never felt so alone, so betrayed, in my entire life.

I pulled my bag out from under my bed and threw things inside it. I didn't know what most of it was, I was looking through a haze of tears. Maybe I should leave it all here and get away from the academy. And maybe a part of me needed to take the time to pack, in the hope one of my friends or lovers came with words that would heal my heart. Or start to.

2 3

THE KNOCK on the door told me it wasn't Ariana. As strained as things were between us, she would have just unlocked the door and come in.

At first I didn't bother to answer it. I zipped up my suitcase and pulled it to the floor by the handle.

Whoever it was, knocked again. Harder this time.

I sighed and opened the door.

"If I was a Zeta agent, you'd be dead or in captivity," Matt said.

I groaned. "Why did they send you?" Of all people.

He pushed the door open further and stepped inside. On his back, he wore a backpack which was almost as big as I was.

"Because I'm the only one who is going to give it to you straight and not try to spare your feelings." He fixed me with a firm look.

I crossed my arms over my chest. "Go on then."

"You're overreacting and being a brat," he declared.

"Okay. You've told me, now you can leave." I tugged my suitcase toward the door.

Matt made a frustrated sound in the back of his throat. He placed a hand on the doorframe. I could get past, but I'd have to duck.

"Everything everyone has done for you was to keep you safe. What would you have said if they had explained everything earlier? Be honest. With yourself, if not with me."

I frowned. "I would have been pissed off. I don't need babysitting."

"If that phoenix had attacked while you were out jogging, what would you have done?" he asked. "If I hadn't been there today, you would have been taken. Right there, in front of the academy. And no one could have stopped them. By now, you'd be so broken you'd be telling them every detail about this place."

"Fuck off, I would not," I snapped.

I caught a hint of a smile. He was trying to goad me. Asshole. It had worked.

"All right, maybe in an hour or two. The point is, you needed help and you wouldn't have accepted it if you'd known we were offering it. Admit it."

I opened my mouth to protest but sighed instead. "Fine. You're right, I wouldn't have wanted it." I would probably have gone off by myself to prove what a badass I was.

He smirked. "Did you just say I'm right? I should have recorded that, I bet you don't say it often."

I rolled my eyes. "Yeah, yeah, don't let it go to your head."

"Which one?" he shot back.

"The one on your shoulders," I said firmly. "I have no interest in the one in your pants."

"That's only because you've never tried it." He grinned. "Believe me, I could have you screaming for hours."

"Says you." I stepped closer to the door, which meant closer to him. He did smell good, like soap and testosterone. "Shouldn't we be evacuating?"

"After you promise to speak to your friends. Ariana in particular is beside herself. Kane too. When I left, he looked like he was about to cry." Matt lowered his arm and stepped back.

"Not that there's anything wrong with men crying," I said sternly.

"If you say so." He grabbed the handle of my suitcase from my hand and pulled it down the corridor.

"What, too much of a big man to show emotion?" I asked teasingly.

"No, I don't waste my time with crying over people and stuff." He stopped to push the button beside the elevator.

"That's actually really sad," I told him. "What about things like love?"

"No time for that either." The elevator doors slide open and he pulled my suitcase in, in front of me.

"Or basic manners," I muttered.

"What? I'm pulling your suitcase, aren't I?" He pushed the button for the ground floor.

"So we'll move faster, not because you're nice."

"True," he agreed.

The elevator started down with a jolt.

"Where are the others?" I asked.

Before he could respond, the elevator jerked to a stop and the lights went out.

"Oh crap," he murmured.

"Let me guess, that's not a coincidence." I leaned against the wall and rubbed my face.

"It's highly unlikely to be one, yes," he agreed. "We're going to need to get out of—"

From outside the elevator an enormous bang sounded. The floor shook so hard I was thrown off my feet. I hit the wall with a thud and cried out in pain.

"Shit." A ball of magic lit Matt's face. He held out his palm to illuminate me. "Are you okay?"

"Yeah." I pulled myself to my feet. "It's just my dignity that's bruised."

"Good. As I was saying, we need to get out of here," he said. "Can you open the door?"

I nodded and reached for my phone. I knew just the spell. We'd been working on it in class.

"Uh, fuckity-crap," I swore. My phone screen must had been smashed when I fell. It flared for a moment, then what looked like a trickle of magic rose from the broken screen. It hovered in the air in front of my face for a moment, then shot up through the elevator roof and was gone.

"Just when you think things can't get worse," I growled.

"That was a—" Matt pointed upward, his mouth agape.

"I know what it was," I told him. "It's a tracking spell. The question is, why was it there?" I groaned inwardly. That must have been what was causing havoc with my phone, and why Zeta knew where to look. Why hadn't Madame Luc recognised it?

"Actually, the question is how long will it take before Zeta finds us here now that spell has broadcast your presence to any paranormal who knows to look for it?" He rubbed his face and shook his head. "There's no point in being subtle now. We can just blast the door open." He raised his hand.

"Wait." I grabbed his arm. "There might be people out there. You could kill someone."

"Right." Beads of sweat coated his brow.

"Claustrophobic?" I guessed.

"Yeah." He swallowed audibly.

"In that case—"

Something thudded onto the roof and the elevator jolted. Whatever it was started to scratch just above our heads.

Matt's face paled.

I squeezed his arm. "We'll get out of here, don't worry." I tried to sound reassuring, but the scratching increased. "Maybe I should blast that?" I pointed upward.

Before Matt could respond, the maintenance hatch above our heads moved. We shrank back into a corner. I know, it was pointless trying to hide in a space so small I could touch either wall with my arms outstretched. Instinct is what it is.

The hatch slid aside to reveal Dyson's smiling face. "Hey strangers. You look like you need a hand."

"Are you naked?" I asked without thinking. Fear does strange things to people's minds. In my case in particular.

He grinned. "I had to shift to get down here. Sorry I don't have a change of clothes stored on top of an elevator."

"Of course," I muttered. "You should help Matt out first. He looks like he's about to pass out."

Matt shot me a dirty look and drew himself up taller. "I'm fine."

"Sure you are," I said dryly. "Now is not the time to pull that macho shit. Get up there. You can help pull me out afterward."

Dyson lay on his stomach and offered Matt his hand.

"I don't need help," Matt grunted. He pulled off his clothes and tossed them to me.

I caught them and held them in front of me, high enough to give him some privacy. Okay, I did peek and ye gads, he was big. I mean, *huge*. My mouth went dry at the thought of him sliding into… Ugh, that was Matt I was thinking about. I reminded myself I couldn't stand him and looked away.

I glanced back in time to see him shift into his gargoyle form. Up close, he was impressive. Rippling muscles and midnight dark hide. His back legs bunched under him and he leapt just as Dyson moved out of the way.

In one leap he was atop the elevator and shifted back into human form.

"Here." I threw his clothes up toward him. He caught them and moved out of sight. Judging by the way the elevator moved, he was getting dressed.

Priorities.

I rolled my eyes and pulled my suitcase under the hatch so I could climb up onto it. Hopefully the hard plastic would support my weight.

"We heard an explosion," I said when Dyson reappeared above me.

He looked over at something beside him and grimaced. "Yeah. We need to hurry up. Things are getting—"

The elevator jolted again and I was thrown off my suitcase and hard against the wall. Pain blossomed through my shoulder and down to the rest of my arm.

"Peyton!" Dyson called out. "I don't think this thing is going to hold much longer."

"Get yourselves to safety," I shouted back. Tears poured down my cheeks. I didn't think my arm was broken, but it sure hurt like hells.

"We're not leaving without—shit!"

The whole elevator shook like we were inside a snow globe. I was tossed against one wall, then the other. Just as I decided I would probably die here, the elevator car went completely still.

"Matt's holding it," Dyson said. "Come on!"

Wincing, I pulled my suitcase back into place and climbed onto it again.

The elevator gave an ominous creak.

"This is why you should take stairs during an emergency," I said under my breath.

Teetering on top of the suitcase, I put my hand up above my head. It took two tries before Dyson was able to grab hold.

With a grunt, he pulled me up though the hatch. I flopped down beside him to catch my breath.

Matt stood an arm span away, half dressed, a look of concentration on his face. Magic danced around him like an aura. "Hurry up," he growled.

"We'll have to climb up to the next level." Dyson gestured.

I followed the direction he pointed. We were a couple of metres down. The cables that should have held us were frayed as if they'd been hacked. If Matt faltered…

"You go first," I told Dyson. "I'm guessing your dog form can jump that distance."

He nodded. "Unless you can conjure a ladder."

"If my phone wasn't smashed, I'd try that," I assured him.

He looked regretful. "Mine is with my clothes. Matt?"

"What?" Matt grunted.

"Do you have your phone with you?" Dyson asked.

"It's in my jeans pocket," he replied.

Since he wasn't wearing any jeans, I crawled over to the pile of clothes near his feet. I searched his pockets and pulled out his phone.

"Passcode." I glanced toward him.

"Six, nine, six, nine," he said.

"Of course it is," I muttered. I pressed in the code and opened the browser. Either he didn't search up anything, or he'd cleaned his history recently. I tapped in the website we'd used in class and scrolled down to the advanced lessons. Yes, conjuring creatures is a basic skill, go figure.

I found a selection of objects and clicked on the link. "Boxes, tables, chairs..."

"Hurry up," Matt urged.

"I'm trying," I replied. "Why the fuck would I conjure a temporary waterslide?" I shook my head. "Ah, there was go. Ladder." I clicked and focused on the floor between my feet and the level above us.

After a moment, a ladder shimmered into existence.

"Perfect." I tucked the phone into my pocket.

"Ladies first." Dyson gave me a bow.

I don't know about lady, but I was the one who couldn't shift and get myself out, so I grabbed the ladder and climbed up and out of the shaft.

Grateful, I flopped down onto the carpet and took a few breaths.

Before I could even move out of the way to let Dyson up, footsteps approached.

"We've found her!"

The words were followed by a snap and the sound of the elevator dropping to the floor below.

2 4

I ROLLED over and jumped to my feet. My first instinct was to run back to the elevator shaft and make sure the guys were all right. Instead, I froze. I had other things to deal with first.

What I assumed were Zeta agents stood with guns trained on me. They were both dressed from head to toe in black. Total cliché, am I right? Black is such a badass colour, it didn't deserve to be appropriated by an evil organisation. They should wear a hideous colour, like muddy brown or olive green. Maybe a nice orange.

I eyed their guns. "Hey guys. Nice of you to come and help."

"Hands up." The agent on the left—a guy with a butt-chin—gestured with his weapon.

In spite of the pain in my arm, I raised my hands slowly but kept my gaze on them and their weapons. I wasn't used to dealing with guns, but I figured if they were going to fire, I would see it in their movements before they pulled the trigger.

"Turn around and walk toward the stairs." Butt-chin ordered.

I considered for a moment. On one hand, I didn't want to have my back to them. That would put me at a distinct disadvantage. On the other hand, Matt said they didn't want me dead. If they knew who I was, I was better off going along with them until the right moment came to fight back.

"Now," the other agent growled. She had a twitch in one eye that gave away her nerves.

I turned slowly and started to walk.

From other parts of the academy the sound of shouting echoed. Every now and again, someone would scream, or a crash would resound. The floor shook under my feet. That couldn't be good.

"Faster." Twitchy-eye poked a gun in my back.

"Hey, I'm going as fast as I can," I replied. The smart ass in me was tempted to slow down, but instinct to survive overrode that. I didn't want to die if the building collapsed and I didn't want to get shot. What I did want was to be sure Dyson was all right. Okay, maybe I was a bit worried about Matt too. Who would I argue with if he was gone?

I chewed my lip. Where the hells were Nash, Kane and Ariana? I wished I hadn't wasted so much time being angry with them. It seemed so silly now. All they had been trying to do was save me from…well…this exact situation. Here I was anyway. Just great.

Hopefully they all got out and ran. Knowing them, they stayed to look for me, but I hoped they had more sense. Firstly, I didn't feel I deserved to have them risk themselves more than they already had, and secondly it wouldn't help anyone if they got killed. Or taken.

I stepped around a corner and found the first of the bodies. One looked to be a student I didn't recognise. The other was a Zeta agent, a frozen look of fear on their face. Score one for our team. And one for theirs.

I shuffled around them and down the first few stairs. Here, there were another two bodies. Another Zeta agent and… I swallowed hard.

Madame Luc.

If the gaping hole in her chest was anything to go by, she'd been shot. The Zeta agent was missing a large amount of their face, so I guessed she won that round.

At the bottom of the stairs, the shouting escalated. If I had to guess, I would say Zeta had us outnumbered. The only way to take on a bunch of witches, wizards, shifters and hybrids would be to do it with strength of numbers. Anything else would be suicide. Unless they had a lot of hybrids on their side. I couldn't discount that possibility.

"Down the next set of stairs," Butt-chin ordered.

"I think that would be a bad idea," I said. "It sounds like people are dying down there. Would it be better to, I don't know, hide for a while?"

"Walk," Twitchy-eye snapped. She jabbed me with her gun again.

"If I fall and break my neck, you're going to get into trouble," I pointed out. "Whoever or whatever your boss is, they want me alive."

"Quiet," Butt-chin said. "Move."

"Charming," I said under my breath. I walked, but as I did, I drew back my sleeve, under the pretence of scratching an itch. I licked my lips and waited.

Five steps.

Four steps.

Three steps.

Two steps.

I turned and conjured the gargoyle. As soon as it appeared, I threw myself through the door at the bottom of the stairs and slammed it shut behind me.

The ear-piercing scream that followed wasn't even slightly satisfying. I took no pleasure in hurting or killing anyone, even if they would happily kill me first.

I ran from the stairs to the elevator just as the doors were blasted outward. I threw a hand over my eyes to shield them from flying shards of metal.

"Peyton, there you are!" Dyson said cheerfully.

I lowered my hand to see him stand in the remains of the doorway in all his naked glory. He caught me up in a big embrace.

Matt, still half-naked, was right behind him.

"You're all right?" I asked once Dyson loosened his hold on me. I fixed my gaze on his and drank in the warm, tender look in his eyes.

"More or less," Matt replied. "Thanks for caring."

I stuck my tongue out at him. "I'm glad you're okay too," I told him, "even if you are a pain in the ass."

"Back at you," he said gruffly. Maybe he didn't hate me after all.

"Fuck." Dyson's eyes widened. He cocked his head like a dog listening to something.

"What is it?" I asked.

The doors to the stairs burst open and a creature leapt out. Head of an eagle, body of a lion, twitching eye, the griffin looked pissed off. Claw marks ran down the side of her face. Butt-chin lay near her feet, or at least his head did.

Two points to the gargoyle. Or maybe one and a half, since Twitchy-eye was still around.

She thrust her head forward and made a strange, low cry.

"I hate griffins," Matt muttered.

"I think the feeling is mutual," Dyson said.

She stalked toward us.

I reassessed the danger to the academy. The numbers of Zeta agents might not be as high as I assumed, but if they had enough hybrids like this, we might be in trouble.

"What can we use against her?" I stepped back until the wall was right behind me.

The griffin licked her lips. Of course, she could understand every word. She seemed to be enjoying this. I guessed in her normal form, she didn't get as much respect as she did as a griffin.

"Maybe her insecurity," I suggested. I stepped toward her. "Hey, there's no reason we should be on opposite sides. We're all paranormals here. We could be—"

She lunged at me and swung an enormous paw.

Only instinct let me duck aside in time for the swing to pass over my head close enough to slice off a few hairs.

"Opposite sides it is then," I said under my breath. I fired a ball of magic and threw it while I rolled out of the way and back on my feet.

She hissed, but formed a bubble fast enough to deflect the worst of my magic.

"Peyton." Dyson grabbed my hand and tugged me toward the door leading out of the academy.

I made a bubble around us both, in case she threw any magic back at me. What we gained in invisibility, we lost with the noise we made as we ran across the tiled floor.

"Ouch!"

A voice cried out at the same time as I stepped something soft. "Sorry." Apparently we weren't the only invisible ones making a run for it out of here. No doubt whoever's foot I stepped on would be okay.

We ran out to the road, Matt behind us.

The road was filled with discarded items left by students who had fled the Zeta attack. Several agents lay dead or dying.

Dyson pulled me down behind a car and Matt crouched on the other side.

"This is why they want hybrids?" I guessed. "They're bloody hard to kill."

"Let's hope some of us are," Matt said.

The griffin ran past us, then stopped and turned back. She cocked her head and stuck out a pointed tongue as though to taste the air. Or our fear.

"I need a distraction," Matt whispered.

I nodded and I pulled his phone out of my pocket. I tapped on the screen, grimaced as I entered the passcode and clicked on our magical website.

"No offence, but maybe a bit faster," Dyson said, "she looks like she wants to bite off my dick."

"Well, we can't have that," I said without looking up. I found what I was looking for and clicked.

A magpie appeared in the air above the griffin. The little black and white bird let out a squawk and dove at the griffin. It managed to deliver a series of pecks to the griffin's head before she swatted it away.

It was enough to allow Matt to shift and throw himself at her. He fastened his great jaw on her neck. His claws gripped her body until blood coated his front feet.

In spite of that, the griffin only shook her head and batted at Matt with her huge claws. They raked down his skin, drawing shining blood on his black hide.

"Matt!" I stood and tossed a ball of magic at her, then another. They struck her, but she had a bubble up before I could blink.

"Fuck, she's fast." I crouched back down.

"Stay here." A moment later, Dyson was in his dog form. He jumped toward the griffin. He was a wolfhound, I realised. Big, shaggy and apparently nasty when they're pissed. He grabbed hold of one of the griffin's legs with his teeth and growled.

She shook her leg to try to shake him off, but he held on fast.

"Good dog," I muttered.

The griffin loosened her grip on Matt and he fell to the ground with a thud. Blood seeped from his wounds and spread across the road.

"Gods." I swallowed hard. I wanted to run out there and drag him to safety. Even as I thought that, he groaned, lifted his head and shifted. Naked, he forced himself to his knees and crawled toward me. His back was marred with gouges, but they were already starting to heal.

The griffin screeched, then screeched again. She shook her leg so hard I thought Dyson might fly off, but he stayed attached.

A new sound reached my ears—a low growl and the sound of wings. Very large wings. A shadow passed overhead.

I licked my lips and looked up as the body of a dragon flew over the top of the car and over us. He swooped down toward the griffin, who looked terrified for the first time.

She turned and attempted to run, but Dyson's weight held her back.

The dragon opened his mouth. Huge teeth shone in the afternoon sun like a set of knives. He huffed out a breath of what looked like magic. That was even more badass than breathing fire.

When Nash was close enough, he leaned down and bit off the griffin's head. Blood squirted from her neck and onto his muzzle and the street around her.

Her body teetered for a moment, then fell.

Dyson just managed to let go and leap out of the way before she crashed to the road.

"And that's how you kill a hybrid," Matt said wearily.

"That's good to know," I muttered, before I leaned over and threw up my breakfast on the ground beside me.

25

The street was quiet now. The residents who had peeked out of their homes had all been reassured they'd witnessed nothing more than filming for some Hollywood blockbuster. Later maybe someone would realise they would have had to sign release forms and vacate the premises while filming was going on. Then there was the lack of cameras. By the time they figured any of that out, we would be long gone, along with anything they'd filmed on their own phones.

All of that was left to the teachers and administrators. The students who weren't dead or evacuated already, huddled together near the front doors.

"I'll organise the bus for the rest of us," Nash had said before he'd hurried away to do his teacherly stuff and find some clothes. Matt and Dyson had found shirts and underwear, neither of which fit well, but at least they weren't naked. Not that I minded, but they looked uncomfortable walking around outside like that. And let's face it, there was much more chance of having a dick bitten off when it was uncovered.

I leaned against Kane, who sat with his arm around me. Ariana sat on my other side, her face pale.

"So what happened to you two?" I asked.

Kane looked embarrassed. "We got trapped on the third floor when the elevator stopped working. We hid until it was safe to take the stairs."

"Oh, that's good," I said awkwardly. "Um, I mean I'm glad you're both okay." So what if they hadn't fought? They'd done well to stay clear of trouble.

Ariana turned to me, her eyes bright with tears. "Really? I'm so sorry I lied to you. I was…I was…" She sniffed.

I patted her shoulder. "You were trying to keep me safe. I get it now. I'm sorry I was a bitch."

Kane gave me a squeeze. "You're allowed to be angry. No one would blame you. And you were never a bitch."

"Yes I was," I said. "I blame me." I sighed through my nose. I had gone off half cocked and that could have gotten us all killed. I wouldn't have forgiven myself if anything bad had happened. Well, anything worse than what already had.

I looked from one to the other, then at Matt and Dyson. "Can we agree from now on, to keep each other safe, and to be honest about everything?"

"I agree." Dyson sat near my feet, wearing an oversized purple t-shirt with a fairy on it. It looked more like a nightgown than a shirt, but he was adorable in it.

"I agree," Ariana said softly.

"Me three," Kane agreed.

We all looked toward Matt, whose shirt was lime green. I had no idea who he'd borrowed it from, but it suited him. For a guy who loathed me, he was pretty cute.

"What? I was always honest with you." He shrugged. "Besides, we don't like each other, remember?" He gave me a look which suggested otherwise.

For some silly reason, my heart did a little flip. Gods, as if I wasn't busy enough with Kane, Dyson and Nash. Still, I wondered what it would feel like to run my hands down his abs, to take his cock…

I cleared my throat. "You didn't tell me you were following me, when you started doing it."

"What kind of secret agent would I be if I revealed myself to you like that?" he asked. A smile tugged at the corners of his mouth.

"Is that what you are?" I asked. "A secret agent?"

"What else?" He raised an eyebrow at me. "We're supposed to be secret, but some of us are already working against Zeta." He nodded toward Ariana.

"I think we all have a score to settle," Dyson said, as if he was talking about the weather.

"I'm not sure if this was what I signed up for," I said carefully.

"It doesn't seem like Zeta gave you a choice," Ariana pointed out.

"They'll come again," Matt said darkly.

"When?" I bit my lip.

"It could be days, it could be decades." Matt shrugged. "In the meantime, they'll find us a place to study which should be safe."

"*Should*," I echoed. "That's the keyword there."

"While paranormals exist outside their control, they'll be looking for us. They won't like having so many of us off their leash."

My tongue darted over my lips. "I'd rather die than take part in whatever they have planned."

"You might get that option," Matt said.

"That's a cheerful thought." I nestled down deeper in Kane's arms. He gave me a kiss on my cheek.

"We won't let that happen," he assured me. "To you, or to anyone."

"Yeah, what Kane said," Dyson agreed. "We'll take care of each other, like a little family. Ariana is the little sister, Nash is the uncle who isn't related to any of us by blood. And Matt is…"

Matt shot him a look. "What is Matt?"

"You're that cousin who pretends he's too cool for the rest of us, but is really just as much of a geek," I told him.

He snorted and shook his head but didn't seem to mind the assessment. "For the record, I *am* that cool."

I laughed, but it faded when Nash stepped out of the academy doors. He looked exhausted and haunted. It didn't take magic to know he was thinking about the griffin he'd killed. The fact he'd had no choice didn't mean it wouldn't trouble him, probably forever.

"The bus will be here soon," he said. "They'll take us to a safe location where we can all rest. They'll decide what to do with us after that."

The fact he included himself made my heart sing. At least, as much as it could on such a heavy day.

"At least we got final exams out of the way," Dyson said.

"Very thoughtful of them," Kane said ironically.

Nash forced a faint smile and turned at the sound of an approaching engine.

A long bus drew to a stop outside the academy and a large man with arms covered in tattoos climbed out of the driver's seat.

"Dick!" he said loudly.

Nash scowled at him. "It's Nash to you, Johnny."

Johnny grinned. "Oh yeah. Well, whatever. Rob and Marion send their regards. Rob's found a place to stash you all for a while."

I found myself smiling at the man. He seemed like the kind of guy people adored on sight. Not like a lover, but as a friend and ally.

"Thanks Johnny." Nash gave him a curt nod and gestured toward us. "Everyone on before they wonder what happened to the attackers and come looking."

From what I could gather, fifty Zeta agents had come against us. As well as the griffin, they'd had two more hybrids. The academy's own hybrids had teamed up to behead them as Nash had done. Well—with claws and a sword, rather than teeth. I reminded myself to have a sword tattooed on my arm the moment we found time. I never knew when that might be useful.

We held back until the rest of the students climbed aboard. Some of them looked in worse shape than we were. One had gashes down her cheek. Another was covered in blood, but I didn't know if it was theirs or someone else's.

Ariana climbed the stairs into the bus ahead of me. Before I could take a step up, Nash grabbed my hand and pulled me to him. He pressed his mouth down hard on mine. He thrust his tongue into my mouth, withdrew it and ran it across my lips.

Just as my knees went weak, he pulled back and gave me a push toward the bus. "Hurry up," he growled.

I snorted at him but licked my lips in what I hoped was a provocative way.

He gave me a look that clearly said the moment we were alone, he was going to tear off my clothes and fuck me senseless. That was fine by me.

Johnny grinned and gave me a wink.

I blushed, grabbed the handrail and climbed up into the bus. Kane, Dyson and Matt followed close behind.

We all tumbled into seats near the back of the bus. Kane and I shared a seat. Dyson and Matt shared the seat behind us. Ariana sat in front, with Violette.

"Hey look, someone even thought to give us blankets," Kane said. He waited until we were seated and draped one over us both. He drew me closer and draped his arms around me. With the blanket covering us, no one could see him slip a hand inside my shirt to caress my nipple.

I gulped.

The bus door closed and we pulled away from the academy. From the outside, it didn't look like it had been a war zone recently. Even the street looked like a place of relative calm in a big city.

"So much for the Academy of Modern Magic," I sighed.

"We're still academy students," Kane replied. "We're just moving to a new campus, that's all." He leaned in to nibble my earlobe. "I'm glad you're okay," he whispered. He rolled my nipple between his thumb and forefinger. His other hand slipped down between my legs.

"Me too," I replied. I parted my legs and let him rub lightly at the front of my jeans.

"I've never met anyone like you." He undid the button of my jeans and tugged the zipper open.

"I could say the same about you." I lifted my hips for long enough for him to push my jeans down my hips.

"I want you to choose me," he said softly. He pulled my panties aside and dipped his fingers down to my entrance.

Oh, that whole choosing thing. The problem was, I didn't want to have to choose. I liked Kane, Dyson and Nash equally. They all drove me wild and made me hot as hells. Even Matt wasn't without his charm.

Kane slid his fingers inside me and rubbed my clit with the back of his hand. With the other, he pulled down the blanket and my shirt to expose my breasts. If the guys behind us peeked in between the seats, they would get a nice little show. For some reason, that made me more aroused than ever.

I glanced back and caught a sign of movement, but I couldn't tell which guy moved or if they were watching. For some reason, my imagination conjured Matt, his hand under the blanket of his lap, fingers wound around his cock, his grip sliding up and down as he pleasured himself while he watched. The thought made my mouth drier than ever. Gods, what these guys all did to me.

I bit back a moan and bucked against Kane's hand. He rubbed harder while his fingertips toyed with my nipples.

My imagination pictured Dyson's mouth on my hard peaks, suckling and licking, running his tongue over my breasts. Beside him, Matt pumped harder until Nash appeared and took his cock into his mouth. Holy fuck, where did *that* come from, and was it wrong that I wanted to see that in real life?

I gritted my teeth to hold back a moan as I came, hard and intense. Pleasure flooded me, wiping out all thoughts of our horrible day, at least for a while. It washed away any thoughts of moving to a new campus and having to choose a lover.

When I came down, I would think about that. For now, I would let myself be lost in the moment, the excitement of being alive and having three incredible guys who seemed to like me as much as I liked them. We had defeated Zeta and passed our final exams.

Second year would be very different, but we had each other. That would get us through anything.

Let them come.

We'll be ready.

EPILOGUE

OUTSIDE THE HOUSE was dark and still. I stopped to glance out the window. In spite of the relative peace of the last few weeks, I was still jumpy. I took a deep breath in and told myself to calm. I was safe here, in my parent's house. I was—

A shadow crossed in front of the moon.

Shit.

I froze. Whatever it was, it was big. *Really* big.

It banked and passed in front of the moon again, then out of sight.

I stood and waited, my breath caught in my throat.

The only thing which broke the silence was the wind and my racing heart. I strained to see, but the night was still again. Nothing moved but the leaves on the trees.

That didn't help me shake the feeling something was out there waiting.

Waiting for me.

WILL PEYTON CHOOSE? Will Zeta catch her? Who has the bigger dick, a dragon or a gargoyle? To find out, read on.

VIRTUAL MAGIC

ACADEMY OF MODERN MAGIC, BOOK 2

1

"YOU ARE *NOT* GOING BACK THERE."

My mother's face was an interesting shade of blotchy pink. Not cute like Kane when he blushed, but uneven like her voice when she spoke to me.

I tossed a shoe into my bag. "Of course I am. Well—" I stood up straight and toyed with my hair for a moment. "I'm not exactly going back. The Academy of Modern Magic has moved to another campus."

"I'm well aware of that." Lucinda Knight-Chapel gave me a look which would have reduced most other people, paranormal or otherwise, to a blubbering mess at her feet. Probably not literally, though who knows. Others seemed to find her intimidating.

As for me, I shrugged off the look and searched for my other shoe. "Are you trying to say the University of Arcana campus isn't safe?" I shot her a challenging look. She had gone there herself. Not only that, She had been fifteen when she graduated. Surely I should get bonus points for stepping foot on a campus where she was all but revered? To be honest, I would rather put my head in a blender, but after the Zeta attack, the academy needed to be moved. Apparently, the university was the safest place for us. Besides, my lovers and my best friend would be going.

"Of course it's safe," she snapped. That was followed by a deep sigh. You know, the kind mothers do when their children refuse to listen. "I just want you to be careful and not get harmed. Is that such a terrible thing?"

Now *I* sighed. The kind daughters do when their mothers are being, well, motherly, but the daughter is nineteen and wants to make her own mistakes.

I flopped down on my bed. "I know you're just worried about me, but I can look after myself, remember? The best place I can be is where I can learn more about using my magic."

She perched beside me. "You shouldn't have to look after yourself. They came after you because of me."

"They" were Zeta. A more or less secret government organisation, whose goal it was to bring normals and paranormals under their heel. Part of that meant taking witches like me and using us to create hybrids—witch and shifter cross. None of that was part of my life plan.

"They would have come after the whole academy sooner or later," I reminded her. "Me being there was probably a coincidence." Except I knew it wasn't. My best friend Ariana and my friend-cum-nemesis, Matt, had been told to protect me. Even my lover and teacher, Nash, was supposed to be keeping an eye on me. Just thinking about seeing him again made my heart race.

My mother eyed me. "Peyton, even if it was a coincidence, I wouldn't want you to go back there."

"How else am I going to learn how to use magic better?" I asked. "Do you have the time?"

She flinched. "I have to leave for North America in the morning. Your father—"

"Isn't as trained as you or my teachers are," I finished for her. I felt bad for saying that. I loved my father dearly, but he hardly bothered to use the power he had. It wasn't that he couldn't, but he never seemed interested. I never gave it much thought until now. From the look on my mother's face, neither had she.

"I will find someone—" she started, but was interrupted by the sound of the doorbell.

"It sounds like my escort has arrived." I rose and zipped up my suitcase.

I thought she might argue further, but she stood and gave me a hug. She didn't look happy in the slightest. She held a lot of power in the paranormal community. I knew full well she could have forbidden me from going back to school and no establishment would dare take me. If nothing else, her indifference had shaped me into the independent woman I was. I don't know if it was that indifference which led her to let me go now, or the knowledge I would never forgive her if she didn't.

Either way, she stepped aside to let me zip up my suitcase. I grabbed my backpack off my bed and headed downstairs.

Standing beside the door, face bright red, was Kane, one of my boyfriends and one of the sweetest guys I know. Beside him stood his brother, Dyson, the clown of the family. Twins—fraternal—were both shifters. Right now, however, they were both smiling, in spite of my father's scrutiny. He must have let them in.

"Hey," I greeted them. I handed my backpack to Dyson and gave both guys a warm embrace and a kiss on the mouth.

My father cleared his throat and gave me a funny look, but smiled. "Are you going to introduce me?'"

I gave him a please-don't-embarrass-me look and nodded. "This is Dyson and Kane Gill. They're both, um, friends of mine." Gods, what were they exactly? I was dating them both and sleeping with Kane. Dyson and I had agreed to take things slowly. I didn't know if any of that meant they were my boyfriends. I mean, who has two boyfriends anyway? Or three if you count Nash. I was definitely sleeping with him, too. The fact he was a teacher complicated things, but we made it work so far.

"This is my dad." I jerked a thumb toward him.

"Nice to meet you, sir." Dyson held out his hand and Kane followed suit shortly after.

"You too, boys." Dad shook their hands and gave them a nod.

I winced. *Boys*? I suppose they were to him.

"So," Dad went on, "you'll take good care of my little girl?"

I groaned. "Dad!" I drew the word out like a whiny child.

Dyson just grinned. "We'll take very good care of her, sir. She's in good hands with us."

I heard Kane swallow and had a pretty good idea where his thoughts had gone. We hadn't seen each other since just after Christmas and the dry spell after a couple of semesters of getting laid regularly... Let's just say my trusty vibrator got a workout.

"Yes." Kane's agreement came out as a squeak. "She'll be safe with us."

Dad blinked at him several times. "Well...good. See that she is, otherwise—"

"They know Mum will hunt them down and have them flayed alive," I assured him. I gave the guys a wink, which probably looked more like I was squinting with both eyes. Winking was never a skill I had mastered.

Dyson grinned. "I hope not. I'm attached to my skin." The mischievous look in his eyes made my heart skip a beat. I knew exactly which piece of skin he was referring to.

I resisted the urge to look in the direction of his dick.

He gave me an innocent look as if he knew what I was thinking.

"Anyway," I drew the word out, "we should get going. We have to beat the traffic."

"Yes, we do." Dyson took my backpack from my father and Kane grabbed the handle of my suitcase.

"Gentlemen, I see." Dad looked pleased.

I was perfectly capable of carrying and dragging my own things, but it gave me a chance to hug my dad and kiss his cheek.

"Stay out of trouble, little witch," he said affectionately.

I caught Dyson's smile and gave him a warning glare over Dad's shoulder. If he thought he'd use the term of endearment as a nickname, he had better think again.

He just smiled more broadly and stepped out into the cool of a Melbourne morning in March.

I followed both guys and closed the door behind me. Something about it felt final, although I knew I'd be back at the end of the year.

"New car?" I asked, eyeing the red Ford something-or-other. I am no expert on cars.

"It's Kane's," Dyson replied. "It matches his face."

"Hey!" Kane protested. "I didn't choose the colour."

"I'm sure you didn't," I assured him. "As long as it goes..." I peered into the back as we got closer and groaned. "What is *he* doing here?"

Matt wound down the window and smirked back at me. "I'd say it's nice to see you too, but..." He shrugged.

I gave him the finger. Evidently we were going to start the academic year the way we'd left the last one.

He rolled his eyes and raised the window again.

"Officially, he's going the same way we are," Kane said. He opened the back of the car and lifted my suitcase inside.

"And unofficially?" I asked.

"He insisted," Dyson said, his hand cupped around his mouth as if that would stop Matt from being able to hear. "He was sure you'd get into some kind of trouble on the way there."

"You *know* she would," Matt called out.

I grimaced. "I would not." Trouble might find me, though. "Do I have to sit in the back with him?"

"Dyson gets carsick," Kane said regretfully. "And I'm driving, otherwise I'd sit in the back with you."

I knew what that meant. While the guys in front watched the road, he'd have his hands down my top and my shorts. No such luck sitting beside Matt.

I sighed loudly and pulled the door open. "Fine, but no funny business." I shook my finger but I was mostly joking. Matt was a dick, but he was hot as hells, especially dressed from head to toe in black. His muscles bulged in a way that made my eyes pop. I would totally go there. Maybe.

He snorted. "Like that'll happen."

I slipped into the seat and stuck my tongue out at him. "Always the charmer."

"That's me," he agreed. "Now shut the door. You never know when we might come under attack."

I gave him a look, but closed the door quickly. Zeta could be waiting anywhere. I couldn't afford to let my guard down.

I hunkered down in the seat and clicked the belt into place. My father stood in the front window. I waved. He waved back. I saw no sign of my mother.

With a shrug I turned back around. "So, we're all second years."

"Yep," Dyson said. He kept the window down beside him, his face in the breeze. I wouldn't have been surprised if his tongue lolled out.

"It's remarkable you managed to survive first year," Matt said. A smile tugged at the corner of his mouth.

I gave him a sidelong look. "Is this where I say thank you for saving my ass, or you're welcome because I saved yours?" I asked.

"Or where we remind him Nash saved us all by biting the head off a griffin." Dyson glanced over his shoulder.

"That was pretty cool," I said. Nash wouldn't agree. He had killed before and it haunted him. Doing it again…

I hated that I hadn't been able to talk to him since the bus picked us up at the academy. I hadn't seen or heard from him for weeks. With any luck, he would be at the combined university slash academy campus, waiting for us.

I sighed softly. If I called him a boyfriend then I was a pretty crap girlfriend. I had tried to contact him over the holidays, but I hadn't managed to reach him. I didn't know what number to call or what email to try. I had casually asked my mother about dragon shifters, but she had laughed it off. A high pitched, nervous laugh, to be sure, but I got no answers.

"As long as he can tell a good gargoyle from a bad one," Matt muttered.

I leaned over to pat his arm. "It's easy to tell. You were the one who was always getting injured."

He gave me a long look. "Only to keep you safe, remember?"

"I didn't say I didn't appreciate it," I told him. "I'm glad you're not dead and stuff."

"Gee, thanks," he said sarcastically.

"Um, guys," Kane said from the driver's seat. "We're being followed."

2

I SWIVELLED AROUND in my seat and looked out the back window. "How do you know?" I was looking for a black SUV with tinted windows, like the one my mother drove. Except, you know, driven by bad guys.

"That blue car has been behind us since we pulled out of your place," Kane said.

"It's a busy road," I pointed out. "They might be going the same way we are. Can you do that swerving through traffic thing to see if we can throw them?"

"You've seen too many movies." Matt waved a hand toward the window. "This is Melbourne traffic. You can't just swerve around without hitting anything. The moment we get to the lights, they'll be right behind us."

"They're not going to risk a magical battle in the middle of morning traffic." I wasn't so sure about that.

"They might assume the same thing about us," Matt said softly.

The blood drained out of my face. He was right. They may think we'd come quietly, so no one else got hurt. The assumption was a reasonable one. We were the good guys, after all.

"We need to stay ahead of them," Dyson said. He closed the window beside him. "And head in a different direction. There's no point in leading them toward the academy."

I chewed my lip but nodded. I wished Nash was here. Between us we had a dog, an owl, a gargoyle, and my gargoyle tattoo, with which I could conjure a magical creature to fight with me or for me. A dragon would turn the odds in our favour, even if it meant asking him to kill again.

"Right." Kane changed lanes and flew around a corner just before the lights turned red.

That move would have lost anyone law abiding, but the blue car swung around behind us. They ultimately worked for the government; they probably thought they were *above* the law.

A truck coming the other way beeped its horn and narrowly missed hitting the blue car. Shame, that would have slowed them down.

"Shit." Kane swerved to avoid a delivery van parked at the side of the road. He pulled back into our lane before another truck took out the side of our car. The driver stuck his finger out the window at us. I kept my hands on my lap to avoid doing the same thing back.

"We need to get out of the city," Matt urged.

"Have I mentioned this is my first time in Melbourne?" Kane asked. "I don't know where we're going unless it's programmed into the GPS."

"Turn left at the end of this street," Matt said. "We'll go west."

"Isn't that the direction we were going?" Dyson asked.

"Yeah, but we can get on a different road and head toward Ballarat. At least out in the country we can fight back without risk to too many others."

"If they realise that, they'll—" I stopped when another blue car rounded the turn in front of us and skidded to a stop. "Try to keep us from doing that," I finished.

"Hold on!" Kane spun the wheel and jammed his foot down on the accelerator. The car leapt forward and flew toward the second car. At the last moment he wrenched the steering wheel, but it wasn't enough. The side of his car scraped down the side of the blue one. The squeal of metal on metal made me wince and throw my hands over my ears.

"Dude!" Dyson shouted.

"Sorry!" Kane gunned the engine and we flew clear, but right into the path of another car.

We struck with a crunch of metal and glass. The airbags in front of Kane and Dyson inflated.

Apparently the car was too old to have any in the back. I was thrown forward hard. My seatbelt jerked and I came to a painful stop against the strap.

"Everyone out," Matt ordered. "Split up. Witch to shifter, shifter to hybrid."

Dyson groaned and rubbed his head, but he had his door open before I did.

He helped me out and grabbed my hand to pull me away from the car.

I glanced back once. "Fuck, there goes another suitcase full of clothes," I muttered.

Dyson snorted. "If that's the worst that happens…"

"Yeah, I know. We should stop talking now, I'm making a bubble." I drew magic from a few small trees beside the road and made us both invisible. Our pursuers could hear us if we made a sound, but they wouldn't see us.

I turned my face just as Matt and Kane disappeared behind a bubble Matt made.

"Which way do we go?" Dyson whispered in my ear. Thank the gods magic allowed us to see each other and around ourselves.

"Anywhere but here," I said, "as long as we do it quietly."

Around us, Zeta agents, dressed from head to toe in black, climbed out of their cars, guns in hand. They stopped to listen, then moved in the direction they had seen us last.

I pulled Dyson in the opposite direction as fast as we dared to go.

"Give it up, witch," one of the agents called out.

Yeah, for real. As if that would make me surrender, just like that. It wasn't even worth a try. No witch I knew was that dumb. I certainly wasn't.

"Maybe I should let my gargoyle loose," I whispered.

"Can you do that and hold the bubble?" Dyson asked.

"I have no idea." I wasn't going to drop the bubble to find out.

One of the Zeta agents turned in our direction and pointed.

I froze. The only way they'd know where we were was if they had incredible hearing, like that of a dog.

The hybrids Zeta created were all what we would consider mythical creatures—phoenixes, griffins, gargoyles and, yes, dragons. What the hells kind of hybrid would a dog be?

"Have you ever heard of a Cerberus shifter?" I asked nervously.

"No, but that doesn't mean they don't exist," Dyson replied. "If you drop the bubble for long enough, I can distract him."

"I can't let you take that risk." I pulled him forward a few more steps.

The agent turned his face as though following our movement. His brow was creased. He moved toward us, slow and deliberate.

I stopped again.

The agent sniffed the air. He might be able to follow our scent as easily as any sound we may make. I could drop the bubble and blast him with magic, but that would draw the attention of every other Zeta agent on the street, not to mention the normal people who had stopped to gawk. Evidently a car crash was a novelty.

"We need some kind of distraction," Dyson whispered. "I can—"

Whatever he was about to say was interrupted by the flapping of wings. Not big wings, so it wasn't a dragon come to rescue us. No, these were small wings, but fast. An owl, about the size of my forearm, shot across the road and into the face of the Zeta agent.

The agent flailed his arms and tried to strike the bird, but Kane was gone as quickly as he'd arrived. He circled above the Zeta agent and came in for another dive.

"Shoot the fucker!" someone shouted.

Dyson squeezed my hand and dragged me up the street at a run.

A gunshot rang out.

I spun in time to see Kane soar away to the safety of a rooftop before he disappeared.

"Gods, Kane," Dyson muttered,

"You can thank him later." In the meantime, we had to keep running.

"We need to split up," Dyson insisted. "I'll throw that fucker off your scent."

Before I could protest, he let go of my hand and pushed his way out of the bubble.

"What the hells…" I almost lost my magic, but drew it back at the last moment. I hated the idea they would risk themselves because of me, but I wouldn't throw it back in their faces by exposing myself.

Dyson shifted into his dog form and let out a long, low howl.

"Over there!" an agent shouted. Three or four of them set off after him, including the dog hybrid.

"Peyton!" Matt's voice out of nowhere made me jump. Surrounded by his own bubble, I couldn't see him either. "Head west. I'll be right behind you."

"How do you know? You can't see me," I pointed out.

I was certain he grinned before he said, "I'll probably hear you trip over your own feet."

"I am not that clumsy," I retorted. Maybe he was the one tripping. In spite of that, I checked where the sun was and went in the opposite direction. A shadow passed overhead and I was relieved to see Kane land on a tree up ahead. I assumed Matt had told him which way we'd go. It seemed unfair I could see him and not vice versa, but there wasn't much I could do about that at the moment.

With one eye on him and the other on the sidewalk ahead, I ducked around passers by and hurried away from the scene of the accident.

A big, furry figure bolted between a few cars in front of us. A couple of Zeta agents followed, but the gods knew where the rest were. I glanced back. The man I assumed was a dog hybrid was only fifty metres behind me and closing fast.

"Shit," I muttered.

"Take the next street," Matt said. "It'll be busy enough. Maybe we can throw him off."

"And if we can't?" I hissed.

"Then he'll meet with a nasty accident," Matt replied. He almost sounded as if he relished the idea.

"Right," I said under my breath. I hurried forward at a jog until I reached Clarendon Street. There, the roaring traffic would cover a lot of the noise and the exhaust fumes were thick. Hopefully thick enough to cover my scent.

I checked the sun and headed west toward the freeway. I hoped Matt had a plan. Dodging traffic doesn't generally result in a good life expectancy.

From the corner of my eye, I saw Kane on a roof up ahead. He looked around, obviously wondering where Matt and I were. Even in the middle of this craziness, I had to admit he was a cute owl. All brown and fluffy, I would have loved to give him a cuddle. Who am I kidding, I quite enjoyed cuddling his human form as well.

Something bumped into the back of me. I was about to curse when I realised it was Matt.

"I'd say you should watch where you're going, but..." I shrugged, then reminded myself he couldn't see that either.

He snorted. "We need to ditch this guy."

Sure enough, Cerberus was still following us.

"He's persistent," I agreed.

"Yeah. Hold on."

"To what?" I frowned. Matt grabbed my hand and pulled me toward him. At the same time, he expanded his bubble to incorporate us both. I let my magic go with a sigh of relief. Holding onto it for long periods of time was exhausting.

"I figured it would be easier if we could see each other," he said.

"I guess so," I agreed. He was still fully dressed, so he hadn't shifted into his gargoyle form during any of this. That was probably just as well, naked Matt would be distracting.

"I know you're there," Cerberus called out. "There is no escape. Give yourselves up now."

I rolled my eyes and mouthed, "No way, motherfucker."

Matt grinned. "Let's try something," he mouthed back.

He gripped my hand and we bolted into the traffic.

3

THE CARS COULDN'T SEE us, so none of the drivers were any wiser about how close they came to hitting us. A side mirror grazed my ass and I bit back a yelp. Later, they might wonder why it sat at a different angle. For now though, the driver drove on, seemingly oblivious.

Matt tugged me across the last lane in front of a huge truck. We managed to leap onto the sidewalk with a hair's width to spare.

"Now I know you're crazy, as well as an asshole," I said lightly. I rubbed my backside. That would bruise later.

"We made it, didn't we?" He loosened his grip on my hand and jerked his head back. "Him, on the other hand—"

Cerberus stood on the opposite side of the road, a scowl on his features. He sniffed the air. His scowl deepened. I assumed he could still smell us, but the fumes from the cars confounded his doggie senses.

"Come on," Matt tugged me away from Cerberus and toward the highway. "We need a car."

"You're not suggesting we steal one, are you?" I frowned at him.

He ignored the question. "Do you have your phone?"

"Of course." I patted the back pocket of my shorts. "Do you want me to try to conjure a car?"

He gave me a funny look. "No, can you order a ride share car?"

"Oh." Now I felt silly. "Only if you have cash. Zeta would trace any cards we use."

He gave me a look as if I'd said the sky was blue. "I've got us covered for that."

I shrugged with my spare shoulder and tapped the details for the ride share into the app with my thumb. The moment I pressed, "enter" my breath caught in my throat.

"What if they're tracing my phone?" I asked.

"Then our friend over there would know where we are. But just in case—" Matt grabbed the device from my hand and tossed it onto the road. It was promptly run over and crushed by a pizza truck.

Yes, a pizza truck. I have never felt so betrayed by my favourite food in my entire life.

"What the fuck?" I asked.

"Would you rather be in a Zeta lab? I can leave you to it, if you'd prefer." He made to step away.

"Don't you dare," I hissed. I gritted my teeth and shook my head. "It's just a phone."

"Exactly." He nodded. "Now hurry up or we'll miss the ride share car altogether."

We trotted down the block and around a corner. Finally out of sight of the Zeta agents, Matt dropped the bubble and my hand.

"We can't leave without Dyson and Kane." I looked around, but saw no sign of either of them, dog, owl or naked men.

"We can and we will," Matt insisted. "They can both take care of themselves. My job is to get you to the academy in one piece."

I swallowed. On one hand, he was right. We couldn't afford to take the risk of waiting for them to find us. On the other hand, I adored them both and if anything happened to them because of me…

I gave my head a little shake. If they were injured, or worse, it would be because of Zeta, not me. The fact they found it necessary to protect me was Zeta's fault. However, I would blame myself until the end of time.

I sucked in a breath. "We can wait until the car arrives." If I still had my phone, I would know how long that was. Since I didn't, I crossed my arms over my chest and kept my eyes open for the guys.

Matt placed a hand on my shoulder. "They'll be fine. They're both tough as nails and slightly more intelligent."

I snorted. "I thought you guys were friends?"

"We are, but I was trying to make you smile." He shrugged indifferently.

"Why bother?" I asked. "We loathe each other, remember?"

He grinned. "Yes, we do. That doesn't mean we can't be nice, though."

"I suppose." I scanned the rooftops. Gods, please don't let them catch the guys. A bird took off and my heart leapt until I realised it was just a pigeon.

A moment later, a car drew up alongside us. A man with spiky blue hair and about a bajillion facial piercings stuck his head out the window and smiled.

"Hey, you ordered a Broomer?"

"Yeah, we did," I opened the door to the back seat, while Matt sat beside the driver.

"Where to, guys?" the driver asked cheerfully.

Matt gave him the address while I fastened my seatbelt and watched out the window.

"Wacca's restaurant, Werribee," the driver repeated. "Okay, great! That'll take us about half an hour in this traffic." He pulled his little yellow car away from the curb.

Mat nodded. "Okay, Broomer."

"Call me Bruce," the driver said. "It's my name, but don't wear it out." He laughed, which would have been infectious under other circumstances.

"Hilarious," I muttered.

"Yeah, my friends agree. They tell me I should stop talking so much, but what can I say? I'm a friendly guy."

I hunkered down in my seat and kept my eyes on the city as it passed by. Bruce kept up a monologue the entire time, while Matt responded with a word or two here and there. I didn't hear a thing they said until Bruce pulled his car into a parking space at Wacca's.

Matt handed over a couple of notes and we climbed out of the car.

"Have a great day!" Bruce waved out the window as he drove off.

"I think he might be more annoying than you are," Matt remarked.

"Is that even possible?" I asked ironically.

Matt looked thoughtful. "You're right, it probably isn't. You set the bar pretty high."

"If I had a bar right now, I'd shove it up your ass," I murmured.

He chuckled. "We have quite a walk in front of us. Let's get something to eat first. My shout."

"It will have to be, since I have no money and no phone." I gave him a look.

"You're welcome," he said lightly. "This isn't quite how I expected our first date to go."

I gave him a funny look. "You expected us to have a first date?"

"No. That's exactly my point." He opened the door.

I stuck my tongue out at him and marched past.

"Always with the class," he said reproachfully.

"Maybe a Zeta lab wouldn't be so bad." I sat at a more-or-less clean table near a window so I could watch while we ate.

Matt's eyes flashed with anger. "Trust me, it wouldn't," he said in a tight voice before he stalked away.

While I regretted my words, I glanced at the few people around the small restaurant. None looked in my direction. They were either lost in conversation or, more commonly, engrossed in their phones. I couldn't see what they were looking at, but I wasn't sure they'd notice if Kane and Dyson walked through the door, naked.

Matt slammed a tray down in front of me, making me jump.

"I'm sorry about what I said. I didn't mean to—"

"Yeah, whatever." He slipped into the seat opposite me. "I get it. You ran your mouth off about something you know nothing about."

"And you do?" I asked as gently as I could.

"I'm not talking about that with you, especially not here," he snapped. He pushed a box of food and a cup of tea toward me and started to eat.

I sighed and opened my box. Bacon, eggs, toast—all the essentials for an early lunch.

"Eat fast, we shouldn't linger around here for too long."

I was too anxious to be hungry, and still full from breakfast, but I managed to down everything in record time. I picked up my tea to wash it down when Matt rose.

"Bring it with you. You can sip and walk."

I grabbed up my cup, put my rubbish in the bin and followed him out. "How did you know I drank tea?"

He shrugged. "Lucky guess."

I gave him a disbelieving look. "Bullshit. If you were guessing, you would have given me coffee. Or water."

"You must have mentioned it in passing then." He led us back to the road and we started off to the south.

"Well, thanks," I said awkwardly. "It saved me from having to tell you coffee is disgusting."

He gave me a sideways glance and sipped his. "I knew there was something wrong with you."

"Fuck off," I retorted. "There's probably a lot of things wrong with me. Not drinking coffee isn't one."

"Oh yeah? What are the others?"

I sniffed. "I'm not going to dignify that question with a response."

"Coward."

I glanced toward him to see his eyes shining and a smile tugging at the corners of his mouth.

"Has anyone told you you're an asshole?" I asked.

"Yes, you have. Recently, too."

I smiled sweetly. "Has it sunk in yet?"

He grinned. "Honey, it sank in a long time ago."

I blushed. "You wish."

He let out a choking laugh. "Not a chance."

"Liar."

He shrugged. "Keep telling yourself that. In the meantime, can you walk a little faster?"

"Can you shift and I'll ride on your back?" I was only half-joking.

Rather than dismiss the suggestion offhand, he looked thoughtful. "I don't think it's come to that yet. We'll call that plan B."

"Fine. As long as we don't get to plan F."

"The day I go to plan F with you…" he started.

"Yes?" I prompted.

He gave me a look which suggested only the animosity between us was stopping him from dragging me into the bushes and screwing me silly.

He shook his head. "I'll know I've lost the last of my common sense."

"You said 'willpower' wrong." I stepped over a fallen log.

"Lucky I have plenty of that," he shot back.

"Oh really?" Without thinking, I turned and pressed my palm to his cheek. I don't know who moved next, but our lips were pressed together, and his tongue slipped inside my mouth.

I only kissed him back for the count of three. Okay, four. All right, maybe it was thirty seconds, tops. I pulled back and smiled. "Yep, you're totally willpower man."

He scowled at me as though I had done something horribly wrong and stalked on ahead.

"Hurry up, we're nearly here," he growled.

I shrugged to myself and followed. "There's nothing wrong with being attracted to someone."

"It is when they're a pain in your ass," he said over his shoulder.

"I'm not that bad when you get to know me," I said. "I—"

"Shhh," he hissed.

I immediately froze. Every centimetre of me watched and listened for…anything. "What is it?" I said finally.

"The University of Arcana."

"Is it under attack?" Please gods, don't let it be that, after all we've been through already.

"No, I'm just not sure I should take you there," he replied.

I frowned and stepped up closer to him. "Why not? What's wrong?" A heavy feeling started to settle in my stomach. Had he sensed some kind of danger I couldn't? Did he have heightened gargoyle senses, like Cerberus seemed to have dog instincts?

"If I take you there," he said slowly, "I'll be stuck with you around for the entire academic year."

I punched him on the arm as hard as I could.

While he grinned, I stomped past him and onto the university slash academy grounds.

At last.

4

THE UNIVERSITY WAS HOUSED in a mansion which was over a hundred years old. A number of signs dotted the driveway which led to it. One read, "Danger." Another said, "Condemned." Fortunately trees and hedges obscured the view from the road or people would notice it was neither of those things. At least, the building *looked* safe enough.

The inhabitants, on the other hand, were probably a different story.

A group of students strolled past and didn't give us more than a glance. At least, I assumed they were students. They were all dressed in blue jackets, blue and white ties and blue trousers or skirts.

"For real? UA has a uniform?" I snorted.

"Yeah, and we have to wear it, too," Matt replied.

My smile faded. "You're kidding?"

He shrugged with one shoulder. "Not this time. At least the skirts aren't plaid."

I made a face. "Thank the gods for small mercies." At this point I was distracting myself from worrying about Dyson and Kane. "We need to tell them about Zeta coming after us again."

Matt nodded. "Let me deal with that. You go and get settled."

"What about you?" I asked.

Before I got an answer, he was gone, marching toward what I assumed was the admin section of the campus. As for me, I was engulfed in a hug.

"Peyton, you got here finally!"

"Ariana." I gave her a squeeze, then leaned back to look her in the face. "You got here, too."

She smiled. "Last night. Where are the others? I saw Matt's back as I stepped out of our dorm." She wrinkled her nose. "If you can call it that. They've brought in temporary buildings for those of us who decided to stay with the AMM."

"Are there so few of us?" I fell into step beside her.

She led me toward a series of low buildings set off to one side from the mansion.

"Of the original six hundred or so, there's only about three hundred coming." She opened the door and stepped into a long, narrow corridor. "Just under thirty students died in the attack last spring. I guess the rest didn't feel safe here."

"Or they know Melbourne winters suck," I said dryly.

"That too," she agreed. "Where is all your stuff?"

I told her about the attack on us and explained about the guys. "I'm sure they'll turn up sooner or later." I sighed.

She gave me another hug. "I'm sure they will. They're tough, smart guys."

"Yes, they are." I remembered what Matt said and flipped him a mental bird. What did he know anyway?

"So, this is our room." Ariana pulled out a regular key and unlocked it.

I stepped inside and gaped in dismay. The room was tiny. So small it only contained two small cupboards, side by side and a bunk bed. I doubted a heater would do much for the chill in the air.

"I took the top bunk. I hope you don't mind?" She looked tentative, but I didn't think it had anything to do with which bed she'd chosen. We'd left the previous year on uneasy terms and had only seen each other via video chat since.

"I don't mind," I said. "Your snoring might be muffled by the ceiling, with any luck."

She giggled. "And yours might be muffled by the underside of my bed."

"Not a chance," I said lightly. "I'm guessing there isn't a bathroom connected to this room?"

Ariana grimaced. "It's not even in this building. Everyone has to shower in the next one over. Meanwhile, the UA students live in a nice warm mansion." She wrinkled her nose.

"Oh good, elitism," I said sarcastically. "Maybe I should tell them who my mother is. They might take pity on us and give us better accommodation."

"You can try," she said wryly. "But I have a feeling they won't care."

I exhaled through my nose. "Do we really have to wear that uniform?"

"So I'm told." She looked just as happy about that as I felt. "At least you'll look cute in it."

I barked a laugh. "Is it too late to transfer to Melbourne Uni?" They, like everywhere but here, had no uniforms for students. Shame they didn't teach magic.

"Probably," she replied, "there are other options, like getting a job arranging flowers."

I looked at her in surprise. "Why flowers?"

She shrugged. "Why not? It might be fun."

"I suppose so." I ran a hand over my face. "I should go and check in with the academy admin and see about a new phone and a uniform. Have you seen Nash?" My blood heated at the idea of seeing him again, being alone with him, his hands on my…

Ariana cleared her throat and brought me back to reality. "Not yet. I've only seen Hamish and a few others." Her face went slightly pink.

"Hamish? Really?" The last I heard, he was interested in her, but she didn't feel the same. Apparently things had changed.

"We came here together," she explained. "We might have bonded on the drive down. He's sweet."

I smiled. "I'm thrilled for you." He was nice and she deserved to be happy. "Just let him know if he hurts you, I'll conjure a gargoyle to tear his nuts off."

Ariana giggled. "Come on, I'll show you where the academy admin is. They're a little hard to find."

"Don't tell me, they've been shoved down into the university basement?" I said, half joking.

She gave me a funny look. "How did you know?"

"Lucky guess." I had a feeling the academy was the university's poor cousin and would be treated accordingly until we got a new, more permanent campus. Hopefully that wouldn't take long. I hated wearing uniforms, especially ones that screamed, "repressed private school girl." I was too old for that.

Before Ariana led me out the door, she handed me a key. "Apparently we have to learn to do a few things the old-fashioned way."

I pocketed the key and grimaced. "Welcome to the nineteen hundreds. Population: us."

"BASEMENT" was an understatement. The space allocated for the academy admin was dark, dank, and smelled as if they kept rats locked inside for a few decades. Two tiny windows at the top of the wall would allow for an emergency escape, but didn't let in much light. A handful of bulbs hung from the ceiling, but several flickered. Instant headache stuff right there.

The man behind the desk looked weary. They had probably spent the holidays trying to pull enough resources together to get the academy ready in time. Their surroundings wouldn't have inspired them much.

"Can I help you?" he asked.

I explained the situation. As I talked, he seemed more and more interested.

"Zeta came after you, you say?" He clicked his tongue. "Terrible business, that." He reached into a drawer and pulled out a new phone, still in its box. "Try not to let this one get damaged. We should have a uniform in your size. The university has been very generous with *those*."

I didn't miss the inflection. Nor did Ariana, judging by the look on her face.

I grimaced. "It is a bit cozy in here."

He snorted. "It's only temporary."

"Fingers crossed," Ariana said lightly. "Can Peyton try on some clothes?"

"Sure." He waved us toward what looked like a storeroom. "Take whatever you need." He rubbed his chin. "Are you all right for a ride into town to replace your other clothes?"

"I should be fine, yes," I said. I wanted to ask for someone to drive me around to look for the guys. Instead, I just said, "Thank you."

He gave a nod and turned back to his work.

THE LIGHT in the storeroom was as bad as the rest of the space, but it was enough to see shelves with bags of shirts, pants, skirts, and ties. Jackets hung from a rack to one side.

"At least it's better than being chased by Zeta," I remarked. "Although they might laugh if they saw me in this stuff." I shut the door and pulled out a few bags marked with my size. "Surely there are pants for women in here somewhere."

"If you find any, let me know." Ariana reclined against the door. "I feel silly in this skirt."

I glanced toward her. "You look cute. I'm sure Hamish would agree." I gave her a sly smile.

She flushed and muttered, "He said he did."

I grinned and pulled on a stiff university shirt and skirt. The skirt fell to just above my knees. I frowned at it for a moment.

"I guess it's not too bad. It *could* be ankle length." The shirt hugged my breasts in a way I actually liked. Maybe naughty schoolgirl wasn't such a bad look after all.

"That would be very impractical when running away from bad

guys," Ariana said. "For the record, it makes your legs and ass look amazing."

"Thanks." I wondered what the guys would think. To be fair, they would all be dressed more or less the same, except Nash. Unless this place had a dress code for teachers, too. Maybe they'd make him wear a suit. My mouth went dry at the idea and I actually licked my lips.

"This should be your size." Ariana handed me a jacket. "The good news is, I've seen plenty of students without their jackets on. I think they're only for when it's cold."

I took the jacket and shrugged it on. "I miss my oversized *Harry Potter* sweater already." It was old and worn, but comfortable. The jacket was stiff and cold, but better than nothing.

"I hear you," she sighed. "I miss my pink hoodie. It was my favourite thing to wear, by far."

I remembered a pale pink hoodie with paint stains and holes. I'm not sure I would miss seeing her in it, but comfort was a good thing.

"Okay, I think I'm done." I grabbed two more shirts and another skirt before we stepped out of the storeroom. "No sign of the guys yet, I suppose." If they turned up, they weren't here, looking for clothes to wear. The idea of the twins naked made my heart race again.

"They'll turn up," Ariana said. "I promise."

"I hope so," I replied. "Otherwise, I might have to go out and look for them."

"I'll come with you," Ariana assured me. "If it comes to that. We'll stick together and look after each other."

"You mean you'll keep an eye on me," I said, more tersely than I'd intended.

She blanched and her tongue darted over her lips. "I said I was sorry—" she started.

I put a hand on her shoulder and squeezed lightly. "No, *I'm* sorry. I don't want you to think I'm holding a grudge. I'm really not. You were trying to look out for me and I adore you for it. I didn't mean to be a bitch, it's just been a difficult day already." That was a lame excuse. I needed to try to be a better friend.

She leaned over to put her arms around me. "I adore you, too. I'm sorry they came after you. I should have been there. My unicorn could have stabbed them with her horn." She raised her arm. Her sleeve was rolled back to show the tattoo of a unicorn with a multicoloured mane Matt inked on her last year.

"Thank you, but too many humans would have seen it. We don't want to have it broadcast on the evening news." I could just imagine it. *Unicorn spotted in peak-hour traffic, authorities baffled.*

She grinned. "I suppose not, but she's ready if we go looking for the guys."

I chuckled. "So is my gargoyle. Let's wait a few more hours, then if they're not here, we'll go and hunt them down. I'm sure Kane and Dyson can't be too far away."

"Absolutely not," a new voice said. "You're *not* going back out there to look for them."

I turned to see Nash. Holy fucking instant orgasms, he looked good in a suit. Better than good. I wanted to tear it straight off him and…

I cleared my throat. "I beg your pardon, sir?"

His pupils dilated at that, and a bulge formed at the front of his pants. He liked it when I called him sir.

"Ariana, will you excuse us please?" Nash said, his voice tight. "I need to talk to Peyton alone."

"Yes, sir," she squeaked and hurried away.

Nash took my arm. "Come with me," he said softly.

Fuck yeah, I thought you'd never ask.

5

NASH LED me to a room on the ground floor of the main university building. His body was tense the entire walk there, eyes darting back and forth.

"Are you expecting another Zeta attack?" I asked after the third time he stopped to look around.

"No." He pulled me into a room and closed the door. "Things are different here. The academy might have frowned on us associating, if they had known, but the UA strictly forbids it, under threat of being fired."

I raised both eyebrows at him in surprise.

Before I could speak, he held up a hand. "I know. We're two adults conducting a consensual relationship." He stalked to the window and drew the curtains closed over it.

"Does that mean we can't see each other anymore?" My heart sank. I was falling for him hard, and I was falling for Kane and Dyson. Nash would still be my teacher, so I would see him whenever we did self-defence training, or practice for the hand-to-hand combat team. None of that would be the same.

He turned back and licked his lips. "I thought it might be a good idea if we stopped for a while, but seeing you in that outfit makes me want to tear it off and screw you silly." He stalked toward me. His eyes blazed with desire.

I couldn't imagine even trying to resist him when he looked like that. My whole body ached. I needed him inside me, buried deep. I needed him to touch me.

I sucked in a deep breath. "Oh, really?" I toyed with the top button of my shirt. The back of my wrist brushed past my hard nipple. "Naughty schoolgirl does it for you, hmmm?"

He snorted. "*You* do it for me. I don't care what you're wearing. Although, the uniform does add a certain something."

I cocked my head to one side. "Yeah. That suit is pretty hot, too, sir."

He glanced down and grimaced. "I feel ridiculous. I teach self-defence, I'm not a lawyer."

"Flashbacks to your police days?" I asked. I regretted the words the moment I said them. In his past life, he had had to kill to defend himself and people he cared about. At the academy, he had done it again, in his dragon form. Reminding him of those dark days wasn't fair to him.

A frown crossed his face, but it was quickly gone, replaced by pure desire. "I don't want to think about that now." He grabbed my hand and pulled me to him. His deft hands made quick work of my buttons. He slipped my shirt down my arms and carefully placed it over the back of a chair. He hated mess.

He claimed my mouth with his. His tongue probed deeply while he reached around to unhook my bra.

I let it slide off my arms and pressed my bare nipples to the front of his suit jacket. One of my hands wandered down to the front of his pants. He was already rock hard. I undid the front and slipped my hand inside. My fingers curled around his hot erection.

He groaned and broke off our kiss just long enough to shed his jacket and shirt, then took my wrists in one hand and turned me around. He pushed me toward a table and bent me over the top. With one hand, he pinned me to the wood while with the other, he slid his hand up my skirt and tugged my panties down.

I kicked them aside just as he positioned himself and slid his cock into me. I let out a moan of pure pleasure.

"I've missed you," I said, breathless already.

"I missed you too." He clamped a hand on my hip and drove himself deeper inside me.

The thrill of doing something truly elicit sent a thrill down my spine and all across my body. Without meaning to, I came. Pleasure wracked my whole body and I cried out. I bit my lip to keep from making too much noise. That would give us away for sure.

"It seems you missed me a lot," he said, uncharacteristically teasing.

I laughed softly, but it quickly turned into a groan as he began to thrust more rhythmically. I leaned down to rest my cheek on the cool wood. At this angle he was filling me fully. With each stroke, his balls slapped against me.

"Gods," he whispered. He pulled out and let my wrists go. His hands slid down my body as he lowered himself to his knees. His tongue flicked at my folds.

I reached out to grip the sides of the table as his tongue delved deeper. He rubbed the tip hard against my clit. I wanted to rock against him, but between his mouth and the table, I was pinned, helpless to do anything but let my passion rise again.

"Sir, I'm going to come again," I said in a rough whisper.

"No you're not." He pulled away just before I went over the edge.

I groaned in frustration.

He chuckled. "Not yet." He peeled me off the table and helped me out of my skirt. "You look better out of that uniform."

"You look better out of that suit, sir."

He was slender, but fit. His arms and legs were defined by muscle. A light sprinkle of hair dusted his chest and abs and ended in curls at the base of his stomach.

I looked at him sideways. "That is particularly adorable, sir." I pointed to his feet. He was completely naked except for a pair of superhero socks.

He grinned and leaned on the table to tug them off. "I had other things on my mind," he said unapologetically.

He took my hand and led me to his bed. He sat me down on the side and knelt in front of me to bury his face between my legs. His lips and tongue masterfully lapped against my clit and between my folds. He slid two fingers into my wetness, then three, and started to stroke me inside and out.

I gathered up small sections of blanket in my hands and gripped tight while he drove me to another orgasm. This time, he let me come so hard I had to grit my teeth to keep from screaming.

I hadn't even come down fully when he drew me the rest of the way onto the bed.

"Get on your hands and knees," he said, his voice deeper with lust.

"Yes, sir." I did as he asked before he settled himself behind me and slid into me up the hilt. He reached around to cup my breasts with both hands.

"I don't care what they say," he growled between thrusts. "I'm not going to give you up. I'd rather lose my job."

"We'll be careful." The way his palms rubbed my nipples made it hard to think, much less talk. "You won't have to give up anything."

His strokes came faster and faster. "Gods, Peyton, you feel so good."

"So do you, sir," I replied.

He let out a long, low grunt and with a few more frantic thrusts, he came inside me. The heat of his cock and his cum made me come for a third time.

We both flopped down and panted for a while, his hands still on my breasts, cock deep inside me.

"I could stay like this forever," he said with a sigh.

"I don't know about forever, but we have a while." I lay with my back to him, one leg over his to hold him inside. There was something incredibly intimate about lying there full like this.

He lightly caressed my breasts and traced circles around and over my nipples.

"Sometimes I wish we could run away and find a place where we could lie in bed naked all day." He sounded wistful. "Of course if we do, you'll want to bring the others."

"Right." That brought me back to Dyson and Kane, but they fled my mind when Nash started to move inside me again.

"I wouldn't object, as long as you're happy." He thrust a little faster. "And make some time for me." And faster.

"And call you 'sir'?" I asked.

His thumbs and fingers tightened on my nipples, painful but pleasant.

"And that." His strokes became quicker and firmer.

His hold on my nipples became a pinch which filled me with ecstasy I had never felt before.

"Mmmm, harder, sir, please."

He grunted and obliged by ramming into me so hard it hurt.

"Again," I pleaded. "Harder."

He did it again and again until I was caught between begging him to stop and coming harder than I ever had. In the end I cried out as I was swamped by a fourth orgasm, then a fifth. Both swept me away until I could no longer think. Every nerve, every muscle was given over to absolute pleasure.

Somewhere in the back of my awareness, I heard and felt him come again. He cried out my name and then all the pain was gone, replaced by lethargy in every last little bit of me.

I lay like a rag doll, my eyes half open, panting for a long while.

"Oh my gods," I breathed. "That was..."

"Yes," he agreed, "it was. You're incredible."

"No, you, sir," I replied sleepily.

He slid out of me. I would hurt like hells later, but I had no regrets.

"Are you arguing with me?" he asked.

"Would I dare?" I rolled over to face him.

He regarded me for a moment. "Yes. Yes you would. Lucky I'm here to keep you in line. Otherwise you'd tear off and do gods only know what."

That brought Dyson and Kane right back to my mind with a jolt which made me fully awake.

I sat up. "We need to go looking for the guys."

"No, you need to stay here where it's safe," he said firmly. The crease between his brows deepened. I probably imagined the slight glow of his eyes and the hint of scales on his cheeks.

"Is that what this was about? Distracting me from them?"

He blinked. "I needed you. Wanted you. You wanted me, too." He averted his eyes.

He was right, my brain had been firmly in my clitoris.

I sagged. "If anything happens to them..."

Nash put his arms around me and drew me close. "If anyone can take of themselves, it's those two." He placed a finger under my chin and made me look at him. "They're resilient. They will be fine, okay? And if they don't turn up by morning, I'll go out there myself."

"Are you going to go all dragon on them?" I asked, half teasing.

He hesitated. For a moment, I thought he might be angry, but then he smiled. "Would it turn you on if I did?"

"Yes," I replied firmly. "But only after I've replenished my energy." I covered a yawn with my hand. "You've worn me out, sir."

He chuckled softly. "I have? I haven't even begun yet." He rolled me onto my back and moved down my body to suck my nipple.

"Maybe one more time," I said breathlessly. Gods, the man would drive me crazy and I would enjoy every moment of it.

6

MIDNIGHT CAME and went before I finally crawled into bed. Thank the gods I had the bottom bunk. I doubt I would have made it to the top one.

I fell asleep to the sound of Ariana snoring and woke as the sun slanted in through the window.

I shot up and hit my head on the bunk above me.

"Shit." I rubbed my head and leaned against the wall.

"Are you all right down there?" Ariana's face appeared, upside down.

"Yeah, all good. I'll just have to remember to sit up more slowly from now on." I rose carefully and grabbed a change of clothes.

I had showered—yes, with Nash—the night before, so I just dressed and brushed my hair. I caught a glimpse of myself in the mirror and grimaced.

I still had the streak of green hair. I had gotten used to it. Mostly. Truthfully though, I looked tired. Satisfied, but tired. My body ached in the best way possible. Even so, I would have killed for a long soak in a hot bath.

I had to step to one side to let Ariana climb down and dress. We were both all but pressed against the walls in an effort to keep out of each other's way.

"This is a little too cozy," I said after ducking her elbow for the third time. "At least they've given the teachers more space." I told her about Nash's room and how we'd have to keep our liaisons secret.

"That's exciting," she grinned, her eyes wide. "The thrill of the forbidden."

I sighed. "I suppose so, but it's a bit silly to make consenting adults hide. I mean, who are we hurting?"

She paused for a moment. "You could be hurt if he fails you."

"He would never do that," I replied quickly. After a moment I added, "And I wouldn't give him an excuse to."

"I know you wouldn't on purpose, but you could pass without going to his classes if you wanted."

I was about to argue, but realised she was right. I did have an unfair advantage over the other students. "I'll make sure that doesn't happen," I said firmly.

"I know you will." She gave me a hug and opened the door. "Ready to face the dining room?"

"Why does that sound as if I'm going to my execution?" I grabbed my jacket and followed her out the door.

"Because you haven't really met any of the UA students yet," she replied. She wrinkled her nose. "It's like we smell of AMM or something."

"What does AMM smell like?" I hung my jacket over my arm and followed her toward the main building.

"I don't know." She laughed, but it faded almost immediately. "Dyson might."

I sighed. "He's probably in the dining hall, eating all of the bacon."

"That's possible," she agreed. "We should hurry, before it's all gone."

I didn't think either of us thought that was true, but we walked faster anyway.

～

THE DINING HALL WAS HUGE; probably bigger than the accommodation UA set aside for us. The chatter didn't skip a beat as we entered, but eyes turned to stare at us anyway. I saw what Ariana meant. They seemed to know we were from a different school, even though we all wore the same uniform.

I lifted my chin and walked toward the food service area. "I'm having flashbacks to high school," I muttered. "Bad ones."

"Same," Ariana replied. "They really don't want us here, do they?"

I met a few hostile glances with my own and they turned away.

"Too bad, they have to deal, just like we do," I said firmly.

There was no sign of either Dyson or bacon amongst the warming trays of food. Rather, everything looked... I groaned softly. Healthy.

"Are they trying to kill us?" Ariana asked. She grabbed herself a bowl of oats and fruit and made a face at the bottles of skim milk before she poured some onto her cereal. "There's not even coffee."

"Thank the gods there's tea," I said, until I realised it was all the herbal stuff. "You're right, they *are* trying to kill us." Or have us kill each other in a caffeine-withdrawal induced rage.

"It might do you some good." Matt appeared behind me, his usual guarded expression on his face.

"Not a chance," I replied. "But remember that when I'm ripping your head off because I need the carbs."

He chuckled. "I would have thought a fitness fanatic like you would enjoy this kind of food." He gestured toward the large variety of fruit.

"I like fitness," I agreed, "but I also like flavour." In spite of that, I snagged two bananas and a tub of yoghurt. A girl had to eat. Later I might ask Nash to smuggle me some chocolate. "Any word on the guys?"

"*Now* you ask," he said reproachfully. "No, there's been no word."

"I should be out there looking, too."

"That's a good idea," Matt nodded. "You should absolutely put others at risk again, just to satisfy your ego."

I rolled my eyes. "Fuck off. I just want to help. It's my fault they're missing."

"Your help won't find them sooner," he replied. He picked up an apple and bit into it.

"You don't know that." I picked up a spoon and resisted the urge to stab him in the eye with the blunt end.

"I know Zeta will be looking for you."

"As if I need reminding of that." I made a face.

"Then go to class and let people more qualified deal with Zeta. The guys will be fine without your help." The look on his face made me want to slap him. So much for our uneasy peace.

"I don't..."

I stopped talking as a UA student with a broad chest stepped between us.

"Don't mind me," he said, his voice a pleasant rumble. He picked up an orange and started to peel it. "I couldn't help but overhear. You're the one Zeta came after?" His ocean blue eyes held no hint of his opinion of either me or Zeta.

"They came after the whole academy," I snapped. I was in no mood for more accusations.

"But because of you, they knew where to look?" Still, his expression gave away nothing.

"It's not that simple." I frowned.

He smiled, just slightly. "Simple enough that your presence puts us all in danger. Apparently it's already done that, if the mention of missing guys is an indication." His brow quirked upward in question.

I flushed. "It's complicated."

"It's really very simple," he said slowly. "You should leave before you get anyone else killed." With that, he turned and stalked away.

Tears prickled at the corners on my eyes. "Maybe he's right."

"Hey." Ariana put her cereal on the table beside her and put an arm around me. "He's *not* right. You deserve an education as much as he does. Maybe more. This place should be safe, right?" She looked toward Matt.

"It should be," he agreed. "It's been here for at least a hundred years, teaching paranormals and breeding bigots like that." He patted my arm. "Do what I said—go to class and forget all about this."

I swear, if he had said, "Don't trouble your pretty little head," I would have decked him then and there.

"I will go to class, but I'm not going to forget. Not until the guys are back here, safe and sound."

Matt shrugged and walked away. Damn, why did he have to be such an asshole with a perfect ass? I didn't know what I wanted to do more, cup it or kick it.

"Is it possible they decided not to come back?" Ariana asked as we searched for a place to sit. "Maybe they agree with that guy." She gestured to where Asshole 2.0 sat with a group of friends.

Every now and again they would all look in our direction and glare. I fought down the urge to climb onto a table and scream at the top of my lungs, "This isn't fucking high school, you morons!"

Instead, I slid down in my chair and sliced banana into my yoghurt.

"If there's one thing I know about those two, it's that they'll be back." As long as they are able to. "They're both dedicated to their educations."

"And to you," Ariana said slyly. "I know they're both hoping you'll choose them some day."

I blushed. She was right. They made that clear enough. I told them I wouldn't choose either of them if I came between them, but they still vied for my attention.

"Right. If they don't come back, you-know-who would win by default." This place had far too many ears for me to say Nash's name out loud.

"I'm sure he wouldn't mind." She smiled.

"Hey." Hamish Small flopped down in the seat beside her and kissed her cheek.

While she flushed, I smiled. It was nice to see her happy and Hamish was a nice guy.

"Looks like AMM has its own table," he remarked.

That proved accurate when more and more of our fellow academy students filed into the hall and sat with us. Violette, Mustafa, and

Carter I knew already. Some other faces looked familiar, some not. Everyone seemed as anxious as I felt.

"Do we have to take classes with them?" Violette moaned.

"I don't think so," Carter replied. They had changed their hair to solid black during the holidays. It was an interesting look. "They have their own lecturers."

"I heard Mr Nash will be working with them as well as us," Mustafa remarked.

I swung my head to look at him in surprise. "Who did you hear that from?" I asked.

He shrugged. "One of the UA girls. They were talking about how hot he was." Mustafa made a face, but he watched me carefully. A couple of dozen AMM students had seen him kiss me outside the bus before we were evacuated from the old campus.

I shrugged. "Student-teacher relations are forbidden here," I said as lightly as I could. "So all they're going to get to do is look."

Mustafa nodded, but he didn't look convinced.

I wasn't either, truthfully. The idea of Nash touching another woman made me want to claw her eyes out, but technically he owed me nothing. I was seeing two other guys, after all. When they weren't missing, that was. I told myself jealousy was stupid, but I didn't believe it.

"We'll mostly be relegated to our classrooms," Carter said. "At least until they find us somewhere else."

"Let's hope that's soon." Asshole 2.0 stopped at the table to regard us as if we were a nest of cockroaches. Did cockroaches even have nests? I didn't know, but that was what his expression looked like.

One of his friends laughed. "My father said they should just close the AMM and be done with it. It's nothing more than a second rate university to begin with."

"You're right, Jacob," Asshole 2.0 said. "Second rate at best. Maybe third."

"You know Xav, I think you might be right." Jacob sneered and moved on.

Xav—short for Xavier, I assumed—lingered for a while longer, hostile eyes on me.

I gave him an eye roll. "Are you done with your preschool crap? If so, then fuck off."

A flash of anger crossed his eyes. He stepped closer to me. "You'll leave here, if it's the last thing I do."

I stood and drew myself up to my impressive height, which brought my face all the way up to his chin—he was tall, okay, be quiet —and glared.

"Don't make idle threats," I hissed.

He snorted. "It's not an idle threat, bitch. You're a danger to everyone here. You'll leave if I have to carry you out of here myself."

Before I could respond, or punch him, he turned and walked away.

Fucker.

7

THE PARANORMAL HISTORY classroom was freezing. I ran my hands up and down my arms to keep warm.

"I think I know what I want to do when I finish studying," I said.

"Heater installer?" Ariana said hopefully. Her lips were slightly blue and her hands trembled.

I laughed, but it was almost as bitter as the cold. "No, I think I want to teach."

"Like Dyson?" She gave me a meaningful look. "Are you choosing him?"

I frowned. "No. I mean, I'm not not choosing him, I just..." I shook my head. "I mean, teaching at a place like this."

"What, cold?"

I chuckled. "No, like a university. Maybe not one where people are assholes to other paranormals, but..."

She nodded. "I get it. You want to work with Nash. Are you—" She stopped talking as my eyes widened in warning. "I was going to ask if you're inspired by him?"

I held back a snort. *Sure* she was. "Yes, very inspired. Who wouldn't want to teach young paranormals to defend themselves?"

"Can you teach me?" she asked. "I think Mr Nash has pretty much given up on me."

It was not in his nature to give up, but I was happy to give her extra help. "Of course, I—"

"Shhh," Violette hissed, "I'm trying to listen."

"Sorry," I mouthed. I rubbed my hands up and down a bit faster and tried to focus on the lecturer who paced back and forth at the front of the room, probably trying to keep warm as well.

She had introduced herself as Ms Dannon and apologised for the room temperature. Evidently our former history teacher had decided not to return to the academy. I wasn't sure I blamed them. Wherever they were, it was warmer than this. Gods help us in winter.

"And that brings us to your research project for the semester." She pressed a button on her projector—the kind normal schools used twenty or more years ago—and brought up the details. "This will all be on the website, but we can go through it all now."

I sighed and tried to focus on what she was saying. I enjoyed history, but knowing the guys were out there made it hard to concentrate.

"And so, being second years, you can choose your own study project." Ms Dannon's words got my attention.

"Anything?" I asked.

"Anything pertaining to paranormals, yes, but run it past me first." She smiled, then nodded. "All right, I'll see you next time."

"What are you thinking?" Ariana asked while we filed out of the room into the warmer air. "Please tell me you're not going to study the rise of Zeta."

I slipped my jacket off and hung it over my arm. "Why not? I know at least two hybrids."

"Neither who seem interested in talking about their upbringing," she reminded me.

I hesitated. "I suppose you're right. I could—" I was interrupted by the appearance of Matt in front of my face.

"I did not step in your way," I told him immediately.

He snorted. "Not this time, no. You're both wanted in the Chancellor's office."

"Which one?" Ariana asked.

Valid question. Unless the AMM Chancellor had resigned. Honestly, I would be surprised if my mother hadn't demanded his job after I was almost killed last year. That was precisely the kind of thing she'd do and she would probably get away with it.

"Mr Ridgeway," Matt supplied. He gestured for us to walk with him.

"Ah." So he'd kept his job. For now. Maybe no one else wanted it. Paranormals with the credentials to run a tertiary institution must be few and far between. I added that to my list of ambitions. "They gave him an office in the mansion?"

"They couldn't very well..." Matt stopped and sighed. "Yes, I suppose they could. It's on the ground floor, though."

"Right. No fancy view of the grounds. Are you his assistant now?"

"That's what I was wondering," Ariana said. "Shouldn't you be in class, too?"

"Yes," he replied dryly. "I'm trying to help clean up the mess from yesterday. And last year. The repercussions... It doesn't matter, just hurry up." He walked faster and I had to almost trot to keep up.

"What repercussions?" I asked as we drew closer.

"Having a campus here, for one thing," he replied tersely. "The Paranormal Council is hunting for a suitable alternative. They're also dealing with different factions. Some want to..." He stopped outside a door and knocked.

"Some want to what?" I asked.

When he pushed the door open, I knew I wouldn't get an answer. Not now anyway.

"Come in." Mr Ridgeway looked tired. He had more grey in his hair than he'd had when I saw him last, and more lines around his eyes. He must be around my parents' age, but he looked older.

He only drew my eye for a moment though, until I saw a figure huddled under a blanket on a chair opposite the chancellor.

"Kane!" I hurried to embrace him and kiss his mouth as he stood.

Judging by the way he held the blanket with one hand, he was still naked underneath it.

Hashtag shifter life. Under other circumstances, it might be funny. Not today, though.

"Where is Dyson?" I leaned back to look into his eyes.

Tears shone and he blinked until they trickled down his cheeks. "Zeta has him." He sniffed.

My heart sank. "They… Is he…" I swallowed hard.

"He was alive when I saw him last," Kane whispered.

My head spun and I felt faint. Zeta didn't tend to keep shifters alive, from what everyone had told me. They couldn't siphon off their magic, and they couldn't breed a male in the same way they could with a woman.

"How?" I whispered.

He shook his head. "They surrounded him. Shot him with a tranquilliser dart, or something…" He leaned against my shoulder and sobbed a couple of times.

I glanced toward Matt. "We shouldn't have left."

"If we hadn't, we would have been taken too," he replied.

"We might not." I looked away from him and held Kane tight.

"Kane has suggested you could help him to get settled here," Ridgeway said after an uncomfortable silence.

"Of course. I'll show him where the uniforms are." I grimaced.

"Here's your room assignment and classes." Ridgeway handed him a sheet of paper and a new phone. "I assume you've misplaced yours?"

Kane smiled slightly. "Yeah, it's back in the city with my car. It's probably been towed by now. Thanks."

Ridgeway nodded and waved us out. Only Matt stayed behind. I didn't bother to ask why. I doubted he'd tell me anyway.

I gripped Kane's hand and led him around to the uniform storeroom.

"So what's the plan?" I asked.

"Matt said he'd meet us in the common room after dinner," Kane said, his voice low.

"What?" Ariana asked. "Why?"

I frowned at her for a moment. "Because we're going after Dyson."

She formed an O with her mouth. "Isn't that dangerous?"

"Of course, but we can't leave him with them," I replied. "If they'd wanted him dead, they wouldn't have used a tranquilliser. They must need him for something. We need to get him out before that happens." Whatever that was. It didn't bear thinking about, but Cerberus sprang to mind. Maybe they wanted a legion of magic dog soldiers. If that was the case, they'd take blood from Dyson, lots of it. Hopefully they would need him for long enough for us to save him first.

Although, would blood be enough? I could easily picture him coming, but not in a cup and not while under duress.

I shuddered.

"Are you okay?" Kane asked softly.

"I should be asking you that," I told him. "What happened to you?"

He shrugged. "After they caught him, I followed for a while, but I got tired. I lost them when I landed in a tree, so I spent the night there, fending off possums. First thing this morning, I flew here." He looked rueful. "I might have gotten lost a time or two."

I squeezed his hand. "At least you got here." I glanced around. This would normally be where someone like Xav would appear and make derogatory remarks about Kane being unsafe because of me. I even prepared a retort, but he was nowhere to be seen. Good, I was in no mood for his bullshit.

"Yeah." Kane sighed.

"We'll find him and bring him back," Ariana said firmly. "There's no way those bastards will beat us."

"Exactly," I agreed. "Although Dyson is probably telling terrible jokes as we speak."

"Right," Kane said with a half smile. "They might let him go so they don't have to listen to him anymore."

"If anyone could make that happen, it would be him." I leaned against Kane for a moment and reminded myself that if the guys hadn't been escorting me here, they would both be safe. I should have tried to get here alone. They would have taken me instead, but they wouldn't stop until they did that anyway. Maybe Xav was right, I was a liability to everyone here.

"He might even turn up before we can plan," Ariana said. She opened the door to the storeroom and rummaged through the shelves for pants and shirts for Kane. "They don't stock underwear," she said apologetically.

He shrugged. "I'll just go commando. It wouldn't be the first time."

I forced a smile. "It really wouldn't be. He likes to let it all hang loose."

While Ariana had her back turned, he let the blanket slip and wiggled his hips. His cock flapped back and forth.

I held back a laugh. Before he pulled his pants on all the way, I ran my fingertip down his length to watch it rise.

"Tease," he mouthed.

I gave him my best innocent-but-not-that-innocent smile and took a shirt out of its bag.

"It's a shame to cover those," I said about his abs. Damn, his body was as gorgeous as the rest of him. Abs I could do washing on, a firm V that slanted down his hips like an arrow pointing to his groin.

"I'll put it on so you can take it off later," he told me.

"Count on that," I replied.

"I will," he replied. "Isn't what those skirts are for?"

I grimaced. "I don't think that was the original intention, no." Guys and their schoolgirl fetishes. If he had a thing for girls in short skirts, it was overshadowed by his thing for wanting to have sex in front of other people. Fortunately it was a thing we shared.

"Gods, I miss jeans." Ariana turned back and handed Kane a jacket. "I'll grab some for Dyson too. He's about the same size, right?"

"More or less," Kane agreed. "I'm bigger in the dick." His face was deadpan, but I smiled, remembering Dyson's fondly.

They were about the same, but I wouldn't be so mean as to say so. Let him have his moment.

"There are no socks either." Ariana handed him a pair of shoes.

"I'll make do." He sat and pulled them on, while trying to catch glimpses up my skirt. No luck there, boyo, Ariana had spare panties that fit me. They were pink, with some kind of cat slash unicorn, but they were better than nothing.

"All right." He stood. "I guess I have to go to class and pretend I'm not worried about my brother."

I gave him a hug and kept one arm around him while we headed back toward the classrooms. "If you're lucky, they will have set up a lab for you science geeks."

8

———————

"So, what's the plan?" Ariana settled into one of the ancient but surprisingly plush chairs.

I was about to sit beside her when Kane pulled me onto his lap and sat with his hands right over my sex. I swallowed hard and resisted the urge to writhe with the warmth of his touch.

Matt flopped into a chair opposite and rubbed his face. He looked worse than I felt.

"When did you sleep last?" I asked gently.

He shrugged. "I don't know. I'll sleep after this." His mouth pressed in a tight line and I knew that was all I would get from him.

I leaned back into Kane and rested my head against his chest.

Movement in the corner of my eye caught my attention.

Hamish stuck his head into the room and smiled tentatively. "Hey, can I help?"

Matt groaned. "Who invited him?"

"I did," Ariana replied. "Come in Hamish, of course you can help."

"The more people who know about this—" Matt shot her a warning look.

"He's the only one I told. I trust him." She moved over to give Hamish space.

"You'd better be right," Matt muttered. He crossed his arms over his chest and scowled.

I was about to ask what he was waiting for when Nash stalked into the room and closed the door behind him. He had changed into track pants and a t-shirt which hugged his torso in a way that made me want to drool.

He gave me a half smile and perched on the edge of the chair beside Matt.

"For the record, I would prefer none of you were in on this," Nash said. His brow furrowed.

"If not us, then who?" Matt asked.

"I know people," Nash said tersely. "Unfortunately they're currently too far away to be much help." He ran a hand over his hair. "That leaves us. However, if any one of you want to opt out, now is the time." He looked at each of us in turn, his attention lingering on me.

"I'm not changing my mind," Ariana said firmly.

"Me either," I agreed.

"I'm certainly not," Kane said. His fingers tightened on the inside of my thigh.

I knew it was from anxiety, but it still sent a jolt of heat to my belly. What was wrong with me that dangerous situations didn't diminish my libido? In fact, it seemed to have the opposite effect. I forced myself to stop thinking with my groin and focus. Dyson needed us right now.

"What do you want us to do?" I asked.

I saw in his eyes that he was itching to say, "Stay here, out of trouble," but knew that would get him nowhere.

"There are a few places in the city they might keep him," Nash said. "We need to find out which one it is first. We'll split up into teams and look, then come back and discuss tactics." He squinted at us. "We have two hybrids, two witches, an owl shifter and—" He raised an eyebrow at Hamish.

"Just a regular wizard, sir," Hamish replied. He looked as though he'd stepped into the lion's den, but only now realised the danger. I gave him credit for not running away. Yet. He must really care about Ariana.

"Right," Nash nodded. "Kane, you'll be good at reconnaissance, but you have no power, defensive or offensive, to speak of." That sounded harsh, but accurate. Nash was teaching him to fight the way normals did, but that wouldn't help against guns. "You'll work with me."

"Yes, sir." Kane sounded a little disappointed. He might have been hoping to be paired with me, but he was safer with a dragon. Nash wouldn't let him come to any harm.

"Ariana and Hamish, you're together."

They both looked pleased at that.

Matt looked less pleased when he realised he was paired with me. His lip curled and he gave me a quick look through half-lidded eyes.

"I'm just as thrilled as you are," I said tartly.

"I could go with Kane," Matt said. "A gargoyle hybrid is only slightly less badass than a dragon."

The corners of Nash's mouth twitched. "If I worked with Peyton, I would get distracted."

"Same here," Kane said. He ran his hand down the inside of my thigh.

"What makes you think she wouldn't distract me, too?" Matt snapped.

When I glanced at him in surprise, he snorted. "The same way a mosquito bite on the ass is distracting."

I rolled my eyes. "Maybe I should just go by myself. Or take someone friendly, like that Xav guy."

"No one is going alone," Nash said firmly. "You two have worked together twice before and lived to tell the tale. You can do it again."

"They will," Ariana said. "So Dyson can live to *wag* the tail."

I snorted with laughter.

Matt groaned, but he was holding back a smile. Even Nash looked amused.

"Yes, exactly so. I left a bag outside the door with changes of clothes. I expect UA won't want you creeping about in their uniform." Nash rose.

"Please say there's some jeans in there," I said hopefully.

Nash opened the door and tugged it inside. "See for yourself. I'll see you all tomorrow at dawn."

"We're not leaving now?" Ariana asked.

"Nothing says suspicious like us all sneaking around in the dark," Nash said dryly. "No, we'll draw less attention during the day when places are busy. The noise will cover us if we need to become invisible."

"I guess so." Ariana sighed. "I suppose we should…um…go to bed then?" She looked meaningfully at Hamish.

"Yes." He shot up out of his chair. "Bed. For, um sleep." He offered her his hand and they slipped out the door.

Matt followed closely on their heels.

"Thank you," I said to Nash as I opened the top of the bag.

He gave me a nod and Kane an envious look, then he, too, left the room. The door clicked shut behind him.

"So, I guess we should see what might fit us in here, hmm?" Kane let me up, then knelt beside the bag. "You know you're going to have to take your clothes off before you can try on anything."

"I thought I might," I replied. "So do you."

"That's awful." He grinned. "Maybe we could help each other?"

"That sounds like a good idea." I nodded slowly, then gave him a slow smile and crept closer. He wasn't wearing a jacket or a tie, so I started on his shirt buttons first.

While I teased them through the holes, one by one, he returned the favour with mine. We almost tangled arms pushing them down each other's shoulders.

I laughed and pulled off my own sleeves while he did the same with his.

He leaned forward to kiss my mouth and unhook my bra. Without breaking our lips apart, he threw it aside.

He cupped my breast while his tongue traced the outline of my lips.

He broke off and took my hand to help me to my feet. Smiling slightly, he led me over to the window. The UA mansion was bathed in darkness, except light which glowed in several windows. Anyone looking out would have a full view of us.

Kane faced me toward the window and worked my skirt and panties down my hips.

I had no idea if anyone was watching, but the idea they might be sent my heart racing. I never thought I would be an exhibitionist, but here I was. Part of me wished there was a face in the window so I knew someone saw Kane run his hands from my neck, over my breasts and down to my sex.

He parted my legs and rubbed lightly over my mound and down toward my clit.

Did I imagine seeing a figure in a window near the top of the mansion? They stopped and looked down toward us.

Well, enjoy the show.

Kane turned me around so he faced me, but wasn't blocking too much of the window. He ran his hands all over me, while I wound my fingers around his erect cock.

He moaned, cupped my ass and lifted me so I was pressed against the wall beside the window.

"I didn't want to rush," he whispered, "but I need you."

"I need you, too," I said. "I want you inside me." Gods knew I was already wet.

No sooner had I finished speaking than he drove his cock into me.

I gasped aloud at the suddenness. After a moment I relaxed and let him push himself in deeper.

He closed his eyes and exhaled deeply for a few moments. Then, as if by some silent signal, he began to thrust with increasing rhythm.

I glanced toward the window. Whoever was watching from the mansion still stood, backlit in the glow of the light. Evidently they liked what they saw. Was it Nash? I didn't think so, but it might be easier to pretend it was. I doubted Nash would be shy. He'd watch and not hide that he was doing it.

Kane put his hand on my waist to guide me to keep the rhythm.

I put a hand to my own breast and rubbed my nipple to drive myself closer to the edge.

He moaned. "Gods, you are so hot."

"You too," I panted.

He dipped one hand between us to rub my clit in time with each stroke.

I half closed my eyes, but cast another look at our watcher. I would almost swear I saw a hand full of cock, sliding up and down as they observed. Just when I thought this couldn't get more hot, it did.

I cried out as I crested for the first time. As I was coming down, movement outside caught my eye. Someone, maybe more than one, had stopped outside to watch.

Gods, I was as aroused as ever.

Kane moved faster inside me and rubbed at the same time. "I want you to come again," he panted. "Come for me."

So he had noticed them, too.

I arched my back so they got a better view of my breasts and rock hard nipples. A bit of me wanted one of them to join us, to run their hands over me. Knowing they saw me would have to be enough.

"You too," I said, my throat in my mouth.

He moaned. "I'm going to…"

Desire rose again, almost as fast as the first time. I bucked against his hand so hard I was on the edge again in moments.

I toppled over at the same moment he grunted and came with me. He pounded a few times, then stilled as he spilled himself into me.

We fell into each other's arms then, both holding each other up so we didn't fall in a worn heap on the floor. On the edge of my consciousness I thought I heard applause, but my pulse was louder.

After a while, we lowered each other to the floor.

"Can I ask you a favour?" he asked shyly.

"Of course," I said. Right now I might give him the world if he asked. As long as he didn't ask me to choose. I wasn't ready for that.

"Can I take a photo of you?" he asked.

I smiled slowly. "Like this?" I glanced down at my naked body.

"Yes. I swear I will never send it to anyone else." He propped himself up on one elbow.

I licked my lips. No one had ever asked me for anything like this before. After a while, I nodded.

"Okay, but if it ends up online without my permission—"

"I promise it will only go on the net if you put it there," he assured me. He pulled the phone out of the back of his pants and focused on me.

I sat with my legs together, but at an angle where my breasts would be clearly visible. I blinked as the flash went off.

"Perfect," he declared, "just like you."

I doubted that, but he went a long way to making me feel sexy.

9

"I KNOW it's only been one day, but I missed jeans." I toyed with the hem of my black t-shirt and tried not to appear as if I was looking over Matt's shoulder at the building behind him.

He shrugged. "It's better than those uniforms." He was back to head-to-toe black. His eyes scanned the road behind us. No, he didn't look suspicious at all.

"What, you don't think the short skirts are cute?" I cocked my head at him.

He squinted at me. "No."

"Why not?" I pressed.

He looked uncomfortable. "They remind me of high school."

"Ah." I nodded. Did *anyone* have fond memories of high school? "Yeah, that makes everything about a thousand times less sexy, doesn't it?"

"At least that much," he grunted. "Are you sure this is the place?"

I pulled a piece of paper from my pocket and checked the address. "Yeah, number one hundred and thirteen. I don't suppose Nash would have sent us somewhere Zeta wouldn't be?"

Matt frowned, but I knew he was thinking the same thing. "If he did…"

"You'll write him a sternly worded letter?" I suggested.

He looked surprised, then barked a laugh. "Something like that. Maybe we should go—"

"Wait," I said quickly. A gate beside the building groaned open slowly and a black SUV pulled out. "Oh look, a cliché."

Matt gave me a funny look.

"It's black," I pointed out and peered inside as subtly as I could. "Why do the bad guys always dress that way and drive cars like that? What's wrong with pink or yellow?"

"Not just the bad guys." He gestured toward his own outfit.

I arched an eyebrow at him. "Says you," I teased.

He smirked. "It's not like you're perfect."

"Thank the gods for that." I ventured a look toward the SUV. It headed down the road toward a set of traffic lights. "Should we follow it?"

"You heard Nash. We're only here to watch."

Now I gave him a full, double brow rise. "Since when did you listen to him?"

"Since…" Matt hesitated. "Since he's the leader of this…whatever this is."

"Don't tell me you're not at least tempted to follow. Or go inside those gates before they close?"

"Of course I'm tempted, but he would kill me if I got you killed or captured."

"So you only care about what he thinks?" I asked. "Not because you care about me?"

My question obviously took him by surprise. For a fraction of a second I thought I saw something in his eyes. It was gone before I could be sure I had seen anything. A moment later, his haughty mask was back.

"You're like the pesky little sister I can't ditch," he replied.

"Right." Only I was almost certain the look he gave me smouldered. There was nothing brotherly about it. Whatever though, he was still an asshole. "I'm going in anyway. You can stay here if you like."

I drew magic from a nearby tree and formed a bubble around myself.

"Peyton," he hissed. "You stupid, fucking…"

"See, I knew you cared." I grabbed his hand and pulled him inside the bubble.

"Nothing says conspicuous like two people suddenly disappearing," he growled softly.

I shrugged. "No one was looking our way." I hoped.

"Your recklessness is going to get you killed," he stated. "Or worse, get *me* killed."

"Is that your prediction?" I stepped quickly but quietly toward the gate.

"Just stating a fact," he replied. "Now will you stop talking. They'll hear us."

It was my turn to give him a sarcastic smirk. He was the one still yabbering.

He rolled his eyes and pulled me forward just as the gate started to close.

The driveway led to a yard with enough garage space for maybe ten cars. Right now it housed four, all of them black. A couple of Zeta agents, all dressed in the same style of uniform, walked back and forth, oblivious to our presence.

The door to the rear of the building stood open at the top of a short flight of steps.

I stood on my toes to peek in. A corridor led deeper inside. Nothing looked remarkable about anything here. Just your standard, garden variety evil, government-funded-organisation building.

"I'm going inside. You're staying here," Matt said in my ear.

"Not a chance," I whispered back.

He gave me a long-suffering look and sighed. "I'm not leaving you here for your safety. I want you to watch and see who comes and goes. If they move Dyson, you'll see it."

"Oh." That actually made sense, damn him. I nodded. "Fine."

He formed his own bubble, let my hand go and stepped out of mine. The relief of not having to shield two of us was immediate. It was like not knowing you're carrying a weight until it's gone.

"Stay safe," I whispered in his general direction.

"You too."

I sensed him move away and did the same. Along the line of the fence would be a safer place to be, as long as I didn't touch it. The chance of an alarm of some kind was too great.

A third agent walked down the steps leading from the building. She must have missed bumping into Matt by a hair. She made her way across to the other agents.

"Has the parcel arrived?" she asked.

"Yes, ma'am." One of the men—tall and with bright red hair—gave her a nod. He had small eyes and a narrow nose. For some reason, he immediately gave me the creeps. It was more than just his job, there was something about him.

This was also the first time I'd known they had any kind of hierarchy, but of course they would. They acted like an arm of the military. A chain of command was only normal. Who then, was at the top?

Meanwhile, what parcel were they referring to? Dyson? Someone else? An actual parcel, like an online purchase? Maybe they needed to stock up on toothpicks or toilet paper.

"It's ready to be loaded into a car, ma'am," the agent continued. He spoke as if he only barely respected her position. In this day and age there were still some men who couldn't handle a woman in command over them.

"Good," she nodded. "See to it, Agent Fitz."

I bit my lip to keep from snorting.

"Yes, ma'am." Fitz gave her a clumsy salute. If she noticed, she didn't respond. She simply walked around the side of the building and disappeared.

Fitz squinted after her, then finally turned and trotted up the steps and out of sight. Whatever this parcel was, I assumed he was going to get it. That suspicion was confirmed a few minutes later when Fitz returned with another agent. Between them they supported Dyson. They all but dragged him down the steps toward the cars.

My heart raced.

Dyson was alive, his chest rose and fell slowly. He looked to have been drugged. If they let him, he might shift and tear their throats out. He would hate himself for it later, but that wouldn't stop him from breaking free if he could. They would know that, too, and probably kept him sedated since they caught him.

They hauled him over to one of the cars and opened the door. Together, they heaved him inside.

I winced as he grunted in pain. At least he had some awareness left.

Fitz and the other agent, a blonde with a long scar down his cheek, stepped back from the car. Blondie opened the driver's side door and got inside, while Fitz trotted back to the building and went inside.

I licked my lips. I had an idea but I didn't know who would kill me more, Matt, Nash, Kane, Ariana, or Dyson himself if I acted on it.

I hesitated only until I heard Fitz heading back, then I ran on my tiptoes and climbed into the car beside Dyson.

He leaned against the opposite door, eyes closed, a trickle of drool on his chin. He didn't look to have been harmed, but pulling him to safety would have to wait until he woke a little more.

Just as I had that thought, he cracked open an eye and peered around. Judging by the frown, he'd felt the car move slightly, but wasn't sure why.

I grimaced to myself. I wanted to reassure him, but I couldn't just yet. Blondie was too close to risk speaking, even in a whisper.

When Dyson sniffed the air a moment later, I smiled to myself. Of course he knew I was there, he was a dog shifter and knew my scent.

He hid his own smile by ducking his head down to his chin and closing his eye.

The passenger side door opened. A moment later, the car dipped when Fitz slipped into the passenger seat. Thank the gods he had. He could have sat in the back beside Dyson. If he'd done that, he would have sat on top of me. The door slammed shut.

Just a wild guess here, but that would probably have given me away.

Blondie started the engine and pressed a button which seemed to open the gate. The faster the car went, the more uneasy I felt. Not only was I in a vehicle with evil agents, I was traveling without a seatbelt on. I'm paranormal, not immortal.

We passed through the gate and headed west.

Clinging onto magic for this long was tiring, but I had no choice. I almost lost it when Dyson flopped over toward me and ended up with his head on my hand. He peered upward, but of course he saw nothing. He still smiled.

Silly me, I smiled back. I snorted softly at myself, but pushed away the self-reprimand. I had a feeling he knew my response, even if he couldn't see it. I was probably lucky it was Dyson I was with and not Kane. Kane would probably have found a way to make me come, even if it put us both in danger.

I leaned back against my seat and put a hand on Dyson's head. If I was careful, the magic wouldn't obscure any part of him. Making half of his head invisible might expose us both.

He nestled into my hand and closed his eyes. I stroked my thumb across his hair and sighed softly. I wouldn't mind a sleep too, but I couldn't let my guard down for a moment.

Instead, I watched out the window as we wound through the streets. After a while I realised we weren't going in a straight line. Going around bends notwithstanding, this wasn't the straightest route to the west. Or north, or south... We traveled around in a wide square before we headed west again.

"Doesn't seem like anyone is following," Blondie said.

"Good," Fitz replied. "As long as those vermin fuckers can't make cars invisible, we should be fine."

Vermin fuckers? Screw you, too, asshole.

"What do they want that for anyway?" Blondie jerked his head back toward Dyson.

That? These guys really were evil.

Fitz shrugged. "Dog DNA or something. Maybe they have a bitch ready to go into heat." He chuckled.

"Ah." Blondie nodded. "Do they need to go into heat?"

Fitz shrugged. "I don't think so. We can breed them whenever we want to."

"Oh, I see. I suppose that's easier for everyone." Blondie pulled the car up at a red light.

"It's easier for us," Fitz replied. "Don't forget, they're little more than animals anyway. Cows and sheep. They'll do as they're told, like it or not." He looked smug.

"And, if they don't like it?" Blondie asked tentatively.

"Who cares?" Fitz replied. "This is for the good of all humankind. We're making the world a better place." He actually sounded as though he believed it. "It's as much for their benefit as ours."

"Of course," Blondie said so fast I wanted to be sick. "I was just curious."

"Yeah, well, you'd be better off not to ask too many questions," Fitz advised him. Then he added, "If you don't have the stomach for this—"

"I do," Blondie said. "I know what we're doing is right. Hybrids are important to the whole world."

"Yes, they are. It would be a lot easier if—"

Whatever he was going to say was interrupted by a grinding sound coming from the roof of the car.

10

The grinding increased, like something was trying to tear the roof off the car. A giant talon poked a hole the size of my hand half a metre from my head.

I almost lost hold of my magic as I ducked aside.

"What the fuck?" Fitz turned to look over his shoulder. He pulled out his gun and tried to aim, but Blondie swung the wheel so hard the gun almost flew out of his hand.

Another talon gouged a hole near the first. It scraped backward, taking chunks of roof and interior fabric with it.

"Get rid of the bloody thing!" Fitz growled. "Shake it off."

"I'm trying," Blondie grunted. "Can't you kill it?"

"If I can get off a shot." Fitz aimed again and squeezed the trigger. The bullet missed both talons and lodged in the roof between them.

"Bulletproof goes both ways," Dyson whispered and gave a snort.

I grinned, but joking aside, we really needed to get out of this car.

The talons tugged harder and the roof groaned. The car shuddered with the strain of being pulled in two different directions.

I held on to my magic long enough to pull my phone out of my pocket.

My sudden appearance must have caught Blondie's eye, because he glanced back and gaped before returning his attention to his driving.

"Shit!" he shouted out a moment later.

"I knew that would come in useful someday." I nodded toward the road in front of the car. A moment later we slammed into the temporary concrete and plastic waterslide I had conjured in the middle of the quiet country highway.

I cried out as I flew hard into the seat in front of me. Pain exploded through my shoulder and down my arm.

Through watering eyes I watched a scaled, black form roll over the windscreen and down the front of the car. The dragon would have struck the waterslide, but the structure disappeared as quickly as it had come. Instead, he tumbled onto the tar in a tangle of legs and wings.

He slowly rose and shook it off before he stalked back toward the car.

"Shit," Fitz said from behind his airbag.

"We should go," I told Dyson.

He nodded and opened his door. "Are you all right?"

"Yeah." I rubbed my shoulder before I climbed across the back of the car. "Nothing broken I don't think." At least, I hoped not, but it hurt like hells.

He gave me his hand and tugged me out just as the dragon stepped up onto the front of the car.

"He looks pissed," I remarked.

"When does Nash not look pissed?" Dyson asked.

"I don't think now is the time for me to answer that," I replied.

Nash scraped at the windscreen with one huge talon and peered in at the two terrified agents.

"I think you've made your point," I told him. They would have a hard enough time explaining this accident to the police. The front of the car was smashed up, but no hint of what it had struck remained. The cops wouldn't be likely to believe a waterslide had appeared out of nowhere only to disappear again. That was even more bizarre than the presence of a dragon.

Nash turned huge eyes to me and bobbed his head, but still scratched the glass one more time. The agents cowered in the car until Nash climbed down and stalked away, toward Dyson and me.

He jerked his head toward his back.

"You want us to ride you?" I asked.

Nash bobbed his huge head. Even knowing who he was, I was a little intimidated. I mean, it wasn't every day you saw a dragon in Melbourne, much less rode one.

Nash snorted out his enormous nostrils and jerked his head back.

"Okay, okay." I stepped closer. "How do I get up there? Just... climb?" He didn't disagree, so I put a hand on his warm scales and considered the best way to do this.

"Here." Dyson laced his fingers and leaned down to make a stirrup.

"Thank you." I winced as I stepped onto his hands and threw a leg over Nash's back. I settled onto his warm body and wound my arms around his neck as best I could.

"There's room for two." I assumed Nash could support us both, or at least thought he could.

"Uh, no offence," Dyson took a step back, "but I'd prefer to run." He glanced back toward the car as though he really wanted to rip the agent's heads off. Under the circumstances, I applauded his restraint.

He shed his Zeta prisoner attire, shifted into his wolfhound form, and stood with his tongue lolling out of the side of his mouth. No doubt about it, he was cute in both his forms.

Nash spread his wings just as Fitz managed to work his way past the airbag and mangled car. He staggered onto the road and raised his gun.

"Hold it right there," he ordered. "Don't so much as twitch or I'll shoot."

I turned my arm so my tattoo was upward and readied myself to bring my guardian to life.

Before I could act, another gargoyle leapt onto the back of the car. He jumped from the roof onto Fitz and knocked him clear off his feet. The gun flew out of his hand and spun across the tar.

Dyson ran for it, picked the weapon up in his jaws and disappeared into the bushes.

Matt stood over Fitz and growled deeply, his muzzle a handspan from the agent's face.

Fitz's eyes widened in terror. A puddle formed on the road around his pants.

Yeah, I would have wet myself too, if I thought a gargoyle might rip my throat out.

Matt looked toward us and jerked his head upward. The message was clear: get out of here.

Nash bobbed his head and with a stroke of his wings, we were airborne and hovering over the wreck.

Another car approached from the east.

I held my breath until Matt bounded away in the direction Dyson had gone.

Nash banked hard and took us both toward the shelter of the trees.

I didn't envy Fitz and Blondie having to explain all of this to whoever arrived on the scene next. That was their problem. Maybe they shouldn't have chosen the wrong side. Although, I had a niggling doubt in the back of my mind that Blondie had. He didn't seem convinced what he was doing was right.

I gave myself a mental shrug. He wouldn't have been merciful to me had he known I was there. I owed him nothing in return.

Sirens in the distance suggested someone had called the police or an ambulance.

That led to another thought.

"Nash, would they have—"

I squealed when he dropped several metres. I slipped to one side a little before I managed to catch myself. A fall from this height would suck.

"What are you— Fuck!"

A form few right over my head. Had Nash not seen and dropped the way we had, the phoenix would have snatched me off his back. I'd be a snack as we spoke.

"Have I mentioned I don't like phoenixes?" I cried out.

Nash snorted his agreement and dropped lower, so we wove between the trees, barely off the ground. If I had ever envisioned flying on the back of a dragon, it wouldn't have been like this.

I leaned further forward and gripped him tighter. One slip and things might end badly for me.

I screwed my eyes shut and sat like that for a solid minute or two. My breakfast threatened to rise. Only the idea that I might puke on Nash made me reopen my eyes.

The trees passed by in a blur.

I glanced over my shoulder.

The phoenix, feathers a stunning shade of blue, was right behind us. He'd be beautiful if he wasn't trying to kill us.

"I guess that answers my question on whether or not they called for backup," I said ironically.

Nash banked suddenly. Over my shoulder I spied another phoenix.

"Crap. I don't suppose there's any chance that one is on our side?"

That question was answered a moment later when the second phoenix gave chase.

"Well shit," I muttered. Hanging on for dear life with one hand, I pulled out my phone and clicked on the spell app Madame Luc had taught us to use. I pushed away a pang of grief for the teacher who had died defending the academy last year, and scrolled.

"Magpie? Too small? Goat? Too on-the-ground." Unless the phoenixes got hungry. "Elephant? Let's call that plan B. Oh, this wasn't here last year." I grinned to myself, pointed my phone over my shoulder and clicked as I drew magic from the trees to put into the spell.

The pterodactyl appeared with an ear-piercing shriek and dove straight at the first phoenix. The hybrid never stood a chance. Clearly he hadn't anticipated anything appearing in front of him, much less a carnivorous, winged dinosaur.

I winced at the crunch of prehistoric teeth on bone. The phoenix hit the ground a few moments later, without his head.

I swallowed hard and glanced back as the second phoenix evaded the pterodactyl.

"Damn," I muttered, and again when the phoenix narrowly missed slamming into a tree.

I scrolled through my phone again for something else I could conjure. Snake, hippopotamus, bicycle—that sounded like a crash waiting to happen—table, chair… Nothing which could fly or was capable of defending us against the big hybrid.

We flew low until I caught sight of Dyson and Matt. Both stood under the shelter of a tree, their eyes raised toward us.

I didn't realise what Nash intended until he hit the ground with a jerk that pulled my grip free. I rolled over the side of his wing and landed in the ground with a thud. I cried out with pain—of course had I landed on my already hurt arm.

"What the fuck, you—" I wasn't even on my feet before Nash was off again, phoenix in his wake, the pterodactyl right behind. "Bloody idiot," I muttered.

"Peyton!" Dyson, back in human form and deliciously naked, came running toward me. "We need to get you out of here."

"Hey, who was rescuing who?" I retorted.

Matt growled. I'm sure that was directed at Dyson or Nash. I totally hadn't ditched him back in the city to jump into the car. Nope, not me. Okay, so I had, but he didn't need to growl about it now.

"Look." Dyson pulled me under a tree and pointed.

Unencumbered by my weight, Nash turned in mid-air and raked his enormous talons in the direction of the phoenix.

That slowed the hybrid long enough for the pterodactyl to catch up. It screeched and fastened its own claws into the phoenix's back.

The phoenix gave a very human-like scream and writhed to escape from the pterodactyl's grip.

The dinosaur held fast, then shook the phoenix until a loud snap rent the air.

I grimaced as the phoenix sagged.

A second later my spell ended and the pterodactyl disappeared. The dead phoenix fell from the sky and landed with a ground-shaking thump.

"What a way to go," Dyson muttered.

"Yeah." I leaned against the tree trunk and tried not to spew. Who else would die before this was over?

"I think we're late for class," Dyson added.

I laughed. It started soft, but ended up sounding hysterical. We were late, but at least we had Dyson back. I stopped laughing for long enough to look into his eyes. What had they done to him? Whatever it was, I would pay them back for it some day. All of that and more.

But first, I needed a drink.

I nodded to the west. "The academy is that way. You're going to love the uniforms."

What a horrible way to cover a perfectly good dick.

11

NASH GAVE me a look that left me somewhere between wet panties and wanting to hide behind the chair.

"What were you thinking?" he growled.

I returned his glare without flinching. "I was thinking Dyson needed help to escape," I replied evenly. "The chance presented itself and I took it. How did you know where to find me anyway?"

"I saw them take Dyson out of the building," Matt said. "They put him in the car and left. When I couldn't find you, I figured you'd done something stupid." He gave me a scathing look.

I narrowed my eyes at him, but heat rose up my cheeks. "Dyson needed my help."

"Yes, Dyson did," Dyson agreed. "Without Peyton, the car wouldn't have crashed. Well, not like that." He turned to me. "Good job, by the way."

"Thank you." At least someone appreciated me.

"Thank you for helping my brother." Kane sat beside me on the couch and squeezed my hand.

"We would have managed perfectly well without her," Matt said darkly. "Nash could have just pulled the roof off the car and grabbed Dyson. You were there to help *find* Dyson, that was all."

"Right," I replied, "and there's no way you would have done what I did, hmmm?" I stared him down until he glanced away.

"For what it's worth, I think Peyton is very brave," Ariana declared. "If I had been there, I probably would have peed my pants."

Hamish nodded his agreement.

I shot them a grateful smile. "I might have almost done that." After a moment I sighed deeply. "All right, fine. I admit jumping into the car wasn't the smartest thing to do, but it seemed right at the time."

"Did it ever occur to you," Nash said, his tone menacingly soft, "that the whole thing was a trap to draw you in?"

It hadn't. It should have. The blood drained out of my face and I swallowed.

"Of course not," I said after a while. "You wouldn't have sent me there if it was."

His eyebrow quirked upward. "Never assume." He knew I was right though, I saw it in his eyes. He had chosen the safest place to send me. He and Kane had gone to the most dangerous. Only, he had miscalculated. Or had he?

"What did you find?" I asked bluntly. "Where you went. What was so terrible you had to risk yourself?" If he or Kane had gotten hurt, I would have been devastated. My heart ached at the very idea. Would any of them mind if I locked us all away somewhere Zeta couldn't find us?

Of course they would. None of the guys would let Zeta stop them from living their lives.

Nash looked away, toward the window. The same window where, just last night, Kane and I had...put on a show.

I swallowed hard at the memory. "Nash." My voice squeaked a little. "What did you find?"

He exhaled heavily. "It was..."

"It was empty," Kane finished for him. "Whatever they had been doing there, they're gone now."

"Empty is better than—" I paused. "Wait, you think they knew you were coming?" For some reason, my gaze went to Matt.

His face reddened and he scowled. "If you're thinking I told them, you can fuck off right now."

"No, I know you didn't," I said quickly. He had risked his life over and over. If he worked for Zeta, he wouldn't have done that. "Nash, you thought someone told them about where the academy was when it was in Sydney?"

Nash nodded slowly. "The only people who knew about our excursion are in this room." He scrutinised everyone. "Hamish, how did you come to be here with us?"

While Hamish's face turned white, Ariana sat forward in front of him.

"He's with me," she said firmly. "I trust him."

"Can we trust you?" Nash asked.

"Yes, you can!" Ariana's eyes shone with tears. "All I've wanted here was to help, and to keep Peyton safe."

"She's on our side," Matt said firmly. "Her aunt is on the council. Has it occurred to anyone, maybe Dyson didn't get caught?"

"What the fuck, man?" Dyson shook his head. "You can't be implying what I *think* you are?"

"I watched him get caught," Kane said, his face pink with fury. "My brother would never—"

"What about *you* then?" Matt asked.

Kane launched himself out of his chair toward Matt.

Nash was faster. He leapt up and caught Kane's shoulders and held him back.

"Let me go," Kane growled. "I'm going to deck the motherfucker."

"That's what I'm afraid of," Nash said, more calm than I would have been under the circumstances. "We don't need to resort to violence. Matt, Kane, and Dyson, I trust you all implicitly or you wouldn't be allowed in Peyton's company."

Now it was my turn to get angry. "You don't get to decide who I spend time with."

Nash stepped back from Kane and fixed me with an unapologetic look. "If I knew they were working with Zeta, getting expelled from the academy would be the least of their worries."

I swallowed. I had no doubt he meant what he said. If anyone betrayed us, Nash might just bite their heads off.

He glanced around the room. "Consider that a warning. Neither I nor the council have patience for spies, especially ones who would lead to any of us ending bac...ending up in a Zeta laboratory. Understood?"

"Yes, sir," I replied.

He gave me a smouldering look, then glared at Hamish and Ariana before he took his seat again.

Kane flopped down beside me. I put an arm around his shoulder and leaned into him.

"Are you all right?" I asked softly.

He glanced toward Matt. "Yeah. I just don't like anyone casting aspersions on my brother."

Matt shrugged. "Sorry, I guess. Emotions are high right now."

"Yeah." Kane gave me a squeeze, then locked his gaze on mine. "Yeah they are." The look in his eyes turned from anger to desire.

I raised my eyebrows. I knew exactly what he was thinking. Right here, in front of all these people?

He gave me a nod and dipped his mouth down toward mine. He slipped his arms around my neck and let his tongue dance with mine.

"I guess we're done here," Matt remarked. I thought he might get up and leave then, but he didn't. Fine, he couldn't blame me for anything he saw.

Kane pulled his mouth from mine and kissed his way down my cheek to my neck.

"If you don't want to watch, you should leave," he said, his voice muffled. "But we don't mind if you stay."

I murmured my agreement. It turned into a moan as he cupped my breast and rubbed his palm over my nipple.

Ariana and Hamish snuck out of the room. I assumed they had their own plans.

From the corner of my eye I saw Dyson stand, too. I assumed he was leaving. I was disappointed, but I understood. Instead, he moved toward the door, locked it and returned to his seat.

Well then.

Kane lay me back on the couch and kissed my mouth while he tugged my shirt up off my breasts.

I flushed slightly, but at this point I dared not look at anyone. Knowing they watched excited me enough to almost make me come on the spot. I sat up just enough to pull off my t-shirt and drape it over the arm of a chair.

When I lay back down, Kane crouched beside me, his body angled so as to not block the view too much. He kissed my mouth, my jaw and down my chest to claim a nipple between his lips.

I groaned softly and turned my face. I caught sight of Matt, his eyes wide, hand on the bulge in his pants. Nash sat with a raised eyebrow, but he seemed to have forgotten how to blink.

I turned my attention back to Kane and helped him out of his shirt before he undid my jeans and worked them down my hips. I kicked them off while he ran his fingers over the front of my panties.

"You're amazing," he said softly.

I smiled. I wasn't sure if I was that amazing, but I knew this was pretty much his wildest wet dream coming true, right here.

"So are you," I replied. "I want you."

He licked his lips and hooked his fingers into the sides of my panties. In one motion, he had them down my legs to my feet. I kicked them aside.

"Sit up a bit," he said, breathless. He took my arm and leaned me against the side of the couch. He knelt beside me and parted my legs with his hands, opening me up for everyone to see.

If you'd told me a year ago I would want to do this, I would have laughed. Now, I wanted it very, very much. I half closed my eyes, but left them open enough to see Matt's hand disappear down the front of his track pants. Nash watched with interest, hands crossed over his chest. Dyson's face was unreadable, but he didn't look away.

Kane slipped a finger inside me, then another. In full view of everyone, he thrust in deep. He rubbed the heel of his hand against my clit while his fingers massaged my g-spot. With his other hand, he rolled my nipple between his thumb and forefinger.

I bucked against his hand, well aware my breasts rose and fell with each movement.

"I'm going to come," I said loud enough for everyone to hear.

"Come for me," Kane urged. "Come for *us*."

That was enough to push me over the edge. I crested hard, but left room for more.

Kane pulled his fingers out of me and removed his jeans and boxer shorts. He frowned for a moment, then sat on the couch and pulled me onto his lap, facing away from him. His hands on my hips, he guided me down onto his cock.

I moaned as he filled me. I almost lost it again at the look on Dyson's face. He watched my whole body rise and fall as Kane helped me ride him.

I held out a hand toward Dyson. I didn't want to pressure him. I knew he wanted me, and preferred to take things slowly. I respected that, but I wanted him to touch me, too.

He hesitated, then took my hand and moved over slowly to kneel beside me. Almost reverently, he cupped one breast, then the other. He rubbed my hard peaks, then replaced his hands with his mouth. He licked and sucked my nipples like a man who hadn't eaten in days.

His hand slipped down between my legs and rubbed my clit in time with his brother's thrusts.

I moaned loudly. Between them both, I was hotter than I could ever imagine.

"Dyson," I whispered.

He looked me in the eyes and licked his lips.

I gave him a quick nod.

He rose and pushed his track pants down his hips to expose his rock-hard erection. He cupped my cheek with his hand and eased his cock into my mouth.

The groan I heard this time was from Matt. His eyes looked glazed and he wasn't even trying to hide that he was pleasuring himself. That only drove me wilder still. I remembered my fantasy on the bus about Nash's mouth on Matt's cock, but Nash hadn't moved.

I closed my eyes and teased the tip of Dyson's cock with my tongue.

He panted and wound his hand through my hair. "Gods, woman, your mouth is…" He panted again.

I sucked hard and reached up to massage his balls.

He thrust between my lips. His hand held me tight.

Somehow both brothers moved in perfect synch. Having both of them inside me at once drove me hard and fast toward the edge and over. As I came again, I wondered what it would be like to have Nash or Matt in my rear hole. That made me come for a third time.

Kane grunted and thrust harder before he too came. Dyson was a moment behind him, his hot cum filling my mouth.

I sagged back against Kane and let Dyson slide himself loose.

"Wow," Kane breathed.

I murmured my agreement. "We should do this again sometime."

"Definitely." Dyson sat beside us and lightly rubbed the back of his hand over my nipples. "Sometime soon."

12

"So, your boyfriends got back alive, huh? How many died for that?"

I turned off my phone and glanced over my shoulder. "What do you want, Xav?"

He flopped down beside me. "You know what I want."

I sighed. "I'm not leaving until the rest of the AMM leaves too."

"I'm sure that could be arranged," he said dryly.

"Again with the threats." I crossed my arms over my chest. My gargoyle tattoo was clearly visible. He eyed it with what looked like amusement. This from a guy who had—I glanced over. Damn, he wore long sleeves. If he had any kind of guardian, I couldn't see it. Hells, for all I knew, he might be a shifter. Probably a lame one, like a flea.

"I told you before, it's not a threat," he said coolly. "But that's actually not what I'm here for."

Don't ask, don't ask, don't—

"What *are* you here for?"

Damn it, Peyton.

"I want to challenge you to a duel." He watched me through half-lidded eyes.

"A duel? As in, pistols at dawn?"

He chuckled. "Nothing that barbaric. I meant a magical duel. I'm a wizard, you're a witch. Neither of us is a hybrid."

"You assume."

"I know," he said firmly.

"For someone who doesn't like me, you seem to know a lot about me."

"I make it a point to know my enemy."

I raised my eyebrows. "Enemy? That's a bit dramatic, don't you think?"

"Not at all. It's the name I give to anyone who might get me killed."

"Ahhh." I nodded. "I would call them Zeta."

"If you don't leave, they could kill us all." His eyes darkened.

"If I leave, they still might," I pointed out.

"If they do, it will be because you led them here."

I leaned toward him, almost nose to nose. "I can assure you, with absolute certainty that I did not." I sat back. "Mr Nash surmised there was a mole in the academy. Someone who is working for them."

"So you brought that mole here?" His eyes snapped.

"Not me personally, no," I said as calmly as I could. "The UA administration invited us. If you're looking for someone to blame, maybe you should start there."

My words hit home, I saw it on his face. He sat back and rubbed his chin.

"Go onto Twitter and rant," I suggested, fully knowing he couldn't.

He curled his lip at me. "I still want you and yours gone. In the meantime, my offer of a duel stands."

"Are we allowed to duel?" I asked.

"Of course not," he said lightly.

"Let me guess, if we get caught, we get thrown out?" I cocked my head at him.

"We won't get caught."

"I'm sure you'll make sure *you* don't get caught."

He narrowed his eyes. "Whatever you might think of me, I don't cheat. I want you gone, but I'm not going to set you up to do it."

"I'm supposed to buy that?" I asked. "To be honest, it sounds like the perfect way to ruin my life."

He considered for a moment. "You're right, it does, but that's not how I roll. Duels have rules we both have to follow."

"Let me guess. If you win, I leave."

He nodded.

"And if I win, what then?"

He smirked. "You won't."

"Cocky bastard, aren't you?" I rolled my eyes. He was at least as annoying as Matt, without the mysterious gargoyle shifter thing to make him more appealing.

"I know my own abilities," he said. "If you win, I'll back off."

"How about you just back off?" I suggested. "Surely you have better things to do than bother me every day?"

"You'd think so, wouldn't you," he agreed. "But I'm driven. I won't stop until UA is safe again."

For a moment I seriously considered getting up and walking away. Not just from him but from the academy. I could study teaching at a normal university. Maybe one out of reach of Zeta. Was there a university in the South Pole? Everyone could get on with their lives without me to put them in danger.

I almost laughed out loud at myself. Zeta wouldn't give up. As long as they and I existed, they would be after me. More than that, they would be after every paranormal on and off campus. Whatever they wanted Dyson for, they would still need him or some other dog shifter.

This whole thing was much, much bigger than me.

I shook my head. "I would need something more when I win. More than you leaving me alone." I rubbed my forehead. A headache was threatening at the edges of it. "What about a favour you can't refuse?"

He knitted his brows. "What kind of favour?"

I shrugged. "I don't know. If you're so sure you'll win, there's no risk of you having to worry about it, is there?"

He nodded slowly. "That's true." He stuck his hand out to me. "I'll see you out on the running field at ten pm."

"What, not midnight?" I eyed his hand before I shook it.

"No reason not to hold it at a civilised hour." He held my hand a few moments too long before he let it go and stood. "You can bring two others. One to peel you off the grass when we're done and one as a judge. Your judge and mine will confer and decide on a winner if it's not too obvious. You know, when you run away screaming."

I laughed. "As if that will happen."

He shrugged with one shoulder. "You say that now." He took a few steps away before he turned back. "Oh, and no teachers."

"Why would I bring one of them?" I asked, trying to keep any thoughts off my face.

He regarded me for a long moment, as if attempting to figure something out. "No reason," he said finally. He gave a curt nod and walked away.

I was almost certain he didn't know anything about Nash and me. Perhaps he *thought* he knew, and had been hoping to catch me off guard. He'd have to try harder than that. I was always on the lookout for anyone who might ask about him and any relationship we might have. Still, knowing Xav was suspicious was a good reason to be extra careful. I doubted he'd pull any punches when it came to anyone from AMM, teacher or student.

"What did he want?" Dyson flopped down on the grass beside me. Kane joined us a moment later.

I told them about the duel and the deal Xav and I had made.

"Do you think I'm crazy for agreeing to it?" I gave them a tentative look.

Kane returned it with a lopsided smile. "It's not as if you'll lose." He sounded so confident I almost believed him.

"I might," I replied.

"You won't." Dyson leaned in to kiss my mouth lightly. "You'll leave him all over the grass out there." He waved toward the running field.

I chewed my lip. "I hope so, or I'm out."

"If you're out—" Kane started.

I pressed my fingertips to his lips. "Don't say it. You need to be here. Both of you. What you guys want to do with your lives, you can't learn at a normal university. You belong here."

"We could defer until AMM has a different campus," Kane said. He and Dyson exchanged glances.

"Right, we could," Dyson agreed.

"We could have done that to start with," I pointed out. "If we did, then Zeta wins. Or the UA brats win. Either way, someone else is deciding things for us. Why let that happen? We have as much right to be here as anyone else."

"And that's why you'll win," Dyson said. "But you should see Matt before you do anything else."

"Why?" No doubt Matt would call me a bloody fool for even thinking of accepting the challenge. Who was I kidding? He would take any excuse he could find to lecture me on whatever failing I had that day.

Dyson gave me an adorable lop-sided smile which made my heart skip. He really was so stinking cute. Both twins were.

"Because," Dyson said slowly, "he can add a few more tattoos to your arm."

My eyebrows shot up. "Is that allowed?"

Dyson shrugged. "I don't see why not. Xav has kept his collection close to his chest, so to speak."

"Right." I remembered his long sleeves. They could be hiding almost anything. I hadn't even seen an outline under the fabric.

"Without knowing what you're up against, you have to be ready for anything," Kane concluded.

"Exactly." Dyson nodded. "He might have a giant reptile tattooed on himself."

"You think he might fight with Godzilla?" I asked. What a cliché that would be.

Dyson grinned. "Why not? I know I would."

"He really would," Kane agreed. "He's been obsessed with Godzilla since we were kids."

"I always preferred King Kong myself," I replied, "but no judgement either way. I mean, better those than Mothra." I grinned at the look on Kane's face. "Don't tell me, you're a Mothra guy?"

He shrugged. "At least Mothra could fly."

"True." I half switched off as the guys chatted about various super-heroes and monsters they enjoyed or reading about. I love a good monster or superhero movie, but my mind was on the duel.

Honestly, I had a better idea of what Zeta might throw at me than Xav. Phoenixes, griffins, jerks with guns. Xav might have—the gods knew what. I would need to have something up my sleeve. As much as I didn't want to admit it, that meant asking Matt for help. He would probably have a much better idea about all of this than I did.

I sighed to myself. Undoubtedly he'd give me all the information I needed, while telling me off the whole time for getting involved in something I shouldn't.

And getting him involved.

And—

"Wouldn't you agree?" Kane asked. He draped an arm over my shoulder.

"With what?" I asked, confused.

Dyson chuckled. "I told you she wasn't listening."

I socked Dyson playfully on the arm. "Maybe you two should get more tattoos, too."

Kane looked thoughtful. "Of what? A unicorn like Ariana?" A grin tugged at the corners of his mouth.

I smiled slightly in return. "Sure, why not, that would be cute. Rainbow mane and all. Although, I think you'd suit pink better."

Dyson laughed. "I dare you."

Kane grimaced. "Not a chance. Unless you do it first."

Dyson held up his hands. "No way. A Pegasus maybe. A black one, with a streak of red in its mane."

"That would be cool," Kane agreed. "We could all get one."

I wondered if all would include Nash. If so, where would he have it? Somewhere no one would see it but me, most likely. Maybe his ass.

I licked my lips at *that* visual image. I would happily run the tip of my tongue over his taut skin and...

"Come on, let's go and find Matt." Kane stood and offered me his hand.

Dyson did the same a moment later.

I grabbed a hand in each of mine and let them pull me to my feet. Hand in hand, we walked back toward the academy building, a growing sense of unease in my belly.

This duel could go badly, very badly.

13

"THE RULES ARE," Xav's friend Gunter regarded all of those gathered with the same disdain, even Xav, "no deadly hand to hand combat. No conventional weapons like guns and knives. The combatant must recall any creature they create prior to the death of their opponent. Failure to do the latter will award the victory to the opponent."

I grimaced. Winning wouldn't be much use if one was dead.

"They don't usually end in death," Matt said helpfully.

I eyed him sideways. Once I'd told him what was going on and he'd finished telling me I was an idiot, he had insisted on being my judge. If anyone would be impartial, it would be him. He knew what I had at stake, but he wouldn't make a ruling in my favour just because we were...whatever we were to each other. Friends, maybe, in spite of sharing a kiss. Friends with sexual attraction. That was frustrating, but undeniable.

"Usually?" I asked.

He shrugged. "Accidents happen. Don't worry, that won't happen here, I'll make sure of it."

"Are you trying to say you care?" I asked, giving him a half smile.

He arched an eyebrow and gave me a look which I couldn't quite interpret. Something which suggested his feelings for me ran deeper than he let on, or wanted to admit to himself.

My eyes locked on his. Warmth traveled through me. It was more than sexual attraction. I had come to care for him, even though he drove me crazy. Maybe *because* he did. At least life wasn't dull with him around.

He broke the contact first.

"Of course not, but I'd get my head bitten off if I let you come to any harm," he said easily.

He didn't need to say who would do the biting. We both knew Nash would be furious if anything happened to me.

"I'd peck his eyes out," Kane said with a nod toward Matt. He and Dyson had played rock, paper, scissors to determine which of them would accompany Matt and I. As consolation, Dyson would take me out to dinner. I guess that meant I won either way, as long as I didn't lose the duel.

"Of course you would." Matt shot Kane a flat look. "If you could catch me to do it."

Kane grinned. "I could wait until Dyson had you pinned down first."

Whatever Matt thought of that, he didn't get the chance to say.

Gunter cleared his throat loudly and gestured toward the field in the middle of the running track.

"Duellers, take your places."

Matt gave me a wave to move to my designated spot—a line of paint sprayed on the grass. It glowed softly, but would fade in daylight so no one would know what we'd been up to.

Xav swaggered to his line and curled his lip at me. "A little over-dressed, aren't you?"

I cocked my head at him. "Huh?"

He smirked. "I hear you like to put on a show. At least you'll have a career as a porn star when this is over."

I hoped the darkness hid my blush. "That's your angle? Slut sham-ing? You'll have to try harder than that."

He grinned. "I bet you say that to all the guys."

I shrugged. "Not really. My lovers know what they're doing. Do I sense some insecurity in that department?"

His smile faded. "No. I'm fully secure in my manhood."

"Sure you are." I nodded slowly. "Are we going to do it or not?"

"We're not..." He spluttered before he must have realised what I was actually referring to.

I smiled. In the corner of my eye I saw Matt and Kane laughing. Even Xav's support, a woman named Kylie, looked to be chuckling.

I was so distracted I almost missed Xav's arm shoot up. Magic poured out the end, to land on the grass in front of me. Before it could even form into anything cohesive, I threw up a bubble of magic around myself and went invisible.

"Cheat," Xav hissed.

"There's no rule against it." I ran several steps to the side as a giant snake appeared on the grass. It hissed and looked around itself, tongue out as if to taste the air.

What did I know about snakes? Didn't they sense vibrations? I stomped my foot on the ground. The snake's head swung toward the sound. I tiptoed away so when the snake slid over and struck, it touched only air.

How was its eyesight? I dropped my bubble and gave it a wave. No response. Well then, I could conserve some energy.

I tiptoed further away while Xav grumbled under his breath. I dearly wanted to strike back, but Matt and I had discussed my plan— okay, he'd told me what I needed to do to turn the odds in my favour, but it made sense.

With a faint pop, the snake disappeared. Xav stalked toward me, his brow creased in a scowl. He looked like he wanted to aim a blast of magic at me and end this here and now. He didn't. He must have known killing me would probably result in him getting kicked out of UA.

That, and I didn't believe he wanted me dead. No, he wanted to humiliate me and beat me fair and square. He wanted to watch me leave the academy grounds, my lovers a step behind me. In this scenario, he wanted to be some kind of hero.

What an asshole.

"That the best you've got?" I taunted. "Your snake? It was a bit small, wasn't it? Not very efficient, either."

Xav gave me an ugly smile. "I figured you'd stop and suck it. I bet you'd like it deep down the back of your throat."

"Again with you projecting your thoughts onto me." I clicked my tongue. "Have you ever considered therapy?"

"Since I met you I have," he said.

I shook my head. "And they say sex addiction isn't real."

"As if I'd fuck you," he sneered.

"Right back at you," I told him. I watched his body carefully so when he raised his arm again, I was ready.

An enormous spider appeared on the grass a couple of metres away.

I shuddered.

"Scared of a little spider?" Xav taunted.

Little spiders, no. There was nothing small about this thing. Or its...were they teeth? Fangs?Whatever, they looked wicked sharp.

It turned toward me and started forward on all eight, hairy limbs. It scurried faster than I would have thought anything that big could move.

I struck out with a blast of magic when it was barely a hand's length away.

Magic struck the creature on the front of its head and made it recoil. It threw up its front two legs as if to ward off another blow.

I might have felt sorry for the spider, but it wasn't real. For a bug created by magic, it was impressive, even though it was creepy as hells.

I took a few steps back.

The spider lowered its front legs and matched me step for step.

I thought I heard Xav snicker. I assumed he was ready to call off the spider the moment it had me pinned, ready to bite. That would give him the win, probably in record time.

He wished.

I aimed another blast of magic, but this one landed behind the spider.

Xav barked a laugh, but the spider turned toward the gouge in the grass, its attention drawn long enough for me to direct a long blast toward the middle of its body.

The spider shuddered, then popped out of existence.

Xav swore. The spider was replaced by a bear.

I made myself invisible and ducked just before a claw swiped past my head. That would have taken off my face if I hadn't been so quick. Matt had been right, Xav was getting angry and sloppy.

The bear growled. Any louder and it might have woken the academy. So much for secrecy.

It turned and sniffed the air, reminding me of the Zeta agent I'd nicknamed Cerberus.

I backed up a few more paces. It followed, tracking my scent.

A waterslide might be handy right now, to distract the bear. Maybe with enough water, it would wash away. I had considered asking Matt to tattoo one on my arm, but decided against it on the grounds it would look bizarre. I wanted to defend myself, not look like an idiot while I did it.

I caught sight of Xav, arms crossed over his chest, a cocky expression on his face. He was obviously convinced the bear would hunt me down and pin me. It might do the first, but I wouldn't let it do the second.

I circled around behind Xav, until he was between the bear and me. I dropped the bubble of magic and waved my arms in the air.

"Hey, over—"

Xav must have anticipated the move. He spun and shot off a blast of magic. Perfectly contained for maximum punch without being deadly, it threw me off my feet.

I flew back several metres and hit hard enough to knock the wind out of me.

I lay stunned as Kane shouted for me to get up.

"Peyton! The bear!"

Fuck.

I rolled in time to avoid missing a paw that would have pressed me to the ground. It was a much more controlled manoeuvre than the initial paw swipe. That suggested Xav managed to draw back his emotions somewhat.

The bear stumbled forward and almost fell. Before it hit the ground, it disappeared.

Xav growled and aimed another blast of magic at me, but missed. Apparently his emotions were volatile.

Good.

I jumped to my feet and blasted Xav with my own magic. He jumped aside with more agility than I would have expected for someone of his size, and shot back.

I nimbly sidestepped.

If I was going to do something, it would have to be soon.

He came at me again, with blast after blast. Each one got slightly weaker than the one before. He was starting to tire. The effort of creating the magical beasts had started to tell on him.

Just as Matt said it would.

"He's an arrogant hothead," Matt has explained while he inked my arm. "He'll try to throw everything at you in the hope of overpowering you quickly. Hold him off and let him wear himself out. Then you can go at him with everything you have. And this—this will do the trick."

I raised my wrist. In striking detail, like all of Matt's work, the tiger stood ready to strike. Silent, precise, powerful...or so I hoped.

The big cat leapt off my arm and stalked Xav. He backed away, eyes wide, even though he must have known the big cat couldn't kill him. Or at least, it wouldn't.

He jumped to the side as the tiger leapt. It landed lightly and twisted, immediately continuing the hunt.

Xav raised trembling hands and blasted the tiger on the chest.

The tiger let out a soft growl and faltered slightly.

Xav grinned and blasted it again. "Is this your secret weapon, bitch?" he taunted. "It's a bit useless."

"Not as useless as yours," I replied. I focused on the tiger, reinforcing it so when it swiped at Xav with its paw, the blow was careful and aimed well enough to knock him off his feet.

Xav let out a squeak as the tiger pounced. It pinned him to the ground with an enormous paw.

"Judges!" I beckoned them over.

Matt was grinning.

Gunter still looked bored. "It's clear, the winner is—"

Xav blasted the tiger in the face. It roared and rolled off before it disappeared.

"This isn't over yet." Xav climbed to his feet, hands raised. "Not even close."

I glanced toward Matt, who shrugged.

"Keep duelling."

Fuck.

14

I MADE a bubble and disappeared just as Xav did the same. I anticipated the move after I had used it. That would make this all the more challenging.

I took a shallow breath and stood completely still, eyes and ears open.

I thought I heard a shuffle. I heard my breath. There it was again. I grinned.

Xav was taller and heavier than me. Every step he took pressed the grass down under his shoes. He might as well have announced his presence. Lucky for me, the moon had done that for me.

Footprint, footprint, footprint. The grass bounced back behind him, but I watched his slow, careful process as he went. The shuffling stopped. He must have realised the sound was audible. As long as he didn't realise the grass betrayed his presence, I could use it to my advantage.

The question was, what did I do with this information? I chewed my lip and thought.

I couldn't blast him while he was in a bubble. His bubble could absorb my magic and give him the chance to throw it back at me.

While possibly not deadly, it would knock me off my feet again, and make me vulnerable to whatever else he had up his sleeve.

I rubbed the new tattoo on my arm, carefully crafted beside the first one. No creature I created would get past his bubble, no matter how badass.

Unless…

I followed his steps with my eyes as he circled around to where I thought he might be. I pictured him waving his arm in front of him, but touching nothing. I almost felt his frustration. I smiled. Good, let him get angry and careless.

I stalked toward him on tiptoe, each step silent and light. When I got close enough, I turned to the side and stuck out my leg.

Xav stepped forward and tripped.

"What the fuck?" In his surprise, he dropped his bubble and appeared in front of me on his hands and knees. Shame I didn't have time for any snide remarks. A few good ones came to mind.

Before he could think to respond, I dropped my own bubble and slammed him the rest of the way to the ground with a fist of magic. He flailed his arms and legs, but I wasn't going to let him up, not until this was done.

"How long do I have to wait?" I asked over my shoulder.

"For the count of ten," Gunter replied.

I was glad he was the one who answered. It made Xav even more furious, and gave more legitimacy to my win.

Xav muttered something I couldn't make out. I pressed my magic down a little harder.

"What was that?" I cocked my head at him.

"Piss off," he growled.

"Charming." I smiled sweetly. "One. Two. Three…" I counted slowly.

"Four. Five." Matt moved to stand beside me, a grin on his face.

We counted together. "Six. Seven. Eight. Nine."

"Ten." Gunter said firmly. "Peyton wins. Let him up." Without another word, he turned and walked away.

I shrugged and lifted the magic from Xav's chest.

He jumped to his feet. For a moment I thought he might leap at me. Instead, he curled his lip and stalked back toward the UA building, Kylie on his heels.

"Nothing like a good loser," I said sarcastically. A moment later I was almost bowled over by Kane in his enthusiasm to hug me.

"I can't believe you actually won by tripping him." Kane laughed and kissed my lips. "I bet he didn't expect that."

I kissed him back, then leaned back to smile at him. "That was the general idea. Use your enemy's weakness against them. He was bigger, heavier and cockier."

"I don't know about cockier," Matt said.

I stuck my tongue out at him. "If I'm a handful, it's only because you're rubbing off on me."

"You wish," he murmured, but the look he gave me suggested he was the one doing the wishing.

I didn't know what to say to that. It wasn't as though I hadn't imagined us tearing each other's clothes off. Gods, just the thought made me wet.

"It's a little cold out here for that," Kane said, sounding regretful.

I blinked. It was? I felt kinda hot… Oh, I guess he was right, when I thought about it.

"Yeah, um, I guess we should go inside then." I glanced at Matt, but his face was turned away.

"Dyson will want to know you won," Kane said, seemingly oblivious to whatever this was between Matt and I.

"Yes he will," I agreed. Thinking about Dyson was a lot less complicated than thinking about Matt. Or Nash for that matter. If he found out what I had done, he'd be furious. Thank the gods I had won. Maybe now I wouldn't have to explain.

"WHAT THE HELLS WERE YOU THINKING?" Speak of the dragon… Nash stood beside the door which led into the UA, arms crossed over his chest. His gaze took me in, mouth set in a firm line, but eyes betraying the depths of his feelings for me. He was worried. More than that, he cared about me as more than a lover. I could have happily drowned in that look. What did I do to deserve the affection of any of these guys?

I gave Nash a smile. "I was thinking…it might be a nice night for a walk, sir."

He didn't buy it for a second, I saw that on his face as well. He glared at Kane and Matt. "Both of you as well. I should have you all tossed out on your asses."

"But you won't, will you, sir?" I stepped closer, put a hand on his chest and looked up at him. "I did win after all. Xav will leave us alone *and* he owes me a favour."

"You could have lost." Nash was still angry, but the edge came off his voice slightly.

"Then we would have dealt with it," I said firmly. I stopped and frowned. "How did you know anyway?"

Nash gave me a soft, but somewhat sheepish look. "I came looking for you. Imagine my annoyance when Ariana told me what you were up to."

"Oh." What was done, was done.

"I guess you better make it up to me," he said softly.

"No offence, sir, but Dyson will want to know Peyton won," Kane said.

"Then go and tell him." Nash didn't take his eyes off my face.

"But—" Kane sighed. "I don't think that's fair, sir, pulling rank. Maybe we should ask what Peyton wants."

Oh great, now I was under pressure. I glanced at Kane and frowned.

"Maybe I don't want to choose."

"Rock, paper, scissors." Kane held out his hand.

Nash arched an eyebrow at him. "Really? Are we in high school?"

"It feels like it sometimes, sir." I pointed out. "I mean, Xav acted like it."

"That doesn't mean we should." In spite of that, Nash stuck out his hand. Both guys shook their fists and revealed their choice.

"Paper beats rock, sir," Kane said, delighted.

Nash scowled, but stepped back. "Fine. I'll step aside gracefully. For now."

I shot him a smile as Kane laced his hand in mine. "Sorry, sir. Later."

He nodded. "Be glad there will be a later."

I grinned and turned away to see Matt still standing behind me. His expression was unreadable.

I let Kane's hand go and moved toward Matt.

"Thanks for all your help," I said softly. I leaned up to kiss him lightly on the mouth.

As least, that was my intention. One of us deepened the kiss, and before I knew it, we had dancing tongues, and breath coming in pants.

I don't know who pulled away first, but we snapped apart. Before I could say another word, Matt turned on his heel and was gone.

"Okay then," I said under my breath.

"Try not to let him bother you," Kane said. "He's confused."

"*He's* confused?" I asked. "He's not the only one. I don't know whether I'm coming or going with him." Although I was pretty sure I wasn't coming.

Kane slung an arm over my shoulder. "At least with me, you know where you stand. And in case you don't, I'm head over heels for you."

I gave him a soft smile. "You're a special guy and I care about you a lot." Was it love? It was pretty damned close. The only problem with love was, I'd have to make a choice. Wouldn't I? I still wasn't ready for that. I wasn't sure I would ever be. Life was complicated enough without having to break anyone's heart.

Kane gave me a soft kiss on the mouth and we walked together across the grass.

"You did amazing tonight, er, this morning," Kane said. "The tiger was cool, but using something as simple as tripping a guy..." He chuckled. "I wish more people were around to see it."

I grinned. "I bet Xav is glad there wasn't. Beaten by a girl, with the help of the oldest trick in the book."

"He was so sure he would win. He'll be licking his wounds for a while." Kane opened the door leading into his room and gestured for me to go first.

"I hope so," I replied. "Where's Dyson?"

Kane frowned. "He should be here." He poked the top bunk with a few fingers, but no grunts of protest came in response. "It looks slept in."

"Maybe he went to the toilet?" I suggested.

"I guess so. Or he decided to give us some privacy." Kane stepped closer to me and wound his arms around me.

"That's possible, but we would have found somewhere else if he wanted us to."

Something about this didn't feel right. We had surmised that someone from the AMM had been working for Zeta. They could have snuck onto campus while Kane, Matt, and I were distracted and snatched Dyson from under our noses. If they still wanted him for their experiment then they could have—"

"Oh hey, guys." Dyson walked in through the door as though nothing was up. He tucked his phone into his back pocket. "How did things go?" He seemed distracted.

"Good. I turned Kane into a purple elephant and he stepped all over Xav," I replied.

"Great, great." Dyson nodded, then frowned. My words apparently sunk in. "Wait, what?"

I chuckled. "I won."

"Right, good. Of course you did." He kissed my cheek and pulled off his shirt. "Well, it's late and I need my beauty sleep."

I exchanged confused looks with Kane, who shrugged.

"We'll go somewhere else for a while then," Kane said awkwardly.

"Okay." Dyson stashed his phone under his pillow, slid out of his pants and climbed up onto his bunk.

"Are you feeling all right?" Kane asked him.

"Sure, just tired." Dyson rolled over so his back was to us and pulled the covers over himself.

"Oookay." Kane rubbed his forehead.

"Maybe we should do this another time," I suggested. Dyson was right about one thing, it was late. We'd have to be in class in a few hours.

"I'm sorry," Kane whispered.

I patted his shoulder and pressed a kiss to his mouth. "It's fine. It'll give me something to look forward to." As much as I enjoyed getting down and dirty with Kane, his place was here with his brother. "Let me know if either of you need anything."

I gave Dyson, or his back at least, a long look. He seemed to be asleep already, but I sensed he was at least partially aware I was still in the room. Had I done something to offend him? I hoped not. At least if I had, I'd like to think he could tell me, so I could fix it.

"I guess I'll see you both at breakfast." I flashed Kane a quick smile, then ducked out the door and closed it behind me. I stood in the corridor for a moment and listened. If the guys were talking, I couldn't hear it.

I realised I shouldn't be eavesdropping and hurried off toward my own room.

15

THE MOOD in the dining hall was strange. I felt it the moment I stepped inside. People stopped talking and looked in my direction. Of course they would; word of the duel would have spread faster than fire on a pile of dry leaves.

But... there was something else. When I looked back, no one would meet my gaze. Phones, which students had been looking at intently, suddenly clicked off.

I frowned at a couple of people, but their eyes were always lower than my face. Always on my...

I flushed. There was no way...

My heart racing, I grabbed some breakfast and hurried to slip into the chair beside Ariana.

"What the hells is going on?" I whispered.

She stared at me with wide eyes. "You haven't seen?"

"Seen what?" I searched her face, but my heart sank deeper and deeper.

"Check your phone," she said in a rough whisper.

I pulled mine out of my pocket and pressed on the screen. "Just a message from—" I peered closely, but didn't recognise the sender. "I have a feeling I shouldn't click on that." I wished it was something as benign as a virus which would wipe all my data before sending itself to all of my contacts and wiping all of theirs. Even a visit from fully armed Zeta agents might be preferable.

I swallowed and pressed on the message.

"What the fuck?" There, in living colour, was the photo Kane had taken of me. I had been halfway to thinking someone had filmed us and sent the video around to the whole school. Somehow, this was so much worse. This photo had been taken in a moment of intimacy, between two people who meant it to stay between them.

At least, that was what I had thought.

Tears prickled my eyes. "How could he have done this to me?" I closed the message and slammed my phone down on the table. How it didn't shatter, I don't know.

"Maybe it wasn't him?" Ariana suggested. She didn't seem even slightly convinced. Kane had taken the photo, how else would it have been sent to—as far as I could tell—the entire, fucking academy?

"I can't decide," I said between clenched teeth. "If I should kill him fast or slow." A little of both, perhaps. I had *trusted* him. Cared about him. What a bloody idiot I had been.

"I'm sure there's an explan—" I cut Ariana off when I leapt to my feet.

"I'm not hungry." I snatched my phone off the table and stomped toward the door.

Every step was followed by snickering and whispers. Didn't they understand? This wasn't some great joke. It wasn't just about me being humiliated. I had been violated, as sure as if I'd been held down and forced. My body, my trust…

Tears slid down my cheeks. I wanted to turn around and blast the entire room until every snide smile and nasty word was gone.

Instead, I swallowed and stepped outside into the autumn sunshine. The moment I felt concrete under my feet, I started to run.

I ran until the concrete gave way to grass. The stupid, fucking skirt flapped at my legs and the tie threatened to wind around my neck. I didn't stop until sweat trickled down my back and breathing became more difficult.

The pain settled into a dull ache in my chest, but I slowed to a walk.

"Peyton!"

Kane's voice was barely audible over the pounding of blood in my ears. That and I didn't want to see him, much less listen to anything he had to say.

"Peyton!" He was closer now.

I ignored him.

"Peyton, please stop and listen!"

I glanced over my shoulder. "Go away, Kane. There's nothing you can say to me I'd want to hear." I caught a look of hurt before I turned away.

"It wasn't me," he called out after me. "I swear on…on my entire collection of Godzilla comics."

I stopped and looked back again. "You have Godzilla comics?"

He shrugged. "We, they're graphic novels. Don't tell anyone I called them comics."

"Right now, I'm inclined to tell *everyone* you called them comics," I said dryly. "But I don't think anyone would care. They're more interested in staring at my tits."

He flushed. "I promised you I would never share that photo, and I didn't. Scout's honour."

"You were a Boy Scout?" I raised an eyebrow at him.

He smiled. "No. Geek's honour then. That's unbreakable." He raised a hand with his fingers spread apart, Vulcan style.

I sighed. I was half way to believing him, but I felt as if that photo had ripped a piece of my heart out. The thing was, I *wanted* to believe him. Not just because I didn't want to think my judgment was so flawed, but because I cared about him. The very idea that someone would stab me in the heart…

I swallowed down a new round of tears. "If you didn't, then who did?"

Kane licked his lips. "I don't know," he said tentatively.

I frowned. My mind conjured up a very unwelcome image of Dyson and his strange behaviour last night.

I shook my head. "You can't possibly think..."

"I don't know," Kane said quickly. "But he was acting weird. This morning, too. He barely looked at me. I tried to talk to him, but he hardly said a thing before he went off to breakfast. He didn't even wait."

My legs gave out. I plopped down on the grass. "I didn't see him at breakfast." Surely I would have noticed him amongst the other students? He certainly hadn't been at the table with Ariana.

"I don't understand why he'd do something like this. Unless..."

Kane sat beside me and put a hand on my knee. "Unless what?" he asked gently.

I shook my head. "Is there any chance Zeta got to him in some way?"

"Why would Zeta want photos of you spread around?" Kane asked.

I shrugged. "To humiliate me?" Yeah, that sounded bizarre to me too. "Maybe they wanted to drive a wedge between us. This would be one way to do it."

"I suppose so." He gave my knee a squeeze. "You do believe me though, don't you? I would never do something like this. Not to *anyone,* but especially not to you. You're not like anyone I've ever met. I wouldn't hurt you, not for anything."

"What if you had to do something to me, in order to save Dyson?" I asked. It wasn't a fair question, but he had to mull over the possibility. The gods only knew what Zeta might try to push us into.

Kane hesitated. "I don't know," he admitted. "I'll do whatever I can to make sure it never comes to that. We can't let them beat us."

"And what about Dyson?" I asked. "If he's working with them..."

Kane looked stricken. "I can't believe he would. There must be some sort of logical explanation for all of this."

"Such as?"

"He could have been sleep walking?"

"Has he ever done that before?" I cocked my head at him.

"No," Kane admitted. "There's a first time for everything though, right?"

I exhaled softly. "I suppose it's possible, but that wouldn't explain why he wouldn't talk to you this morning."

Kane rubbed his chin. He had just enough stubble there to be a little rough, but I liked it. He looked sexy.

"I'm sure it was something which isn't a big deal," he said slowly.

I looked down at the grass, then back up again. "Is it possible he's seeing someone else?" He had told me he wanted to take things slowly with me, but that could be because another person was in the picture.

"No," Kane said so quickly I flinched. "He cares about you as much as I do. He told me so yesterday. Or was it the day before?" He frowned. "Either way, if there was someone he would have told you. And me."

"So, why the photo?" I lay back on the grass and looked up at the blue sky. A cloud scudded above me, wisps of white like lace trailing out behind it.

"We still don't know it was him." Kane lay down beside me and snuck a hand up my skirt. "We should try to talk to him."

"Right, we should," I agreed. "Before we get sidetracked." This was a bit too public for my taste, especially after the morning I'd had.

"I'm sorry." He stroked inside my thigh. "I kinda wish I hadn't taken that photo. Then none of this would have happened."

"If it hadn't been that, it would have been something else."

"I guess so." He snuck a finger under the side of my panties.

I covered my hand with his. "I can't, not out here."

He stopped, then drew out his hand. "I understand. Whoever sent that photo really did a number on you, didn't they?"

I sighed. "Yeah, they really did. Fuckers."

Kane chuckled. "That's my Peyton. Nothing holds you back for long."

I smiled. Part of me wanted to strip and screw him silly, right there in the middle of the running field. To hells with idiots like Xav, or whoever had circulated that photo. Another part of me wanted to pack my belongings and go home to my parents. I try to be badass, but a girl can only take so much humiliation.

"Let's go and find Dyson and get this cleared up." I stood and offered Kane my hand. "Then we can figure out who really sent that photo around."

"Atta girl," Kane rose and squeezed my hand. "I'm sure it'll all be a big misunderstanding."

"Yeah."

But I doubted it. Whoever had sent that message was trying to make my life hells, I was certain of that. If this didn't work, they'd try something else. Then there was the problem of Dyson. Photo or no photo, he was acting cagey as fuck. I thought I knew him well enough to know he didn't act like that without a good reason. The problem was, I wasn't sure I really knew him at all.

"Where would he be right now?" I asked.

"Hmmm. If he's finished breakfast, he's probably in one of the computer labs, studying."

One thing I had to give UA credit for, they had the best computers of any school I had attended. Every centimetre was the latest of everything, and they had granted the AMM students full access to all of it. Oh sure, some of their students bitched, but we ignored them. It wasn't as though we had anywhere else to go to use them. Even if we have computers as good as theirs, our rooms were too small to work in comfort.

"Okay, let's go and see." I took Kane's hand and ignored the looks we got when we approached the school and stepped back into the corridors.

Someone whistled, but I suppressed the urge to send my gargoyle or tiger after them. That would be the perfect way to get thrown out and I might regret the damage my creature caused.

Maybe.

Kane sighed. "I'm really, really sorry. If I'd known..."

I shook my head. "It's not your fault some people are assholes." I hesitated for a moment before I added, "Do you really have a Godzilla comic collection?"

"Graphic novels, but yes." He nodded. "Do you want to read them some time?"

"Sure, why not? My geek card might lapse if I don't take it out for a spin once in a while."

He grinned. "Great. Can I teach you the Vulcan salute?"

I laughed and gave him one. "I nailed that long ago," I said proudly. "Geeks unite."

We laughed, but the sound was strained. It probably would be until we got everything straightened out.

If we did.

16

"HEY, DYS." Kane sounded cheerful, but with an undertone of anxiety in his voice.

Dyson glanced up and smiled. "Hey." His gaze lingered on me, laced with warmth. "What's up? You two look as though you lost that duel last night."

Kane and I exchanged confused looks. His brother seemed to be his usual, jovial self, with no hint of the distance he'd shown earlier.

"Are you feeling okay?" Kane asked him.

"Of course," Dyson replied. "Are you?" He closed the computer in front of him, but I hadn't seen anything on the screen but classwork.

"Did you see the photo someone spread around the school?" I asked. I watched his expression carefully.

Dyson sighed and looked regretful. "I did. I'm sorry about that. Are you okay?"

"You're sorry?" Kane echoed.

Dyson frowned. He picked up a pencil and toyed with the end of it. "Of course. As in, I'm sorry someone was such a dick to you. Who was it?"

I considered for a moment, then pulled over a chair and sat beside him. "We don't know. We hoped you might have some idea."

Dyson tapped the pencil against his lip. "Ideas, sure. Evidence? Nope, none. I would suggest their enrolment form says University of Arcana, rather than Academy of Modern Magic. After what we all went through last year, none of us would attack you. Except..."

"Yes?" I prompted.

"Whoever told Zeta where to find us." Dyson shrugged and placed the pencil down on the table beside the computer.

I shook my head. "I hate to say it, but I think this is old-fashioned schoolyard bullying. Well, the modern version of it. Xav is probably pissed I beat him. The fact he or his friends would hack Kane's phone to get back at me is pretty fucking childish, if you ask me."

"It is," Dyson agreed.

"Why were you acting weird last night?" Kane blurted.

Dyson cocked his head at his brother. "What are you talking about?" He seemed genuinely confused. He looked at me, then back at Kane.

"After the duel, you seemed uninterested. Then again this morning, you barely said a word." Kane leaned against the wall and crossed his arms. "It's not like you. I usually can't shut you up."

Dyson frowned. "I don't even remember seeing you after the duel. I didn't know about it until..." He scratched his head. "I don't know."

"Are you stoned?" Kane asked bluntly.

"Fuck no." Dyson looked horrified at the idea. "You know me, I prefer to be high on life, not illicit substances. Besides, drugs and dogs don't mix."

"That sounds like a bumper sticker," I remarked.

"It does, doesn't it?" Dyson agreed. "Or a t-shirt."

"Or—"

Kane cut me off. "Can we focus, please?" He paused for a moment before he added, "Owls and opiates don't mix sounds better."

Dyson leaned over in his chair to sock Kane on the arm.

"So anyway," I sat back in the chair. "What's the last thing you clearly remember?"

"Um." Dyson rubbed his chin. "I remember having dinner. You looked extra cute with your hair in a ponytail."

I flushed but waved for him to go on.

"I was watching you eat spaghetti and thinking about your mouth. The way you slurp those noodles." He fanned himself with his hand.

"Right?" Kane said. "I've never seen anyone look so hot while eating pasta."

"You guys will give me a big head," I told them.

Dyson pointed to his lap. "It's too late for me."

My gaze ventured lower, to the front of his pants. "So I see. We should probably focus, though."

Both guys sighed simultaneously.

"You're right," Dyson said. "After dinner I came here and got some work done on an essay. After that—" He frowned. "It's foggy."

Kane and I shared a look of concern.

"Is mind control magic a thing?" Kane asked.

"Not that I'm aware of," I replied. "What about shifters? Is there some way to influence your actions?" Kane was studying paranormal science. If anyone would know, it was him.

Kane shook his head slowly. "Just the usual substances normals are susceptible to: alcohol, narcotics, sugar."

"Kids and sugar is universal," Dyson remarked. "But the only sugar I've had all week was a donut."

I immediately started to crave one of the sweet treats. AMM would have had them on the menu, but no such luck here.

"How did you get a donut?" Kane asked. "I don't remember you leaving campus for a sugar hit."

Dyson frowned. "One of the women in my history class had some. She was handing them out. She even brought in a pink one for me, because she knew I can't eat chocolate."

I frowned. "Who is this woman?"

"Jealous?" Kane asked.

"Suspicious," I said firmly, "of her."

"She's new to the academy," Dyson supplied. "She transferred from somewhere..." He shook his head. "I don't remember."

"Funny that," I said sarcastically. "Just a wild guess here, but she's left already."

Kane frowned. "That's not nearly as important as why she was here. If Zeta has found a way to control shifters..."

My blood ran cold. "You're right. That would mean they know we're here. Instead of attacking with a full-scale assault, they're testing to see what they might do to us."

Dyson shuddered. "Drugging me so I'll send a naked photo of Peyton to everyone seems a strange thing to do though."

I shook my head. "I don't think those things are related. The photo was just some asshole thinking they could get to me. The drugging... that's something else entirely." It was a bizarre coincidence, but I was sure that was all it was.

"It wasn't a very good attempt," Kane said.

"No. Drugging someone against their will usually isn't," I agreed.

"No, I mean—" Kane looked thoughtful. "We knew something happened. He was acting stranger than usual."

Dyson gave him a lopsided smile. "Thanks for noticing. I think."

"You're welcome." Kane flashed him a smile. "The question is, is it still in your bloodstream, and what is it? Do you feel different or odd in any way?"

Dyson's brow creased in concentration. "No more than usual."

"Can you shift?" I asked.

"Is that related in some way, or do you want to see me naked?" Dyson grinned. "I'm happy to oblige any time."

"We know you are," Kane groaned. He covered his eyes with his hands and rubbed his forehead. "I guess it's a relevant question. Go ahead and try."

"Thanks for permission, bro." Dyson stood and pulled his shirt off over his head.

"Yeah. You're welcome, bro." Kane slumped into a chair and turned away.

For someone who liked having sex in public, he really didn't like seeing his brother naked. Maybe it was all about context. Like how I didn't mind people seeing me having sex, but I didn't want nude photos shared around. If I had done the sharing, I might be okay with it.

Unlike Kane, I didn't look away while Dyson stripped. His body was firm and perfectly toned. I wanted to pour chocolate sauce over his abs and lick it off slowly.

I might have licked my lips.

Dyson saw and grinned. For as long as I had known him, he had never been shy about strutting around naked in front of people. Far from it. I would bet he was the kind of kid who pulled his clothes off as soon as he was old enough to do it by himself.

It was just another part of his charm.

"Okay, let's see." He folded his pants and tossed them onto a chair along with his underpants. He gave me a wink when he noticed my eyes on his dick.

I shrugged. What can I say, I liked his dick.

Smiling, Dyson lowered his face and stood still.

His smile faded, brow creased.

He closed his eyes and bared his teeth. "What. The. Fuck."

Eyes wide, he stared at Kane.

Kane jerked to his feet, his face pale. "You can't shift?"

I gaped at him. Oh gods, what had Zeta done to him. If they…

"I—" Dyson shifted into his big, shaggy dog form. He bared his teeth and huffed out a breath which sounded like he was laughing.

"Fucker," Kane muttered.

"For once, I might agree with you," I told him. I willed my heart to slow from its painful pounding. "That was a mean trick." I had been half way to assuming Zeta had discovered a way to prevent shifters from…well, being shifters. The idea made me shudder.

"He should definitely be in the doghouse for that one." Kane flopped back into his chair so quickly it almost rolled out from under him.

Dyson shifted back. "Sorry, I couldn't resist."

I gave him a dark look from behind my eyebrows. "Try harder next time." I wasn't really that angry with him, but I probably should be. He had scared the living daylights out of Kane and I.

"I guess that answers that question," Dyson said, his expression apologetic at least. "Unless the pink donut wore off already."

"If there's anything I know about donuts, it's that they don't just wear off," I said dryly. "They have to be worked off."

Dyson chuckled, but Kane still looked as if he might be sick all over the floor.

"I need some air." Kane stood on unsteady legs.

"We'll go with you." I offered him my hand.

He waved it away. "It's okay, I need a few moments alone. Then we're going to the lab to take some blood from Dyson. If you're lucky, I'll leave a little."

"My blood seems to be busy." Dyson looked downward.

"Put your pants on and keep it in there," Kane said. "Peyton is right, you might work off the donut. If we can find even a trace of whatever it was, it'll help."

Dyson pulled a face, but picked up his underpants. "You're the science geek."

"That's right." Kane nodded. "Get dressed and I'll meet you in the lab."

"Yes, sir." Dyson gave him a sarcastic salute.

Kane sighed and muttered something about Dyson being his usual self before he hurried out the door.

"Was I really that different?" Dyson asked. He leaned against the wall while he pulled his underpants on.

"You were...distant," I replied. "It felt as though you weren't all there. Like—maybe you had a lot on your mind."

"Well," he said lightly, "we all know that's not true. It's me we're talking about."

"Hey." I gave him my best stern-possible-future-teacher face. "You can be deep when you want to be."

"Except right now." He pouted.

"What happened to taking things slowly?" I asked.

He shrugged with one shoulder. "That was BPD. Before Pink Donut," he added when I gave him a questioning look. "If Zeta can really get to me here, then life might be too short."

I swallowed back a ball of emotion which threatened to leave me choked up. "Don't say things like that." He was right though. If we weren't safe here, and apparently we weren't, then we could expect Zeta to attack at any moment.

He pulled on his uniform pants, which hugged his ass like a glove and took my hand.

"Fine, how about I talk like this," he said softly. "I'm falling for you. Every day I feel more and more, until I don't know why it doesn't swallow me. I wanted to take it slowly because I didn't want to screw this up. You're more than a fling. You're someone I could see myself being with for a long, long time. Even if I have to share you with Kane and whoever else is in your life."

I wiped a tear from my cheek. "I care about you, too. If anything happened to you..." I sniffed.

"It won't," he assured me.

If only I felt so confident.

17

THE LAB WAS COLD. That wasn't surprising, most of the UA was, especially the places the AMM students used. Maybe I shouldn't be so paranoid, the UA students looked just as cold as the rest of us. They sat around the tables and workbenches, huddled in their jackets. Some of them even wore scarves. Unlike the rest of their clothes, the scarves apparently didn't need to be a regulation colour or length. One woman wore a bright pink one, while another looked like a House from Harry Potter.

"Figures she'd be a Slytherin," Dyson muttered.

I grinned. "Yeah, hashtag not shocked."

In spite of that, I gave the group a smile. They nodded in return. Perhaps not friendly, but not outright hostile, either. One or two even gave me glances which suggested they were impressed. They weren't even looking at my breasts, so I guessed it was about the duel, not the photo. Thank the gods. If they wanted to talk about me, I preferred that topic.

"Science geeks," Dyson said under his breath.

"Are you geek shaming?" I asked, one eyebrow arched at him.

"Not all all," he said breezily. "I love geeks. I am one too."

"Sure." I drew the word out. "I hope you're not science shaming then, because I happen to think science is cool."

He held up both hands in surrender. "You're right, it is, but people who study it are a whole other level of geeky. Take Kane for instance. He's bordering on being a nerd."

"Is there a difference?" I sat on a stool, my back to a workbench.

"It's subtle, but it exists." Dyson nodded. "Geeks are the cool version of nerds."

"Okay, thanks for clarifying that." I gave him a funny look, but grinned.

"Anytime." He placed his hands on the bench, one to either side of me. He leaned in until we were nose to nose. His breath brushed my cheek.

"I'd hate for you to think I was working for the enemy," he said softly. "I'd hate to *be* working for the enemy and not realise it."

I put a hand lightly on his cheek. "I would hate that, too, but we'll get to the bottom of this." I wasn't sure we shouldn't run like hells if there was any chance Zeta knew we were here, but we needed the information this lab could give us. As labs went, it was the only one we had any access to. For all we knew, Dyson had really just sleep walked, and all the worry was for nothing. Deep down, I suspected there was much more to this than that. I hated the idea they might have gotten to Dyson, not just for my sake, but for everyone's, especially his. Who knew what they might do to him, or with him?

I swallowed down a knot of emotion which built up in my throat.

"Yeah." He pressed a kiss to my lips, then stepped away, his expression unreadable.

Of all the guys, Dyson was the one I had always struggled to understand. At times he seemed so laid back and open, but much of the time I couldn't guess what was going on in his head. If I was honest with myself, I might admit it scared me a little. If he was working with Zeta and planned to betray us all, I wouldn't know until it was too late. I doubted even Kane would know.

My stomach turned at the idea.

"Are you all right?" Dyson asked. Evidently I was easier to read.

"I'm fine." I was mostly not lying.

"Great. Here comes Kane." Dyson nodded toward the door.

"Roll up your sleeve," Kane told him.

Dyson supported his elbow with his opposite hand and cupped his chin. "Are you qualified to take my blood?"

"No, now roll up your sleeve." Kane grabbed a needle and a vial and nodded toward his brother.

"See what I mean about science geeks?" Dyson said cheerfully. He pulled his sleeve up to his bicep and held out his arm.

I smiled. "Yeah, but he's helping you, so down boy."

"Yes ma'am." He gave me a sly smile.

I responded by sticking out my tongue.

"I can think of better uses for that," Dyson said.

I wiggled my tongue, then drew it back to say, "I'll bet you can. That will have to wait." I caught Kane glancing over to the other students. His Adam's apple bobbed up and down. With him, I knew just what he was thinking, and he'd do it, too. Right there on the workbench. I wondered what the other students would think or do.

I sighed. I wouldn't dare to try to find out. There was enough tension between the UA students and me as it was, without alienating ones who seemed more tolerant.

Kane sighed a moment later. I suspect he'd come to the same conclusion I had. He shook his head slightly and jabbed the needle into Dyson's vein.

Dyson winced. "Ouch, dude."

"Sorry." Kane filled the vial with blood, then drew out the needle and handed me a bandage to put on Dyson's puncture wound. "Don't shift until you stop bleeding."

"Where did you learn to take blood?" I asked while he capped the vial and took it off to a corner full of equipment.

"I watch TV," Kane said. He smiled faintly. "Our mother is a nurse. She wanted me to be a doctor, so she taught me a few things. If I'm going to study paranormal physiology, it's something I'll need to do."

"He used to practice on me," Dyson remarked.

"Only with syringes without needles," Kane said. "The needles were reserved for our teddy bears."

"Mine you mean," Dyson said. "He would never practice on Mr Snuggles."

I grinned. "You have a bear called Mr Snuggles?"

Kane blushed bright red. "I was three when I named him. Anyway, Dyson's was called Miss Pussy. He couldn't tell a bear from a cat."

I smothered a laugh. "I suppose they could look a bit alike."

"For your information," Dyson declared, loud and firm, "nothing else looks like a pussy. I was young and naive at the time. That's my excuse and I'm sticking to it." He crossed his arms over his chest and nodded.

I patted his shoulder. "I believe you."

"This might take a while," Kane said. "Maybe you two can go and study, or…whatever."

"I like whatevering," Dyson said. He glanced toward me.

"I'm fond of it myself," I agreed. "I could whatever all day."

"Me too." Dyson grinned. He held out his hand. "Come on, let's leave Captain Science Geek to solve the mysteries of the universe."

I took Dyson's hand and gave Kane a kiss on the cheek. He responded with a distracted smile. I guessed he was in his element here and we should leave him to it. I would have liked to help, or at least watch, but I really had no idea what I was looking at. Besides, we'd probably distract him and slow him down anyway.

"Oh," Kane said before we'd taken more than two steps. "Be careful and don't take cake from strangers." He shot Dyson a frown that seemed laced with further meaning. He trusted his twin implicitly, but was worried about what influence he might be under.

"I'm fine, I swear," Dyson assured him. "I feel like my normal, paranormal self. I haven't done anything strange for at least a few minutes." He smiled sweetly and batted his eyelashes.

Kane took a moment before nodding. "Fine, but still be careful. If they tried anything once, they might well try again."

"We will be," I said firmly. "We'll be all about being careful and trusting no one." Even each other. That sucked, because I really, really wanted to be alone with Dyson. Naked. And sweaty. "Although, we should fill Nash in on what happened."

"And Matt," Kane said.

I grimaced. "Him too, I guess." I nodded and headed out of the lab and into warmer air.

"Nash is probably teaching right now," Dyson remarked.

"Right. And Matt is probably in class. What is he studying anyway?"

Dyson frowned. "Would you believe, I have no idea? Knowing him it's something to do with killing Zeta agents."

"Is there a degree for that?"

"Bachelor of Death and Destruction to Assholes?" Dyson suggested. "I'm not even sure what faculty that would come under."

I shrugged with one shoulder. "I suspect it comes under humanities."

"Right," Dyson drew the word out. "He could double major in death and destruction and minor in something fun, like theatre."

"That sounds accurate." I nodded and tried to hold back a smile. "I can imagine him up on stage, makeup and all." Honestly I couldn't imagine anything more unlikely, but the idea cheered me up a little.

"What sounds accurate?"

Matt spoke so suddenly behind me, I jumped and whirled around.

"Speak of the devil," Dyson drawled. "We were just discussing what you might be studying."

"Ah." Matt didn't seem interested in elaborating, so we drew him to the side of the corridor and told him everything that had happened after the duel, up until now. He eyed Dyson with the mistrust he gave to pretty much everyone anyway.

"Should we be packing?" The gods knew why I always deferred to Matt. He seemed to have connections to the Paranormal Council, but when it came down to it, he was a second year, like me. One whose ass I had saved in the Zeta attack on the AMM.

Matt rubbed his forehead. "I'll look into it. In the meantime, just keep doing what you normally do. It's possible they don't know we're onto them yet. If we start acting strangely… More than usual, they'll realise."

"If there's anyone watching," I said.

Matt's brow creased. Damn, why was he so adorable when he did that?

"There's little doubt someone is watching," he said slowly, but firmly. "They could be anyone, anywhere." He gave Dyson a meaningful look.

Dyson bristled. "I'm not working for them."

"I didn't say you were," Matt replied coolly, "but you'd say that if you weren't."

Dyson stepped toward him, hands in fists.

I gripped his hand to hold him back. "Don't. Fighting amongst ourselves is what they want."

"How do you know what they want?" Dyson dropped my hand.

I stared. "I beg your pardon? Did you just suggest *I* might be working with them?"

"No," he said hastily. "Of course not, but it would explain a few things."

"Like what?" I demanded.

He looked toward the floor. "Like how they always know where to find us."

"You working with them would also explain that," I pointed out coldly. "Remember the whole "Dyson acting weird" thing?"

His head jerked back up, eyes wide. "I already said—"

I cut him off. "I know what you said. You think I'm the one who is betraying us."

"I don't, I just—" Dyson glanced toward Matt, who raised his hands to indicate he was staying well out of this conversation.

"Someone is doing it," Dyson said finally.

"Well it's not me." I crossed my arms and stepped away from them both. Tears prickled in my eyes.

"But you're okay with thinking it might be me," Dyson said bitterly. "Don't deny it, I've seen it on your face since you stepped into the computer lab."

"I—" I couldn't deny it, and I loathed myself for it. "At least Kane is trying to find out what's going on."

"Yeah, he is. He'll prove I did nothing wrong."

"I'm sure he will," I said. I wasn't that sure and I knew it showed on my face.

Hurt filled Dyson's eyes before he turned and stalked away.

"Fuck," I muttered. If division was what Zeta wanted, they certainly had it. Dyson would probably never talk to me again.

My heart ached. I wanted to curl up in a ball and cry.

18

<hr>

MATT SHRUGGED. "Is there any point in telling you not to let him get to you?"

I gave him a sour look. "None." I sagged against the wall and bit back tears. "Is there really any chance he's involved?"

"There's a chance any of us could be," he replied. "Except me. I know I'm not."

I opened my mouth to make some kind of smart ass comment, but sighed instead. Having been offended only a couple of minutes earlier, I could hardly go around throwing stones at Matt. Besides, after all I had seen him do, I was ninety-nine percent certain he was on our side. It would be a hundred percent, but he didn't tell me everything about Zeta and the Paranormal Council and I suspected he withheld things I should know.

"I know you know I can be trusted," I said finally. He and Ariana had been asked to protect me after all.

"When it comes to Zeta, yes," he agreed. "Not with other things." A smile played around the corners of his mouth, so I knew he was teasing.

I wasn't much in the mood for it though. I grunted and started off down the corridor.

"Where are you going?" His long stride caught up with me quickly.

"I don't know, just walking."

"Do you want some company?"

"Not especially." This whole day sucked, winning the duel notwithstanding. To be honest, I couldn't care less about the stupid duel right now. Everything since then went to crap.

"If it's any consolation, the photo was very tasteful."

I stopped so suddenly the students walking behind us almost ran into the back of me. I expected them to give me a dirty look, but they wove around us without so much as a glance back.

"Tasteful?" I echoed.

"Sure. You know, more like art than porn." Matt's expression was completely unapologetic. He actually seemed impressed.

I gaped at him for a moment, then kept walking. "I suppose it was. Do you know who hacked Kane's phone to send it to everyone?"

"No, but it's easy enough to find out."

I almost stopped again. "It is?"

"Yeah. Well, it'll be harder here than at the AMM, but it was probably a magical hack. The academy keeps a record of spells used on campus."

"Uhhh, like making tigers appear so they can attack other students?" Shit. How much trouble would I be in if they looked up *those* records?

"Making the tiger, yes, but not the why," Matt replied. "But don't worry, I have that covered. Or rather, Nash does. If anyone asks, he'll say you were training under his supervision."

I frowned. "He shouldn't have to lie for me."

"It won't be the first time, or the last," Matt said easily. "But it goes both ways. It probably already has."

"I guess so," I agreed uneasily. He was right though. I would lie for any of my friends or lovers, as long as no one was hurt as a result.

"Come on, let's find ourselves a hacker."

To my surprise, he grabbed my hand and tugged me toward the basement the AMM admin had been relegated to. A bigger shock was the intensity of the jolt of heat his touch sent to my core. I felt as though he had ignited an inferno I hadn't known existed. One I suddenly, desperately, wanted to burn with him.

He gave me a look which suggested he felt it too, and dropped my hand.

"Sorry," he muttered.

"No you're not," I replied. "You're just sorry you like me more than you want to."

He looked over at me before we stepped into the basement. "Interesting theory. Liking you would be a conflict of interest. And probably a bad idea."

"That doesn't stop," I mouthed, "Nash."

"He makes his own choices," Matt replied. "I never said I thought they were good ones." He stepped inside and plonked himself down in front of a computer. None of the staff so much as gave him a second look.

"You'll have to explain that to me someday." I wheeled a chair over and sat beside him.

He glanced over his shoulder. "Yeah, someday." He turned on the screen and tapped in a password. "This is my personal account, so don't think I know the AMM's password."

"That thought hadn't crossed my mind." I had memorised his, though. I never knew when I might need to get access. "How many people would know spell logs are kept?"

He tapped on the keyboard. "It's not a secret, but they don't go around announcing it either."

I crossed my legs. "How does someone hack a phone?"

"With another phone," Matt replied without looking away from the screen.

"The UA doesn't use phones to do magic," I pointed out.

"No they don't," he agreed.

I blinked a couple of times. "But that would mean..."

Matt sat back and regarded me. "Don't assume you can trust everyone, just because they're AMM students."

"I wouldn't," I said quickly. "I didn't, I just..."

"Prefer to assume a UA student did it?" He turned back to the screen.

"Yes, I suppose. Dyson *did* say the pink donut woman was one of us."

"Trust no one," Matt said simply.

"Except you."

"Except me," he agreed.

"Trust the one person who doesn't like me."

"At least I'm impartial."

"Great." I snorted.

"You can trust Ariana and Nash," Matt added. "They like you, for some reason."

I would have stuck out my tongue at him, but his attention was all on the screen. Instead, I made a rude noise with my tongue.

He smiled and clicked the "return" key. "Okay, this should give us some idea. Although, I'm not sure if you're mature enough to deal with whatever we find."

Asshole.

"I'm plenty mature enough, so there."

"Mmmhmm, sure," he replied. The reflection of the screen showed in his eyes, words flickered upward rapidly.

"I had no idea so much magic was done here." I probably should have realised, but I had never given it any thought.

Matt looked as though he might say something, but his gaze snapped toward the screen. He pointed to a line of text.

"There, someone did a hacking spell at one am."

I peered where he pointed. "How can you tell?"

"It's a phone to phone transfer. If it was done voluntarily it wouldn't have needed magic."

"So…you're guessing?"

"Yes, but's an educated guess." He lowered his hand and scrolled down a few more lines. "There's nothing else here like it. Here's your tiger conjuring. There's Xav's two magical creatures." He leaned in closer and squinted. "That's odd."

"What?" I looked too, but I didn't know what I was looking at. "Is your major magical computer science, by any chance?"

He glanced at me. "Yeah. I worked on the development of this program."

"Oh." That made sense, and explained why he was trusted to use it. He was probably here all the time, updating it. "So what's odd?"

"Someone cast a protection spell. Like the magic bubbles we use."

"I know what a protection spell is," I said impatiently. "Why is that odd? I used one and so did Xav, remember?"

"Yes, but no one else there did."

I rubbed my forehead. "Are you saying someone else was out there, watching?"

"Exactly. Someone who didn't want us to know they were there."

"Can you tell who it was?"

Matt shook his head slowly. "No. It might have been a random passerby, who thought they'd stick around to watch. Or…"

"Someone who meant me harm?" I finished for him.

"It was probably someone who wanted to keep you safe." Matt exhaled loudly.

"That's not a bad thing, is it?" I asked.

"Only if they helped you in some way. Then you'll have to forfeit. Xav will have won the bet."

"No one helped me," I said insistently. "You were there, you saw the whole thing."

"I didn't see you when you were invisible," Matt pointed out.

I frowned. "I didn't have any help," I said again.

"Can you prove it?" he asked.

"Ye—no, I suppose not. Xav can't prove I did, though. They might have been there to help him."

Matt snorted a laugh. "If they did, they didn't do a very good job. But if anyone knows about this, they could insist you won by cheating."

I growled. "Please tell me we'll leave high school behind at some point."

"I've heard it lasts until you're forty and give away your last fuck," Matt said.

I grimaced. "Figures. Can you delete the record of whoever it was?"

He frowned. "I can, but I'm not sure I should."

"Do you want me to be accused of cheating?" I asked.

He hesitated.

I glared.

"Fine, but you owe me one."

"One what?" I said with thinking.

His Adam's apple bobbed. "I'll think of something."

Did I imagine the catch in his voice?

He deleted the line of text and updated the program. "There, your tracks are covered."

"Not *my* tracks," I commented. "So what about the phone hack? Can you see who did it?"

"That one is a little easier," he said. "Phones have numbers."

"No shit," I replied dryly. "So what?"

"So, just like calls are logged, so is magical use. Here is the number of the phone the photo was taken from." He pointed to the screen.

"That's Kane's number," I said after I checked it with my phone. "Whose is the other one?"

Matt grabbed a piece of paper and a pen and scribbled down the number. Or rather, wrote it quickly, but in neat, precise writing. "I don't know off the top of my head."

"Of course you don't. Who knows anyone's number from memory these days?" I gave him a look of disbelief. I quickly followed that with a snort. "Let me guess, you even remember your own number?"

"Of course I do, you don't?" He arched an eyebrow at me.

"I don't call myself, " I reasoned, "so, no."

He looked as though he might say something, but closed his mouth and shook his head instead.

"So...I already know it's not my number," he said slowly. "Because I would know it by looking, and I'm not a hacker. At least, not in regard to this matter." He smiled slyly.

"I think I'll file that under "things you probably shouldn't say in a university administration area." Unless you want to get arrested?"

He grinned. Damn him, he was too cute for his own good. Or mine.

"Not especially. I'm not into being restrained." He peered down the piece of paper and luckily missed my blush.

"Have you tried it?" I asked in spite of myself.

I knew I had said the wrong thing when a haunted look crossed his eyes.

"That's a whole other story I won't get into," he muttered. "Cross check the numbers on your phone and see if it matches anyone." He pushed the paper across the top of the table toward me.

"Okay." I opened my contacts and scrolled with one eye on the screen the other on the page.

"It's not Dyson's," I noted with some relief. "Or Ariana's." I hadn't considered her for a moment. "Not Hamish either. Or Nash. It's obviously neither of my parents', or..." I checked my phone, the paper and back again.

"This makes no sense."

"What? Whose is it?" Matt leaned over and squinted at my screen. "Why does that name seem familiar?"

I shook my head in confusion. "Jess is my best friend outside the academy. It couldn't have been her, she can't use a drop of magic."

"Just because she can't, doesn't mean it wasn't her phone," Matt said softly.

"But how—" My heart sank. "This wasn't bullying, was it? They're using her to get to me."

19

Matt put a hand on my shoulder before I leapt to my feet and ran out the door.

"What are you doing?" he hissed. "Apart from jumping to conclusions."

"They have her." I jerked away from him.

"They have her *phone*," he corrected. "Or had it at one in the morning. Apart from that, we know nothing."

"We know someone is trying to screw with me," I said bitterly. I sagged back in the chair and rubbed my face.

"We might know that," he conceded. "Going off half-cocked isn't going to help. We need more information."

"So we can go off full-cocked?" I suggested.

"Exactly." He smiled faintly. "When did you hear from her last? Or better yet, see her?"

"During the holiday. I...I've been busy." Yeah, okay, I sucked as a best friend. For all I know, she had been kidnapped by Zeta and I hadn't known.

Matt shrugged. "It happens. You haven't texted her or received a text from her?"

"No." I double-checked my phone just in case. The last text we'd shared was weeks ago.

"Social media?" Matt sat back and curled his hands around the arms of his chair.

I opened an app and clicked on her profile. "She posted two nights ago. She was off to some party with a group from Melbourne University." The post included a selfie of Jess with a big smile on her face, black hair, and a yellow t-shirt.

A wave of sadness washed over me. Even if she was fine, I missed her and the parties we used to go to together. We had been inseparable before I started at AMM.

I liked the post and closed the app.

"There's nothing after that." I tapped my fingers on the table. "Maybe I should shoot her off a text. It might—"

My phone beeped with the text tone. I frowned at the name of the sender.

"It's Jess." That couldn't be a coincidence. I had just liked her post. That might have alerted her, or whoever had her phone, that I was looking for her.

"Open it," Matt said.

I sucked in a breath and clicked on my messages.

"Shit."

"What?"

I turned the screen so Matt could see the photo of Jess. She stared at the camera with wide eyes, full of fear. She wore the same yellow shirt she had on in her selfie, but her hair was a mess and her face was pale.

"Fuck," Matt muttered. "Any idea where she is?"

I looked back at the photo and searched behind her. She seemed to be on a stool in front of a table, or a bench of some kind. The detail was blurry, as if the sender didn't want me to see too much.

After a while, I shook my head. "It's nowhere I recognise. Maybe I should ask."

I thought Matt might laugh, but he looked thoughtful and nodded.

"Yes, but not yet. We can call them, but we should have Nash in the room as well. He'll know what to listen for."

I nodded. I would feel better with Nash involved. Who was I kidding; he'd be in charge. I might like to think of myself as a badass, but this was way beyond my field of experience.

"What, you're not going to argue?" Matt sounded amused. I want to slap the look off his face.

"Arguing might get her killed," I replied. I shoved the chair away from the table and stood.

"Yes, it might." Matt shut the computer down and nodded to the admin staff before he steered me out of the room. "That might happen anyway. Nash might insist we not try to rescue her."

I stopped and stared at him. "I beg your pardon? We can't just leave her there."

Matt looked unapologetic. "If it means risking a few paranormals to save one normal, then we might have to. If it was my call—"

"Well, it's not," I snapped.

"And what if that's the call Nash makes?" Matt asked evenly.

"Then I'll go without you all." I resumed walking.

"You'll get yourself killed."

"Then you won't have to put up with me anymore," I told him. "I'm sure you'll be relieved."

He caught my arm and turned me to face him. "I would *not* be relieved." He searched my face with eyes laced with something I couldn't read. It almost seemed as if he cared or something. More than he'd let on.

"I don't want to see anyone die," he said finally. "Not even you."

"You said "especially you" wrong." I gave him a sarcastic smile.

He snorted. "You wish."

"Ha. Hardly." Okay, I did, but wish it a little bit, even though my hands were full enough with the guys who admitted they cared.

I pulled my arm back, but he held it firmly. "Here's where you let go so I don't kick you in the nuts," I said dryly.

"Well, if my nuts are at stake." He loosened his grip and stood back.

"Wise choice." I rubbed my arm. "I'd like to have a deep and meaningful conversation about why you looked at me the way you did, but my friend is currently being held hostage."

He rubbed his chin. "You imagined it, but yes, now is not the time. I trust you know where we're going?"

"Of course." I started toward Nash's room. "How do you know?"

"I make it my business to know."

"Some day you're going to have to explain a lot of things to me." I knocked on Nash's door.

"If you're alive to hear it, I might," Matt said, his voice tight.

I glanced over my shoulder in time to see that haunted look he got in his eyes. I knew Zeta had done something to him, but I didn't know what. I suspected he'd been born in a lab and had tests run on him for at least a part of his life. I had no idea what else they had done or even how he had escaped that existence. I was sure Zeta wanted him as much as they wanted me.

"I'll be alive all right," I assured him. "I'll survive if only to hear your backstory."

"I'm flattered." Matt gave me a funny look. He might have said more, but Nash's door swung open.

Nash gave me a hungry look, but it was quickly doused when he saw Matt as well. "I guess this is business," he said quietly. He ushered us inside and closed the door before he kissed me deeply.

"No offence, but this is important." Matt sounded unimpressed.

"So is this," I retorted, but I stepped away from Nash and leaned my hip against the table. I told Nash everything we knew.

"Show me the photo." Nash held out his hand for my phone. He peered at the text and frowned. "It's nowhere I know either. Did you try to trace it?"

I frowned at him, then at Matt.

"It wasn't sent with magic." Matt shrugged. "I'm not familiar with the use of normal's tracking software."

"We'll have to rectify that," Nash told him. "In the meantime, call them." He handed the phone back to me.

Trembling, I took it and opened my contacts. "Are you sure? This might provoke them."

"It might," Nash agreed, "but it's most likely what they're waiting for. Until we make contact, we don't know what they want."

"We know exactly what they want," I said bitterly. "They want us all under their control." They wanted to use me and my magic to breed hybrids. My stomach twisted into a knot.

"We'll make sure that doesn't happen," Nash said fiercely. A flash of green lit his eyes, but it was gone a heartbeat later. I suspected, given half a chance, he'd shift into his dragon form and blast Zeta off the face of the planet. If I thought it was that simple, I might let him. It wouldn't be simple though. All his retaliation would do was slow them down a little and destroy him.

I exhaled deeply and pressed on Jess' number. The phone rang. And rang. Just when I thought it would ring out, it clicked.

My heart kicked into overdrive.

"Hello?" I said into my phone. "Who's there? Jess?"

"Peyton?" Her voice on the other end of the line was tiny.

"Jess! Are you all right?" I lifted frantic eyes to Nash's face. He looked so calm it was almost contagious. Almost. He gave me a nod and waved for me to keep talking.

"What have they done to you?" I asked. "Are you injured?"

"No, I'm okay." She spoke louder now, but high with obvious fear. "They want you to come here."

Of course they did. "Where are you?"

"They'll text you the address. They only want you to come."

"Right." I've seen enough movies to know how this goes. Arrive alone, tell no one, especially the cops. "When?"

The line was silent for a moment before she added, "They'll text that, too. They'll destroy the phone afterward so you can't call me again."

"I'll get you out of there," I assured her. "You're going to be fine. I promise."

"Peyton...don't come, save your—" The line went dead.

"Shit." I pressed the call button again, but no one answered. A couple of minutes later, a text popped up from her number.

Then...nothing.

I flopped down onto a chair and placed my phone on the table. It was that or throw it at the window in fear and frustration.

Nash stepped over, checked my phone, and made a note of the address they'd sent. "It's not far from here. They haven't given us much time to plan."

"Is there any point in me reminding you they said to come alone?" I asked wearily.

The guys exchanged looks.

"No," Matt said.

"None," Nash agreed. "Since Dyson and Kane are indisposed, it'll be just us. I don't think it's necessary to bring in Ariana or Hamish."

"It would be better to keep this small anyway," Matt said. "Just us three."

"I meant two," Nash said, "Peyton and I."

"Not a chance," Matt said immediately. "She might get you killed."

"She won't," Nash said firmly.

"No, I won't," I agreed. "I'm going alone."

"The hells you are," Nash growled. "If I have to tie you down to keep you from doing something crazy, I will."

"While that might be fun, I'm done putting everyone else in danger."

"We can take care of ourselves." Matt's face was slightly flushed. Was it all that talk about tying me down? "It's three of us or no one. If I have to, I'll go to the council and have them—"

Nash threw up his hands. "Fine, we're all going." He pointed a finger at Matt. "But if you ever threaten me again, it'll be the last thing you do here at the academy."

"That wasn't a threat," Matt replied coolly. "Just a matter of fact. I—"

"All right, can you stop?" I rubbed my temples. "Your dicks are about the same size, but if you want to pull them out and compare them, that's fine by me. In the meantime, make your plans and do it quickly. If Jess dies while you two are arguing—"

I sucked in a breath and wiped a tear off my cheek. I felt as though my life had started to implode, and it was dragging everyone else down with it. Maybe they'd be better off without me. They'd certainly be under less risk.

Okay, that was an assumption. Zeta had been operating for longer than I had been alive. It would be around after I was gone, unless we could bring it down. I suspected all we would ever do was make a dent on their armour, but I sure as hells wasn't going to let them kill my best friend.

Nash nodded. "It'll be tricky, but here's what we do..."

2O

<hr>

"THIS IS A BAD IDEA," I muttered to myself. If I had a shred of sense, I would make myself invisible, ditch the guys and go after Jess by myself. What I lacked in sense, I made up for in reason. Both guys were hybrids. Both could do magic as well as shift. I needed their help. Besides, they'd kill me if I tried to lose them. Not literally. I hoped.

I approached the warehouse, eyes peeled for any movement. The place looked deserted. I know that was just for appearances, so no nosy people sniffed around. That would be the theory, at least. If I was looking for a hideout, or a place to live so I didn't have to sleep on the streets, this was exactly the kind of place I'd come to.

I sucked in a breath, squared my shoulders and approached the small door on the side of the building. The only other entrance was a huge set of roller doors which looked locked down tight.

I half expected to be grabbed by an invisible witch or two before I even got near the door. My body was tensed for it. The only sound was that of my feet walking on gravel, and the whisper of wind. Every so often a car would pass, or a dog would bark in the distance. I heard no voices, no approaching army of invisible boots.

I stopped a metre from the door and listened again. Was this even the right place? The idea that this might be a wild goose chase occurred to me. They could have moved Jess to some other location by now. Hells, she might never have been here.

My skin tingled. The hair on the back of my neck rose. This was all kinds of wrong. Not just because I was risking my own life, but because at least three million things could go wrong with Nash's plan. Okay, maybe not that many, but I stopped counting after eleven.

"Who's there?" I called out.

No answer.

I rubbed my arm absently and stepped forward. My breath held, I tapped on the door. Once, twice, three times, just as instructed. The sound echoed inside the building, as though the whole place was empty.

The door swung open without a sound. Definitely not the rusty groan I was expecting. That in itself said a lot. How many not-so-deserted warehouses did Zeta have? How many contained hostages or paranormals held against their will?

"Hello?" I stepped closer, but not through the doorway yet.

Back out the street, a driver beeped their horn and I jumped.

"Bloody hells," I muttered. I was tense, obviously. Who wouldn't be in a situation like this? I glanced over my shoulder, but the car was already gone.

I counted to sixty, stepped inside the warehouse and made myself invisible.

Okay bastards, game on.

The room just inside the door must have been an office of some kind. A long desk was built into one wall. The door behind it was the only way into the rest of the building. It sat closed at the moment, but I heard raised voices beyond it. I stopped to listen but couldn't make out the words. The tone was obvious enough—they were angry.

Things which could go horribly wrong number five. The first four hadn't eventuated. Yet.

I held onto the magic while I clambered over the desk. I just managed to land silently on the other side when the door flew open. It clanged against the opposite wall and bounced back half-shut.

A familiar red-haired man stalked through the doorway.

Fitz.

"I know you're here, you fucking bitch," he snarled. "Show yourself!"

When he put it that way…

Even though he couldn't see it, I flipped him the finger and stepped lightly toward the door.

"I'm going to kill your friend." He turned a slow circle, hands raised, so I knew he had no idea where I was. "And then I'll make sure you're locked away, where you belong, in Zeta's laboratory."

I rolled my eyes at his tirade.

"Once you're safely in Zeta custody, I will make it my personal mission to break you."

Okay, now this guy was pissing me off. How much trouble had he gotten into for losing Dyson that he was so vindictive as a result? To be fair, he was a dick before the car crashed into the waterslide. Now he was an angry, vengeful dick.

I bit back a retort and snuck past him and through the door.

If he suspected anything, he gave no sign. He climbed onto the desk and jumped down the other side, muttering to me as he went.

On the other side of the door was a large room.

Jess sat tied to a chair, confused, but hopeful. Every so often her eyes would dart around as though she somehow knew I was there.

Several people in Zeta uniforms lay still on the ground nearby. Not dead, but unconscious for a while. Nash must have succeeded in reaching the roof and dumping a cylinder of gas into the air vents. The gas would only work on shifters, and only for a few hours, but it was enough. Thank the gods it worked on hybrids, too. On the other hand, the number of hybrids working for Zeta was breathtaking.

Only a handful of agents remained standing, or crouched beside hybrids. They might all be normals, but they might also be witches or wizards. This war went deeper than normals versus paranormals. It was more like…paranormals and normals who wanted the world under their heel and those who didn't.

I swallowed down my outrage and focused. Without knowing what I was dealing with, I had to be careful. Neither Matt nor Nash could help me until I got Jess clear of the building. That was the most difficult part of this plan, and the place where the most things could go wrong.

I stepped over closer to her, my steps as silent as I could make them.

Three metres.

Two metres.

One metre.

I dropped to a crouch behind her.

"Whatever you do, don't flinch," I whispered.

She startled slightly, but not enough to draw attention to herself. She lowered her head as if to nod and raised it again. She wriggled her hands, but they were bound hard with cable ties.

Of course, why couldn't it be rope, loosely knotted? Evil bastards.

I was ready for this, thanks to Matt, but I would have to act quickly.

Heart racing, I dropped my magic and conjured a small knife from the new tattoo on my wrist. It wouldn't last long, but it was sharp enough to cut through the ties.

They fell away just as one of the agents noticed my presence.

"She's here!" she shouted. She pulled out a gun and aimed it at Jess' head. "Don't move or I shoot."

"You won't shoot," I moved closer to Jess. "You might hit me. You know your boss wants me alive."

The agent hesitated.

I used the time to grab Jess' wrist and form a bubble around both of us.

The agent pulled the trigger.

I dropped to a crouch and pulled Jess down with me. The bullet sailed over both of our heads. Judging by the clang and subsequent echo, it slammed into the wall behind us. A small part of me regretted the fact it hadn't hit Fitz or someone like him. The rest of me didn't really want to see anyone dead, although better them than me and Jess.

"We have to be quiet and move slowly," I said in her ear.

She nodded and smiled in a way that made me feel like a fraud. She seemed so sure I was in control here, that I knew exactly what I was doing.

Girl, I don't have a clue.

I nodded toward the door and we rose, hand in hand.

Every Zeta agent was on their feet now, all alert for where we might be. A couple still had guns, but most now had tranquilliser guns in their hands. Barrels were aimed roughly in our direction, but they waited.

One little mistake and we would… Shit, I needed to sneeze.

No, that was *not* a part of this plan.

I screwed up my face and pinched my nose with the fingers of my spare hand.

The sneeze receded, but I knew that trick. The moment I lowered my hand, it would come back, twice as hard.

I held my breath and pulled Jess along a little faster.

Unfortunately faster meant Jess accidentally scuffed her shoe on the floor. The sound was tiny, but enough to be heard.

Half a dozen Zeta tranquilliser darts flew toward us.

I pulled Jess down again, but not before a dart struck her arm.

She let out a tiny squeak, but bit her lip to keep from making any more noise.

I tugged her to her feet and hurried toward the door. I needed to get her out, over the desk and out to where Nash and Matt waited. All before the dart took effect.

No pressure.

"You should save yourself," she said in my ear.

"I'm not leaving without you," I said, mouthing most of the words. I hadn't come all this way to leave her behind. "Just a little further."

I pulled her into the office.

She started to slump slightly. "I don't feel so…"

"We're nearly there." I hesitated. How the hells was I going to get us both over the desk? I thought for a moment.

"You go over first. I'll keep the magic going and give you a shove if you need one." Easy to say. Doing it…that might be different.

She nodded and leaned against the desk. She managed to raise one leg high enough to place on the desk, but I had to push her up the rest of the way. Once there, she closed her eyes and sagged.

Shit.

"Jess?" I shook her, but she didn't wake.

Okay, I can do this. Somehow.

With one hand on her, I climbed up, trying hard not to put too much weight on her. With all the elegance of a hippopotamus, but hopefully none of the noise, I jumped off the other side of the desk.

Right, easy. Now, to pick her up somehow. I glanced toward the door. What I needed right now was to have Nash or Matt come running in, ready to help. I was a kickass woman, but I would struggle to lift someone who weighed a bit more than I did.

They didn't come.

Okay, improvisation time.

I could... No, that wouldn't work. *Maybe I if I...* Nope, bad idea.

Fuckity fuck, every idea I had involved making too much noise, or making myself visible. I was getting tired from holding magic for so long, but I couldn't just leave Jess here.

I chewed my lip.

I had no choice. I grabbed her under her arms and pulled her down from the desk. Her feet hit the floor with a thud that drew the Zeta agents to the door.

"We know you're there. You have nowhere to go."

I ignored them and dragged Jess over to the door. If we could just slip out...

A shadow fell over us both.

"Going somewhere?"

I glanced over my shoulder and dropped my magic in surprise.

Dyson stood beside Fitz.

Dyson aimed a tranquilliser gun at me.

"WHAT THE HELLS?" I raised my hands. "Dyson, what are you doing?"

I noticed then his eyes were glazed.

"He's doing whatever he's told," Fitz said with a smile. "Just like you'll learn to do."

"You've drugged him," I said. My eyes never left Dyson.

He blinked. I was sure I saw him deep inside, trying to fight this—whatever they had done to him. Maybe if I could buy him some time…

"In a manner of speaking," Fitz replied. "Now, we can do this one of two ways. You walk to the car I have waiting outside and get in, or your boyfriend here will put you to sleep and drag you in there for me."

"I don't like either of those options," I said, calm on the outside, mind and heart racing on the inside. "How about you leave us alone? Things aren't going to end well for you if you keep working for Zeta." He'd be lucky if Nash bit his head off cleanly.

"On the contrary, I'll be very well rewarded when we bring you in." He looked so smug, I wanted to punch him in the face.

"What I don't get is why," I said. "Why me? There are tons of witches out there who are more powerful, skilled, and probably better looking. Seriously, if this is about my mother, then maybe take it out with her. We're not that close. If Zeta thinks I would be a good bargaining chip—"

"Enough." He made a slicing gesture with his hand. "Maybe if I kill your friend, you'll understand I'm serious." He turned his gun toward Jess.

"An innocent woman who can't even fight back," I said in disgust. "Your balls must be tiny."

I saw the bullet leave the gun before I registered the sound of it going off.

"No!" The word tore from my throat.

The bullet slammed into the ground a hair from Jess' head.

"Next time, I'll put a bullet in her brain," Fitz said coldly. "Get in the car and she can wake up here, alone but alive. Resist and she dies. Your choice."

My heart was in my throat. I had no doubt he meant what he said. I had come too fucking close to getting her killed. I glanced toward Dyson, but his expression was blank. Whatever they had given him, it was in control at the moment.

"Fine, I'll co-operate." Part of me wanted to see if Dyson would pull the trigger, but I didn't dare to risk being asleep for hours. I believed what Fitz had said about breaking me. I wouldn't let him touch me without a fight.

"If you hurt her in *any* way…"

Fitz gestured toward the door with his gun. "You're in no position to make threats."

I opened my mouth to point out I had friends in the vicinity, but shut it again. He would know I had help, because someone put all the hybrids to sleep, but he probably didn't know both guys were out there.

I brushed past Dyson on the way out the door, but his body was stiff. The drug was winning, for now.

I wished I believed all of that. Kane was smart, but Zeta could have spent years on it. It might take him that long to work out what it was, much less what to do about it. Dyson could be like this forever. The idea choked me up. What would they ask him to do to me? My stomach churned.

"Open the door," Fitz barked at one of the Zeta agents who stood near the SUV. Black, of course, just like Fitz's soul.

She jumped to tug the door open and stepped aside as if I was some kind of wild animal. I bared my teeth at her, just to see her flinch.

"I've changed my mind," Fitz said just before I climbed into the car. "She's too dangerous to keep awake. Dyson, tranq her."

I whirled around. "But I said I would cooperate."

"And I don't believe you." Fitz nodded to Dyson.

Dyson's hand twitched. A flash of apology crossed his eyes.

I shook my head. "Don't do it. You can fight this. You're stronger than whatever they've given you."

He looked pained. "Don't...want...to..." He squeezed the trigger. The dart flew out of the barrel and hit my shoulder.

"Ouch! Fucking hells." I gripped it and yanked it free before throwing it to the ground. It clattered before it came to a stop at Fitz's feet. Empty.

Shit.

"Get into the car." Fitz ordered.

I raised my chin. Where the hells were Nash and Matt? This would have been the perfect moment for them to sweep in and do a bit of clawing and biting.

My eyelids were heavy already. My body insisted I lie down and sleep. I fought the urge.

"Get her into the car," Fitz ordered.

Dyson moved forward and pushed me inside. "Sorry," he said, his voice groggy. Or was that my head?

"You have to keep fighting," I told him. At least, I think I did. I wasn't sure if the words passed my lips.

He lifted my legs and placed them on the seat.

I caught sight of Fitz's amused face before the door slammed shut, followed by my eyes.

~

I AWOKE IN A COOL, dark room. That was a small mercy because my head pounded like someone hammered a nail into my temple. I opened my eyes a crack.

I lay on a narrow bed in what looked like the laboratory at UA. Was there any point in hoping that was where I was? The guys could have swept in and rescued Dyson and I while I had a little nap.

I raised my head, but winced and put it back down when the pain increased.

Gods, it hurt. I squeezed my eyes shut and rolled onto my side. Nothing felt broken and I was still wearing the same clothes I'd had on when I fell asleep.

I opened my eyes again. I was almost certain I wasn't at UA. At least I was alive.

For now.

I rolled over onto my back and stared at the ceiling. It was only then I noticed a bandage on my left arm. Tentatively I touched it.

Son of a bitch. I was almost certain it was right where my birth control was. Or, if I guessed right, had been.

I shivered. Were they really serious about using me to make hybrids? Between that realisation and the pain in my head, my stomach turned. I rolled over and threw up on their pristine, white floor. Shame it wasn't Fitz's shoes, or someone equally nasty.

"Ah, you're awake." A soft voice spoke from the doorway. "Don't try to use magic, it'll hurt like the blazes."

The speaker was a woman around my age. Her eyes were rimmed in dark shadows and her belly was heavily swollen. Something about her was familiar, but I couldn't put my finger on it.

I forced myself to sit up. "They're so badass they sent a pregnant woman to make sure I behave?" My tone wasn't even slightly friendly.

She stepped inside and gave me a bitter smile. "I think the idea is to show you that you can't win. No matter how much you fight." Her hand went to her belly. She looked as though she might cry.

"They think I won't blast you out of the way and escape?" I said coldly. I had no reason to believe she wasn't on Zeta's side. There had to be some women willing to make hybrids for them. She might just as easily be one.

"If you do, then at least make sure I can't get up again." She looked away. She was so convincing I almost believed her. Part of me wanted to.

I frowned, but instantly regretted it. I waited until the worst of the throbbing in my forehead receded before I spoke again. "How do I know you're not one of them?"

She hesitated, then shrugged. "You don't, but I'm not. I was like you, young and full of fight. After the first baby—"

"First… How many have you had?"

She swallowed audibly. "This is the third. They might let me see this one, if I can convince you to do as they ask."

I gaped. My stomach rolled again. "I'm not going to just…" Gods, if they thought I would just let them violate me and not fight with everything I had…

She sniffed. "I didn't think you would. Why would you? But it will make them work twice as hard to break you. Personally I think some of them prefer it."

"Some of them?" I echoed. "How many?"

She shrugged. "Enough."

"Hybrids?"

"Sometimes," she agreed. "Sometimes it's just a needle with shifter DNA. Those are better. Easier."

"Yeah, it would be." A needle versus getting raped. What a choice.

"If you're lucky, that's all you'll get. It's more reliable that way. Higher chance of impregnation with the right combination of DNA. So they said anyway." She rubbed her belly again.

"That's what they did with you the last time?" I asked.

She nodded. "They're trying to make a dragon hybrid. They're hard to make. If this works, they'll do it again."

And again and again until they wore her out. She didn't need to say any of that, it was written on her face.

"Right." Would they try that with me? If Nash fathered my child, we might have done that naturally. Ironic. Zeta could have simply waited a few years. We might have done it on our own.

"They seem to be especially interested in me," I said softly. "Have you got any idea why? Why did they want you, of all the witches?"

She blinked. "It was something about my blood. I don't really know."

I rubbed my aching forehead with my fingertips. All of this thinking was painful and tiring. "I'm just a witch. My parents are just a witch and a wizard. There's nothing unique about me."

"Perhaps there is and you didn't know?" she suggested.

"That's possible," I said doubtfully, "but I have no idea how Zeta would know."

"They will have taken your blood." She pointed to my bandage. "They might tell you, if you cooperate with them."

There she was again, asking me to be good. As if that would happen.

"We'll see." I lowered my hands. "What's your name?"

She hesitated. "Thora."

"Peyton." I held my hand out to her. "I wish we'd met under better circumstances."

"Me too." She shook my hand, but looked over her shoulder while she did it. "I should go."

"Yes, you should," Fitz agreed as he stepped through the door. He jerked his head at her.

She gave me a wide eyed look, but hurried out as quickly as a heavily pregnant woman could waddle.

Fitz closed the door behind her and locked it. "Try to do magic."

"Why should I?" I remembered Thora telling me it would hurt.

"Aren't you going to defend yourself?" He stepped closer.

I shivered at the look in his eyes. I squinted and felt around for magic in the room and outside it. The moment I touched some in the metal of the doorframe, a searing pain flashed through my head.

I cried out and dropped the magic immediately.

Fitz chuckled and stepped closer while I waited for the agony to recede.

"Big man, huh?" I choked out. "You need to incapacitate a woman to feel good about yourself."

"Zeta has blocked your access to magic," he said easily, "but you're far from helpless. I'm sure you have lots of fight left." His tongue darted over his lips. He grabbed my arm in a tight grip.

"I look forward to *pounding* it out of you."

2 2

I GRITTED MY TEETH. "And risk me having a *normal* baby? No offence, asshole, but your hair is bright red. No one would miss the resemblance."

Fitz smirked. "What risk? That birth control will be in your system for days, possibly longer. Besides, there's more than one way to prevent pregnancy."

"Yeah, like celibacy," I retorted. "Or losing your nuts." I aimed my knee but he grabbed it and used that and my arm to slam me to the floor.

Fuck, that was a stupid, rookie mistake. If I wasn't still groggy from the tranquilliser, I might not have made it.

While I was still catching my breath, he straddled me and pinned my arms above my head. The smile he gave me was one of contempt.

"I thought you'd fight harder than that."

"Sorry to disappoint you," I said sarcastically. "Let me up and we can have a do-over."

"Tempting." He ran a hand down my side and across my belly. "Maybe we can do that next time."

"Well, that's something to look forward to, isn't it?" I didn't move while he touched me, not even a twitch. I suspected he got off on women struggling. The more I fought to get free, the more excited he'd become. And the more violent he might get.

He tugged my shirt up and pinched my nipple through my bra.

I forced myself not to react.

"Tough girl, hmmm?" He twisted my nipple until tears sprang to my eyes.

I clenched my teeth. At least the pain in my head lessened in comparison to this.

"Maybe you like it rough," he suggested. "You enjoy a little pain?" He twisted the other way until a cry involuntarily escaped my lips.

He grinned.

I swore then and there I was going to kill him. Quickly, slowly, it didn't matter. I wanted him to look me in the eyes and know his life was ending, and I was doing it. My stomach rebelled. I had never wanted to hurt anyone before, but he was a sadistic bastard. Had he violated Thora? I would almost bet on it.

"Good," he said smoothly, "get angry."

I wanted to spit in his face, but I bit back my fury.

He reached for the button of my jeans. While he tried to work it free, he loosened his grip on my wrists.

With a grunt, I rolled us and drove a knee into his groin.

He let out a cry of rage but rolled me onto my back before he pinned me with the length of his body.

His eyes watered, but he growled. "Fucking bitch, you'll pay for that." The pain in his voice gave me some satisfaction.

Not as much as I got from slamming the heel of my hand into his face.

He rolled off me and staggered to his feet, his hands over his nose. He turned and kicked me hard in the side as I tried to get back to my feet.

"Bitch. I'm going to break you so hard you'll beg me to kill you."

Before he could say another word, or act on his threat, the door swung open.

A man and a woman in laboratory coats stepped inside.

"Agent Fitz." The man gave him a look, as though he knew what the man had been up to. I couldn't tell what his opinion of it was though.

"Dr Yates. Dr Taylor." Fitz nodded. "Watch this one. She attacked me."

"Unprovoked?" Yates asked over his clipboard.

"I was simply trying to explain her place in this program," Fitz lied.

"I see." Yates nodded. "Perhaps you should have your nose seen to."

"Right." Fitz shot me a dirty look before he hurried from the room.

"That man," Taylor muttered once the door was closed again. "His temper will be a liability some day."

"But it would have been fine if he was a hybrid?" I snapped.

Yates placed his clipboard on the bed and crossed his arms. "The change to insemination by needle was a slow one, but ultimately beneficial to—"

"You're using witches as breeding cows," I growled. "Why do you care if it's a needle or a cock? It's a violation either way."

Taylor turned her face away.

"You're even worse," I told her. "You're letting it happen to other women."

"For the good of humanity," she muttered. "I've borne five children for the cause myself."

I shook my head. "You folk are sick."

"Be that as it may," Yates said, "we can't take the chance you'll be damaged."

"I'm glad my wellbeing is so important to you," I said bitterly.

"Yes, well, today we merely have questions," Yates said.

"Fuck off," I replied.

Yates ignored my response. "Why were you immune to the gas which immobilises shifters?"

I frowned. "Because I'm not a shifter." Wasn't that obvious?

"Oh, but you are a hybrid," Taylor said.

I blinked and shook my head. "I beg your pardon?"

Taylor repeated herself.

"I think I would know if I could shift."

"You may not be able to," Yates said. "Or at least, not yet. It was always going to be a question for second generation hybrids. Your father—"

I jerked my gaze back toward him. "What the hells? What does *he* have to do with this?" I rubbed my forehead. The ache was only dull now, but my head was spinning.

"You father is a hybrid," Taylor said, as if I should know that already.

I shook my head. "No, he's not. He's a wizard. Just an ordinary wizard."

"You're mistaken." Yates glanced down at his clipboard. "He's a phoenix."

"You two are out of your minds." I stepped back and sagged back against the wall. "I think I would know if my father was anything like that." After two had tried to kill me, I wasn't a huge fan of the giant birds, but the idea my father might be one was laughable. He hardly ever did magic, much less shift and fly around.

"Your father became embittered with Zeta and convinced your mother to leave. That was before you were born. Zeta paired them in the hope of creating...well, you."

Taylor nodded. "Zeta has been trying to work with you ever since. Your mother has been reluctant."

"You knew where I was, my whole life?" I guessed. When Taylor nodded, I asked, "Why wait until now?"

"We hoped your mother would bring you to us willingly," Yates said. "As a member of the board of Zeta, she—"

"What the *absolute fuck?*" There was my stomach, threatening to empty again. "She is *not*."

"Oh, but she is," Yates said. "She chose not to take further part in the breeding program, but she understands the importance."

"Wait." I took a moment for several long breaths. "My mother knows witches are being raped and bred?"

Taylor looked uncomfortable. "As I said, the needle—"

"Is still rape!" I raged. "Women are forced to have children they don't even get to meet." I couldn't believe my *mother* would have any part of it. Tears stung my eyes. I shook my head. "I don't believe she would allow it to happen. Does she know I'm here?"

"Not yet. She'll be informed when we've finished testing you."

"She won't let you keep me here," I said weakly.

"We have that time to convince you of the importance of the program," Yates said.

"By that you mean break me until I have no strength left to argue."

Neither denied it.

I sucked in a breath. "What did you mean when you said she would take no further part?"

They exchanged a glance. "That's something you should ask her."

"I'm asking you," I said coldly.

Taylor sighed. "She had two children before you. The first was stillborn. The second…"

"What?" I had siblings? This was becoming too much to process. I sucked in a breath to slow my mind a little. "What was wrong with the second?"

"Not wrong, exactly," Taylor said slowly. "She was a chimera. Technically she still is."

"She's alive," I said softly.

"Yes, but she doesn't see other people," Taylor said. "She's a danger to herself and others."

"She wants you Zeta assholes dead too, hmm?" I had zero sympathy for any of them. Let her rip their heads off.

"She almost killed your parents," Yates said dryly. "She can't control herself when she shifts, that was part of the reason your mother stopped breeding." He shrugged one shoulder. "She had you anyway."

"Yes, me, just a regular witch with no ability to shift."

"But with hybrid DNA," Yates said insistently. "And yet, the immunity I mentioned earlier. You're unique. Valuable."

He sounded so covetous, I took a step away from him. "That's what this is all about, isn't it? You knew what I was and you want to see what kind of babies I'll make. Well let me tell you, I won't play your sick games."

"Oh, you will. You're too important to the cause for us to let you do otherwise." Yates picked up his clipboard.

"We could find out what happens when a second generation hybrid breeds with a human," Taylor said coldly.

I swallowed at her thinly veiled threat. "What happened to your precious needles?"

"Whatever it takes to bend you to our way of thinking," she said.

"Bend," I said slowly, "or break?"

She shrugged indifferently.

Gods, these people were monsters. "And if I choose to go along with your shitty plan, then what?"

"Shifter DNA," Taylor replied. "We have been experimenting with dog DNA. The results are fascinating. I believe you're acquainted with Dyson? Your impregnation could be quite…pleasurable."

"Considering you had to drug him to get him to cooperate, I doubt that," I said dryly. I had thought about having children with Dyson some day, but it involved a whole lot of consent.

"I suspect bird DNA would be a better match for phoenix DNA," Taylor went on. "That was how it began after all. We know you have a bird more than happy to copulate with you."

I started. "How did you know about that?" Gods, don't tell me they were standing outside the window on one or both occasions? "Don't tell me, you have an informant at UA?"

They exchanged glances again.

"Not exactly, no," Yates replied. "Not in the way you're thinking. Zeta runs the University of Arcana."

If he'd told me I could shift into a three-headed, pink rhinoceros I couldn't have been more surprised.

"The evil government organisation who wants to kill shifters and enslave witches, runs a university for paranormals? You know shifters go there, right?" Under other circumstances I might have laughed, especially at the thought of Xav's face when he found out. His precious UA was more a danger to him than I had ever been. What a trip. Pun intended.

"Of course. It's an excellent source of recruits and knowledge," Yates replied.

I swallowed. Did Nash know about this? Did Matt? Surely they didn't, or they would have made sure I was as far away from the place as possible.

"Kane is studying science. He worked in the lab." He studied the very things they might use against us.

Yates confirmed that with a nod. "His findings have been very useful. Especially in helping us to discern how long the shifter control drug actually works. Thanks to him, we knew to increase the dosage. With help, we'll make the effects longer lasting."

"He would hate it if he knew he was helping you," I hissed.

"He might. Until we offer him a lot of money to help us. When you tell him you've decided to cooperate, that will sweeten the deal."

I crossed my arms. "I won't ever tell him that."

"You will, we'll make sure of that," Taylor said. She seemed almost bored, as if she'd held this conversation a hundred times before. They were certain they'd beat me because they beat gods knew how many others before.

"I want to see my mother," I demanded. There was no way she'd let them do any of this to me, if she knew I was here.

"In time," Taylor said with a nod. "Behave and that time will come sooner. If you decide to be difficult...you'll wish we let Fitz have you."

"I would never wish for that," I said firmly. Gods, what did they have that was worse than being violated by someone like him?

23

LEFT ALONE, I had nothing but time to consider everything they had told me. I would take it all with a grain of salt. Hells, a whole fucking barrel of it.

I slumped against the wall on the other side of the room and watched the door while my brain turned over and over. At least my stomach settled. For now.

Methodically, I teased out everything they had said, bit by bit. The first was the suggestion I had two sisters. I'd never laboured under the illusion my mother wanted me particularly much. This would explain why, but a dozen other things would as well, including her busy schedule. A schedule I was almost certain didn't include being on the board of an evil organisation. Surely she would know all about Zeta's involvement in the UA and stop me from going?

I ran a hand over my hair.

She tried, but I ignored her. I put it down to some kind of maternal need to protect me, but if it was my kid, I would have locked her in her room until she came to her senses.

I snorted to myself. She probably would have done just that if there was a chance of it working. I would have broken out and left anyway. She knew that. I was nothing if not headstrong.

Still, none of that meant she was involved with Zeta. Gods, they tried to kill us last year. There was no way…

I shook my head, but the seed of doubt had sprouted already.

Okay, so maybe I had a dangerous, living sister and an evil mother. What about my father? It sounded as though he might be involved in this up to his eyeballs as well. That was the hardest thing to swallow. My father was the most kind, gentle, decent man I knew. He wouldn't have locked me up, he would have sat me down and explained everything. Assuming he knew.

I chewed my lip. Or would he? Was it possible he really was an actual hybrid and had never told me? That seemed like the kind of thing you tell your child.

Hey, kiddo, you might shift some day, because I can. And by the way, I met your mother in a lab. We bonded over a nice bottle of DNA and an IV.

I snorted to myself. The truth was, I didn't know what was the truth. It was possible every word the agents said was a lie, designed to make me do exactly what I was doing, freaking out. I needed to stop and think about what I knew to be fact.

Fact, Kane cared about me and he would never play along with their sick games, unless they drugged him. Same with Dyson.

Fact, Nash also cared about me and he was probably out there planning to break me out of here. Same with Matt, even if he wouldn't admit it.

Fact, Ariana—I winced, I almost forgot about her. My mother arranged for her and Matt to keep an eye on me. By leaving her out of Jess' attempted rescue, we kept her safe from this. For that I was grateful, although including her might have increased the chance of success. Maybe I wouldn't be sitting here right now, waiting for…

I stopped myself before I spiralled into a black hole.

"Fact, I'm a badass," I muttered. I could wait for them to take me or I could get myself out of here.

Tentatively, I tried to draw magic again. The searing pain wasn't quite as bad as the first time, but it still sucked.

Fine, old fashioned escape plan it was then.

I rose and tweaked aside the curtain which hung over the small window.

Barred. No surprise there.

I grabbed two of them and pulled.

Nothing. Whoever put them in place intended them to stay there. I doubted even a blast of magic would make them budge. Even if they would, the drop once I got out the window would probably kill me. Unless I was an actual phoenix, but on the way to my death was no time to test that theory.

I peered out, just in case a dragon hovered outside the window.

Nope, just a whole lot of blue sky and trees.

That left the door, but leaving through a building full of Zeta agents would be difficult, even with magic.

I tried the knob, but the door was locked, as I expected. I could try to kick the door down, but it looked as solidly made as the bars.

"Fuck you, good workmanship," I muttered. Why couldn't this place have been made by a cowboy builder? It was the government, for the gods' sake, they were all about cutting corners.

Apparently not today.

I looked up for a vent, skylight, anything I could climb into. The ceiling was unbroken except for the lights and they were too small for anything but a flea.

"Ladies and gentlemen," I said under my breath, "the situation was looking difficult for your hero, but she's not giving up yet." *She is, however, talking to herself.*

The door clicked and swung open. I had to force down the urge to jump back, especially when I saw Fitz's bandaged face and furious eyes. I wasn't sure if the two armed agents with him were a good thing or a very bad thing.

"This way." He jerked his head toward the corridor.

Rule number one, never let a potential attacker take you somewhere else. Did that rule even apply here? I didn't know, but I didn't immediately comply.

"Why?" I asked instead.

His face turned pink. Not a cute pink like Kane, but an ugly, blotchy pink.

"Move," he snarled.

"Have you ever tried saying please?" I asked.

"You enjoyed being tranquillised that much?" he replied.

I only paused for a moment longer before I stepped out of the room. I couldn't risk being asleep around a vengeful man like Fitz.

"Where are we going?" I asked cheerfully. I walked behind one of the agents, with Fitz and the other behind me. I took note of every turn we made until we reached the elevator and waited.

"You'll see. Keep your mouth shut." Fitz poked me in the side with his gun, right in the spot he'd kicked me.

I winced. Through watering eyes, I saw him smile.

Fucker.

"I guess your nose is broken." I peered at it.

Blotchy pink turned to blotchy red. I suspected if we were alone, he would have struck me across the face. As it was, he poked me again in the same place.

"If you know what's good for you, you'll keep your mouth shut," he growled.

"Is he always so grumpy?" I asked one of the other agents, a man with curly hair. I knew to move away from Fitz before he could touch me again.

The elevator pinged and the door slid open.

"The last time I was in an elevator with Zeta agents, they both ended up dead," I remarked. "Are you sure you want to take that risk?"

"Inside," Curly instructed. "No one needs to die today."

"He does." I nodded toward Fitz. "He's a nasty piece of—"

Fitz took a swing at my face, but I ducked and he missed. He staggered forward a few steps.

"See what I mean?" I said to Curly. "That would have hurt."

"Keep your mouth shut and it won't happen again." Curly ushered me inside the elevator.

"Victim blaming much?" I muttered. I eyed the last agent, a woman with wheat-blonde hair and striking blue eyes. I couldn't tell what she was thinking about any of this.

I leaned against the side of the elevator, arms crossed, every bit of me as far from Fitz as I could get.

The elevator moved down. Two floors. Three. Four. Five.

It stopped on the twelfth floor. I know, I would have guessed they'd take me to the thirteenth too, but maybe they were superstitious.

"Out, please." Curly nodded.

I immediately moved to comply. "See where having manners gets you?"

For some reason, Curly smiled at that. He would have been cute if not for the whole evil organisation thing.

"To the right," Fitz barked. He led the way down the corridor.

I felt safer behind him, with Curly and the woman on either side of me. Safe, of course, was a relative term. I was far from safe, really.

Fitz pulled out a card, slid it through the reader beside a door and pushed it open.

"Inside."

I hesitated. If I stepped into this room, I would be locked in again. I had already determined that only led to being trapped.

"Please." Curly sounded amused.

Fitz shot him a dark look, but Curly shrugged and gestured for me to precede him into the room.

I sighed and took a step forward.

A ringtone broke the silence of the corridor and Fitz swore. He pulled a phone out of his pocket.

"Blake, get the bitch inside and ready for the doctors." He stalked off down the corridor, the phone to his ear.

"Saved by the bell," Curly said with a smile.

"Blake…" the woman said, her tone clearly a warning.

"No, Corinne, it's time." Blake grabbed my arm and pulled me into the room.

Corinne followed and closed the door behind us.

I managed to jerk my arm from Blake and turned to face him,

hands up, ready to fight back. Had I traded one wannabe rapist for another?

"It's okay." Blake put his gun away and raised his own hands. "We won't hurt you. We work for the council. We're here to help you."

Corinne sighed and put her own gun away. "I told you you're too soft for this undercover stuff. The first pretty face and you fold."

Blake shrugged and held out his hand. "I'm Blake Jordan. This is my cousin Corinne." He smiled, forming a dimple in his cheek.

"I knew you were too cute to be a baddie," I said without thinking.

Blake laughed. "I don't know about that."

Corinne snorted. "Yes you do and you know it. Now stop wasting time, we need to get out of here."

"About that." I pointed toward the door. "We're in enemy territory here. There's some kind of dampening field on magic."

They exchanged nods. "We need to bring down that field and get the witches out of here. We need your help for that."

"Hey, I'm as badass as the next girl—" Corinne did seem pretty badass, "but they have guns, tranquillisers and the numbers."

"And we have a phoenix," Corinne said softly.

It took a moment to realise she was talking about me.

I shook my head. "I know they think that, but I've never shifted in my life."

"They brought you here for that," Corinne said.

I looked around the room now. It was another lab, this one bigger than the one at UA by at least twice.

"They've developed a formula to make shifters shift."

I blinked, but it made sense. They would have been searching for a way to stop them. Perhaps they'd stumbled upon the opposite during their research.

"So you want me to take it?" I grimaced. None of this seemed like a good idea to me.

When Blake nodded, I added, "And what if it doesn't work?"

"Then we'll try plan b," Blake said.

"There is no plan b," Corinne said.

Blake looked at her sharply. "There isn't?"

She shook her head. "No, just plan a. They were sure this would work. I wasn't going to try this yet, but bringing you here has forced our hand." She frowned at Blake.

He shrugged. "It felt right."

"So, if I'm not a shifter, we go straight to plan f?" I asked. "As in, we're fucked."

2 4

"HOW HORRIBLE IS this going to taste and why should I trust either of you?" I frowned at the vial of white, cloudy liquid.

"Do you want the answers to those in that order?" Blake asked.

I held the vial to the side so I could look at him through one eye. "Either way is fine."

"You can trust us," Corinne said quickly. "But even if you don't, they'd make you drink that anyway. If Fitz were here, he'd tie you down first, just in case."

"Right." I could just imagine what else that would entail.

"This way we can be ready when he comes back." Blake glanced meaningfully toward the door. "He won't be much longer."

"Did you organise that phone call?" I asked.

"I wish." Blake leaned against a workbench. "That was just dumb luck."

"Speak for yourself," Corinne said.

Blake gave her a surprised glance, but his expression quickly changed to impressed. "Nice."

Corinne shrugged. "Drink up. I'm going to pull my gun so it looks like we're forcing you into it." She nodded at Blake to do the same.

The doorknob turned.

I opened the vial and gulped down the contents. It tasted like the kind of medicine you usually take from a needle, not by mouth.

"Ugh, disgusting. Leave it to you evil people to make everything taste like crap." I stuck out my tongue and gave Blake a look as if I still assumed he was on Fitz's side.

The door opened. Fitz stepped inside. He stopped, took in the scene and his mouth twitched to the side.

"She should be bound," he said coolly. "For her own protection." He stalked toward me and pulled a cable tie out of his pocket.

I shit you not. Apparently he carried them around with him like he thought he might need one at any moment.

"No need." I held up a hand. "I told you I'm not a shifter." My hand turned blue and sprouted feathers. Where a moment ago I'd had an arm, I now had a wing.

"Fuck."

At least that's what I would have said if I had a mouth and not a beak.

Apparently they were right.

That was the last coherent thought I had before my mind became a tumult of emotion and sensation. I had wings.

I could fly.

I had been lied to.

I could rip Fitz's head off.

I started toward him.

Eyes wide with fear, he backed toward the door. "Get the tranquilliser!" His voice was so high I thought his balls might have retreated into his body. "Use it on the bitch!"

I lifted a foot… No, giant, taloned claws.

I stared at them for a moment, then shredded Fitz from the top of his head right down to his calves. He didn't even have time to let out a squeak. Blood rained out of him, covered the floor. Gore stained my claws.

I let out a bird-like squawk. The phoenix part of me revelled in the smell of blood, the joy of killing. The rest of me was shoved so far back into my head I could barely register my own existence. All I wanted was to kill again.

I turned toward the other agents. Stalked toward them.

One shouted something, but I couldn't make it out. It didn't matter, I just wanted to kill.

"Peyton!"

What was that? *Who* was that? Who dared to try to break through to me? I was a phoenix, made to destroy. Made to burn the world down.

"It's me, Dyson. I fought back. Now *you* have to."

Dyson? Did I know that name?

I swung around. He stood near the door. I sensed the warmth of his body.

I stepped toward him. I was a creature of fire. I needed to take his heat, to leave him cold. When they were all cold, I would burn what was left and then burn the ashes.

"Peyton! You need to shift back to yourself," Dyson called out. "It's hard the first time, but you can do it. You don't want to hurt anyone else."

I hissed. Yes I did. Why didn't he understand that?

I shook my head. My mind was a jumble. All I could think of was death. No, it was more than that. I wanted to be sure I'd done the job right.

I stopped over to Fitz's corpse and tore his mangled head from his shoulders with my beak. I spat on the floor, leaving a splatter of blood and saliva. Let that be a warning to them all not to fuck with me.

I shook my beak. Droplets of blood flew everywhere, but my thoughts were clearer now.

"Come back to me," he urged. "I love you. We need you to be you so we can all get out of here."

Out of here. The words resonated. Dyson was wrong, they didn't need me in witch form, they needed me like this.

I tried to speak, but my shifter form wouldn't make words. I put a clawed foot to my head instead.

"The dampening field." Corinne appeared in front of me and nodded. "It's a level down." Specks of blood coated her cheek, but she didn't seem to notice. At least it wasn't hers. Thanks to Dyson, I came back to myself in time.

I tapped at the floor with a claw while I thought. I wasn't going to fit in the elevator like this, but I had to bring down that field.

I bobbed my head and stepped over to the window. What a dragon could do, surely a phoenix could as well.

I gripped the bars in my claws and tore them clean out of the wall. With barely a heave, I tossed them through the window and jumped out after them.

Okay, here's the bit where I should have practiced flying first. I plunged like a stone for several floors until I managed to throw out my arms and catch myself.

I flapped like crazy and rose back to the twelfth floor. Dyson all but hung out the window.

"That's my girl." He grinned.

I let out a little creel and dropped the floor below. As easily as before, I tore the bars off the window and threw them into the room.

The three or four occupants screamed and ran for the door. I thought about killing them. I *wanted* to, but if they ended up being on my side…

I let them go and turned toward a panel on the side of the room. I had expected to find a mechanism attached to the brain of a witch, or at least some kind of complicated machinery.

Instead, a large, black stone, like a huge pearl, sat in the centre of the panel. I heard about witches using stones, but I had never seen one. It was considered an antiquated way to use magic. Evidently it was also efficient.

I landed on the cool floor with all the elegance of a brick and knocked the stone out of the panel with a flick of my claw. It rolled out and clattered onto the tiles where it lay still, barely a metre from the wall.

Was that far enough to stop it from working?

I had just finished that thought when a wave of energy washed over me. It felt like hot wind that made my skin tingle. I fell to my knees, suddenly groggy, but not like when I had been tranquillised. This was something different altogether, something much more powerful.

I felt as if the stone was absorbing every bit of magic inside me, witch and shifter. I was vaguely aware of returning to witch form before I slumped down on the cold, hard floor.

I WOKE BRIEFLY.

I wasn't sure what woke me until I heard voices nearby.

"...damaged the stone."

"...she's going to be furious."

"...have our heads."

"I'll handle her."

She who?

I opened my eyes a crack. As far as I could tell, I hadn't moved from where I'd fallen. I was very aware I was now fully naked. Fitz was dead, so I didn't need to worry about him, but that didn't mean I was safe.

I wriggled my fingers and toes. Could I shift again if I needed to?

The stone. I should be able to use magic now. Unless...the sensation of the stone sucking it away had actually done that.

Before I could try, the speakers stepped closer. One bent down and picked up the stone in a black bag.

"Don't touch it." A voice spoke from behind me.

"Of course not, love. I'm no fool." The man with the bag closed the top of it and turned so I caught a look at his face.

What the fuck?

His skin was red. Not flushed like a blush or sunburn, but red like... Nothing I had ever seen. Narrow eyes, like slits shone with an orange glow.

Part of me wanted to get up and run like hells. I wasn't sure if he knew I was watching, but I sensed he did. For some reason, he didn't see me as a threat.

Shame I can't say the same for you, buddy.

He stepped around me and headed toward the door with his companions. I wanted to see if they were like him, but I dared not roll over to find out. I preferred not threatening and alive to satisfying my curiosity. For once.

The door clicked shut and the darkness claimed me again.

"PEYTON? Hey, come on, wake up. Shit, do you think she's hurt? I can't see any sign of injury. Peyton?"

I groaned. Once again, my head pounded. Great. This day sucked.

"She's alive!"

"Stop shouting, Dyson." I peered up at him. "I love you, too. Why aren't you wearing a shirt?"

He smiled, but it faded quickly. "I had to shift. We dealt with an agent or two. We need to get out of here."

"Right." I sat up and winced. "Are you all right?" I gave him a speculative look.

"I'm drug free," he said firmly. "Corinne gave me an antidote."

I nodded. I'd have to remember to thank her later. "Say, did you see a redhead go past?"

"Fitz is gone, remember?" Blake stepped into view. His eyes widened as he saw me naked. He promptly took off his agent jacket and draped it over me.

Aww, I guess chivalry isn't dead after all.

"Thanks." I pulled it closer. "I don't mean red hair, I mean..." Maybe I had imagined it. I looked over to where the stone had lain. It was gone now.

"What was that?" I let Dyson help me to my feet and took a moment to admire his dick. Hey, I wasn't dead. "The stone. It was here..."

Corinne glanced around before exchanging looks and shrugs with

Blake. "Rumour says the dampening field was created by an ancient artefact." Her blonde hair was messy and flecked with blood. "If my grandmother was to be believed, it was crafted by demons."

"Demons?" I laughed awkwardly. "There's no such things as demons." Or was there? Gods, I didn't know anymore. Redhead certainly looked—well—demonic, even if he hadn't harmed me in any way. Not that I knew of. I hadn't become his lunch at any rate.

"Come on, we need to hurry. Once the field dropped, a bunch of witches started to fight back, but they won't be distracted for long." Corinne led the way to the door and peered out.

"Um, wouldn't it be easier to fly out?" I asked.

"Can you carry us all?" Dyson asked.

I blinked at him. "Stairs it is then."

"This is all too familiar," Dyson remarked as we headed for the door to emergency stairs.

"Isn't it though?" I grimaced. All we were lacking was Matt, also naked or in gargoyle form. "We really have to stop Zeta from chasing us around places with multiple floors."

"Agreed. Stairs are so claustrophobic. A firefighter pole would be good right now."

"Or a…wait." I pulled him back into the room and gestured for the others to follow. "Has anyone got a phone?"

"I do." Blake unlocked his and handed it to me.

I opened the magic app.

"Oh no, please say you're not," Dyson groaned. A smile tugged at the corners of his mouth.

"Oh, I most certainly am." I grinned. I walked to the window and aimed the phone. The magic came rushing to me faster than ever. Maybe the stone had had some kind of impact on me. I couldn't think about that right now. I focused, clicked on the screen and watched the magic come to life.

"Other people might be cool," I handed Blake back his phone with a flourish, "but they're not "escaping from an evil organisation's secret compound by gigantic, magical waterslide" cool."

"You're fucking crazy," Dyson told me. 'And I love it. Now, let's get out of here."

I climbed out the window and onto the top of the slide. It was still a long way down and I was held up by nothing but magic, but I sat in the flow of water and let gravity take me toward the ground in a blur.

Wheeee.

2 5

I SLID out into a pair of arms. As we fell in a tangle of legs and confusion, I thought I must have bowled down a Zeta agent.

I drew magic, ready to blast them back.

"Woah, steady there, loveliness." Nash raised his hands in surrender. He was wet from where I ran into him, but apparently unharmed.

"What the hells?" I pushed myself to my knees. It was good to see him. So good my heart skipped a beat. "It's about time you showed up."

He frowned.

"Sir," I added.

He smiled. "It took a while to find where they'd taken you. I—" He grabbed my hand and rolled us both to one side just as Dyson slid out of the end of the slide.

"Maybe we should find somewhere safer to talk," I remarked.

"This works for me."

Of course it did, I was lying on top of him, his arms around me.

"Save it for when we're not outside a building full of Zeta agents," Matt suggested.

I glanced over. I hadn't seen him until now. "He has a point."

"I always do," Matt replied. He drew back as Corinne landed neatly on her feet.

"She's with us." I got to my feet but held on to Nash's hand. I wasn't ready to be apart from him yet. He felt like…safety. "Him, too."

Blake slid out a moment later, uniform drenched, huge smile on his face. He looked like a little boy who had just discovered adrenaline hits.

The waterslide disappeared a moment later.

We followed suit, just as a pair of agents appeared in the window we had used to escape. They peered around, spoke words I couldn't hear, then disappeared back inside.

"They'll be down here before long," Nash said softly. "Everyone head north. We'll meet at the car."

"Roger that," Matt replied. I hadn't seen him take Dyson's hand, but he must have. Good, he would be safe with Matt.

Nash squeezed my hand and we started walking.

"I guess you guys took out any alarms on the perimeter fence," I said conversationally.

"Alarms and guards," Nash replied in a tone which suggested he'd killed or at least maimed them.

He would be in a dark mood later, but I wouldn't let him be alone to brood.

"Are you all right?" he asked softly.

I took a moment to respond. "Physically I am. The rest will take a while." I gave him a brief rundown of what had taken place, including what they'd said about my mother, my father ,and the UA.

"Did you know the University of Arcana was run by Zeta?" I asked. "I guess the horrid uniforms they made us wear should have been an indication. I mean, who would make us wear those unless they were evil?"

Nash mouth quirked upward, but he didn't look surprised. He chewed his lip and led me toward a copse of trees. "I was starting to suspect as much. They knew how to reach you and Dyson. We surmised that someone had told them, but I wondered if there was more to it than that. The pink donut wasn't so much an infiltration as it was an experiment."

"One Kane inadvertently took part in with his work in the lab." I sighed. "Where is he anyway? And Ariana and Hamish? They won't be safe there anymore."

"Right." Nash pulled out his phone, punched in some text with one deft thumb and slid it back in his pocket.

I waited for a moment but when he didn't say anything else, I asked, "And?"

"And what?"

"Will they be okay?"

"My priority is to get you somewhere safer—"

"Lincoln Nash." I stopped mid-step.

He frowned at my use of his full name. Or the name he went by, at least. I was almost certain it wasn't his real name.

"You know I can't rest until I know they're safe too."

He sighed and tugged me onward. "Shhh." He looked back over his shoulder.

"Don't—" Then I heard them. Shouts and the baying of dogs.

"Shit. I don't want to kill any dogs," I whispered. "That's bad juju."

"Assuming they're actually dogs," Nash replied.

"Oh." I froze.

Heads appeared, bounding over the terrain we'd just crossed. Three heads. One body.

Cerberus. Trust Zeta to have an actual fucking hellhound!

"What do we do?" I asked frantically. My phoenix form could probably rip the hound's heads off, but that was if I could shift and was willing to kill again. Which I wasn't if I could help it.

Cerberus stopped and bared three sets of teeth and a whole bunch of saliva. He growled deep in the back of all of his throats. He definitely meant business.

He stalked forward.

"What else are you going to fight a dog with?" Nash asked. How did he sound so calm?

"Uh." It took me a moment. "Right."

"On three. One. Two. Three."

He dropped the magic bubble from around us just as I conjured the tiger from my tattoo. Was it bigger than the last time? It certainly seemed more solid somehow. I suppose I was getting better at conjuring.

Cerberus skidded to a halt in front of the tiger.

"Now, we run." Nash snapped the bubble back around us, took my hand and we bolted as the sound of two large animals clashing rang out.

A canine howl of pain made me wince, especially when it was cut short.

"One head down, two to go." Nash sounded grim.

I grimaced and kept running, even though the ground was tearing up my bare feet.

"Not much further," he told me. "Can you climb?" He waved toward a wire fence as we rounded some trees.

"Just try to stop me," I replied. I released his hand as I drew to make a bubble around myself. The magic felt as though it flew into me. I caught a look of surprise on Nash's face before our bubbles separated.

I didn't take time to think about it, I just scaled the fence. My small feet fit nicely into the holes and over the top. I dropped to the ground just as the fence started to buzz.

"It looks like they got the power back on," Nash remarked. "Hopefully the others got over in time."

"Yeah." I glanced around but saw no sign of them and no indication any guards had seen a naked shifter climbing the fence. I could only hope they'd make it to our meeting point.

"I'm right beside you," Nash said.

I felt a hand brush my chest. I dropped my bubble for just long enough for Nash's to envelope me again.

"Hey," he said softly. "I think I forgot to mention I'm glad you're alive." His lips brushed mine and sent a jolt of heat through me. "Come on, let's get somewhere safer."

"Good plan," I replied, although part of me wanted to tear off his damp clothes and let him take me up against a tree. More than that though, I didn't want to get caught. My libido would have to wait.

Breathless, we trotted the rest of the way to a small SUV parked amongst the bushes maybe a kilometre from the Zeta building.

To my relief, Matt and Dyson were already sitting inside, Dyson wearing a blanket. Blake and Corinne trotted up shortly afterward.

"We can't go with you," Corinne said. "We need to report to the council. They'll need to know what happened here. They may also reconsider recommending the UA to young paranormals."

"Good idea," I said dryly. They would still go there, though. The education they got at the university was second to none. Well, except the Academy of Modern Magic. And maybe the College of Advanced Magical Education.

"We did good here today," Blake assured me. "You especially. A lot of witches owe you a debt of gratitude."

"Thanks," I said awkwardly. Some wouldn't though; those who thought they were doing a good thing.

"I'm sure I'll see you again." He gave me a dimpled smile and a kiss on the cheek before the pair clasped hands and disappeared.

"Yeah," I said softly. "I'm sure."

"Hey." Dyson climbed out of the SUV. "Kane called. He said Ariana had insisted he go with her and Hamish to the city for lunch. Then she told him why he can't go back."

I glanced at Nash, who shrugged as if he wasn't behind all of that.

"I guess we'll meet them there."

"There's a little matter of all our belongings," Matt said, as if this was all my fault.

"Don't worry about that," I said, "Xav owes me a favour. I bet he'll be thrilled to pack up everything we own and ship it off to…wherever we're going."

"The council will find a place," Nash assured me. "At least we don't have to hide anymore." He pulled me to him and kissed me deeply. He slipped his hands under the jacket and cupped my rear.

"I guess I'm driving," Matt remarked.

"You guessed right." Nash guided me to the back of the car and closed the door behind us.

I vaguely heard the front doors close as Dyson and Matt got in.

Nash eased off the jacket I had been wearing and kissed my neck.

Slowly, he moved down my body. He teased my nipple with the tip of his tongue and slipped a hand down between my legs.

I parted them for him.

"Shouldn't you two have seatbelts on?" Matt asked dryly.

"Drive carefully," Nash growled. He dipped two fingers inside me. I was already as wet as hells.

I moaned softly. And again when we stopped at a set of traffic lights and a truck pulled up alongside us. The driver peered down at us. His eyes widened as I unzipped Nash's pants and freed his erection. I ran my hand up and down his hot length.

I gave the truck driver a smile and closed my eyes. I rocked my body against Nash's touch. My lips dropped apart and I panted as I came.

The truck drew away a moment later.

"You're so beautiful." Nash carefully moved himself up the car seat until he lay over me. I wound my legs around him.

"Even when I'm not tied up, sir?" I teased.

"Even then." He slid his cock into me and groaned.

I sighed with the pleasure of him filling me fully. I opened my eyes a crack to see Dyson watching from the front seat. He gave me a smile. Someday I wanted to have him inside me. If I was honest, I wanted Matt too. I almost insisted we pull over so they could join us in the back, but there would be time for that later. That didn't stop me from picturing them pushing back the seats and lying beside us. I imagined taking Matt's cock into my mouth, while my fingers curled around Dyson's. Then Kane was there in my mind, his fingertip teasing my rear hole.

Nash pulled almost all the way out and slid back into me. He went still, then drew back again.

"Peyton," he said, his mouth beside my ear. "I'm falling so hard for you."

I swallowed. "I'm falling for you too, sir."

Gods, what was I going to do with all of these guys and my feelings for them all? Part of me was even eager to see Blake again. I was certainly looking forward to seeing Kane, safe and sound.

Nash grunted and moved faster. Every thrust drove me closer and closer to the edge.

"Say that again," he said, breathlessly.

"Sir," I said. "Fuck me harder, sir."

He grunted and came, spilling hot seed into me and driving me over the edge again. I arched my back as pleasure washed over me.

"Gods, yes…sir."

I had barely started to come down before he relaxed his weight on top of me and sighed.

"You're amazing, but they won't stop hunting us," he said softly. "We got away, but this isn't over."

I closed my eyes to keep from looking out of the car. If someone was following, I didn't want to see them, not yet.

***

Will the AMM find a new home? Who is the guy with the red face? Will Blake return? Find out by reading on.

LOGICAL MAGIC

ACADEMY OF MODERN MAGIC BOOK 3

1

"WE'RE GOING WHERE?" I looked up from my book to frown at Nash.

He had an, "I've got this, don't question me," look on his face, which was as sexy as hells. Of course, it never stopped me from asking before and it didn't now.

"Illusion Bay," he repeated.

"I like the sound of that," Dyson remarked. "Very mysterious." He paused before adding, "Are you sure it's really there?"

I had spent the last hour sitting between Dyson's legs, his arm around me while I read. Apparently reading was now such a dangerous pastime I needed a guard for it.

Not that I was complaining.

Nash shot him a look and Dyson's body shook with laughter.

"Isn't that up near Byron Bay?" Matt frowned. While the rest of us were holed up in a safe house Nash organised, Matt lived somewhere else, but dropped by almost every day. I asked him where he was staying, but he refused to answer. I suspected it was somewhere close, but apart from that, I had no idea.

"Yeah." Nash lowered himself to the chair opposite me. Like Kane and Dyson, he was never far away from me, apart from the odd night he spent away on council business. Or so he said.

I had no reason not to believe him, but he wouldn't give any details either. Some days it seemed as though they forgot how badass I was. On other days it just seemed as though they were trying to save me from stress. No matter how much I growled or asked nicely, neither Nash nor Matt would tell me anything more.

"Illusion Bay is what Byron Bay used to be," Nash added, "before all the celebrities moved in and made it expensive."

"Surf all day, smoke weed all night?" Dyson asked. "Sounds great. When do we leave?"

"That sounds like a strange place for a university." Kane closed the comic he'd been reading and sat forward.

"Exactly," Nash replied. "But that's where the College of Advanced Magical Education campus is. Amongst the bushes and the beach."

I snorted. "And who came up with that name?"

Dyson chuckled. "What's wrong with CAME?"

I grinned. "Nothing at all, unless you're trying to be taken seriously."

"Life is way too short for that," Dyson replied.

"Hells yeah to that," I muttered. "So, the AMM still has no campus of its own?"

"The council is working on it," Matt replied. He jumped up and started pacing. "They want to find a place away from Zeta influence."

"Right." Last year I was told, by two Zeta agents, that my mother sat on the board of Zeta and the Paranormal Council. So far, neither Nash nor Matt found further information to prove or disprove the claim. I could ask my mother face to face, but Nash preferred I didn't see her, or my father. Until he knew which side she was on, he didn't trust her. Truth be told, neither did I. The suggestion I might be a hybrid had turned out to be accurate after all. What else was true?

"The council is keeping an eye on your mother," Nash said softly. "And looking for any connection to Zeta."

I sighed. "It's the last bit that worries me." Why would anyone want their own child to be locked away and bred like a prized racehorse? Did Zeta have something over her, apart from influence? I had to believe they did. I didn't want to think she would willingly want me used in any way.

Dyson gave me a squeeze. "We'll get to the bottom of it, one way or another, okay?"

I snuggled into him more. "I know. It's the uncertainty that's difficult. I mean, why didn't they tell me I could shift? That seems like the kind of information you tell a gal."

He rubbed his thumb over the back of my hand. "My guess is they weren't sure either. Magic isn't an exact science."

"You sound like Kane," I teased. I grinned at Kane, who smiled back.

"Dyson is right, though," Kane said.

"Can I get that in writing?" Dyson asked. "Or better yet, on camera." He reached for his phone.

Kane flipped him off. "Your friend Jess is from a paranormal family and can't do magic. There are no assurances children will follow in their parent's footsteps."

I grimaced at the mention of Jess. She nearly died, thanks to Zeta holding her hostage to get my attention. Nash assured me she was safe, but I hadn't seen or heard from her since that day. She was probably too scared to try to contact me. I didn't blame her. That didn't stop me from missing her terribly.

I shook my head. "I know, but they could have warned me about the possibility."

"Given how hard it is to control the killing urge of the phoenix, they might have been in denial," Matt said flatly.

"Thanks for that vote of confidence." I grimaced at him.

He shrugged, unapologetic. "Why do you think they sent them after us?"

"Because they're pretty?" I asked sweetly.

Matt raised an eyebrow. "They might be pretty, but they're also vicious. You would know that better than anyone."

I suspected he was implying I was nasty in witch form too. I stuck out my tongue at him. He wasn't wrong though, at least about the phoenix. When I had first shifted, I had wanted to kill everything in sight. Only Dyson telling me he loved me had brought me back to my usual, adorable self.

"So anyway," Kane interrupted, "when do we leave?"

"When our escort arrives," Nash replied.

"I assume you're not referring to ones who charge by the hour," I said lightly. "So why an escort? Between us we have two witches, three hybrids, a kickass dog, and an equally kickass owl."

Kane looked pleased at being called that. I knew he didn't think his shifter form was especially intimidating.

"Who's kicking whose ass?" Ariana walked into the room, her boyfriend Hamish in tow. As far as I could tell, they hadn't been apart for a moment since we left the UA.

Nash sighed. "I was just explaining to Peyton that the council was sending an agent or two to accompany us to Illusion Bay. We can't all travel together, there are too many of us to go unnoticed."

"Is this my life now?" I asked, a little snappy at being babied. "Not allowed to go outside without every step being watched?"

"You're allowed outside whenever you like." Nash gestured toward the door.

"The house is in the bush, a bajillion kilometres from anywhere," I pointed out. "There's no one to see me."

"Tell me about it," Kane said, looking sulky.

After a moment I broke into a laugh. He got off on people watching us fuck; the more the merrier. Out here, the audience was greatly reduced, unless we were filmed and put on Porn Hustle. I wasn't quite ready to have myself recorded on camera again. After the photo he took of me was hacked and went viral, I was reluctant to do it again. Although, if I could disguise my face…

The idea of thousands of people watching me made me swallow hard. My core throbbed.

"Anyway." I blinked to return myself to the present. "I can take care of myself."

"I know you can," Nash replied. "Maybe the escort is for the others." His mouth quirked up in a faint smile. He rarely joked, but when he did, he melted my heart a little more.

Who was I kidding, he made my heart a hot puddle a long time ago, along with my sex. So did Kane and Dyson. What I felt for Matt was more complicated. I had feelings for him, to be sure, and I wanted to get him naked and sweaty, but he could be such a jerk. A part of me hoped to see Blake—a guy who had helped me out of the Zeta compound—again at some point.

Yeah, okay, I don't know what was up with me either. Although we didn't talk about it, I know they all hoped I would choose them some day. The problem was, I couldn't choose. I wasn't sure I would ever be able to. Certainly not today.

"I guess Matt could use a little help." I gave him a sly smile.

"Fuck you," Matt retorted.

"You wish," I shot back.

His tongue flicked over his lips. I was reasonably sure he *did* wish. I knew he liked watching me and pleasuring himself at the same time.

"You know," he said slowly. "You're right. I might need help to keep from getting killed by Peyton or something she does."

I was sure he meant it as a joke, but it stung. There was far too much truth in his words. Zeta coming after me resulted in the deaths of several students and a teacher, the capture of both Dyson and Jess, and Nash was forced to kill again to save us all. I could add a bunch of Zeta agents to that tally. If I went quietly in the first place, a lot of people, innocent or otherwise, would still be alive. I was a danger to all of them.

Eyes stinging with tears, I jumped up from the couch and ran toward the door. I wrenched it open and hurried outside.

"You fucking idiot," I heard one of the guys say behind me. "What did you have to go and say that..."

"I just..."

I headed toward the trees so I couldn't hear them argue any longer.

"Peyton!"

I ducked behind the first set of trees as Kane called me. I ignored him and kept on walking.

"Wait!" he yelled. "Please!"

I sighed and stopped, but didn't turn around. If he did, he'd see the tears which poured down my cheeks.

"He's a dick." Kane was closer now. "He shouldn't have said that."

"It was accurate." I sniffed. "I should leave before you all get killed."

"We're not going to get killed." His hand rested on my shoulder. "We don't even know if Zeta is after us."

"After I ruined their breeding program? Oh, they'll be after me, if only for that. While you're around me, you're in danger."

He exhaled softly and turned me to face him. "I'd rather be in danger with you than be without you." He swallowed audibly. "I love you."

I wiped tears from my cheek with the back of my hand. "I…I love you, too."

His expression softened. "You're the most amazing person I know. And the only other bird."

I blinked in surprise. "Hey, you're right. About the bird part." I didn't feel particularly amazing right now. "Maybe you can teach me to fly?"

"I'd like that." He wiped his thumb over a new tear.

"I'll promise not to eat you," I said without humour.

"That's a shame, I quite like being eaten." His expression was deadpan until I smiled and socked him on the arm.

"I didn't mean *that* kind of eating. That's the kind I can do." I eyed his groin as his pants tented.

"Thank the gods for that." He sounded a little choked. "Maybe we should go inside?"

Honestly, he was the only guy I knew who would go inside for *less* privacy.

A couple of birds called out from a tree nearby.

"We have an audience already," I pointed out. I reached for the top of his track pants and slid them down his hips. His boxers followed, letting his erection spring free. "And he is ready."

"So ready," Kane murmured.

I sank to my knees in front of him and slid my tongue down the length of his cock.

"Mmm."

I looked up at him as I licked my way back up and circled his already beaded tip. Kane's eyes were closed and a faint smile graced his lips.

I closed my mouth around his cock and started to suck gently.

"Gods, yes," he breathed. He tangled a hand in my hair.

I took him in deeper, almost to the back of my throat.

"Peyton, I'm sorry..." Matt skidded to a stop a couple of metres away. "Oh, I should have known." His face turned slightly pink. "I'll talk to you later." He turned around.

"Why don't you stay?" Kane suggested.

Matt turned back, eyes wide. His cock strained against the front of his pants.

I paused for a moment. Matt and I had an undeniable attraction. I might not admit it, but I liked having him around, including during intimate moments. I wanted to explore that with him. Maybe this was our chance.

I slid my mouth off Kane's cock and licked his tip again. "I want you to stay. If you want to."

Matt groaned. "I really..." His hand twitched beside his groin as though he wanted desperately to grab himself.

Fuck this dancing around. If anything was going to happen between us, someone would have to make the first move. That might as well be me.

I moved away from Kane and crawled the few steps across the mercifully soft grass. I stopped in front of Matt and reached for the fly of his jeans. My heart pounded at my own boldness. I half expected Matt to turn and run. This was a big step for us both. In spite of myself, I cared about him as much as I cared about the other guys. I wasn't ready to tell him that, but I could show him.

When he didn't run, I undid the button and slid down the zip. In a moment his erection was hot and hard in my hand. I stroked his length several times before I closed my mouth on him.

He shivered a little. "Oh my gods." Placing a gentle hand in my hair, he guided me down to the ground, so I lay beside him, his cock deep inside my mouth.

I looked him in the eyes and what I saw there went far beyond pleasure, beyond lust. I let my eyes smile, then closed them and sucked slowly.

Kane moved to lay on the other side of me and slipped my shirt up and away from my breasts. He leaned down to thoroughly lick and suck one firm peak, then the other. He lavished equal attention on both. He was always so considerate in making sure I enjoyed myself.

I rubbed Matt's balls gently while Kane undid my pants and slid them down my legs. The air was cold on my bare ass. I shivered slightly, but Kane warmed me by kissing and nipping his way across my skin. He bent my leg and buried his face between my legs.

I gasped aloud as his tongue tickled against my sex with just the right amount of pressure to drive me wild immediately. Gods, he always knew just what I liked.

Matt bucked slowly and moaned before he pulled away from me. He worked his way down to take his turn at sucking on my nipples.

"I've wanted to do this for so long," he muttered.

I moaned in agreement. Having him touch me felt even better than I'd dared to imagine. Between his mouth and Kane's tongue lapping at my folds, I was already close to the edge.

Kane slid a finger inside me and worked me from the inside and out. Every touch made me want to scream. He played my body like a practiced violinist. I wanted to sing in response.

In moments, I came, crying out so loudly the birds flew squawking from the trees.

At some unseen signal, Kane moved from my sex and back to my breasts. Matt pulled me to him and pressed the tip of his cock to my entrance.

"Are you sure about this?" Matt whispered. His expression was serious, although his eyes were laced with desire. He wanted me, but he needed to know I was sure. He didn't want to see me hurt. That feeling was mutual. I searched his gaze for certainty and found it. He would have no regrets and neither would I.

"Yes," I panted, but was as decisive as I could manage with short breath. "I want you inside me." I pushed myself forward onto him.

He grunted and slid all the way into me.

I groaned with pleasure. He was so damned big I needed to stretch a little more to take him.

Kane, eyes wide, watched for a minute or two, then moved back up to slip his cock back into my mouth.

I took him in and paused for a moment to enjoy the feeling of being the centre of attention for two such amazing guys. How in the hells did I get so lucky? I didn't know, but I was going to enjoy myself.

With both guys thrusting into me, I closed my eyes and savoured the sensation of their cocks. In and out, in and out, in an imperfect rhythm.

Kane grunted. "I'm going to come."

"Mmmhmm," I replied around his length. I sucked harder, took him in deeper, until he cried out and sent hot cum down the back of my throat.

Matt came a moment later with a grunt of pure pleasure and a few thrusts that followed me completely. As his seed gushed into me, I came again, intense and mind blowing, for at least a full minute.

When I finally came down, I sagged onto the grass to catch my breath.

"Does this mean I'm forgiven?" Matt slid out of me.

I suppressed a grin and snorted. "No way. You're still an asshole."

He laughed and opened his mouth to say something. Instead, he stopped and frowned. "I think we have company."

2

I FROZE. After a moment I heard the sound of a car. Distant, but steadily coming closer.

"I'm hoping that's the escort Nash mentioned." I grabbed my clothes and started to pull them on. "Otherwise someone else has found us out here."

"Maybe the neighbours heard you screaming?" Matt suggested. He gave me a lopsided smile so I knew he was teasing.

I stuck my tongue out and pulled down my shirt. "Maybe they heard you moaning."

He laughed softly and handed me my panties.

I leaned against Kane to pull them on and started with my jeans. I had just done up the fly when a car drove up to the house. I just made it out through the trees before I dropped to a crouch.

"They might be friendly." Kane crouched beside me, Matt on the other side.

"The car is black," I whispered.

"Sometimes Zeta drives blue cars," Matt reminded me. "And my mother's car is black."

I glanced at him. That was the first time I had heard him mention his mother.

"Is she evil?" Kane asked.

Matt gave him a dry look. "Of course not. Not that I know of anyway."

I searched his face but he gave nothing away. Since he was a hybrid, his mother might well have taken part in Zeta's breeding program. Whether that was voluntary or not, I wasn't sure even he knew. He might now be wondering how deeply she was involved with Zeta.

I had the same questions about my own mother. I only had a couple of doctor's words that she sat on the board. Unfortunately the not knowing was a good way to let my imagination run wild.

The driver's side door swung open and a figure stepped out. She was dressed from head to toe in black and sported a long golden blonde ponytail.

I breathed a sigh of relief and rose to my feet. Before I could take a step, Matt grabbed my hand.

"She's a Zeta agent."

"She's on our side. Corinne helped me escape from Zeta," I replied, unsure now. "Blake, too." I nodded toward him. His mess of curls shone in the morning sun as he moved to stand beside Corinne.

"Just because someone helped you, doesn't mean they're above suspicion." Matt let my wrist go and rose to stand in front of me. "Are you sure they can be trusted?" He eyed Blake as though he was familiar in some way.

"Are you saying that because you care?" I kept my tone light, but my heart went into overdrive. We had all been through so much, I didn't want to waste another moment on guessing.

He gave me a soft look which melted me a little more. "Yeah, but don't think I'll stop telling you when you're being a pest."

I grinned. "As long as I can keep telling you when you're a dick."

He stuck out his hand. "Deal."

When I shook his hand, he didn't let mine go. Instead, he pulled me around behind him. "Stay vigilant."

I wasn't sure if he was talking to me or Kane, but I nodded and waited for the owl shifter to step beside me. I knew he was trying to protect me, but the truth was he was more vulnerable than I was. I'm not saying owls aren't badass, but he had no magic and wasn't going to rip off anyone's head. He might peck their eyes out though, so there's that.

We moved toward the house as the door swung open. Nash stepped out, followed by Ariana. Her sleeve was rolled up and I knew she would conjure her attack unicorn if necessary. Nash might be susceptible to the gas which put shifters to sleep, so I suspected Hamish would be close by as well.

"Mr Nash," Blake called out warmly.

"Just Nash," Nash replied. "I'll leave the formality to my students." His voice caught slightly and I suspected he was thinking about me.

"Yeah, about that." Blake gestured toward the house. "Maybe we should talk inside."

Nash hesitated, then nodded. He turned toward me, the first indication he knew the three of us were approaching.

Blake looked surprised, but Corinne just inclined her head and grimaced.

"Evidently my cousin needs to work on his secret agent skills," she said, an eyebrow arched at him.

Blake shrugged and grinned. "That's what I wanted to talk to Mr... I mean Nash, about. Amongst other things." He gave me a wink that made my heart flutter. He was too damned cute for his own good.

I smiled and self-consciously brushed grass off my jeans. I probably had grass stains on the knees, but I wasn't about to look. That would be embarrassing. Nope, no looking for me. Okay, maybe a tiny peek. Bingo, grass stains.

I blushed.

"So, I need some tea. Anyone else?" I kissed Nash's cheek as I slid past him and through the doorway. Not having to hide our relationship anymore was one of the major perks of not being at UA anymore. One of many if I was honest.

I hurried into the kitchen and flicked the electric kettle on.

"I could use something hot and steamy," Dyson remarked. He stepped into the kitchen and wrapped his arms around me but kept his hands on my middle. No higher and no lower. He told me back at the Zeta building that he loved me. I said it back. Ever since then, nothing changed. He was still the same cheerful guy who was content to take things slowly. Some day, I'd find the time to talk to him about it. Okay, and the guts. In the meantime, there was no need to rush.

"Coffee?" I offered.

"I'll get it." He stepped back from me to pull mugs out of the cupboards. In spite of all the people who were currently living in the house, everything was always clean and neat. Nash made sure of that. He ran the place like it was a military operation.

We stepped out into the living room with trays of hot drinks, just as Matt spoke.

"I still don't like the idea of splitting up." He nodded his thanks and glared at Nash over his steaming mug. "It makes us all vulnerable."

I looked from Nash to Blake and Corinne, who sat on the opposite side of the room, in chairs they must have pulled over from the dining table.

"Noted," Nash replied simply. "We're sticking to the plan."

Matt scowled, but didn't argue further. Smart move, considering the look on Nash's face. Stony and calm, he was the picture of an immovable mountain. When he looked like that, the only thing we could do was go with the flow.

"What is the plan?" Blake asked eagerly.

Did Matt's scowl deepen slightly? It was hard to tell with him sometimes.

"Do you three know each other?" I gestured toward him, then to Corinne and Blake. I suspected Corinne was a few years older, but Blake was around the same age as the rest of us. If they all worked for the council, then it wasn't much of a stretch.

Matt and Blake shared a glance.

"We've met," Matt replied

"Mathew and I went to school together for a while," Blake said cheerfully. "Before his family moved away."

"Oh really?" I grinned. "I bet you have some great stories."

"As a matter of fact—"

Nash made a slicing gesture with his hand and cut Blake off. "Have your reunion later. We don't have time for it right now. The sooner we're gone from here, the better."

"We weren't followed," Corinne said, her voice tight.

"I'd rather not take the chance." Nash stood and started to pace. "Ariana and Hamish, you know what you have to do?"

"Yes, sir!" Hamish replied. "We're packed and ready to go."

I frowned. "Where are you going?"

Ariana gave Nash a nervous glance. "He asked us to keep it to ourselves."

"The less anyone else knows, the better," Nash said firmly. There was that immovable mountain again, but I *was* going to argue.

"You're going to keep secrets from me?" I asked in disbelief.

"Not the kind you think," he replied.

"Oh, what kind do I think?" I crossed my arms, which might have had more impact if not for the mug in my hand.

Nash sighed. "It's nothing bad. Will you just trust me, please?"

I hesitated. I did trust him, implicitly, but I didn't like secrets, especially amongst my friends and boyfriends. "Fine, but if it's anything bad, I get to tie you down and spank you."

Nash looked surprised, but then a smile crept to the corners of his mouth. "Deal."

"You can spank me anytime," Kane remarked. He didn't bother to hide his grin.

"I'll remember that for next time," I told him. "So, what's the rest of the plan then?"

"Dyson, Corinne, Blake, and Peyton will travel in the car out there." Nash nodded toward the front door. "Your Zeta uniforms should convince any agents you meet that you've recaptured these two."

"They think we have a score to settle," Corinne said. "After you escaped from the facility we went back and told them we lost you. They think we're deeply regretful." She cocked her head so her ponytail fell to the side.

"And are you?" Matt asked. His whole body looked tense, ready to react depending on her reply.

"Not even a little bit," Blake replied.

Matt nodded slowly but his posture only relaxed slightly.

"Right then. You four will go together." Nash said. "Matt, Kane, and I will be a few hours behind, but we'll take the inland route."

"I'd rather travel with Peyton," Matt said, his eyes on me.

Nash fixed him with a frown. "You usually complain when I pair you up."

Matt shrugged. "Someone has to keep her out of trouble."

"I can do that," Dyson said.

"Me too," Blake agreed. "She's in good hands."

"That's what I'm afraid of," Matt muttered.

"Jealous?" I asked.

Matt snorted. "Of course not." His mouth moved for a moment longer, but he eventually closed it, his teeth clicking.

I let the silence hang for a moment before I broke it. "Is there such a thing as demons?"

Every eye turned to stare at me.

"Demons?" Ariana echoed.

"Yeah. At the Zeta facility I saw a guy with red skin, like something out of a movie." I hadn't been sure I had really seen him, or if I had dreamed it. Maybe I'd hit my head and he was a hallucination.

"Red skin," Nash echoed. At least he wasn't laughing. Yet. "What did he do?"

"He took the stone Zeta was using to dampen witches' ability to do magic. He had two people with him, but they both looked human."

Nash rubbed his chin. "Yes, there are such things as demons," he said slowly. "They are…a shifter mutation, if you like. Instead of shifting into an animal, they can change into a form most of us would find repugnant. A mutant ant, for example. Others are almost entirely human except for some minor quirk, like glowing eyes."

"Demons are real," Corinne agreed. "What Nash said is accurate. They tend to live in inner cities and only interact with their own kind. Some are resentful of the fact." She rubbed her hands up and down her arms. "Some of them would like to step out of the shadows, but their elders hold them back."

"Yeah, but mostly they're just normal paranormals like us," Blake said. "I went to school with some."

I exhaled loudly. "Thank the gods. For a moment there I thought we'd have to tackle Zeta on one side and demons on the other."

"We still might," Corinne said. "The stone they took is powerful. The gods only know what they might want it for."

I cocked my head at her. "You told me where to find it."

"Yes, I did." She regarded me for a moment. "I was hoping to get to it first."

"So you knew they were after it?" I asked.

She looked toward Blake, then back at me. "I suspected they might be. Demons, like shifters, can hide in plain sight. They could have been waiting there for months, hoping someone would do what you did and disconnect the stone from the dampening field."

"They could also have been days away," Blake said. "We couldn't be sure."

"So there's an ancient and potentially dangerous artefact loose in the world," I said. "One that does weird things to witches."

Nash frowned. "It stopped witches from drawing magic. Are you suggesting it does something else?"

I swallowed. "I've been able to draw more quickly and with stronger spells ever since I came into contact with it. I thought maybe it was to do with unlocking my phoenix side."

Nash shook his head slowly. "That's not how that works."

"It was the stone," Corinne said softly. "It siphons off power, but it also releases it. It's taken the power from one witch and given it to you."

3

I GAPED.

"So I'm walking around with someone else's magic while they have none?" I wanted Corinne to deny it, but she wouldn't meet my eyes.

"Is it yours?" Kane asked. His blunt question surprised me. Ever the science geek, he looked fascinated, if a little sickened by all of this.

Relatable. I felt the same way myself.

"No," Corinne replied firmly. "Blake and I are fine, fortunately. We were both far enough away not to be impacted. More likely the stone siphoned a Zeta agent's magic, so don't feel too bad. They would have done the same to you, given the chance."

Even knowing she was right didn't make me feel much better. Having someone else's magic inside me felt dirty somehow, although at least it hadn't done me any harm.

Yet.

"So what would a demon do with the stone?" I asked. "Take magic and keep it themselves?"

"Only someone with the innate ability to use magic can absorb it and use it." Corinne chewed on her thumbnail. "They could certainly make a witch more powerful if they wanted, but that doesn't usually end well."

"Oh good," I said dryly. "Now we get to the part where I'm doomed." I should have known. I narrowed my eyes and her and Blake. Surely they understood the risks before they asked me to shut down the dampening field?

Corinne snorted. "Not doomed, no. Not unless you got your hands on the stone and absorbed a bunch of magic. Then you'd probably go insane."

Matt made a choking sound, as if he was struggling to hold back a snarky remark.

I shot him a look and he made a zipping gesture with his fingers in front of his mouth.

Good call.

"They may want the stone for the same reason Zeta does," Nash said slowly. "To stop witches and wizards from being able to use magic for as long as they live."

"There's another explanation," Ariana said, her voice soft as though she barely dared to speak.

I turned toward her and gestured for her to continue.

"They might just want to keep it out of Zeta's hands," she suggested.

Nash looked thoughtful, then nodded slowly. "It's possible." He didn't seem convinced.

"So they're either a bigger threat than Zeta, or they're potential allies," I reasoned. "I'm glad it's all so clear." I slumped into a chair.

"It would have been handy if they'd stopped to tell you which one it was," Blake said lightly.

I gave him an ironic smile. "Yeah, definitely. It would have been courteous."

"Maybe they did," Dyson said. He rubbed his chin. "They could have stopped to siphon Peyton's magic while she lay unconscious on the floor, but they didn't."

"Right. They stepped around me." That begged a question though. "Can the stone siphon from hybrids?"

Corinne frowned. "It must, since it dampened your magic, but if they took it, you'd still be a shifter."

"Cool. I couldn't do magic but I could still rip their heads off," I said bitterly. Killing Fitz gave me no satisfaction. At least, not as much as it had then, when I was in phoenix form.

"Being a shifter isn't so bad," Dyson said. He sounded slightly hurt at my words.

I rose and moved to put my arms around him. "Of course it's not. Shifters are awesome. I just… I didn't like my phoenix self. I wanted to tear the world apart and set the ruins on fire. If it wasn't for you, I might have." I gave him a squeeze, which he returned.

"I'm sorry," he said softly. "I keep forgetting that was the first time you knew you could shift. It must have been strange."

"It was. I'm sure it was for you when you were little."

He shrugged with one shoulder. "A bit, but I knew it was coming. The only question was what we'd shift into." He nodded toward Kane, whose face was characteristically red.

Dyson went on. "I was hoping I'd be a tiger."

"Same here," Kane mumbled.

"Me too," Matt said.

Every eye in the room swung around to look at him.

"What? I wanted to be a normal shifter, not a mythical creature."

"Gargoyles are cool," I assured him. "Dragons too," I told Nash.

Nash sighed softly. "It could have been worse. I had a childhood friend who was a sphinx. He kept his normal face even when he shifted. It was…weird."

"But you would have preferred an actual animal too?" I asked.

"I would have liked to be something soft and cute like a possum," he admitted.

I grinned. "At least your human form is cuddly."

He grinned back. "You think so?"

"Absolutely." I nodded. I moved over and gave him a hug. He wound his arms around me and drew me closer still. At least with him I had no doubt of his feelings for me. It went way beyond lust and sex.

"So anyway," Kane interrupted. "Can magic be taken from Peyton and given back to the witch it was siphoned from?"

"In theory, yes, if we could find him or her," Corinne replied. "If they're a Zeta agent, would we want to?"

"Hells no," I said firmly. "It feels strange, but I'd rather have extra magic than give it to the enemy."

"And if it's not the enemy?" Matt asked. "Would you take the risk?"

I hesitated. "Yes, I would," I said finally. "Without it, they're vulnerable."

Matt nodded. "I'll keep an ear out for any witches or wizards turning up without their magic."

"We should all be watchful in case the demon isn't on our side," Nash said. "That makes this travel north even riskier." He was firmly back in his teacher cum bossman hat. There was no questioning him with that look on his face. He was hot as hells, but more than that, he made me feel safe and loved. I would have preferred to travel with him, but I trusted his judgment. Well, more or less. The last time he had a plan, I ended up in a Zeta laboratory.

Okay, maybe I should have questioned his decisions a bit more.

"Maybe we should fly instead of drive," I suggested. "On a plane, I mean. Unless one of you guys has a helicopter up your sleeve?" I looked around hopefully.

"I have second cousins who have one," Blake replied. "They mostly keep to themselves these days."

Corinne nodded. "They do. By the time any of them checked their phones, we'd almost be in Illusion Bay anyway."

"There are people who aren't glued to their phones?" Hamish said in amazement.

Most of us laughed in reply, but he wasn't wrong.

"As fun as it would be to travel by helicopter, it would make us vulnerable to attack from…" Nash stopped mid-sentence.

"Phoenixes?" I finished for him. "It's all right to talk about them… us. I am what I am. There's no point in trying to hide from it."

He averted his gaze and I realised this wasn't about me. This was about him and his memories. Had he been given the same concoction I had, to force his dragon form to reveal itself? I had several nightmares about shifting since it had happened. And about killing Fitz and ripping off his head.

I reached for his hand. "Are you okay?" I said softly.

His jaw clenched and for a moment I was sure he'd say nothing. Then he gave a deep sigh.

"I think it's time we talked about our childhoods." He nodded toward Matt, whose lips pressed into a tight line.

"Should we leave?" Ariana asked, her eyes wide with concern.

"No." Nash waved his spare hand toward her. "You should hear this, so you all understand." He sucked in a deep breath.

"My mother was a witch. I have no idea what my father was. A shifter of some kind." He pursed his lips. "She wouldn't talk about it."

I squeezed his hand. He offered me a watery half-smile.

"I assume he was a bird of some kind." Nash glanced toward Kane, whose face reddened at being singled out.

"I was literally born in a Zeta laboratory and removed from my mother almost immediately. We were allowed to see each other once in a while, as a reward for good behaviour of some kind." Nash ran a hand over his hair. His expression was pained. Every word seemed more and more strained.

Matt nodded. "It was the same for me, until my mother took me and left." His eyes glazed and I caught him wiping a tear from the corner of his eye.

Nash nodded. "My mother couldn't leave. Or at least, she didn't. I went to school with other young hybrids, where we learnt how we're superior to other paranormals, and why normals need to be brought under control. Every chance she got, my mother told me otherwise. In spite of that, I was recruited into Zeta and joined the police force. They decided I could help them the best there."

He leaned back and closed his eyes. "The more time went on, the more I saw things I couldn't condone. The breeding, the corruption, infiltration of governments, the murder of normals. I couldn't do it anymore. I changed my name and went rogue."

"That must have been difficult," I said softly.

"The choice to do it was easy," he replied. "Actually *doing* it was something else entirely. Zeta doesn't like it when their agents run off, especially knowing what I know."

"They came after you?" Dyson asked.

"Yeah, but I knew all their tricks. The hardest part was convincing other paranormals I was really on their side. Some of us have trust issues." He smiled wryly.

"That sounds lonely." I put an arm around him and rested my head on his shoulder.

"It was." He reached down to cup my ass. "Then I met you and everything changed."

"Yeah, now you're stuck with us crazy folk," Dyson joked.

"I wouldn't have it any other way," Nash said firmly.

"Thank the gods for that." I kissed him lightly on the mouth, then drew back and looked him in the eyes. "I knew Nash wasn't your real name."

He smiled slightly. "It's the third or fourth name I've had. It was given to me by a friend. He organised the job at the AMM to hide me from Zeta. I'm not sure it's what I would have chosen, but it'll do."

"I like him, whoever he is." I nodded. I turned to Matt. "So is Matt your real name?"

He smiled, but his eyes looked haunted. "I'll never tell," he replied.

"So it's not," I concluded. "Is it Bartholomew?"

Matt snorted. "Gods, no."

"Waldo?" I asked with a smile.

Matt chuckled. "No. Like I said, I won't tell you, but it's nothing that horrible."

"If you say so." I frowned. "I don't even know your last name." Strange I hadn't realised that until now.

"Ling," he replied. "That's all you're getting from me."

"Sure it is." I gave him one of my crappy winks, where both eyes almost closed. He responded with a snort but the sides of his mouth tugged upward.

"We should probably get packed and get on the road," Nash said reluctantly.

I suspected he had other ideas of how to spend the next few hours.

Personally I'd prefer it to sitting in a car for a long period of time, but the sooner we left, the sooner we arrived.

"Illusion Bay or bust," Dyson said.

"Let's not bust." Kane grimaced. He shot his brother a look, then glanced toward me. The message was clear: take care of Peyton or else.

Ah, brotherly love.

"I'll help Peyton to pack," Corinne said. "Otherwise I suspect we'll be here for days."

I blushed, but she wasn't wrong.

4

"Is this where we start asking if we're there yet?" Dyson grinned over at Corinne who sat next to him, in the driver's seat.

I checked the time on my phone. "We've only been on the road for an hour." I sat forward and peered at him over his shoulder.

"So I should have started half an hour ago," he joked.

"Only if you want to walk the rest of the way," Corinne said. She shot him a sideways glance.

He looked to be considering that for a moment before he shook his head. "Naw, I'll get too tired."

I snorted. "If you're lucky, you will. If you're not, you'll be found by a family who decides to keep you as a pet."

He cocked his head. "Right. I could spend the rest of my life lying on a bed in the sunshine and being fed from a huge bowl."

"You'd be fed dog food and might have to sleep outside in a kennel," Corinne pointed out.

"Yep, no ice cream for you," Blake said from the seat beside me.

Dyson groaned. "Great, now I'm craving ice cream. Can we stop for—"

"No," Corinne interrupted. "No stopping until the designated time and place."

"But—"

"Give it up," Blake advised. "You won't change her mind. She's a stickler for the rules."

"The plan was designed to keep us all safe," Corinne replied. "If we deviate from it and something happens, the rest won't know where we are. Zeta would be the least of our worries."

"Right," I agreed. "You'd have to face Nash."

Dyson gave a mock shudder. At least, I think it was a mock one. Angry Nash wasn't for the faint of heart. Though Dyson could handle himself.

"Fine." Dyson sat back and looked out the open window beside him. It blew cold air in my face, but I knew he got carsick, so it was a small price to pay. At least he didn't hang his head out and pant.

"Any sign of the others?" I glanced back, but knew I wouldn't see them. Ariana and Hamish left hours ago, on their mysterious mission. Kane, Nash, and Matt were probably leaving now. I hated the idea everyone was out there somewhere where I couldn't see or talk to them. That left me to worry, which wasn't much help to them or me.

"They'll be okay." Blake leaned over and put a hand on mine. His touch sent butterflies through my stomach. He gave me a soft smile. He really was too damned cute.

I smiled back.

"I know, I just…" Under normal circumstances, a girl might worry if her three boyfriends traveled in a car together. Jealousy or animosity might make things ugly. I knew I had nothing to worry about on that account. There didn't seem to be any hard feelings between them where I was concerned. They might envy the guy I spent the night with, if we spent it alone, but none minded that I had strong feelings for them all.

"I'll be glad when we're there," I said finally. "And safe." I looked back again, but saw no sign of anyone following us. Not, I should add, that I really knew what to look for.

"We should be fine, we're—" Blake cut off when his phone rang. He pulled it out of his back pocket and grimaced.

"What is it?" I asked.

"It's Zeta," he replied wryly. "They have a job for us."

"They might be testing you," Dyson suggested.

"It could be a trap," I added.

"Um." Blake frowned toward the roof of the car. "I don't think so, but it's possible."

I blinked. "They play games like that with their agents?" Of course they would. Nothing was beneath them. A burst of anger made my blood hot. That was followed immediately by the fear my inner phoenix would burst loose inside the car. I would rip the car to pieces and everyone in it. Then I'd start on the people in the car behind us and the one after…

I sucked in a breath. Forced the fury to cool. I didn't want to kill anyone, no matter the circumstances.

"We're infiltrating them," Corinne said calmly. "We've helped at least a dozen witches to get free and make it to a safe haven. There's a place…" She shook her head. "It doesn't matter now. We're not on their side, and they might suspect that."

"We're absolutely not," Blake agreed. "Corinne is right though, they might try to test us and we can't afford to fail." He exhaled through his teeth. "What do we do about this though? We're only ten kilometres from… Moruya. What a strange name."

"What do they want us to do?" Corinne asked.

"Capture a hybrid," Blake replied.

I frowned. "What makes them think there's a hybrid on the loose in a rural area like this?" I waved out the window. The view was a combination of lush green and black from recent bushfires.

"They found people dead, with marks consistent with a lion," Blake replied. "There aren't any lions in the wild in Australia. Unless a lion escaped from the zoo, which would have been all over the news."

"Wait a minute. You can't be suggesting you're going after this… whatever it is?" Dyson asked.

"If they're killing people," Corinne said. "What choice do we have?"

"We ignore the message and keep driving," Dyson suggested. "Surely there's someone else who can deal with this kind of thing?"

"A whole team of someones," I agreed. "How are you supposed to handle a dangerous hybrid by yourselves? I mean, no offence, you're both badasses."

"We've been trained." Corinne slowed as we approached a small town. "With any luck, this won't take long."

"Those sound like famous last words to me," Dyson pointed out.

"They really do," I agreed.

We rolled to a stop beside a pretty, green park. At the end of the park a wide river ran.

"They hold a market here every Saturday." Corinne opened her door and climbed out. "I've come here for it a few times. Every other day, it's just a nice place for a picnic."

"Are you suggesting Dyson and I stay here and eat sandwiches while you hunt hybrids?" I asked. I followed her example. The sun was warm on my face and the breeze was clean and clear. There was certainly something to be said for living in places like this.

"There's a nice little café just there." Corinne pointed across the road.

"Why don't we all eat, then find our friend?" I suggested.

"Peyton, Nash would—"

I cut Dyson off with a glance. "He's not here. Whatever is going on is better dealt with by four of us than two."

"Or we could take the car and keep driving," Dyson said lightly. "They could catch up."

"How?" I asked.

"Rideshare?"

"Out here?" I waved around me. "They'd be lucky to have a taxi or two."

Dyson hesitated, then sagged. "Yeah, I guess so. But I agree with Peyton. We go together or not at all." He stood like a dog who wouldn't walk past a strange house, no matter how hard anyone tugged on his leash.

Corinne grimaced. "Fine, but we eat first."

I nodded. "I could eat."

"I'll get it," Blake offered.

"I'll go with you." Dyson fell in beside him.

I sat on the grass beside the car and leaned against the trunk of a small tree. "Are we really doing this?"

"Going after a hybrid?" Corinne asked. "We have to. We need to protect the normals. The police can't manage. There are no other teams close."

"How do they know where you are?" I asked carefully.

"We told them." Corinne raised a hand before I jumped up and started toward her. "The most convincing lies are at least partly truthful. They don't know you're here. As far as they're concerned, we're loyal agents, even if we're not the most competent." She scowled.

She was nothing if not competent. Pretending to be lacking just so Dyson and I could escape must rankle a little. I appreciated her ability to put her ego aside to do the right thing. I knew people who wouldn't have done it.

"What happens if they turn up here and demand you hand us over?" I asked. "Neither of us look very restrained."

"I can tie you up, but we know that won't hold you anyway," she replied easily. "We'll just say you came willingly because you couldn't control your shifter form. You wouldn't be the first. Not everyone gets accepted into places like the AMM. Some shifters and witches are on their own." She sighed softly.

"Someone you know?" I guessed.

"Not exactly. Someone I met in the facility. He didn't know how to use magic until he accidentally killed his best friend. A shifter on the police force told him about Zeta. He had his magic siphoned off."

"And?" I prompted.

"And what?" she asked. "He went back to a normal life with a new name and identity, but with no magical means to harm anyone. I don't know what happened to him after that." She averted her face.

"You cared about him, didn't you?" I asked softly.

"I did," she said. "I tried to talk him into seeking help from other magic users."

"You mentioned a safe haven."

She nodded slowly. "Raven's Gate. They train witches and shifters, sometimes demons. Sometimes just the basics, sometimes more. They also train a handful of normals to hunt wayward demons and shifters, but that's incredibly dangerous work for a normal."

"So there are normals who know about paranormals." I frowned. Part of my mother's job was to ensure they weren't able to tell anyone else. I wasn't sure how she did that, I had never dared to ask. I assumed she had them killed, but maybe I was wrong.

"Some are recruited by the Gate," Corinne replied. "Some stumble upon us. Some are friends or lovers. Still others are paranormals stripped of their magic before they were old enough to know they had it. They always feel drawn toward...something, without knowing why."

I thought I caught a glint of tears in her eyes, but she looked away before I could be sure.

I decided to change the subject. "Do you think my mother is really on the board of Zeta?"

"I'm honestly not sure," Corinne replied. "The board is so secretive, I'm not sure they know everyone who is on it with them."

"So, what, they have code names or something?" I was only half joking.

She nodded in response. "From what I can gather, yes. If one decided to betray the others, it could expose the whole organisation and the paranormal community."

"If it was only about them, I'd blow the whole thing apart," I said firmly. "But I care about too many paranormals to risk them."

"Yeah," she agreed. She stopped and glanced around slowly. "Do you feel that?"

"What—" Now she mentioned it, I did and had for a while. Someone or something was sucking on the edge of my magic.

5

———

I ROSE SLOWLY, hands out to either side. "Can you tell where it's coming from?"

Corinne stood too. She turned her face slowly to the left, then to the right. "I'm not sure. It feels stronger—"

"From there." I pointed roughly to the east. I only knew that because of the position of the sun. I wouldn't have a clue otherwise. Most people don't anyway, right? Well, I didn't.

I took a step in that direction, then stopped.

"Wait, should we be running away instead of moving closer?" I peered ahead. Was there someone there? A couple of someones maybe? I couldn't be sure from this distance.

"Probably," Corinne agreed. She started walking. East. Ish.

"I... Okay." I hurried to catch up, but I kept my arm ready. Or rather, my tattoos. My gargoyle and my tiger were ready to defend me as long as I had access to magic. Here, surrounded by trees and grass, I had lots. Failing that, I could go all phoenix on their asses. That was the last resort, always. I couldn't control that side of me well enough and my jeans were new. I didn't want to risk tearing them. Or worse, losing them altogether. All right, in the scheme of things it wasn't that important, but I *really* didn't want to shift.

378

A figure stepped out from behind a tree when we were less than a hundred metres away.

I braced myself, but they gave no sign of aggression. Well, except for standing with his legs slightly apart, hand out, palm up.

"Is that..." I didn't finish the question because I knew the answer. He held the black stone which Zeta used to dampen magic.

"Took you long enough, darlin'," he said. He spoke with an English accent. The kind you hear on British police dramas, not the fancy, upper class kind.

I did a double take. I knew that voice. He didn't have a red face now, but rather a handsome one, with hazel eyes and buzz-cut dark hair. His short sleeved t-shirt revealed muscular arms covered in a layer of tattoos. He wore track pants which hung loose from his hips.

"You're the demon from the Zeta facility," I blurted out.

Corinne glanced at me sharply. "Are you sure?"

"Is the sky blue?" I asked.

"That depends on the weather," she said dryly. "At the moment it is."

I exhaled softly. "I'm sure." To the demon I said, "Right?"

He shrugged his left shoulder. "Guilty as charged, darlin'. Don't be too concerned though, I'm mostly harmless."

"Considering you're holding that," Corinne nodded toward the stone, "excuse me for having my doubts."

"What, this old thing?" He dropped the stone into a small velvet bag. Its influence immediately vanished as if it hadn't been there at all. "It's harmless too, in the right hands."

"Your hands?" I placed a hand on my hip and stuck it out to the side a little.

For some reason, he seemed to find this funny. He laughed for a few moments, then said, "They absolutely are the right hands. Why don't you come here and find out, darlin'?"

Before I could respond, Corinne spoke. "Enough of this, who are you and what do you want?"

He sighed heavily. "Someone always has to spoil the fun, and they're usually wearing a Zeta uniform." He waved toward her, but looked at me. "Do you need me to get rid of her for you?"

"No," I said quickly. "She's a friend. She does have good questions though. Who are you and what are you doing with that stone?"

He scratched his head. "Those weren't her exact questions, darlin', but I'll humour you both." He placed a hand on his stomach and bowed. "My given name is Leopold Yarinov Donatello Fitzsimmons, the third. You can call me Leo."

"That's a mouthful," I remarked.

He frowned, but his eyes twinkled. "Leo?"

"No, the rest of it. Can you spell it all?"

He chuckled. "Most of it."

I snorted. "What about the rest of our questions?"

"Ah yes. I thought it wise to remove the stone from Zeta's hands. Thank you for helpin' with that, darlin'."

"You're welcome. Why?" I cocked my head at him.

"Why what?"

"Why did you take the stone?" Corinne said impatiently.

"Would you prefer they had it?" he asked.

"I'd prefer *I* had it," she replied.

"The woman in the Zeta uniform? I don't think so." He eyed her speculatively. "Although, you're not working for them, are you, Corinne?"

She took a step back. "How did you know my name?"

"Same way I know her name is Peyton." He nodded toward me. "The Demon Collective—"

Corinne interrupted. "The collective is a myth."

"Not so." He shook his head slowly.

"Apart from sounding like a show I'd binge on, what the hells is the collective?" I asked.

"The Demon Collective," Leo replied. "It's the demon equivalent of the Paranormal Council."

"The council and Raven's Gate have been trying to make contact for years." Corinne glanced sideways at me.

"By "make contact", she means *eradicate*," Leo said, a sardonic smile on his lips. "Rid the world of all things demonic."

"Only the bad ones." Corinne's voice was tight. "Same with Zeta. There are some decent agents—"

"Like you?" he asked challengingly.

"I'm not—" She bit off her words. "I work for the council. They're not perfect either, but..."

"As interesting as all of this is..." And it was. There was apparently a whole world out there I knew nothing about. I fixed my gaze on Leo. "Is there a point to this? You have a stone which could fuck up a lot of witches. What do you want in return for it? Money? Power?"

"Goodwill?" he suggested. "Maybe I just want the council to back off from demonkind?"

"Sounds reasonable." I turned to Corinne. "Doesn't it?"

She replied through gritted teeth. "Demon Hunters recently thwarted a demon plot to murder all of humankind, normal and paranormal, and take over the world. It's those kinds of demons we can't have running around."

"People still use the word thwarted?" Leo asked. He shook his head. "Yes, those kinds of demons we can do without. We're just as happy to...thwart those. What we'd like is for the council to work with the collective to minimise threats to all of us."

"You want me to talk to the council on your behalf?" Corinne looked wary.

"Oh gods no. I want to talk to them myself. I'm coming on this little road trip with you. I'm sure there's plenty more room in the back. Right, darlin'?" He winked at me.

My silly heart fluttered. I couldn't deny he was charming and I had no illusions that he was dangerous. Any sensible girl would run in the other direction. Me, of course, found him sexy as hells.

"You think I'm going to let you in our car?" Corinne asked.

"I can help you find the hybrid you're looking for." He looked smug.

"How did you know about that?" She shook her head. "Let me guess, the collective?"

"That and he was a friend of mine." Leo's expression darkened. "His girlfriend was killed and he went off the rails. He won't listen to anyone now. So you see, you help me and I'll help you. Everyone wins."

Corinne hesitated. "If I consider doing this, you'll be watched closely. One toe out of line and you will be dealt with."

"Noted," he replied. "Although I would suggest you're in no position to make threats."

"She might not be, but I am," I said. No matter how sexy he was, Corinne was right, we needed to keep an eye on him.

He grinned. "The phoenix has claws." He chuckled.

"And teeth." I bared mine, but he only laughed harder.

I couldn't help it. Before I knew what I was doing, I was laughing too. For the first time since I discovered I could shift, I didn't hate it.

Corinne, on the other hand, scowled. "He can sit next to you then."

Leo stepped over to me and draped an arm over my shoulders. "Fine by me. How about you, darlin'?"

"The closer you are, the easier it is to eat you," I replied.

"Promises, promises. What about you?" He waved his hand toward Corinne. "The three of us could have some fun."

She gave him a look which suggested she'd prefer to swallow a bag of nails and turned back toward the car.

"I guess it's just you and me then, darlin'" He moved his hand to the back of my neck and rubbed lightly.

"How about you prove you're on our side first?" I replied.

"That goes both ways," he shot back.

"Of course it does. We just met." I liked to think I was trustworthy, but if witches and shifters had been giving demons a hard time since the gods knew when, it would take time.

"And yet, it seems as though I've known you for a long time." He toyed with the back of my hair.

"It does," I agreed. "So...can I ask which is your real face?"

"Which is yours?" he asked without answering.

I frowned. "This one."

"Are you sure?"

"I was until now," I said uneasily. "I'm pretty sure. I didn't know the phoenix was there until the other day."

He clicked his tongue. "Paranormal parents not being forthcoming with their offspring. That hasn't changed, I see."

"Aren't you also a paranormal?"

"In a manner of speaking," he agreed. "We prefer to hold ourselves apart though. No, wait, witches and shifters preferred to hold us apart. Bigots." He looked toward Corinne's back as if she was personally to blame.

She stopped and turned around. "We could stand here and discuss the past, or we could work to move forward."

Leo scratched his head. "I'll take option two."

"Good, then let's focus on the present and future." She stalked away.

"I'm starting to think she doesn't like me," he remarked. "Was it something I said?"

"It might be the magic sucking stone in your pocket," I told him.

"I'm just happy to see you." He grinned.

I laughed. "Are you like this with all the girls?"

"Only the cute paranormal ones who could rip my head off," he replied lightly.

"You think I'm cute?" I raised an eyebrow at him until I spotted Dyson and Blake heading out of the cafe in the direction of the car, arms laden with food.

"Let me guess, they do too?" Leo asked. He made no move to step away or remove his hand from my neck.

"The feeling is mutual," I muttered.

"With both of them?"

"And three more." I blushed.

"You're suddenly quite the bit more interesting than I suspected, darlin'," Leo said. "It seems I'll have to work harder to get your attention. I don't mind though, I'm sure you're worth it."

"I don't know about that." I swallowed hard and moved away from him regretfully.

"There you are," Dyson called out. His nostrils flared as he took in

Leo. "Sorry, we only bought enough for four."

I had no doubt he knew exactly what Leo was. I would have to ask him later how a demon smelled compared to other people, but that could wait.

"Oh, I've just eaten." Leo assured him. "Rest assured, I'll eat again later." He gave me a look which said he wasn't referring to food.

Corinne said something which sounded like, "Cocky bastard," and drew Blake aside.

While they talked, I sat beside Dyson and gobbled down my sandwich. I eyed Leo, who leaned against a nearby tree. In spite of his assurances, his possession of the stone made me uneasy. It made him a powerful ally, but it could make him a deadly enemy. I wanted to trust him, but for now I would watch him and make sure he didn't screw us over.

"It's a short drive," Leo said after a few minutes. "To my friend the hybrid. We should go before he hurts someone else."

I nodded and finished my sandwich. "I'm ready when you are."

Leo wiggled his brows. "Not yet, but you will be."

6

I jumped as a bird shot out of a tree beside me.

"Shhh." Leo pressed a finger to his lips.

"I'm trying." I dropped to a crouch between him and Blake. Corinne crouched on the other side of Blake. Dyson stayed behind us.

"I didn't mean to step on that twig." The sound was probably tiny, but it sounded loud in the silence around us.

"Are you sure this is the right address?" Blake whispered.

"Yes." It was Corinne who replied. "According to the message from Zeta, this is the place."

"It is," Leo replied. "He likes his privacy."

The small house sat in the middle of a circle of grass. That, in turn, was surrounded by trees. The road beyond those was little more than a dirt track. The highway was several kilometres away. The perfect, isolated country retreat. Not my thing at all, but I appreciated the peace and quiet.

"Peyton, Dyson, this as far as you go unless we come under attack," Corinne ordered.

"Then we rush in and help?" Dyson asked.

"No, you get in the car and get the hells away from here," Corinne replied. "Leave this to us."

She rose and started forward. Blake walked a step behind, his expression anxious, but maybe a little excited.

There was nothing like a good adrenaline rush on a Wednesday afternoon.

Leo stood and followed.

Corinne stopped and glanced over her shoulder. "What are you doing?"

"I'm coming with you," Leo replied cheerfully.

"The hells you are," she hissed.

His eyes narrowed. "He's my mate, love."

She gave him a look like she might deck him. Instead, she said, "Never call me love again."

"Or what?" he asked, looking genuinely curious.

She paused. "You don't want to know."

He opened his mouth but closed it and shrugged. "I'm coming with you," he repeated. "You have no authority over me."

"I'm going to be pissed off if you get us killed." Corinne scowled at him.

"Me too, lov…boss." Leo gave her a half bow.

She looked as though she wasn't sure being called boss was much better than love, but she turned away.

Dyson moved over beside me. "I think I've changed my mind about what I want to do when I grow up."

"Oh? You want to join Zeta?" It was meant as a joke, but I regretted it the moment I'd said it. Only a few months ago, I wondered if he actually was working with them. I knew now he wasn't, he was under the influence of a drug they created to control shifters.

"I'm sorry," I muttered.

He leaned over to kiss my mouth. "It's okay. I meant I wanted to be an action man like Blake, but a teacher is better. Safer."

"It is somewhat," I agreed. "Well, depending on the students."

"That's true," he agreed. "Maybe this is safer." He nodded to the others who were a few metres from the front door of the house.

"If they get in trouble, I'm not going to run."

He grinned. "I didn't think you would."

"I might even fly." As much as I hated the idea, I wouldn't let anyone kill my friends.

"I'll be right there with you." He bit the tip of his tongue before adding, "Have we waited back here for long enough yet?"

"I think so." I stood and stepped out of the trees into the open.

In the same moment, Leo pulled a pouch out of his pocket. He turned to me and smiled before he tipped the stone onto his palm.

"Corinne, Blake!" I shouted. "Watch out, it's a trap—"

Leo raised his hand.

Corinne went for her gun.

I braced for all my magic to be sucked away into the stone. I was ready to shift and tear him to pieces before his friend could leap out and act.

Corinne raised the barrel of her gun.

I held my breath.

Nothing happened.

"It's not aimed at you, darlin'," Leo called out. He glanced toward Corinne. "Bryan is a hybrid. Without his magic, he'll be easier to deal with."

His words were punctuated with a crash as the door exploded into a thousand tiny pieces.

I threw my arm over my eyes, but lowered it when Corinne gave a cry of alarm.

"What the hells?"

The creature that stalked out of the house was one of nightmares as well as mythology. Head of a lion, six legs which looked like they belonged on a bear, and a tail with a stinger on the tip like a scorpion.

"Tarasque," Dyson supplied. "He probably has a shell as well."

"I'm going to have bad dreams tonight," I murmured, but Bryan was living one. This form was hardly one he could go out in public with. Neither was mine, but a giant bird-like creature was slightly less mind-blowing than this.

"There you go, boss." Leo took several steps back and slipped the stone back into the pouch. "You and my old mate Blake have Bryan's magic. That'll help a little." Evidently that was the extent of his assistance, because Leo backed away and came to stand beside Dyson and me.

"Magnificent, isn't he?" Leo enthused.

"That's one word," I agreed. "Have you tried to reason with him?"

"In this form? No."

Bryan took a swipe at Blake, who jumped back and pulled his own gun.

"As you can see, he's not inclined to be friendly when he's like this. Best stay back." Leo shoved the pouch into his pocket. "I think I might wait in the car. The stone and my own awesomeness was my only defence."

"I thought this guy was your friend," Dyson pointed out. "Shouldn't you try to talk to him or something?"

"I might have exaggerated a little," Leo replied. "We're not really friends. I owe him money. Before you get pissy with me, he couldn't go around hurting more people, regardless."

"Yeah." Dyson looked unconvinced. Something caught his eye and he looked away and pointed. "Looks like Corinne has something up her sleeve."

She pulled her sleeve up and a shape formed in the space between her and Bryan. A moment later, a dragon with silver scales uncurled and launched itself at Bryan.

Bryan roared. The sound made the ground shake beneath my feet. He swung his stinger and caught the dragon in the chest. If the creature had been real, it would have been impaled on the spike and died painfully. Since the dragon was made of magic, it simply evaporated.

It was replaced a moment later by Blake's hawk. The small bird flew in rings around Bryan's head. Every now and again, it would dart in and snap at him with its beak. The hawk did no real damage, but it clearly angered Bryan further. The angrier he became, the more quickly he would tire.

He seemed to realise the same thing. He took a step back and aimed a swipe at the hawk. This time he made contact and sent the bird into a spin before it disappeared.

"What about a gargoyle?" Dyson gestured toward my arm.

"Better that than a phoenix." Although I wondered how well one would work if I created one. The phoenix of a phoenix. I never tried before, although I made a pterodactyl and that was awesome. This was a problem to consider later. In the meantime, I raised my arm and a gargoyle leapt off and loped toward Bryan.

For some reason, Bryan seemed confused by its presence. That only lasted until the gargoyle jumped and tried to pin him down to the ground. He flailed his bear-like limbs and growled long and deep. Huge teeth snapped at the gargoyle and his stinger swiped but only found the air.

"Give it up, Bryan," Corinne called out. "You're outnumbered and out… Out-magicked."

Bryan growled in defiance. He rolled onto his side and dragged most of himself out from under the gargoyle.

Corinne raised her arm and made another silver dragon. It stalked toward Bryan's exposed side as if wary after the last attempt. I knew the emotion came from Corinne, but it almost seemed as if the magical creature could think for itself.

Leo yawned loudly.

"Are we boring you?" I glanced over to him.

He gave me a wink and a smile. "Naw, I just have other places to be. Like on a beach up north. Picture it; you and I skinny dipping in the ocean in the moonlight. All your other boyfriends can come too if they like. The more the merrier."

"I can't believe you're talking about things like that right now," Dyson said.

"Oh? Is that usually your thing," Leo asked, "talking about sexy times during a battle?"

"Well, maybe not *during*," Dyson replied lightly.

"Okay then." Leo nodded. "Where was I?"

"Saving it until this is over?" I suggested. The gargoyle faded slightly, so I sent my tiger out to help.

"You're a hard woman, darlin'," Leo sulked.

"You have no idea."

"I can't wait to learn."

"Leo," Corinne shouted. "Get over here and talk to your friend."

"Um."

"Go on," I told him. "Serves you right for lying about it."

"Ohhh, burn," Leo said playfully. He sighed loudly. "Fine, I'll put myself out there if it'll prove I'm not going to screw you over." He walked forward like a man going to his own execution.

"He's dramatic," Dyson remarked.

"Very," I agreed.

"You think he's hot, don't you?"

"Uhhh."

"It's okay, I do too," Dyson replied.

I shot him a look of surprise.

He shrugged. "The reason I wanted to take things slowly was because I needed to figure some things out. I've realised I like guys and girls." He looked at me apprehensively.

"Cool," I said simply.

"Cool?" he echoed.

"Yeah, cool. Who am I to judge anyone else?" I was starting to lose count of my boyfriends and the guys I was attracted to. Well, not really, but it felt like it at times.

"Great." He smiled, but it turned into a tentative look. "So if I and one of the other guys… while you were there…"

I flushed. My body ached at the thought. "That would be fine," I squeaked. So much for not talking about sex at a time like this. "We should probably concentrate on…um…Bryan."

"Right, yes," Dyson agreed.

The tiger and Corinne's dragon had him pinned. He writhed and snapped, but he looked exhausted.

"Come on, old mate," Leo said from a few metres away. "Give it up, you're beaten."

"Shift back into human form," Corinne ordered.

Bryan growled, still defiant in spite of everything. He writhed for another minute or two, then sagged. A moment later he lay on the ground, a naked, defeated human. His expression was one of utter dismay.

"Blake." Corinne kept the gun on Bryan while Blake pulled something out of his pocket.

"Sorry buddy," I heard him say before he slid a needle into the man's arm and pushed the plunger.

Bryan's eyes closed and his whole body relaxed.

I decided it was safe to get closer now. "What's going to happen to him?"

Corinne exchanged glances with Blake.

"He'll escape," she said finally. "There's plenty of evidence of a struggle." She nodded toward the smashed door. "Unofficially, he'll be stashed in the back of the car until we get to Sydney. We'll leave him with someone from the council. They can deal with him."

"And by deal with him, you mean…"

"Reason with him if possible. If not, that's up to them."

"Bugger," Leo said suddenly when we all looked at him, he added, "I forgot to tell him I can't afford to pay him back."

I snorted. "I think he has bigger problems right now."

"That's because you don't know how much I owe, darlin'," Leo said lightly.

I arched an eyebrow at him.

He grinned. "It's a long story. I'll tell you on the way."

"Yeah, let's get out of here before more Zeta agents arrive," Corinne said.

"Uh, guys," Dyson said. He raised a trembling hand toward the road leading to the house.

"Oh bollocks."

7

"THEY GOT HERE much sooner than I would have expected." Corinne sounded frantic.

"They can't take me again." I backed up a step.

"We're not going to let them." Dyson grabbed my hand.

Blake took the other. "Dyson is right, but we all have to play along with the scenario. Leo, can you carry Bryan?"

"Do I look like a weightlifter?" In spite of that, Leo grabbed Bryan's arm and hauled him onto his shoulder. "What is the scenario?"

"You're assisting us," Corinne said. "As a concerned local."

"That's more or less accurate, love," Leo replied.

Corinne gave him a look, but didn't correct him. "Best they don't know you're a demon. They won't hurt an ordinary human."

"I resent any suggestion that I might be ordinary," Leo grumbled.

"You're not even slightly ordinary," I assured him.

"See, you get me, darlin'." He grinned, but was obviously straining under the weight of the hybrid.

"Hurry up," Corinne urged. "Blake, get Peyton to the car. Dyson, you too. If anyone asks, you've been there the entire time." She stopped and frowned before adding, "Dyson, you should probably pretend you're drugged, just in case anyone asks. Peyton, remember you're coming with us willingly."

I grimaced, but nodded. I could play along as much as I had to, as long it meant we all walked away at the end of this. Or drove away. Or whatever. As long as I didn't up back in the hands of the bad guys.

The car drew closer. Through the trees a flash of red appeared.

"Does anyone in Zeta drive a red car?" I asked. I knew they occasionally drove blue ones, but mostly they used black, like any evil organisation.

"They might," Blake replied. "I know an agent who has a yellow one."

I glanced at him. "Really? But yellow is such a happy, non-evil colour."

"Unless you're allergic to lemons," he replied.

"Oh, you are?"

He shrugged. "Yeah, anything citrus. It makes my face swell and—"

"Hurry up," Corinne urged.

"Uh, I'll tell you later." Blake opened the door and gestured for me to sit.

Dyson flopped down onto the seat beside me and sagged onto my shoulder. "A drugged prisoner wouldn't sit in the front," he said without opening his eyes.

"Just don't spew on me," I replied.

I looked back as Corinne opened the back of the car to let Leo place Bryan inside. The back slammed shut and Leo moved around to the door.

"You can sit in the front," Corinne said tersely.

"But—" Leo waved toward me.

"*Front*," Corinne repeated. "A Zeta agent should sit in the back with Peyton."

Leo's face dropped, but Blake smiled.

"I'm happy to." Blake swung the door open just as a red SUV pulled out of the line of trees near the road.

Even from a distance, I made out their Zeta uniforms and the general feeling of bad juju.

"Maybe we should leave before they can stop us," I suggested.

"Nothing says guilty like fucking off from the scene of the crime," Leo remarked.

"He's right." Corinne opened the driver's side door, but stood leaning against it.

Blake slid in next to me and held my hand so no one outside the car could see. "I won't let anything bad happen to you. Whatever it takes."

"Me too," Dyson muttered out of the corner of his mouth.

If the situation wasn't so serious, I would have laughed. "You might want to look more drugged."

"Mmmhmm," he agreed.

"Shhh, they're coming," Blake said.

"Agents," Corinne called out. "It's good to see you, but we have the situation under control."

My heart raced as the agents stepped into view. I knew one wouldn't be Fitz, I killed him, but I was surprised to see one I knew. I had nicknamed him Blondie and last saw him when I made a Zeta car crash into a magical waterslide.

"Kear, Davis, and Singh." One pointed to himself, then Blondie, and finally to a black-haired agent.

Davis peered into the back of the car and frowned at Dyson and I. I wished I could have made us invisible, but I had to stick to the plan for the sake of Blake and Corinne. They had to be seen to be model Zeta agents, regardless of the risk to us.

"You managed to recapture these two." Davis waved in our direction. For some reason, he looked troubled by this. I suspected he didn't care for the way Zeta did things any more than I did, but he was still working for them. That made him the enemy, however anyone wanted to swing this.

"We've recaptured the shifter," Corinne agreed. "The hybrid came willingly. You know how some of them are with their new abilities." She clicked her tongue. "Out of control. She was scared she'd kill someone she cared about."

Davis nodded. "Right. That's...sensible of her." He eyed me as if he wasn't fully buying the story.

I gave him a watery smile and nodded. "It's true. I'm very dangerous."

"I'm sure." He nodded and backed away.

"We have the other hybrid in the back of the car," Corinne said. "You can see for yourself."

While Singh and Kear moved around to the back, Davis hovered near the front, occasionally looking back at me. After a while I noticed him including Leo in his regard.

"How's things, old boy?" Leo asked.

"Um, fine," Davis replied awkwardly.

"He's a demon," Dyson muttered.

"He—" I shut my mouth so quickly my teeth clicked. I had no reason to question Dyson. If Dyson thought Davis smelled like a demon, then he was one. I sniffed the air, but couldn't detect anything different. Maybe phoenixes didn't have a particularly good sense of smell, like dogs did.

Leo moved slowly toward Davis. I barely caught him saying, "We're on the same side, old mate."

"Zeta's side?" Davis asked.

"Of course," Leo said easily, "what else would I have meant?"

Davis looked uneasy. "I know who you are." His voice was barely above a whisper.

"As you'll see, the hybrid put up quite the fight." Corinne led the other agents away toward the house.

"Excellent." Leo grinned. He spoke a little louder now. "This will be much easier then. I know what you are. Don't worry, I won't tell anyone. I assume your counterparts don't know?"

Davis glanced toward their backs. "I would prefer they didn't."

"Naturally, old boy. Us demons have to stick together."

Davis flinched.

"What would Zeta do if they knew?" I asked in Blake's ear.

"Officially, demons don't exist," he replied.

"Unofficially?"

He shook his head. "I don't know. Most don't have magic and they tend to shift into...um..."

"Things from your nightmares?" Leo asked, his face just under the line of the roof.

"I mean no offence..." Blake flushed bright red.

"None taken. The average demon has a face only a mother could love." Leo tapped the car roof with his knuckle and stepped away.

Blake swallowed loudly. "I really didn't mean to be rude."

I patted his arm. "Some shifters are straight out of a nightmare, too."

"If you're referring to yourself, there's nothing nightmarish about you," Blake said firmly.

"He's right," Dyson added.

I looked over to him, but he was still slumped against the seat, head at an angle.

"They're coming back," Blake said. "They don't look convinced."

I peered out.

"We'll take the hybrids off your hands," Kear said. "You can do what you want with the shifter, just get it back to headquarters."

It? Fuck you too, buddy. Wait, hybrids, plural? My hand closed around Blake's. A bubble of anger rose inside me. My inner phoenix threatened to boil over and rip the car apart. And everyone in it.

My nails dug into Blake's hand until he jerked.

"Ouch."

I smelled blood, hot and warm. I wanted to taste it, to drink it, to paint the world with it.

"Peyton," Blake hissed. "Don't lose control. If you do that, they'll kill you. After you kill us."

I turned and looked him in the eyes. To his credit, he didn't look as scared as I might have been. Blood ran down his hand, but he either didn't notice or he was ignoring it.

"Please, take a few breaths."

"They can't kill me if I destroy them all first." I bared my teeth.

"Peyton, please." He put a hand on my arm.

"If you don't get out of my way, I'll go through you," I hissed.

His eyes widened. "If you do that, you'll regret it. I know how you feel about killing Fitz."

"Fitz deserved it," I growled.

"Maybe, but you don't deserve the pain you'll feel after you harm someone else. Let Corinne take care of it."

I gritted my teeth. For a moment I seriously thought about shoving him away, maybe with a talon. I could have ripped him in two without a second thought.

A tiny part of me, right in the back of my mind, pressed itself forward. Sense, rational thought, whatever you want to call it. It told me Blake was right. It reminded me I didn't want to be a murderer.

I blew out a breath between pursed lips. Control gradually took over and my blood started to cool.

"So you see—" I became aware of Corinne speaking and the agents staring into the car. "We have her under control, but only Agent Jordan here can get through to her. He's helping her to tame her phoenix. I can't guarantee your safety if you try to take her."

"If we tranquillise her like the shifter and the other hybrid—"

"You wouldn't get close enough," I growled.

"They seem to have the situation well in hand," Davis said. "Let's just grab the other hybrid and get out of here."

I resisted the urge to shoot him a grateful look. He was probably just trying to save his own ass anyway.

Kear hesitated, then nodded and disappeared around the back of the car. Singh followed a moment later.

"Are we going to let them take Bryan?" I whispered.

"I don't see that we have a choice," Blake replied. "We've done enough to draw attention to ourselves as it is."

"But...what will they do to him?"

Blake shook his head regretfully. "I don't know."

I sat around in my seat and watched them carry Bryan between the two of them.

Leo stood behind them and scowled. "Careful, old boys, he's a mate of mine."

Kear gave him a suspicious look, but didn't so much as slow down.

Evidently they didn't know what he was and didn't plan to find out. They had their orders and they followed them. Bring in Bryan.

I sighed softly. I didn't think things would end well for the hybrid. He'd be used or he would die. Probably both eventually.

"This doesn't feel right," I said half to myself.

"I know, but it's him or you," Blake replied. "I choose you."

"We shouldn't have to choose," I said bitterly.

"I know." Blake gave me a look which suggested he'd kiss me if we weren't surrounded by Zeta agents.

I squinted out at Davis, who looked as happy about this as I was.

"If you need to reach out to the collective, they can help." Leo pressed something into Davis' palm.

Davis flinched, but then nodded. "Yeah. Maybe." He turned and walked back to the red SUV.

"He's a conflicted man," Leo said before he slipped into the front passenger seat.

"Aren't we all?" Blake replied.

"Nope." Leo twisted around to look back at us. "I know exactly what I want." His eyes rested on me. I blushed.

"We should get out of here." Corinne's expression was grim as she took the driver's seat. "We still have a long way to go."

Pressed between Blake and Dyson, I silently agreed. It would be a long, hot drive.

8

WE SLID until the southern suburbs of Sydney about fours later, without any sign of anyone following us. Granted, the closer we got to the city, the thicker the traffic was. We could have a dozen cars on our tails and not realise it. Fortunately the heavier the traffic, the less chance of Zeta trying anything nasty. At least, that was what I told myself. That hadn't stopped them from coming after us in Melbourne.

"So, what happens now?" Dyson asked. He stretched and yawned, his fake sleep having turned into a real one a couple of hours ago.

"Oh good, you've stopped snoring," Leo said from the front seat.

"I do not snore," Dyson protested.

Leo turned around and gave him a wink.

Dyson cocked his head like a dog and let his tongue loll out to the side.

I giggled, but he brought up a good question. "You're not actually planning to take us to Zeta headquarters?" Although maybe I could let my inner phoenix loose there. No, I didn't want to kill, but they might leave us alone if I toyed with them a bit.

Rational thought caught up a moment later. They also had phoenixes and those shifters probably knew how to tear off heads better than I did. I didn't relish the idea of getting us all killed.

"No, this is where you escape," Corinne replied. "But Blake is going to go with you. Officially, you charmed him into your way of thinking."

I eyed Blake sideways. "And unofficially?"

He blushed. "It might be true," he admitted. "I've decided to continue to study at the AMM."

"Oh." My mouth stayed in that shape for a few moments. "I didn't know you'd gone there?"

He shrugged. "A couple of years ago. I left to help Corinne with Zeta, but I think my place is there now."

"Peyton has that effect on people, doesn't she?" Dyson asked softly.

"Yeah," I muttered. "It's all fun and games until you decide I have to choose between you."

"Bah." Leo waved dismissively. "Who needs to make a choice like that? Plenty of folks live in polyamorous relationships."

"By "folk" do you mean it's normal in demon circles?" Blake asked, genuine curiosity on his face.

"Demons, normals, paranormals, hippies." Leo smiled.

"Hippies?" I echoed.

"Sure, why not? They're all about free love and all that."

I glanced at Blake who looked amused. "So what will you study?"

Dyson was studying primary education, I was studying high school teaching and Kane was doing science. Matt was a computer science major and a bigger geek than he looked. Luckily, I liked geeks.

"Biomedical engineering," Blake replied. "It's hard for shifters to work with prosthesis because they can't change them along with the rest of their bodies. I was hoping to find a way to do that. Maybe with engineering, maybe with magic."

"You, old boy, might be the biggest geek I have ever met," Leo remarked. In spite of his words, he sounded impressed.

"That's because you haven't met Kane," Dyson said. "He runs geek rings around the rest of us."

"He really does," I agreed. "Although Matt isn't far behind." *And has an adorable behind.* I sighed, then turned back to Blake. "I'm impressed. That sounds amazing."

"Thanks," he murmured. "We're nearly there."

I glanced out the window. To my surprise we were deep in the city now. The suburbs gave way to...well, higher density suburbs. Those sat side by side with various businesses in a mishmash of styles and states of repair.

"We'll be dropped off at the train and make our way from there." Blake handed out train cards to Dyson and I. When Leo held out his hand, Blake simply looked at it for a moment. "Sorry, old boy, we weren't anticipating you. Besides, aren't you stopping in Sydney?"

"Ahhh, no. I got into some trouble with a couple of Demon Hunters here. It's best I avoid them."

"It's a big city," Corinne remarked.

"I have a big personality," Leo said proudly.

"We've noticed," she agreed. "We're not taking any responsibility for you."

"Great," Leo grinned. "Then no one will mind if I tag along."

"I don't mind," I said.

"Me either," Dyson added.

Blake hesitated. "Fine, but I still don't have a train card for you." He slipped off his Zeta shirt and pulled out a blue one from a bag next to his feet.

Before he tugged it on over his head, I took a moment to admire his physique. Of course he had to be fit to work for Zeta, so he was toned in all the right places. A sprinkling of hair covered his chest, the same colour as that on his head and just as curly. I wanted to run my hands over it, to tangle my fingers in those curls. As for his lickable abs, well...they looked extremely lickable.

To my disappointment he pulled down his shirt. "There's not enough room to change my pants, but I look a lot less Zeta-ish now."

"Yes, you do," I replied. "Much more 'starving student', like the rest of us." I raised an eyebrow at the holes in his shirt, but I smiled to show I was teasing. He needed to look normal now, unobtrusive, and he did. Well, as much as he could when he was still as cute as hells. There wasn't much we could do about that, except go invisible. In a place as crowded as this, that wasn't always a good option, but we'd do it if necessary.

"That's what I was going for," he replied, a dimple forming in his cheek. "My parents would be so proud."

"They like scruffy?" Dyson asked, teasing as well.

Blake grinned, but it faded after a moment. "They like well-educated. They were disappointed when I dropped out. Especially when they found out why." He grimaced.

I winced. "Not the future they hoped for their young wizard?"

"Not so much," he agreed. "They're no fans of Zeta and were even less thrilled at the risk Corinne had dragged me into."

"Hey, you were a willing participant," she said over her shoulder.

"Consensual espionage is so much sexier," Leo remarked.

"Consensual anything," I agreed.

"Absolutely." He nodded.

"All right folks, here's where you get off." Corinne pulled the car into a parking space.

"What are you going to do?" I asked. She was more than capable of looking after herself, but she would still be alone, without any of us to help her if she needed it.

"I'll see you in a few weeks," she replied evenly. In spite of her calm, her voice wavered a little.

"Come with us now," I urged. "We can all just disappear off Zeta's radar." Nash did it. Matt too. Corinne could make a new life in Illusion Bay.

"I can't." She shook her head. "There are still paranormals who need my help. I won't abandon them." She got out of the car and started to pull bags out of the back.

Before I could move to help, Blake put a hand on my arm.

"She's made up her mind," he said. "Trust me, I've tried to change it. She's one stubborn witch."

"I heard that," she called out.

"You were supposed to," he called back. He pushed the door open and climbed out. I followed close behind.

"Hey, darlin', what do you say we ditch this lot and get lost in the crowds ourselves?" Leo jerked a thumb toward the others.

"Tempting," I replied dryly, "but I'll pass. You can come with us or not, but I'm going with them." I raised an eyebrow at him. I hoped he did decide to travel with us, partly because I enjoyed his company and partly because he still had the stone. I'd like to learn more about it, but more than that, I wanted to be sure it was in safe hands. That, as far as I was concerned, was ours. Yeah, okay, there probably were more qualified people to deal with it, but we were doing the best we could. Besides, Nash and Matt would have a better idea than anyone what to do with the stone.

"I wouldn't dream of being anywhere else, darlin'," Leo replied. "Besides, you need me."

"How do you figure that?" Corinne asked. She handed me my bag and closed the back of the car.

"Because I'm me, love, that's why," he replied. He stepped toward the sidewalk with a swagger.

"Are all demons as cocky as you?" I asked.

"Only the handsome ones." He gave me a wink that set my heart racing.

"It's kinda hot," Dyson said.

"Isn't it though, big boy?" Leo wiggled his eyebrows. He grabbed my hand with one of his and Dyson's in the other. "Come on, Curly," he said to Blake over his shoulder before he started to march toward the train station.

Blake shook his head and trotted to keep up.

I glanced back in time to see Corinne pull the car away from the curb. I nodded to her, but wasn't sure if she saw or not. I worried at my lip with my teeth.

"She'll be okay," Blake assured me. "She'll turn up in a week or two, probably with a few witches in tow. She won't rest until she saves the world."

Or dies trying, I added mentally.

"I know. She's pretty amazing, that cousin of yours." I clasped his hand in my spare one and gave it a squeeze.

"She really is. She's been like a sister to me." He gave me a squeeze back, but didn't let go until the crowds became too thick to walk in a line like we were.

The moment I let go of him and Leo, the crowds surged forward and pushed me with them.

I looked back, but only caught sight of Dyson's face in the press. He mouthed something, but I couldn't make it out as I was pushed forward again. I tried to stop and stand in place, but the crush of people almost dragged me off my feet.

I suppressed the urge to shift and tear my way back to the guys. That wouldn't be particularly subtle.

Instead, I went with the flow. They were carrying me toward the train platform anyway. Once there, I just had to find platform fourteen—no three quarters—and wait for the guys. All while hoping Leo didn't decide to choose now to show his demon face. That would clear the station in a matter of moments, but would also be lacking in the subtlety department. I suspected subtle wasn't his strong suit, but we needed it today.

The crowds thinned as I reached platform one. No doubt fourteen was right at the other end. Typical.

I glanced around, but saw no sign of any of the guys. I chewed my lip again, but started to weave through people toward the higher numbered platforms. Three, four, five.

I spied a doorway with a sign above it reading, "Through to platforms ten to fifteen

Figures, I was in totally the wrong place and according to the screen beside the sign, the train would arrive in less than two minutes.

"Fuck," I muttered under my breath.

I hurried forward and almost tripped over someone's bag.

"Double fuck."

"Watch where you're going," an older woman snapped. She brushed my arm in her haste to grab up the bag and hold it to her.

I would have argued, but the screen now said the train would arrive in under a minute.

"Sorry." I shot her a smile and continued toward the other end of the station at a trot.

Platform ten, eleven.

I ran a little faster, my bag bouncing on my back with each step.

Twelve.

Thirteen.

I spied fourteen just up ahead and sprinted around a group of school kids.

Shit.

There was the train. Where were the guys?

I skidded to a stop on platform fourteen just as the train door slid shut and the train pulled away.

Through the window I saw the frantic faces of Blake and Dyson.

I mouthed, "I'll catch up to you," and gave them a wave before they were drawn out of sight.

Fucking fuckity fuck!

9

"It's okay," I said under my breath. "The next train will leave..." I checked the board. "Tomorrow morning."

Crap.

I moved back from the edge of the platform and leaned against a pillar. I could call Corinne and ask her to come back and get me, but she'd taken enough risks on my behalf. I couldn't ask her to take another.

I winced at the idea of calling Nash and seeing how far away the guys were. He would come and get me, but he might tear Blake and Dyson a new one for leaving me stranded. Although it wasn't their fault, he would still be pissed. They must have assumed I'd boarded the train before they did.

No, it would be better to find somewhere to wait, and catch up in the morning. With any luck, I'd arrive in Illusion Bay before Nash. I admit, I also wanted to arrive before Matt. If I didn't, I would probably never hear the end of it. As much as I adored him, he would never stop giving me hells. That was just as well, since I didn't plan on stopping any time soon either.

Okay, I better find a hotel then. I pulled out my phone and shot off a text to Dyson so he knew my plan. He responded a moment later with a string of sad face emojis and a thumbs up. There was nothing he or Blake could do but ride the train to its destination.

"There you are, darlin'. I guess I'm not the only one who missed the train, eh?" Leo's cheerful voice jerked me out of my thoughts. He held a train card in one hand and a newspaper in the other.

"I didn't know people still read those in paper form," I remarked.

He shrugged. "Something to do on the long train ride. I guess I'll save it for later." He tucked it under one arm and pushed the train card into his pocket. "Come on then." He turned and headed toward the exit.

"Where are we going?" I asked, without taking a step to follow him.

"I have a mate who lives hereabouts. He'll let us stay there and give us a feed. Don't worry, he won't bite."

"What about you?" I tried not to look as if I was looking toward the pocket where he stashed the stone. He could do a lot more than bite if he wanted to.

He stopped and looked back at me. "I'm not going to hurt you, I swear on my mother's life."

"Is she still alive?"

He hesitated, then broke into a smile. "No, she's not, but if she was, I would swear on it."

"Right." I eyed him sideways. Call me a cynic, but I wasn't entirely convinced.

He stepped back toward me, his gaze locked on mine. For those few seconds, the world melted away and it was just us. A witch-hybrid phoenix and a demon of dubious integrity but undeniable charm.

"What if I *want* you to bite me?" I asked.

His grin was back. "Then I'd bite you as hard as you want, darlin'. For the record, I don't mind a few teeth marks here and there. Now, come on. I don't know about you, but I'm ravenous. My mate does the best pizza you've ever had. Guaranteed."

My ears perked up at that. "Pizza, you say?"

"I do say," he agreed.

"Best ever, hmmm? That's a pretty high yardstick. I've had some epic pizza."

"Not like this, you haven't. It'll make you come back for more until we have to be rolled out the door. Don't worry though, we can work it off afterward." There he went, winking again.

"Fine, you had me at pizza." I pushed my bag up my shoulder.

"Pizza, the real universal language of love," he said with a dramatic gesture which almost connected with the face of an unsuspecting commuter. "Oops, sorry."

The commuter glared at Leo, but hurried on as a train drew into platform thirteen.

I smothered a laugh with my hand and hurried to catch up with Leo.

"I think we're supposed to be keeping a low profile," I reminded him.

"I never have been very good at doing that," he admitted. "That's why I have debts and Demon Hunters chasing after me. I tend to stick out, even with this face."

I couldn't argue with that. He was tall, handsome, and covered in more tattoos than bare skin. Guys like him tended to draw the eye. His accent and personality cemented him in my memory at least. I wondered what he was into, although at the moment I really needed to worry more about getting to somewhere Zeta wouldn't find us.

"For both of our sakes, try," I told him. "I'm not going back to a lab." I flushed at remembering the first time he saw me was when I was lying naked on the floor, having finally shifted back to human form. As far as I could recall, he hadn't stopped for a look, or anything else, but I was still embarrassed.

"Not going to happen," he said firmly. "Not on my watch. I have more than a few tricks up my sleeve."

"Me too, I guess." I was, after all, still a witch. I could tear the place apart with magic if I wanted to. Better yet, I could go invisible. That might go unnoticed now, with people hurrying past to catch trains or go about their daily...whatever they had to do. I would put that on the maybe pile for now. At the moment I felt safe enough. That is to say, I saw no one in a Zeta uniform.

Yet.

"Of course you do," he assured me. "You're a badass. I knew that the moment I lay eyes on you. That was in your phoenix form, by the way."

"How did you even get in there?" I asked. "Zeta should have the best security the government can afford."

"And then some, given the current government," he replied dryly. "Corinne and Blake aren't the only ones working things from the inside."

"Let me guess, you had a mate there?" I remembered he hadn't been alone.

"Something like that," he agreed. "I called in a favour."

"It must have been a big one, to get you into a place like that." Personally, when I was in there, I could only think about getting out. I couldn't imagine wanting to go back on purpose.

"It's always a big one. Go hard or go home."

"That stone must be important for you to take the risk of going in to get it. I assume Zeta would kill you if they knew what you are?"

He stopped and regarded me for a moment. "You don't pull any punches, do you, darlin'? If you want the stone, you only have to ask."

I hesitated for a moment. "Maybe not out here, surrounded by people."

He gave a curt nod and resumed walking. "For the record, yes, they would have killed me. My witch friend made us invisible for most of our harrowing journey through the building. To be fair, though, they would kill me because I'm me, regardless of my other face."

"You've pissed Zeta off in the past?" I guessed. Who hadn't he gotten on the wrong side of?

"I have a tendency to turn up in the wrong place and relieve them of items they believe are theirs," he said easily.

"There are more stones like that?" I don't know why I found that surprising, but I did.

"Loads. And they all do different things, depending on the magic put into them. Some control the minds of normals. Some can do the opposite and protect the wearer from mind control. Those are tricky, they let the wearer see right through an invisibility bubble. I heard of one used to trap demons inside." He shuddered.

I glanced over at him. "Trapped? How?"

"Trapped," he repeated. "As in, their consciousness is transferred inside." He waved a hand. "It's a long story for another time. We should hurry, I'd hate to be recognised out here."

"Are you really that notorious?" I asked, half teasing. I wasn't sure if he was just playing up to the role of badass demon.

"And then some." He grinned. "I like to live on the edge, it makes life more exciting."

"Hmmm," I said thoughtfully. "It seems I might be safer away from you then."

"Possibly," he agreed, "but then you wouldn't get pizza."

I pulled a face. "Fine, but this mate of yours better not want you dead as well."

"Oh no, not at all. He would probably like to see me inconvenienced, but not dead."

I snorted. "Is that much better?"

"Definitely." Leo nodded. "Death is usually a bit more permanent."

"Usually?"

"I know some demons who can reattach their own heads. Their brains are in their chests."

"That's an interesting place to keep it."

"Right? I keep mine in my groin."

I laughed. "I didn't doubt it for a moment."

"It just means my dick is smarter than average. It knows just what the ladies like." He wiggled his brows and gave me a cocky smile.

"Does it now?" Of course now my eyes had to go there.

"So they say," he replied. "But you're welcome to find out for yourself."

"Has anyone told you you're very forward?"

"If an adjective exists, it's probably been used to describe me." He stopped at the edge of the road and waited for the traffic light to change. "I prefer to concentrate on the positive ones. You know, handsome, intelligent, articulate…"

"Modest." I smiled.

"Never that," he said. "Life is too short not to embrace your best qualities." He eyed my breasts.

"Right." I licked my lips. "How far to this pizza place?"

"Just another few minutes walk." He nodded ahead of us. "A word of warning though. Johan's place is a little…different."

"Different how?" What could be more strange than anything I already saw over the last couple of years?

"It's… You'll see." He led me up the street to an alley. He stopped at a faded red door and tapped on it three times.

"Best kept secret in the city," Leo explained. "Johan's Pizza."

Hidden as it was, I didn't know how it was still in business. It wasn't the kind of place you'd stumble on while walking around looking for dinner. No sign suggested a restaurant, or a business of any kind, operated here.

The door swung open. The smells which rushed out contradicted my assumptions. My mouth watered immediately.

"Leo." The tall man who had opened the door looked unimpressed to see him.

"Johan, my old mate." Leo stepped forward and tugged me inside. "It's been a long time."

"Not long enough." Still, Johan stepped back and closed the door behind us. He gave me a quick look and a nod before he bustled away.

"He's not the chatty type," Leo said.

"You think?" I followed them down a short corridor and into a wide courtyard. Surrounded on four sides by buildings, none of which had windows on this side, the residents probably didn't even know it was there.

Paranormals sat at various tables around the courtyard. A couple had green faces and long noses. Another had a round face and reddish fur. Several looked like normal humans, but I would have bet anything they were demons or shifters, maybe witches or wizards.

"Welcome to Johan's. Paranormals only allowed," Leo placed his bag against the wall.

"I can't believe you'd step foot in here." A man almost as wide and he was tall rose from his chair and launched himself at Leo.

10

<hr>

LEO STEPPED ASIDE and the man staggered past a few steps.

"Gregor, you old fucker," Leo said cheerfully. He ducked as Gregor turned and swiped a meaty fist at his head. "They love me here, as you can see."

"Evidently." I stepped a safe distance away, although I could have had Gregor on his stomach, his arm twisted up behind him in a heartbeat if I wanted to. Failing that, my inner phoenix could tear him in two. "Do you owe him money too?"

"No, Gregor is an old friend from childhood. He's jealous of my good looks."

Gregor grunted. "This man is a double-crossing piece of crap. Told the Demon Hunters where to find me. They wouldn't leave me alone for weeks."

"Oh," I said slowly, "I guess that's bad."

"I'm not even a demon," Gregor growled. "I'm pure, law-abiding shifter."

Leo clicked his tongue. "Law-abiding? That's a stretch." He glanced toward me. "Gregor runs an auction house. Let's just say some of his goods are not legally obtained."

"Where the seller gets their goods is none of my business," Gregor muttered. "I just sell 'em."

"That amulet was mine," Leo said reasonably. "Stolen by some low life and sold by you." He poked a finger in Gregor's direction.

"Who did you steal it from?" Gregor asked.

Leo smiled, but didn't deny the accusation. "That's beside the point, old boy."

"It sounds as if you're as bad as each other." I slipped into a chair and picked up the menu.

"I dunno why I let either of them in." Johan slid up to the table, order pad in hand.

"I was wondering the same thing," I agreed. At least Gregor had stopped trying to beat up Leo. For now. "Can I please get a pizza with everything except anchovies, and a glass of red wine."

"Everything?" Johan echoed. "Including the crickets, banana, and tuna?"

I blinked.

He shrugged. "We have a varied clientele here."

"Right." I checked the menu and chose a pizza with all the regular toppings before handing the menu to Johan.

He backed away and disappeared through a doorway as Leo sat beside me.

"Banana on pizza?" I whispered.

He grinned. "Don't knock it until you try it."

I grimaced. "Hard pass."

"It's not as tasty as the tuna," he agreed.

I opened my mouth to comment, but closed it again. For all I knew, tuna really was delicious, but I'd leave it for sandwiches and sushi.

"So whose amulet was it?" I asked finally.

"I was wondering how long it would take you to ask." He sighed. "It's a long story."

"We have a few hours to spare."

"And you won't let up until I tell you, I assume?"

"Exactly." I propped my elbows on the table. "Come on then, spill."

"Fine. It originally belonged to a member of the collective."

"Is it sensible to steal from one of them?" I asked. Taking anything from people with power didn't seem like it would end well.

"Of course not," he replied, "but they were corrupt. Tried to take over the collective and bring all the demons under their control. The amulet projected them from attack. They needed someone sneaky to get it so they could get him."

"And did they?"

"Not without a fight, but in the end they did."

"Thanks to you."

He puffed out his chest. "Yes, exactly."

"Because you're a sneaky, dishonest thief," I teased.

He pouted. "If you want to call me that. I prefer to be thought of as an undercover operative."

I waited.

"I like to get under the covers as often as possible."

And there it was. I rolled my eyes playfully. "Does your charm usually get you what you want?"

"Not nearly as often as I'd like," he admitted. "But maybe I just needed to wait for the right situation."

"And you think that involves me?"

He looked thoughtful. "I'm almost certain of it. You like me, I like you…"

"You're sure I like you?" I asked.

He pouted again. "I'm reasonably certain. I am very likeable."

I found myself taking his hand. "I do like you," I assured him. "My situation is complicated. Not everyone is going to want to get themselves involved in anything so—"

"Fascinating?" he suggested. "Compelling? Sexy?"

I gaped for a moment. "All of those things. It's anything but straightforward."

"That's okay, I'm anything but straight. And straightforward is boring. You can't tell me your life is that."

"Boring? No, it certainly isn't. Sometimes I wish it was, but I don't see that happening anytime soon."

He stroked the back of my hand with his thumb. "We can take

some time tonight to make things normal for a bit. We can eat, drink and enjoy each other's company."

"With Gregor glaring at you from his table." I nodded toward Gregor and wondered what he could shift into. The size of a shifter's human form didn't dictate what they could become, or I'd guess bear or elephant. He was just as likely to become a chihuahua.

"We could always go somewhere else to be alone," Leo suggested.

"Maybe after we eat." I was starving.

I pulled my phone out of my pocket as it vibrated. "Text from Dyson." I shot one back to assure him I was fine and ask how he was.

A moment later I got one from Blake with much the same question. I replied in the same way.

After a few seconds I got another from Kane. By the sound of his, he had no idea I got stuck in Sydney. I replied and told him to tell Nash and Matt I was okay before they texted me too.

I just pressed send when Dyson responded that he was all right, but missing me.

Blake sent a similar text a minute after that.

"When I said it was complicated..." I replied to Dyson and Blake and sat the phone on the table.

"You mean they all blow up your phone?" Leo finished.

"Not usually, no." We were often together, so there was no need for texting. When we weren't, the guys knew I might be alone with one of them and respected our space. I hadn't been apart from all of them and Ariana, or my parents, except when I was held in the lab. If it wasn't for Leo I would be very much alone. I didn't find the idea as appealing as I once might.

"Peyton," Leo said. I got the impression he'd said it a couple of times.

"Hmmm? Oh, sorry."

Johan stood beside the table, a plate on either hand. I leaned back so he could place mine in front of me. If it tasted half as good as it smelled, it would be wonderful.

"Thank you." I gave Johan a warm smile.

He grunted and moved away.

We can't charm everyone, I suppose.

"Eat up." Leo was already halfway through his first slice before I picked up mine and bit into it.

"Mmmm." It really was that good, even without the banana. I would have to bring all of the guys here sometime. And Ariana. They would all love this place. Well, maybe not the atmosphere. Gregor was still glaring as Leo over his glass of beer.

"What did I tell you, darlin'?" Leo asked.

"You were right?" I said with a mouthful of food.

"'Course I was. I usually am." He wiggled his eyebrows.

"There goes that modesty again."

"Maybe now you'll trust me." He gave me a speculative look and picked up another slice.

"You can lead a girl to pizza—"

"And her heart is yours forever?" he suggested. "It's an old saying."

"Old as in several seconds?" I asked.

He chuckled. "Something like that."

I smiled and plucked up the courage—maybe the wine helped—to ask another question.

"When do you use your demon face?"

"Oh, this?" He sat still for a moment as his skin turned red and rough-looking. Any sign of his tattoos disappeared. His head was completely free of hair of any kind. Even his eyebrows were gone. "Pretty, ain't I?"

That wasn't exactly the word I would have used, but I found him fascinating. Before I could stop myself, I reached out to touch his cheek. His skin was warm, but not as rough as it looked.

He caught my hand with his and raised it to his lips. The kiss he placed was soft, gentle.

"See, I'm not a big, scary demon. I'm a big softy, but don't go tellin' anyone."

"I didn't think you were scary," I said.

He looked a little disappointed for a moment.

"Not even a tiny bit?" he asked.

"Okay, maybe a teeny bit," I assured him.

"To answer your question, I only use this form to remind people of what I am, and when I'm with my mum. She says we shouldn't forget who we are and where we came from and all that." He let my hand go and shifted back to human form. "She says we shouldn't be ashamed. We're just shifters with a twist."

I smiled. "I like that. Shifters with a twist." I picked up my wine and sipped while trying not to look as though my hand was burning where he'd kissed it. Some people might have run when they saw his demon form, but I wanted him as much as I ever had.

He tilted his head. "Does anything scare you, darlin'?"

I snorted. "Lots of things. Zeta. Failing my classes. Losing people I care about."

He nodded. "Crickets on pizza?"

I laughed. "That's more yucky than scary." I regarded him for a moment. "Don't tell me, you like them?"

He shrugged. "They're an acquired taste. Like me."

"From what you've told me, I should probably run away and never look back."

"And yet, you're still here."

"Yes, I am," I agreed.

"And you're finished eating."

"As are you."

Leo waved toward Johan and handed him a couple of notes before he stood.

"There are rooms upstairs." Leo pointed toward one of the walls which loomed over us.

"Right, sounds good." My heart was pounding like a drum at a rock concert. I picked up my bag. "Lead the way."

"Whatever the lady desires." He took my bag and then my hand.

I didn't look back over my shoulder, but I sensed every eye in the restaurant was on us. They probably thought I was crazy and maybe I was, but I did trust Leo as much as I trusted any of my guys. *My guys? Since when had he become one of them?* That didn't matter so much as the fact he was.

The door clanged shut behind us and we headed toward a set of stairs. We had barely reached the landing outside the door to room three when Leo dropped the bags and pulled me into his arms.

Breathless, I let him draw me toward him. Our lips met in a burst of heat. He turned me and pressed my back to the door. His hands slid up my shirt and cupped my breasts. He ran a thumb over my nipple, making it instantly hard and sending a rush of warmth all through my body.

Before I was even aware of what he was doing, he'd tugged off my shirt and tossed it in the direction of our bags. Without any hesitation, he pulled down the cup of my bra and leaned down to close his mouth over my nipple.

"Maybe we should go inside," I suggested. Not because I was modest in the least anymore, but he might be getting carried away.

"I can't wait that long," he said around my nipple. He worked the button of my jeans loose and they joined my shirt on the ground. My panties followed.

"Foreplay next time," he promised. He unzipped his jeans and released his erection.

My eyes widened. He was bigger than I expected, but I ached to have him inside me. I didn't have to wait long. He hooked at am under my leg to lift it, pressed me against the door and slid himself into me.

"Oh gods," I moaned. He fit so tight it hurt at first. Gradually, my muscles relaxed to accommodate his thickness. Once they had, all I felt was good. Every fibre of me burned to feel his touch, inside and out.

He slid halfway out, then back in again. His cock massaged my insides, driving me closer to the edge already.

"You feel incredible, darlin'," he said breathlessly.

"So do you."

One more thrust and I came with a cry. I arched my back and let the fire consume me, burning through my veins and making me writhe against him to hold on just for a little longer.

He let out a hard grunt and came as well with a series of frantic thrusts. The moment I felt his hot cum flood inside me, something changed.

11

"So you and Dyson haven't had sex. Or..."

"Or what?" I pulled the blanket tighter around my shoulders and watched Leo over my glass of wine.

"Or you're not fated."

What the fuck?

"What the fuck?"

"Fated," he said again.

"You can say that all day, but that doesn't change the fact I have no idea what you're talking about." That was a lie, but not a flat out one. I understood it a little bit, just enough to freak me out.

"Is that something to do with whatever you did to me?"

He smiled and leaned over to refill my glass. He sat naked on the bed, apparently not worried in the slightest. Maybe that should have given me comfort, but it didn't.

"I didn't do anything to you, as such. It's a demon thing. Well, demons and dogs anyway."

"Like marking your territory?"

He grinned, but I sensed his desire to laugh. He suppressed it.

"How are you doing that?" I drank a gulp of wine bigger than I should have. Under the circumstances it was warranted.

"It's just part of the bond," he explained reasonably. "I suspected it was you, but I'm still as surprised as you are. Almost."

"I don't know if I need more wine or less for you to start making sense," I said dryly. "We had sex and now I feel your emotions. Can you feel mine?"

"Of course. Don't worry so much, darlin'. The bond won't hurt you. Quite the opposite."

"We'll see," I said darkly. "Did you do this on purpose?"

He threw back his head and laughed. "Nah. A demon can only bond with the person or people they're fated to be with. If they're lucky enough to find that person, a link is formed. It's a kind of magic, but it's older than... Well, just about everything."

"Can it be broken?"

He arched an eyebrow. "You wound me, darlin'. You don't want to sense my innermost feelings?" When I didn't answer, he added, "No, it can't be broken, but it can be minimised with distance."

"So we're meant to be together or something," I said uneasily. "What about the other guys?"

"You can bond with someone else, if they're a demon or a dog of some kind," Leo replied. "It's especially strong for wolves. I guess it's a wolf pack thing." He shrugged.

"But only if it's fated?" I ran a hand over my hair.

"Exactly. Hence my question about Dyson."

I licked my lips. "Would we have bonded if he..."

"Came down your throat?" Leo asked. "No, only if he was deep inside your warm, luscious—"

I held up a hand. "I see." I wasn't sure I did, but it made some kind of sense. I was drawn to Leo from the moment I'd seen him. If magic decreed we were supposed to be together, who was I to argue? The other guys might not be pleased though. I hated to think how Dyson would feel if we didn't form a bond. Part of me itched to track him down and find out. The other half was terrified of what might happen.

Or not happen.

"You can bond more than one person, too?" I asked finally.

"In theory, but one at a time." He smiled and took the glass from my hand. "I'm sorry if I scared you."

I looked at him from under my brows. "A little warning would have been nice, but if you weren't sure anything would happen, I'm not sure it would have helped."

"Would you have fucked me if I told you?" He grabbed the corner of the blanket and started to tease it away from my skin.

"Maybe not so soon," I said thoughtfully. "Although you are pretty irresistible."

"That's true." He kissed my cheek, then tickled my neck with his tongue. "I promised you foreplay, too."

"That's true, you did," I agreed. We had a lot more to talk about, but truthfully I needed to process this first. As strange things went, it was reasonably high on my list of things which happened to me recently. As far as I could tell, the bond was harmless, as long as Leo was. I liked to think I was a good judge of character, especially when choosing who to sleep with.

I put those thoughts aside for now. I would make more sense of it all later.

I hoped.

"Nice and slow then, hmmm?" He drew the blanket away from one breast, but left the rest of me covered.

"I like the sound of that."

He pressed me back against the mattress and let his tongue trail down over my chest. With featherlight touch, he licked the very tip of my nipple. Slowly, slowly, he traced circles around my sensitive peak, only touching it now and again.

"You're going to drive me crazy," I said breathlessly.

"That's the idea," he said, his voice muffled by his tongue. He pulled back and tugged the blanket back over my breast. Before I could object, he opened the other side and started to give the same teasing treatment to my other nipple.

As turned on as I got being exposed, there was something strangely arousing at having the layers peeled back only a little. It felt more intimate somehow, like he was focusing all of his attention on one part of me. At the same time, I felt his own arousal through the strange bond we had formed.

He closed the blanket over both breasts and moved down my body. He looked up and gave me a smile before he pulled the blanket back from my legs. He hooked one arm under my knee and bent it just enough to open me up to him.

He kissed his way up one thigh, then the other, before he tickled my sex with the tip of his tongue.

I shivered with the delicious warmth which coursed through me. From the bond I felt his appreciation for what he saw in front of him. It was a strange way to see myself, but I liked it.

He dove in a little further, licking and caressing me with practiced ease. His tongue darted around and over my clit. His eyes watched me, but I sensed he was using the bond to discern what I enjoyed. I wasn't sure if that was clever or cheating, but in the end I decided to stop thinking too much.

I closed my eyes and arched my back as he slid a finger into me. Then another.

"Gods," I murmured.

He lifted his head up just enough to smile before he lowered it and went back to licking at my clit and rubbing me from the inside with increasing rhythm.

I crested and tumbled over the edge in a wave that wasn't just mine. I felt his delight in hearing me cry out and buck against his hand and mouth. That heightened my orgasm to a place I had never been before. Blood pounded all through me so hard and hot I couldn't hear or feel anything but pleasure.

After a long plateau, I finally came down and flopped back against the mattress.

Leo emerged from between my legs and tugged the blanket off the rest of me. He rolled me onto my stomach and straddled my legs. Before I had even caught my breath, he gently pried my legs apart and slid his cock deep inside me.

He leaned down to whisper in my ear. "Gods, you are beautiful, inside and out." He cupped his hands over mine and started to move slowly inside me.

I felt how warm my insides were around his cock, how soft around his hardness. No wonder men liked sex so much, I felt amazing.

He pulled out and slid back in over and over, his breath becoming more and more ragged. The closer he got to coming, the more aroused I became.

Our breaths and bodies were in near perfect synch by now. The bond drove us closer and close to falling over the edge together. I had never felt anything like it. I didn't want it to end.

"Gods," he said near my ear. "I had no idea…" He thrust harder and harder until with a grunt he came hard. The bond gave me no choice but to follow.

Our voices cried out in perfect harmony. Whether this was fate or some magical bond created by peculiar circumstances, I didn't care. In the moment it was the most incredible sensation I had ever had. I felt myself contract around his cock, felt me milking him, felt his cum squirt out into my body. I sensed his pleasure and his joy.

Of course, he never bonded before either. This was new to both of us. It was something we could look forward to exploring together. As long as he didn't start to read my mind. A girl has to have some secrets.

Still in unison, we came down from the wild high together. He flopped down onto me before he rolled aside and drew me into his arms.

"I guess that's why they call it fate," he said softly. "I would only want to share that with someone I care about."

"Yeah," I agreed softly. The ugly memory of Fitz popped into my brain.

"I sense you're having dark thoughts." Leo propped himself up on one elbow. "Are you regretting this already?"

I frowned at him. "No, nothing like that." I considered telling him, but that would spoil this lovely, intimate moment. "Just ghosts from the past."

"Ah." He lay back down. "We all have those, darlin'."

I snorted softly. "You certainly seem to have a few. I hope you're not going to drag me into any trouble?"

He chuckled. "Of course I am, but you'll love every minute of it."

"Oh? You think so huh?"

"I have no doubt whatsoever. Have I led you astray yet?"

I considered that for a moment. Unless he really had known about the bond, then he hadn't really. It wasn't his fault we missed the train, or that I had been drawn to him in the first place.

"No, but there's plenty of time for that to happen," I said finally.

He nuzzled my neck. "Yes there is and I can't wait for a moment of it. You and me, darlin' and all your other guys, we're in for one hells of a ride."

Honestly, that was what I was afraid of.

1 2

Dyson and Blake were waiting for us at the train station in Illusion Bay when we arrived. The anxious expression on both of their faces could have been due to worry about me and Leo. It might also have been because of Nash, who stood a few metres away from them, his arms crossed over his chest. His face looked calm, but his eyes snapped with fire.

I couldn't tell if that anger was directed at me, or if he was pissed at himself for letting me out of his sight.

"Hey guys." I stepped off the train into humid air and a rush of embraces from Dyson, Kane, and even Matt.

"Trust you to get lost," Matt told me, a sideways smirk on his face.

I stuck out my tongue. "I love you, too." I might have been sarcastic, maybe not. Either way, he looked pleased.

Nash cleared his throat and everyone stepped back, leaving me to face him. After a moment he took my hand and led me off the platform toward a waiting van. It looked like something Scooby Doo would ride around in.

"Why in the name of the gods didn't you call me to come and get you?" he asked, his voice low. "You could have been—"

"I wasn't," I replied firmly. I appreciated his concern, but I was a grown woman, more or less capable of looking after myself. After all, I could shift into a nasty, bloodthirsty creature just like he could.

"I was perfectly safe the entire time. I don't need to be babied." I shook off his hand and narrowed my eyes at him.

His body stiffened. "I'm not trying to baby you. I care about your safety. Evidently more than you do."

I blinked at him a couple of times. "If I didn't care, I would have stayed in the lab and let them rape me," I snapped. "I have no intention of letting Zeta touch a hair on my head for as long as I live. If you think I would, you better think again, buddy."

I stuck out my chin and fixed my gaze on his face.

He seemed conflicted. On one hand, he knew I could be a badass, killing hybrid. On the other, I didn't want to be anything more than an ordinary witch, just conjuring up fluffy bunnies for shits and giggles. I didn't ask for any of this.

Finally, he exhaled. "I know. I'm sorry. I didn't mean to be a dick. It's just…"

"I know, you care, but leave being a dick to Matt," I said, half teasing.

"I heard that," Matt said from the other side of the van.

I chuckled. "Sorry, not sorry."

Nash took my hand and drew me to him. He nuzzled his face into the hair around my right ear. "I should tie you up and spank you for not calling me sir."

A delicious shiver traveled through my body and made my toes curl.

"Why don't you then, sir?"

"Maybe I will, after…" He trailed off and leaned back to look at me, a puzzled expression on his face. "What…" He glanced toward Leo and back.

"Fated mates, mate." Leo grinned.

"You can feel that?" I asked Nash.

"Yes, no…" Nash frowned. "I can feel something. It's like a strand of magic, like a bubble, but…not."

"Well that's as clear as mud," Kane said. He climbed into the front passenger seat and now sat staring at me.

I started to speak, but shook my head. "Maybe we shouldn't talk about this here."

"Yes," Nash replied immediately. "Let's get to the academy. It's an hour's drive from here as it is." He nodded to Matt who slipped into the driver's seat and started the van. It purred like a cat on steroids and smelled faintly like stale weed.

"Where did you find this thing?" I climbed in and sat between Nash and Blake. Blake changed into brightly coloured board shorts and a rumpled grey t-shirt. His curly hair was damp and the dimple in his cheek when he smiled was as cute as ever.

I returned his smile and placed a hand on his thigh, and one on Nash's when he sat beside me.

"It belongs to the college," Matt said over his shoulder.

"Do they use it to solve crimes?" I joked.

"They could now," Dyson said from the seat behind me. "We have a big, goofy dog."

"Awww," I twisted around and looked back at him. "You're not goofy." My gaze went to his lap and wondered if we could form a bond, too. Or he and Leo. They seemed to have taken to each other as well, judging by the looks they exchanged when the demon flopped down beside Dyson and stretched out like he was on a couch, not the back of a van.

"So, about that magic connection," Nash began.

"Right." I sat back around and explained what Leo had told me. Thankfully no one seemed bothered by my having slept with Leo in the first place. Blake and Dyson probably saw it coming—pun intended—as much as I had.

"Ain't never heard of anyone being able to sense a bond before, mate," Leo remarked, his accent thicker as he addressed Nash.

Nash shrugged. "I'm special."

I wasn't sure if he was joking or not, so I raised an eyebrow at him.

"Maybe it's because I'm a dragon," he said slowly. "Or it might be a hybrid thing."

"I can't sense anything," Matt said, "but my brain might be foggy from the second hand weed smoke in this godsdamned van."

I snorted softly. The longer I was in it, the stronger the smell became. "It doesn't run on weed fumes, does it?"

"It might," Kane said. "Technology is changing all the time."

I giggled. "Oh goody, we could all have weed mobiles in a year or two."

"Who needs flying cars when you can get high like this?" Blake asked.

I giggled again.

Nash opened the window beside him to let in some fresh air.

I took the opportunity to peer out at the landscape as we rushed past. Through the trees I caught glimpses of the ocean and the occasional beach. Buildings of any kind were few and far between. Subtropical vegetation dominated the view instead.

"Are you sure there's a college up here?" I asked. "Please tell me there's no uniform."

"I hear on some days, clothing is optional," Dyson replied.

"I'm pretty sure that was an exaggeration," Kane said dryly.

"Why is nudity such a problem for you?" Dyson asked him. "You like having sex in public."

"I don't have a problem with nudity," Kane insisted. "Just yours. You're my brother, I don't want to see your dick."

"I do," Leo said.

"Me too," I agreed. "Dyson has a very nice dick."

"Oh, he does?" Leo asked, sounding very interested.

"Well, I don't want to brag," Dyson said.

Leo leaned forward so his breath brushed my neck. "Is it as nice as mine?"

I considered that for a moment. "I think it best if I don't answer that. I don't want to be seen to favour one dick over another."

"That's fair," Blake replied, "but you shouldn't decide until you've seen mine anyway."

"Oh, is that a promise?" My heart pounded.

He gave me a dimpled grin. "If you want it to be."

"Oh, I definitely do, but I'm still not going to favour one of you over the other."

"Does that mean you won't choose between us?" Kane asked.

The humid air in the van was suddenly hotter, but the guys all fell silent as though each held his breath.

"I…" I chewed my lip for a moment. "I don't want to choose. I care about you all equally. I want all of you. If that's a problem…"

"Not for me," Kane replied almost immediately.

"Me either," Dyson said.

"Or me, darlin'. You're stuck with me."

"And me as well," Nash said softly.

"There are worse clowns to be stuck with," Matt said from the driver's seat.

"Thanks, I think," I said dryly. I glanced over to Blake who was looking down toward his lap.

Without raising his head, he said, "I decided to go back to school so I could be around you. Whatever form that takes. I just hope you can find some time for me."

I put a hand on his arm. "Count on that. I'm looking forward to it."

He turned his head to the side and smiled. "Me too." His mouth worked before he was able to form more words. "Do you think we can make the same kind of bond you have with Leo?"

"Unless you're a dog or a demon, old boy—" Leo started.

"It's possible," Nash interrupted. "If you can form one with Dyson, I might be able to feel how it's done." He swung his head back toward Dyson. "Assuming you two plan to have sex and don't mind me listening in."

"You can watch us any time," Kane said helpfully.

"Noted," Nash replied. "Your twin isn't you. He may prefer privacy. Although as I recall, that one time—"

"Yeah." Dyson's face was pink. "I suppose if we can form a bond, it's not fair if the rest can't. I mean, at least you could try to form one. If that means you have to… Yeah, I guess it would be okay."

"Good." Nash nodded. "I'm sure we can set up something suitably romantic."

"That would be nice," I said. "Because for a minute there I was feeling like a science experiment. I think we've established that I don't want to be in a lab."

Now Nash flushed. "It has to be all right with you as well. If we could bond, I would know…"

"You could keep a closer eye on me, sir?" I asked.

He hesitated. "That would be a benefit, yes."

"It would go both ways," I reminded him. "I would know if you're angry."

"You can't tell now?" he asked. "I need to work on that."

I chuckled. "You'd know how it feels to be spanked."

Rather than be put off by that, he seemed to find the idea appealing.

"Matt, can you drive a little faster?" Nash asked.

"Not without breaking the law now," Matt replied. "We're almost there anyway."

We swung into a narrow road which wound through trees covered in brightly coloured flowers. After a few minutes more, we came out into an open space with a beach on one side and a series of long, low buildings on the other.

"This is the college?" I asked in amazement.

"Yes." Matt said over his shoulder. "Welcome to the College of Advanced Magical Education. C. A. M. E."

I snickered at the acronym, but I preferred this to the original AMM campus or the one which belonged to the UA. Compared to those, this looked warm, relaxed, and inviting, rather like a resort. All it needed was a few hammocks here and there and a cocktail bar. Although, for all I knew, those might be around here somewhere.

"Please tell me we're not in the basement, or sleeping on the beach?" I climbed out behind Nash and reached for my bag.

"Oh no, nothing like that," Dyson assured me. "Come on, you'll love it." He took my hand and sent a jolt of heat through me.

At that moment, I wasn't sure if I could be happier, sounded by a bunch of guys I adored, in the warm air beside the beach and anticipating the night to come. What more could a hybrid want?

Okay, in the back of my mind I was worried whether we'd be accepted at this campus and if Zeta would find us here. I just wanted to finish my education in peace.

Was that too much to ask?

13

―――――――――――

"You don't have to do this you know." Dyson's face was distorted by my champagne glass. Bubbles rose in front of him, slowly sliding upward to burst at the top.

I took a sip and set the glass aside.

He grimaced. "It's not that I don't want to. It's just..." He jerked his thumb toward the curtain which covered the open window. Every so often a breeze would ruffle it and blow it inward a fraction.

Nash and Matt sat outside, ready to see if either could sense anything which might indicate a bond forming. Nash seemed sure he'd know if it worked. Matt—he seemed more curious than anything, but sceptical as well. I suspected he wouldn't believe bonds existed until he felt one for himself. Fair enough, I wouldn't have believed it if Leo had merely told me about it.

I crossed my legs. "They're probably on their phones," I remarked. "Would you feel better if they were in the room?"

"Gods, no," Dyson said immediately. "Any other time I might, but not now." He cupped my cheek gently. "I want this to be about you and me. Well, as much as it can be."

"I could tell them to get lost." I uncrossed my ankles and placed my hand on the bed, ready to push myself to my feet if necessary.

Dyson caught my hand. "I'd never hear the end of it from Kane. He wants to bond with you too. If there's a chance, he would take it with both hands. I'd bet anything Nash, Matt, and Blake feel the same way."

I arched an eyebrow at the direction of the window, but if either guy heard, they didn't respond. At least, not that I could hear. For all I knew, they were using sign language to have an intense discussion on the best cop movie ever made and not paying us any attention.

What? Cop movies are okay.

"That doesn't mean you're obligated in any way," I said firmly. "They'll deal with it." They were all big boys after all, more than capable of handling all sorts of things, including this.

Dyson shrugged. "After tonight, I'm taking you somewhere private so we can take our time with no interruptions."

As if on cue, Leo's voice came in through the window.

"Is this where you ole boys got to?" he asked easily.

Nash replied but his words were muffled.

"Oh, don't mind if I join you then? I love a little voyeurism. Move over then, lads."

"We're not here to watch." Nash sounded annoyed. "We're just observing the bond, if there is one. This all might be for nothing."

"Bet you ten bucks it won't be," Leo replied.

"Ten bucks? What do you know that we don't?" Matt asked.

"A shit ton, probably," Leo said with a laugh. "Seriously though, it's obvious."

"You think?" Nash asked. "If you could tell us how the bond is formed, we could leave them to it."

"No can do, big guy," Leo said. "I don't know either. I just know they have a connection." After a pause, he added, "Don't dragons have dog DNA? That's why you're here, isn't it? Your ego can't stand the fact you don't have a bond. If you're not meant to be, you're not—"

Nash cut him off. "I don't believe this bond is some kind of gods-made gift. It's just a kind of magic and most magic can be reproduced in some way."

"I guess we'll find out, eh?" Leo said.

"Only if you shut up," Matt snapped.

Dyson sighed softly and leaned back against the pillows. "Now I know how lab rats feel."

I snorted. "Maybe we both need more champagne. Or we could sneak out the door and hide somewhere?"

He grinned. "I'm surprised Kane didn't insist on being my fluffer."

I slapped a hand over my mouth to stifle a loud laugh. After a moment or two, I lowered it and said, "That would take awkward to a whole new level. Although, I could ask Leo in to do it if you like."

Dyson chuckled and reached for me. "I have a better idea. How about we forget all about them and focus on each other."

"That's the best idea I've heard all day." I leaned in to claim his mouth with mine. The kiss we shared was searing hot and left me breathless. We kissed before, but never like this.

"Wow," I said against his mouth.

"Mmmhmm," he agreed. "You set me on fire."

"Not literally, I hope." Phoenixes and fire went hand in hand, or was that hand in wing? At least in mythology they did. In real life, I didn't breathe flames, or get reborn from any ashes.

Yet.

Give it time, I was probably not done with the weirdness. Or it wasn't done with me.

He chuckled again. "No, but my insides are burning up." He reached for the hem of my shirt and tugged it up and over my head. He tossed it aside and unhooked my bra after a few tries.

"I've never done that before," he admitted as he cupped my breast and ran a thumb over my nipple. "I've thought about this a thousand times."

"Only a thousand?" I teased.

"At least that."

I helped him out of his shirt and ran my fingertips down his abs. "What do you have under there, rock?"

"Just hard work," he assured me. "And pizza."

"Pizza makes for great abs?" I asked. Hells yeah. If that was the case, I would eat more of it.

"No, but it's a great reward for working out."

"I don't think that's how it's supposed to work." I shuffled down a little and ran the tip of my tongue over his firm torso.

"No?" He tangled his fingers in my hair.

"Nuh-uh." I shook my head and undid the front of his shorts. I thought he might have been turned off by the guys outside the window, but his erection said otherwise. His cock was hard and hot in my hand. I licked his tip and tasted the bead of cum which had already formed there.

"You might want to save some of that." His voice was strained already.

"Good point." But I still sucked the head of his cock a few more times and massaged his balls with my fingers and nails.

When he groaned, I moved away and tossed my shorts onto the floor.

"Tease," he said jokingly.

"You'd better believe it." I grinned and lifted my hips as he pushed my panties off them and down my legs.

His eyes raked down my body, taking in every bit of me. "You're also the most beautiful woman I have ever seen. I'm the luckiest guy on the face of the planet right now."

I felt Leo's response through our bond. I thought he might joke around, but he agreed with Dyson and was turned on. That in turn heightened my own arousal. Bonding with all the guys might get interesting if I was turned on every time they were. I had a healthy enough sex drive as it was.

"You're going to make me blush."

"I'd prefer to make you scream." His mouth closed on my nipple. He drew it in between his lips and sucked like I was a delicious morsel.

"That could happen too." I arched my back, aroused as hells by his touch, but also knowing the guys were listening. In some ways, it was almost more enticing than having them watch. This way they would have to use their imaginations to visualise what might be going on inside. If theirs were anything like mine, it would be wild.

"There's something you should know," Dyson said around a

mouthful of nipple. He swapped to the other, leaving the first to glisten in the light of the candles the other guys had lit for us. "I've never done any of this before. With anyone."

He lifted his head and looked at me as though he was worried about how I'd react.

"I thought you might not," I said gently. "Or you might have bonded with them."

He cocked his head to the side. "That's true. You don't mind?"

I held his gaze with mine and hoped he saw my desire. "I'm honoured," I said firmly.

He smiled with relief. "I want you so bad."

"I want you too." Mostly because I just did, but part of me was dying to know if the bond would form or not. If it didn't, I wasn't sure who would be more disappointed, Dyson or me. Or Kane, who apparently has almost as much invested in this. I was surprised he wasn't sitting outside with the others. Then again, maybe he was and was just more quiet than they were.

The idea of him listening in made my skin tingle all over. My imagination threw Blake in as well, then they started to touch each other...

Dyson rolled me onto my back and lay between my spread knees. With most of his weight on his huge arms, he leaned in to cover my mouth with his.

I returned his kisses with all the heat which rushed through my veins. I opened my mouth and teased his lips.

I rolled us both until I straddled his hips. He looked up at me with such love, my heart reacted a little harder. I sensed he forgot about the guys outside. This was all about us now.

I positioned myself over his cock and slid down his cock. Tentative at first, then a little deeper.

He groaned. "I didn't know you'd feel so amazing." He closed his eyes, an expression of pure bliss on his face. "I mean, I suspected." He caressed my breasts lightly, thumbs brushing over my taut nipples.

I laughed softly. "Same to you."

Let's face it, not all cocks are created equal. They're all epic, but they feel different. Not different bad or necessarily different good, just different. And this one I was enjoying thoroughly, deep inside me.

"You think so?" He cracked open one eye and gave me a lopsided smile.

Of course Dyson would crack jokes during sex. It was another part of his charm.

"Absolutely. I've imagined this since I first saw your dick. This is next level amazing."

"Thank you, on behalf of my dick and I." He closed his eyes as I rose and fell, riding him slowly.

"You're welcome." I closed my own eyes and let my arousal and Leo's carry me closer to the edge of the abyss. I wanted to tumble over, but not yet. First, I wanted to savour the first time between Dyson and I. It had been a long time coming.

Pun intended.

"Peyton," Dyson whispered.

"Yes?"

"I love you."

"I love you, too."

He rolled us over again and pulled out of me and rolled me onto my side.

"I want to be able to see your face better." He gently guided one of my legs over his and opened me up to him. One hand cupped my cheek, the other guided him back into me.

We lay there like that for what seemed like an eternity, eyes locked on each other, his thrusts slow but rhythmic. My passion simmered, coming closer and closer to the boil.

After a long while, he increased his speed. He reached in between us to gently caress my clit.

"Come for me," he whispered.

I drew my lower lip in between my teeth and bit gently. I wanted, needed to come, but I didn't ever want this to end.

He rubbed a little harder, always at the right angle, in exactly the right place. Maybe we had formed a bond already; he was that in-sync with my body. Maybe he just knew where to find a clit.

I puffed a breath out my nose, then another.

The pressure built until I couldn't contain it any longer. I threw back my head and cried out, long and low as my orgasm rocked my from the top of my head to the tips of my curled toes.

"Ohhh, Dyson," I breathed.

"Peyton…" He thrust harder still and grunted.

My eyes snapped open the moment he came.

I felt his body tense.

His cock, hard and deep inside me squirted cum like a fountain of heat and magic. It flooded into me, through me. It traveled from my belly through every drop of my blood, every organ, right up into my heart, my mind.

It was different to the one Leo and I had formed, but it was undeniable.

We were bonded.

The profound silence was broken by Leo's shout of triumph. "You blokes owe me ten bucks!"

14

"So, did you feel anything?" I pulled out a chair and flopped down beside Nash. I stifled a yawn and stole a slice of Vegemite toast from his plate. After Leo's shout, the guys had left Dyson and I to enjoy the rest of the night in peace. And enjoy it we did, twice more. When I crept out of bed, he was still snoring.

I smiled at Kane who had been scrolling madly through his phone, but now put it aside.

"Yeah." Nash scowled as I bit into the toast. "I felt the bond form. I was right, it is just magic."

"It sounds to me like the release of a pheromone," Kane said. "In animals, they help to attract a mate. In humans, too. Basically it… influences the behaviour of the other person, or people."

He gave me a lopsided grin that looked so much like his twin, my heart skipped. I adored both of them so much. I couldn't imagine my life without them.

"So this magic pheromone created a bond?" I asked.

"Pheromones can work to synchronise two creatures, so basically, yes." Kane nodded.

I considered for a moment. "Was it something I did last night that did it? A conjuring I didn't know existed until Leo?" I scratched behind my ear. "That doesn't explain how he and I formed a bond too, though. He can't do magic, can he?"

"He's a shifter, more or less," Nash pointed out. "That in itself is magic."

I nodded slowly. "Of course it is."

"Bond-forming and shifting might be his only magic. Dyson's too, evidently." Kane grimaced slightly.

I leaned over to cover my hand with his. "What you do with your tongue is magic."

He flushed bright red and mumbled his thanks.

"You didn't consciously do magic?" Nash asked, interrupting the awkward moment.

"No, I just…enjoyed myself," I replied. "Why? Did it feel as if I did?"

Nash picked up his mug of coffee and held it without drinking for a few moments. "Not that I could tell, but all I know is magic flashed between you two and the bond was there."

"Magic cum," I mused.

"That or you have a magic pussy," Kane said.

"She certainly has that," Nash agreed.

Now I blushed. "Maybe it needs both."

Nash frowned. "That's something we could try."

I raised both eyebrows at him as high as they'd go. "Are you planning to use Dyson's cum to create a bond?"

His mouth dropped open in surprise. "I wasn't, but now you mention it—"

"I suspect it will only work once," Kane said. "It's caused its chemical—or magical—reaction. It might work with someone else, but not with Peyton again."

"What will then?" Nash asked. "Regular magic?"

Kane rubbed his chin. "It might, but I feel as though if it was that simple, everyone would be doing it."

Both guys let out simultaneous heavy sighs.

"It can't hurt to try though, right?" I finished my toast and washed it down with a sip of water from Kane's glass. I needed tea, but it would have to wait.

Before Kane could move, Nash put aside his coffee and took my hand in his. He closed his eyes.

I sensed him drawing magic from all around us. "What now?" I whispered, not wanting to break his concentration entirely.

He shook his head. "I don't know. I'm thinking about the bond, but I don't feel anything forming."

"Neither do I." I drew a little too, and delved around for where his magic met mine. We could have formed a large bubble, or knocked everyone in the room off their feet. There was no sign of a bond.

After a while I exhaled and let the magic go.

Nash did the same. "Either it has to involve sex, or there's more to it than that. As much as I'd love to find out if it's the first one, I have to get to work. You have classes too, no doubt."

"Ugh, the real world." I groaned to add a little extra melodrama to the moment.

Kane chuckled. "I'm looking forward to it. I hear the facilities here are nice and warm."

"Thank the gods." After the rooms at UA, I was ready for a nice, humid lecture theatre or whatever they had here.

"Just try not to piss anyone off," Nash warned.

"Who, me?" I pointed at myself. "I never *try* to annoy anyone, it just happens." I smiled as innocently as I could.

He snorted. "Just don't mention Zeta or anything about them coming after you and you should be fine."

"I was trying to avoid even thinking of them," I said. Nash was right though. The antagonism between me and some of the students at UA was less about me and more about their fear Zeta would come after them. The joke would be on them though, if they knew Zeta *owned* the University of Arcana. Still, I wouldn't even wish life in a lab on Xav, the guy who had been the biggest dick in UA.

"Don't get complacent either," Nash added. "The council assures me you're safe here, but don't turn your back on anyone. Just in case."

"Yes, sir," I said smartly. I even threw in a salute for good measure.

His eyes shone and I knew he was rethinking having to work. I suspected he'd prefer to tie me down to his bed and spank my ass until it was red.

He placed his hands on the table and pushed himself to his feet. The bulge in his pants confirmed my suspicions.

"I will see you later," he said, his voice heavy. He nodded to Kane and hurried away.

I watched his tight ass until he was obscured from view, and turned to Kane.

"I'm sorry."

He looked surprised. "What for?"

"Because your brother and I bonded, but we haven't. It's not for lack of trying."

"Maybe if we'd known we could, we would have done something differently," he said.

"Your parents never mentioned a bond?"

"No, never."

"Are they dog shifters?"

"No. Dad is a big cat. Our mother is a bird. They think the wolfhound came from our dad's mother."

I ran a hand over my hair. "So shifters can be quite different, even within families. Are any of you part demon?"

Kane considered for a moment. "It's possible. Maybe dogs and demons share more characteristics in common."

"I've never heard of demons humping people's legs," I said with a smile.

Kane choked back a laugh. "Me either, but Leo looks like the kind who would."

"What would I do, big guy?" Leo appeared behind us and slid into the chair Nash vacated. "Oh look, you left me a half drunk cup of cold coffee."

"Feel free." I waved toward the mug.

"I'll pass. I prefer it fresh and hot, just like you, darlin'" He pressed a kiss to my mouth.

Kane cleared his throat.

"Oh, sorry." Leo turned and planted a sound kiss on Kane's mouth which ignited my blood faster than a match.

Kane blushed bright red, but didn't look as though he minded.

Oh gods, now them being together would be in my carousel of fantasies.

"We should be getting to class," I said regretfully.

"Bah, there's plenty of time for class." Leo waved his hand in a gesture of dismissal. "Wouldn't you prefer to sneak out and explore Illusion Bay? Just the two of us. Okay, three of us." He winked at Kane.

"I don't mean to be rude," Kane said, "but why are you here? Apart from your bond with Peyton, I mean."

Leo rubbed his forehead with his fingertips. For a few moments he actually looked serious.

"I'm trying to find my place in the world. I know it involves Peyton and you guys, but apart from that..." He shrugged and the smile returned to his face. He sat back and crossed his arms over his chest. "Maybe I'll get a job. Or I might find the local nudist beach and get a tan."

"Don't get a sunburnt cock," I advised him. "That might hurt."

Kane winced. "Yeah, it does. I mean, it would. I wouldn't know." His face was red again and he looked away.

"I'll bet there's a story there, old boy," Leo said lightly, "but it'll have to wait. We have a town to discover." He held out his hand to me.

"I really can't," I replied after a few moment's thought. "It's our first day of classes and they've been nice enough to let us study here."

Leo huffed. "Responsible adult, hmmm?"

"What can I say?" I shrugged. "One of us has to be."

"I thought that was Nash's job?"

"It is, but he's not here right now, so I have to step up." A smile tugged at the corners of my mouth.

Leo grimaced playfully. "I hope it's not contagious."

"It probably is. Why, are you regretting bonding with me now?"

"Not for a moment, but I should go before I turn into my father."

"Well we wouldn't want that." I nodded.

Leo's nose wrinkled. "Gods no. He's an accountant. So is my older brother. And my younger one. I'm the only fun one in the whole family."

Kane patted his hand. "That must be a terrible burden."

Leo sighed dramatically. "It really is. Family events are so dull."

"I never would have thought of demons as boring," I said.

"Until you saw me, you didn't know we existed," Leo pointed out. "Except on TV and in movies."

"I'm assuming those aren't accurate representations, just like witches and shifters?" I asked.

"Oh, I don't know. I know plenty of demons who…" Leo flinched and looked past my shoulder. "Shit."

"What?" I turned around in my seat and glanced back. I didn't see anything unusual, just a group of students gathered around talking. They all wore t-shirts or singlets and shorts; a refreshing change from the uniforms UA had made us wear.

"Them," Leo said. "They're all demons."

"Oh." I looked at them closely. They didn't look like anything out of the ordinary, certainly nothing to be afraid of.

"Which one did you piss off?" Kane asked.

"All of them," Leo replied.

I turned back around in time to see him stand and push his chair back under the table. Before he could step away, one of the other demons called his name.

"Leo! What the hells are you doing here?" A woman with long red hair and a nose ring walked toward him, hips swaying. She smiled, but her eyes snapped with barely contained annoyance.

"Cordelia." Leo spoke from between clenched teeth. "I thought I'd get an education. Wasn't that your suggestion?"

She smirked. "I believe my words were along the lines of, "if I ever see you again, I'll teach you a lesson." Are you dumb enough to come back for more?"

He raised his hands. "I guess so, love." He loudly whispered, "Cordelia is an old family friend. She likes to think she's queen of the demons. Maybe of all paranormals."

Cordelia snorted. "That's bullshit. I just don't put up with Leo and his crap." She held out a hand to me. "Welcome to the college. Don't believe a word Leo says." To my surprise, she gave me a wink.

I found myself shaking her hand and smiling at her. I had the feeling whatever there was between them was a lot of words, but mostly a friendly rivalry. I hope so. I'd had enough of aggressive students and assholes.

"You *must* come to the party tonight on the beach. We're inviting the entire college, especially you guys from AMM. I've heard whispers that you dealt with an attack from Zeta."

She was clearly fishing for information. Truthfully I didn't know how to reply to that.

I shrugged. "You shouldn't believe everything you hear."

She smiled. "I never do. That's why I want to hear it all first hand. But it can wait until tonight. You will come, right?"

I glanced back to see Kane nod.

Leo made a choking sound, but said, "We wouldn't miss it."

"There you are then," I said lightly. I might tell her a bit about the attack, but if I could, I would also ply her and her friends for information about the bond. This could work in both our favours.

15

THE MUSIC THROBBED HARDER than my heart. The slip and crunch of hot sand changed to a cool squelch under my feet as I reached the waterline. A wave washed up the beach and over my bare feet.

I squealed. "It's so cold!"

"As cold as Cordelia's heart," Leo said. He scowled down at his damp pant legs.

I reached for his arm and tugged him closer to me. "Are you going to be a killjoy all night?"

"If he is, you can ditch him and dance with me," Dyson said easily.

"Me first." Kane took hold of my hand and laced his fingers in mine.

"No way, I—"

I cut Dyson off. "Don't make me throw you both in the drink so you cool down."

"You wouldn't?" Dyson asked with mock horror.

"She might not, but I would," Matt said from behind them.

"I'd help Matt," Nash remarked.

I looked back and caught his eye. He looked good back in track pants and a singlet; comfortable and with more of his muscled body on display. I loved seeing him in a suit, but this was the Nash I knew and loved. I could have torn off his singlet and licked his abs then and there, but instead I gave him a smile full of promise.

"You would?" I asked teasingly.

He shrugged. The corner of his mouth turned up in a slight smile. "Whatever it takes to break up a fight." His expression darkened and I knew what he was thinking. As long he didn't have to kill, he'd take part.

"We'll be good," Kane said in a hurry. "But if you want us to take our clothes off, you only have to ask."

"Take your clothes off." Leo grinned.

Kane blushed, bright red. "Maybe later," he muttered.

"I'll hold you to that, big boy." Leo clapped him on the back. "Oh look, alcohol."

If there was anything that might change the subject, it was that. We all stopped chatting and gathered around a huge table to grab a cup and fill it with beer.

"Here you are." Blake handed me a cup before I could get one myself.

"Thanks." I took the cup and shot him a smile.

"Do you actually dance?" he asked.

I grimaced. "Not very well. I'm more the type to sway, more or less in time with the music. You?"

He looked embarrassed. "I used to do competitive ballroom danc-ing. It's been years since I've done it," he added quickly.

My eyes widened. "You must have been really good. Did you win a lot of the dance-offs, or whatever they're called?"

He chuckled. "A few. It was fun, except…"

"Except what?" I prompted.

"Except the mothers at the dance school used to go on about my curly hair." He sipped and made a face. "You'd think they'd never seen a guy with curls before." He ran a hand over his head absently.

"I like your curls," I assured him. Would it be wrong of me to admit that was the first thing I noticed about him? To be fair, he was pretending to be a loyal Zeta guard at the time. I was hardly going to be looking at his ass. I had done that a lot since.

He looked pleased, but smiled ruefully. "I like your hair better, especially the green streak." He tilted his head. "Is that a permanent colour? You've had it since I've known you and it doesn't seem to be growing out."

I touched my head lightly. "Magic gone awry," I said simply. "Courtesy of Ariana." A flood of emotion filled me. I missed her. Nash still hadn't explained where she'd gone and I didn't push. I knew he would only tell me when he was ready to. While that bugged the hells out of me, arguing with him would get me exactly nowhere.

"I could probably fix that if you want?" Blake offered.

"It's okay, I kind of like it now." I lowered my hand. "I want to hear more about your dancing. Or better yet, see it."

"On sand?" He glanced toward his feet. "It's not exactly the best dance floor."

"Why not?" I tapped my bare toes on the sand. "It's a little wet, I suppose."

"Just a little," he agreed. "Maybe later. Can we sway first?"

I glanced around to see the rest of the guys, beers in hand, talking about some movie we streamed the night before. I fell asleep in the middle of it, but evidently they'd enjoyed it.

"Sure." I offered him my hand and we moved away to let others get to the drinks table.

Blake wound an arm around me and, careful not to spill our drinks, we swayed. His body pressed hard against mine and made my heart race faster than before.

"This is nice," he said near my ear. "It's hard to get you alone."

I snorted softly. "It's hard to be alone," I agreed. "Not that I'd change a thing," Truthfully, they gave me space when I really needed it, as long as it was safe enough. Which translated to not as often as I'd like, but hopefully being here would change things. I was desperate for something close to normal, maybe even boring, for a little while.

"Can I cut in?" a smooth voice asked.

"Uh." Blake stepped back before Cordelia all but shoved him out of the way. "I guess so."

I gave him a regretful look and mouthed, "Later," before Cordelia took my hand and wound an arm around me.

"If you haven't guessed before now, I like girls," she said bluntly. "I want you to know I want to kiss you, badly."

"I…" I swallowed. I wasn't sure how to respond to that. I couldn't say I hadn't kissed girls before, but not recently. Ariana and I were just friends and I wasn't close enough to anyone else to even think about it.

"It's okay if you don't feel the same way," she said lightly. "I just prefer to be honest."

"Right," I replied. "Of course. I appreciate that." I really did.

"There's no need to rush things." She twirled us around. "I'm sure you have lots of questions about demons. You want to know about the bond, right?"

While I stammered, she smiled. "I'm very astute. Besides, I know Leo. He wouldn't hang around long unless there was something in it. It's either a bond or he's running a scam." She cocked her head to the side so her hair fell over her shoulder. "I wouldn't rule out both, just between us. Keep an eye on that one."

"Right," I said slowly. "What kind of scam?" If she was trying to sew seeds of doubt, she succeeded.

She laughed, a tinkling sound which unnerved at the same time it drew me to her. "Oh the gods know with him. Gambling, blackmail… If it's illegal, he'll do it. It's funny how people like bad boys. And bad girls too, of course." She ran the tip of her tongue over her lips.

I swallowed hard. "Yeah, funny about that." I tried to clear my thoughts, but they were hazy, as if I had more than a few sips of beer. "So, you were going to tell me about the bond?" If I didn't know better, I'd think someone slipped something funny into my drink. Blake wouldn't do that and I held my drink myself ever since he handed it to me. Maybe it was just her.

"I could be persuaded to… Are you feeling okay? You look a little pale."

I blinked at her worried face, but she was a blur.

"Maybe you should sit down."

"Yeah." I took a step away, but staggered before she caught me.

"Wow, you must be a real lightweight." She laughed. "One drink and you're tripping over. Come on, I'll help you."

"I didn't…only had a sip." My speech was slurred, as if I'd downed a bottle of vodka and it just hit me.

"You what?" She wound her arm under mine and helped me off the side, out of the lights they set up for the party.

"I only had a bit." I tipped my cup and upended the rest of my beer on the sand. When it hit, it sizzled slightly before it sank between the grains.

"Those fucking idiots," she growled.

"What?" I muttered. I leaned against her and closed my eyes. "Please don't tell me it's Zeta?"

"If it is, I'll tear their heads off with my bare hands. But no, it's not them."

"Hey Cordy." A new voice spoke, smooth, like honey laced with arsenic.

"Sawyer," she replied darkly. "What did you do to her?"

He laughed, deep and low. "Just having a little fun. You know how these witches are. They think they're better than us. It's time to take them down a peg or two."

"I'm not a witch," I mumbled. I felt the familiar sensation of anger burning at me. My inner phoenix itched to get out. Forget tearing heads off, I would rip the demon into ribbons so small his parents wouldn't be able to identify him.

Sawyer crouched down in front of me and crossed his arms. "You're a slut with more dicks than holes. I'm sure you're itching for one more." He grabbed his groin and sneered.

"Fuck off," I said as clearly as I could manage. I tried to draw in magic and knock the asshole off his feet, but it wouldn't come.

"That's the idea. Come on guys, grab an arm each. You can have a go when I'm done."

"No way." Cordelia shot to her feet. "I'm not going to let you do this."

"Get out of the way Cordy. You said yourself she wanted to know about the bond. Who better to show her?"

"Not like this, Sawyer," she growled. "Do you think those guys won't come looking?"

Of course they will, I thought. Any minute now.

Sawyer laughed. "Do you think I'm stupid? They all drank the beer, too."

Fuck.

I reached out to Dyson and Leo through the bond, but found only Leo's befuddled thoughts. Dyson seemed to be out cold already.

A hot tear trickled down my cheek.

Fingers dug into my skin as Sawyer's friends hauled me to my feet. I tried to shrug them off, but my body wouldn't respond with more than a twitch.

Fuck.

"Can't you just tell me about the bond?" I asked, with what spirit I had left.

"Hells no, it's much more fun if we show you." Sawyer leered into my face.

"Sawyer," Cordelia said insistently.

"You can help, or you can get out of the way."

I turned heavy, but pleading eyes to her. *Yes, help. Help me!*

She stood for a few moments, wide eyed and horrified, just in the edge of the light. She let out a long breath, then stepped aside.

"Good girl." Sawyer nodded. "Bring that one, too." He waved toward a figure who lay slumped on the sand a few metres away. Kane.

What the hells? What kind of twisted game were they trying to play? The idea of them hurting Kane made my fury rise like throwing fuel on a fire. I gritted my teeth and tried to shift. To hells with being nice, I would tear them all to pieces and feast on their bones. I suck their veins dry of every drop of blood. I would coat my claws in their gore. If I found brains in their heads, I would eat those too, hot and raw with their last, terrified thoughts.

I gritted my teeth, but the shift wouldn't come. All it did was burn away the last of my energy. I blinked, but keeping my eyes open was almost impossible.

"Give in," Sawyer said in my ear. "Sleep. When you wake, we'll have some fun."

Fuck you. The words wouldn't come though. I slumped and was caught up in someone's arms. The last thing I knew, I was carried into the darkness.

The last thought I had before sleep claimed me was, N*ot again.*

16

"WAKEY WAKEY." A hand tapped my cheek.

I jerked away, but regretted it immediately. Partly because I had the headache from hells and partly because they knew I was awake and regained some use of my body. Had I waited, I could have shifted and torn them to shreds without them knowing I was coming.

"Come on." Fingers pinched my earlobe.

"Fuck off." I lashed out with a punch and connected with a hard thigh.

Sawyer chuckled. He rose and moved away. "The witch has some bite to her, huh?"

"You have no idea," I muttered. I opened my eyes and pushed myself up to sit in the sand. A fire crackled a few metres away. Sawyer's friends sat around it, drinking beer from bottles and passing around what looked like a joint.

"What the fuck?" I squinted at them, then down at myself. I didn't seem to have been interfered with in any way.

Yet.

"You want some?" A guy with blonde hair and what looked like scales on his cheeks offered me the joint.

"Um, no thanks, I'm good." I raised a hand slightly.

"Mmmm-kay." He put it to his lips and took a drag.

Sawyer flopped down in front of me and crossed his legs. "Sorry for the subterfuge, but we can't let any old person know about the bond."

I bared my teeth at him. "The last person who put me to sleep and abducted me died a horrible death. You have exactly three seconds to tell me why I shouldn't do the same to you."

He held out his hand and opened it. On his palm lay two stones, both red and shaped like a circle. Leather necklaces dangled between his fingers.

"Because I have bonding stones."

"So what?" I asked. "If you even try to touch me, I'll rip your throat out."

He chuckled. "Trust me, you're not my type. I prefer demons."

"Bigot." I kept one eye on him and the other on the stones.

He shrugged. "Once bitten, twice shy."

I snorted. "A witch bit you?" I was tempted to do the same. "Did you drug and threaten to assault her too."

He gave me a sideways smile. "Cordy tells me I have a sick sense of humour. The drugging was necessary, so you don't know where you are. We can't have people turning up here."

I frowned. "Where is here?" To me it looked like an ordinary section of beach.

"Why would I go to all this trouble only to tell you that?"

"You still haven't given me a reason why I shouldn't shift and rip your head off, then fly away," I said sweetly. "From the air I'd find out where I am pretty fast."

For a moment his bravado slipped. "I'm starting to think I shouldn't help you at all. Maybe I should have cut your throat while you slept."

"There's that sick sense of humour again," I said. I wasn't sure he was joking until he grinned.

"Yeah, I wouldn't want to mess my clothes with witch blood. Or hybrid." He narrowed his eyes. "What are you?"

"I can't think of a single reason why I should tell you that." I sniffed. With any luck, the rest of the guys were waking up and looking for me. Although, I wasn't sure I really was in any trouble, as such. I mean, apart from the whole abduction thing.

I glanced to the side to see Kane start to twitch.

Sawyer shrugged. "So you want to know about bonding? Let me guess, you know magic is involved?"

"Do I?" I asked. When he didn't reply, I sighed. "Fine. Yes, we know that much. We also know it involves dogs and demons, or some combination of both."

"The bond originated with dog shifters. Some nosy witch managed to emulate it with magic."

I frowned at his continued bigotry, but said nothing.

He tossed the stones in his hand. "She shared the information with her demon lover. Between them, they started the story about fated mates and it went from there. That was over a hundred years ago now. The witch passed the secret to her daughters and to this day, only a handful know how to do it. The Demon Collective keeps a tight rein on them. If every witch knew, she'd have every man under her spell." He made a face as though he'd eaten something sour.

"You keep saying witches," I pointed out, my voice tight with annoyance at his attitude. "What about wizards?"

He hesitated. "As far as I know, it's only witches who can do it. The gods only know if any wizards have tried. I'm not privy to that information."

"So you don't know everything," I said dryly. "There's a shock."

He raised his eyebrows, but then grinned. "Not everything, just most things."

I turned my face as Kane groaned and rolled over, but didn't wake.

"He'll be fine," Sawyer said. "So do you want to try one?" He held up a bonding stone.

"I'm not bonding you." I curled my lip at him.

He snorted. "Thank the gods for that. These stones will allow us to feel the bond, but the moment we take them off, it'll be gone. Careful though, you'll bond any cock that comes inside you before the magic wears off."

"So we'd have to have sex to make the bond permanent?" I asked carefully.

"Yeah, that's what he's for." Sawyer jerked his chin toward Kane. "You're not going to believe me until that happens."

"Why do you care if I believe you or not?" I asked.

"I don't, but Cordy will get the shits with me."

"Cordy likes girls," I pointed out.

"No shit," Sawyer snorted. "She's my sister."

"Oh."

He tossed me a stone and put the other around his neck.

"If this goes badly, I will kill you," I told him. I hadn't ruled out doing that anyway. The sweat from my fear hadn't dried on my skin yet.

I took a closer look at the stone. If I didn't know it was full of magic, I would have just thought it was a cheap trinket. Hells, it might be cheap anyway. It felt warm on my palm, as though it was alive somehow. That was a disconcerting thought.

"We're here for a good time, not a long time," Sawyer pointed out.

"It's the good time I'm worried about." I wouldn't be so quick to dismiss the leer on his face before the drug hit me. I trusted him about as far as I could spit.

"I told you, you're not my type. Now put the bloody stone around your neck and you'll see I'm mostly harmless."

"Mostly," I muttered.

Kane let out a loud snore and nestled deeper into the sand. He looked so comfortable I wanted to curl up beside him and sleep. I wouldn't though, not here. I didn't believe for a second the demons around the fire were just a bunch of chill stoners. They moved fast enough to do what Sawyer said the last time. They might just be lying —or sitting—in wait for the "fun" Sawyer promised them.

I suppressed a shudder, sucked in a breath and, against my better judgement, put the stone around my neck.

The reaction was instant. Just like the bond with Leo and Dyson, I felt Sawyer's presence and his mood. Right now he was amused at something, probably me and my caution.

I sent him "fuck you" vibes and resisted the urge to poke my tongue out at him.

He grinned and sent thoughts of him touching Leo intimately. Maybe they were memories. Either way, I didn't want to know. I pulled the stone off and tossed it back to him.

Mercifully, the bond was gone again.

"See, nothing to it." He tucked the stones into his pocket. "Be careful for a day or two and you'll be fine."

"Thanks for the warning," I said ironically. "I guess you have to be careful too."

He shrugged. "Yeah, see the sacrifice I made because Cordy wanted to help you out."

I frowned. "Why is that?"

"Why did I make the sacrifice?"

"No. Why does she want to help me?" Wanting to kiss someone and going to a lot of trouble for them were two different things.

"I was asking myself the same thing." He propped his chin on his hands. "I guess she likes you for some reason. Maybe she wants you to understand what went on with Leo."

I blinked a few times. "What do you mean?"

"You're bonded, right?"

"Right," I said slowly. "So what?"

"So he must have had a bonding stone. Or you do and all of this is for nothing." He spread his hands.

"I don't." I tucked my legs under me and thought. "I don't think he did either. He was so certain it was fate." He had the magic sucking stone, but so far I had no reason to think they were related. I decided to keep that information to myself for now.

Sawyer let out a choked laugh. "Leo, the hopeless, fucking romantic." He shook his head. "There's nothing romantic about it. Well, not really. In the wrong hands, bonding magic could be a powerful weapon."

"So what are you saying? Leo bonded with me on purpose?" I didn't believe that. He was as surprised as I was. He firmly believed we were meant to be. I had believed it, too, but now I wasn't sure what to think.

"That, or someone made sure it happened. Although, that someone had to be sure you'd screw each other. It's possible it was meant for someone else, not Leo. You do have quite the collection of cocks."

"Do you have to be so crude about it?" I shifted uncomfortably. Sure my relationships were unconventional, but we did nothing without the knowledge and consent of everyone else.

He grinned. "I wouldn't have thought you were a prude."

I snorted. "I'm not, I just don't like feeling slut shamed. Maybe you're jealous."

I thought he might laugh, but instead he looked thoughtful. "Possibly. Maybe I should gather my own harem and see how I like it."

"Suit yourself." At this point I had more questions than answers. "Do you know why anyone would want me to bond?" That made me more uncomfortable than slut shaming. The idea that someone might have forced this on Leo and I wasn't much better than assault. "And how?"

"A touch with a bond stone would do it," he replied. "Did you bump into anyone in a crowd?"

I thought back to the train. "Plenty." Especially the older woman whose bag almost tripped me. Coincidence? Possibly, but I doubted it. I wished I could remember more details, but I didn't pay her much attention. That was probably the idea. Be forgettable, but do what has to be done.

"As to the why," he leaned back and looked up at the sky. "Maybe Leo paid someone off. He must have been very sure you'd spread your legs."

I didn't rise to his bait. "I'm almost certain he had nothing to do with it. I could have been targeted at random."

"Did I mention how expensive bond stones are?"

"And yet, you have two," I pointed out.

"I know a guy."

"Now you sound like Leo."

Sawyer hissed. "I'm starting to regret helping you."

"Why did you?" I asked. "Really. You don't seem like the type to go out of his way for his sister."

Before he could respond, Kane groaned and sat up.

"Hey, are you—"

I was so focused on him, I almost missed seeing a dark shape leap out of the nearby bushes and bound toward us.

1 7

THE GARGOYLE WAS SO BIG, I flinched. He growled and threw himself at Sawyer. His friends leapt to their feet with cries of alarm, and scattered.

"Matt!"

He knocked Sawyer back onto the sand and stood with his front paws on the demon's chest.

"I should have know he was your fuckin' dog," Sawyer spat. "Get off me."

Matt leaned down so his face almost touched Sawyer's nose and growled. Deep and menacing, it sent chills down my spine.

"Let him up," I said after a few moments. Of course I had to let Sawyer squirm for a little while.

Matt turned toward me and cocked his head.

"He's a dick, but he's more or less harmless," I assured him.

Matt let out a gusty sigh and climbed off Sawyer. I thought he might shift, but instead he lay in the sand near the demon and rested his head on his front legs. The message was clear, "I'm ready to bite you the moment she says so."

"Lucky that wasn't Nash," I remarked. "He would have ripped your head off and asked questions later." I eyed the bushes as if a dragon might fly out without warning.

"Dyson too." Kane rubbed his head and scooted over closer to me. "Are you okay?"

"Yeah." I gave him a quick kiss of reassurance and searched the bond for Leo and Dyson. Both were groggy, but okay as far as I could tell. I sent them thoughts of me being fine as well. Both responded with relief.

Sawyer slowly sat back up, his eyes on Matt, and brushed sand off himself.

"Hybrids. Why do they always have bad tempers?"

"Maybe it's not them," I suggested. While he scowled, I said, "You called him a dog. Why did the bond not happen with him?" Or Nash for that matter. From what I gathered, dog shifter DNA played a part in the creation of gargoyles and dragons.

"The dog is too diluted in hybrids," Sawyer replied grudgingly.

I nodded, then asked another question. "Can girls bond other girls?" This whole bonding thing would be horribly judgemental if they couldn't.

"Arousal fluids are arousal fluids," he replied. "It's trickier, but possible. Fingers, dildos, etc."

"Right." I swallowed. The visual image made my blood hot.

"You're not bonding my sister," Sawyer said coldly.

"That's up to her," I replied, my tone matching his.

A shadow passed overhead. It blocked out the moon for several heartbeats before it wheeled around.

Sawyer flinched. "Don't tell me, one of your cocks is a dragon?"

"Yeah, but I'm starting to think the biggest cock here here is you," I told him.

He looked down at his groin. "Believe it. Not that you'll ever find out."

I grimaced. "Thank the gods for that."

I rose and waved toward Nash as he flew over again.

He banked sharply and landed a few metres from the fire, scattering sand with his large, clawed feet. He stalked toward Sawyer until he saw Matt lying near him.

"I'm fine, but I don't mind if you bite his head off." I pointed toward Sawyer.

The demon placed a hand on either side of his face. "Hey, I'm attached to my head. Remind me not to help you again."

"It's not the help that's the problem, it's the method," I said. "As a teacher, Nash is well within his rights to eat you." I was only half joking.

Sawyer snorted. "He's not my type, either."

Nash snorted a hot breath out his large nostrils.

"I think the feeling is mutual," I remarked. "But I don't mean the good kind of eating."

"Yeah, I figured." Sawyer moved away from Nash, but the dragon shifter followed him.

"I think he might like you after all." I watched for a moment, then felt Leo and Dyson getting closer. If this place was supposed to be a secret, Sawyer had brought the wrong person here. We wouldn't tell anyone about the place, but we'd know where to find the demon and his friends.

"Someone is coming," Kane said.

Matt rose and padded toward the bushes just as Dyson, Leo, and Blake staggered through and into the clearing.

"I told you she'd be here," Dyson said happily,

"We believed you," Blake assured him. "Well, I did." He glanced at Leo.

"I knew she'd be close, old boy, I was only off by a little bit." Leo sniffed. He stopped and watched Nash stalk Sawyer, a bemused look on his face. "Looks like we got here just in time."

Dyson grabbed my hand to pull me to him and pressed a long, lingering kiss to my lips.

To my surprise and delight, the moment he stepped back, Blake did the same. His mouth was warm and tasted of beer and promise. His hands slid down my sides and around to cup my rear. He drew me closer still and slid his tongue between my lips.

After a long moment, he pulled back and smiled. "I've been wanting to do that for a while."

"Me too," I said softly. "I… I love you as much as the other guys."

"I love you, too," he said softly. "Should we call off Nash, though?"

I looked over my shoulder to see Sawyer stumble back away from the great dragon.

"I suppose so." I sighed. Hopefully he'd learnt his lesson. Don't screw with me. Any woman, really. "Nash, let him be before he wets himself."

"I would never…" Sawyer spluttered, but he looked relieved when Nash stopped and sat in the sand. "Thank you."

"Yeah." I shrugged and looked toward Leo. "We need to talk."

"That sounds ominous," he said, with a nervous glance at the other guys.

I gestured toward the sand and sat crossed-legged on the edge of the firelight. When he sat beside me, I told him what Sawyer told me about the bonding.

Every so often, Leo would frown toward Sawyer. But the time I was done, he was scowling.

"It's fate, it has to be, darlin'," he insisted. He looked like a man who had the rug pulled out from under his feet. And then he was rolled up in that rug and tossed off a bridge.

I sighed softly. "Nash was right, it was magic. For some reason, someone needed me to bond."

"Maybe the gods came down to Earth…"

"You believe in the gods?" I asked.

He scratched his head. "Not really, but I'd rather believe that than think someone forced me on you."

I placed a hand lightly on his. "They didn't. I wouldn't have slept with you if I didn't see a future with you. Same for all the guys. Call me selfish, but I want to be with all of you."

Leo leaned in to kiss me lightly. "You're not selfish. We all like this…whatever this is. That doesn't change the fact someone made us bond. How did they even know we were there?"

I gaped. "I hadn't even thought of that," I admitted. Of course, it should have been the first thing to occur to me.

"Is it possible Corinne left us there for them to find?" Leo asked.

"She would never do that," Blake said from where he stood near the fire. He moved closer and looked worried. "Not unless they made her talk."

I shook my head. "Whoever it was was there already, waiting for us."

"Or for him." Kane shot Leo an apologetic look.

Leo shrugged. "Or it's a coincidence and they were just up to some random fuckery."

"I rate the chance of that to be pretty low," I said sadly. "It's more likely they knew where we were the entire time, but they were just waiting for the chance. I thought the drive up here was too easy."

"No one should have known," Nash said with a growl. He shifted back and now sat naked in the shadows. "I made sure of that."

"Where are Hamish and Ariana?" I asked without thinking.

"They're supposed to be protecting your friend Jess," he said after a moment. "I suspected Zeta might go after her again if they wanted to capture you. It seems as though they've decided on another tactic instead."

"We don't know if they were even involved," Blake pointed out. "Maybe Leo pissed off someone."

"Leo pisses off lots of someones," Leo said. "If they wanted to punish me, there's worse than having me bond a beautiful woman."

"Leo is right," Nash said.

"About pissing people off?" Dyson asked with a smile.

Nash gave a faint smile in return. "About this not being about him."

"So bonding me was to punish Peyton?" Leo asked.

"Possibly," Nash agreed. "But probably not. I think you were coincidental to all of this. If Corinne was involved—" He held up a hand before Blake could protest. "If she was, it's more likely she intended you to bond with Blake."

Blake flopped down into the sand. "You think?"

"There's a chance Peyton and Dyson would have bonded anyway.

She might have wanted you to do it first. Maybe she thought she could control Peyton through you."

I snorted. "Not a chance."

"Right," Blake agreed. "She knows Peyton is headstrong."

"Unless she planned to use you as bait," Nash said.

Blake looked as though he might be sick. "I can't believe she'd do something like that." Still, he appeared at least halfway to believing it. "She's my cousin. Surely…"

"Apparently my mother is on the board of Zeta," I said simply. "Just because you're related doesn't mean she can't screw you over." I scooted over closer to him. "I'm sorry. We have no proof she is involved. She might be as innocent as…as…"

"As me?" Leo suggested.

I snorted. "No offence, but that's not a word I'd use to describe you."

"Thank the gods for that." He lay back, his arms over his head. "I'd hate to think you misjudged me that badly."

I laughed softly and leaned into Blake.

"If there's any chance she was involved, does that mean we shouldn't bond?" Blake looked despairing.

Unable to answer, I looked toward Nash. Damn, he was hot sitting there all naked like that. He had muscles for days and a body I didn't want to stop touching for as long as I lived. He was also the rock that grounded and guided us all.

Nash rubbed his chin. "It's possible you shouldn't. If there is some agenda, be it hers or someone else's, we should avoid stepping into the trap. However…" He let the word hang for a moment. "There's no reason not to bond everyone else if you so choose."

My pulse instantly started to race. "Right then." I looked toward Blake, who sat with his head hung.

"It's okay," he said before I could ask. "Go ahead. We'll have time. You shouldn't waste this chance."

I squeezed his hand and looked at Kane. While we talked, Sawyer and his friends, each with a tentative look on their faces, returned to the fire and picked up their hastily abandoned beers.

Kane's eyebrows rose. He looked like a man whose birthdays and Christmases all came at once.

"So, how does this work?" he said slowly. "We make love, right here, right now, we should bond?"

"Exactly," I replied lightly.

He eyed the demons who glanced at us every now and again with interest.

"If they don't like what they see, they can leave," I told him.

Kane smiled and drew me into his arms. He kissed my mouth, long and slow, while his hands worked my shirt up to my neck. He broke off long enough to pull it over my head and tossed it toward Matt.

Matt shifted back into human form and pulled my shirt over his lap. He could try to hide, but I didn't think anyone missed his erection. Good, he'd need it soon enough.

To my surprise, Blake unhooked my bra and slid it down my arms.

"Just because we can't bond, doesn't mean I can't take part, right?" he said softly.

"You absolutely can," I agreed. Oh gods, my blood was on fire already.

Blake reached around to massage my nipples while Kane continued to kiss me.

I tugged on the bottom of Kane's shirt and pulled it over his head. With a grin I threw it so it landed on Leo's face.

"Hey!" He sat up and pulled it off.

I giggled and went back to kissing Kane while he undid the front of my shorts. I wriggled out of them and my panties went next. In the corner of my eye I caught the demons watching with interest. Sawyer's eyes were huge. Good, let them watch.

I helped Kane with his shorts and lay back to let him lie between my legs. All without our mouths separating for more than a moment.

Blake scooted around and rested on his elbow. He took one nipple between his lips and suckled gently. Matt, who apparently abandoned his modesty, lay on my other side and licked the other nipple.

How in the world I had gotten so lucky, I had no idea. I never, in my wildest dreams, have imagined being the centre of the attention of so many—let's face it—hot guys. If I wasn't me, I would wish I was.

In the meantime, I would just enjoy myself and let the flood of passion grow and wash me away.

Kane finally broke off and moved down my body. He tickled my bellybutton with his tongue, then kissed his way down between my legs. When he finally licked my clit gently, I was ready to come.

I pushed the sensation down for a few moments, wanting to make this last for as long as I could.

Kane's licks because more persistent, faster, deeper. He teased my clit and flicked at my folds. He pressed the tip of his tongue against my entrance and slid inside a little.

I shuddered with the deliciousness of the warmth flooding every bit of me.

He pulled back and replaced his tongue with his fingers.

While he pumped me gently, Blake pressed his mouth to mine. I opened to let his tongue inside, then reached for Matt's cock. It was hot and hard in my hand. With three guys touching me, inside me, I was closer and closer to the edge.

Through the slit in my eyes, I caught sight of Dyson and Leo talking softly. They only exchanged a few words before their mouths met in a heated kiss. That was enough to drive me over the cliff and into a whirlpool that made me cry out loudly. My body rocked against Kane's hand. My hand pumped Matt harder.

"I'm gonna…" Matt panted. "Not like this."

I pumped him one more time, then let him go. He moved away, his teeth gritted.

To my surprise, Kane moved aside and let Matt lay between my legs. With a look of relief, he slid his cock inside me slowly.

"Gods, this is…" Matt breathed.

"It really is," I agreed. My eyes went over to Leo and Dyson. They had each other's shirts off and Leo's hand was down Dyson's pants.

Dyson caught my look and bit his lip. "Do you mind?" he asked.

I knew if I said I did, they would pull apart and never touch each other again.

"I want to see you two...together," I said in a hoarse whisper. Gods, did I ever.

Leo grinned wolfishly and tugged down the front of Dyson's pants. He bent to wrap his mouth around Dyson's erection.

"Holy gods," Kane breathed. His face was pink, eyes alight with arousal.

Dyson grunted and his hips started to move slowly, pulling his cock in and out between Leo's lips.

Holy gods was right.

"Peyton," Matt panted. "I'm going to come. I want to bond you. I want you...forever."

I turned my eyes back to him. "Come inside me," I said softly. "I want to bond you, too."

He thrust harder and faster then, his cock hitting deeper and deeper inside me.

"Oh, yeah..." He balanced himself with a hand on either side and groaned once, twice. He let out a cry as he came, filling me with hot cum. I came again a heartbeat later, longer and deeper than the first time.

The bond formed immediately, almost faster than with Leo or Dyson. Maybe I was getting good at it or something.

"Whoa." Matt wiped his brow and looked stunned. "I can feel you."

I smiled. "I would think so." Since his cock was inside me.

He grinned. "Yeah, that too." He wiggled his hips and slid free.

"Dude, I'd like to feel the bond, too," Kane said lightly.

Matt rolled aside. "Sorry, mate."

"All good, dude." Kane rolled me onto my side, pulled my leg over him and pressed himself hard into me.

I let out a gasp at the slight sensation of pain, but it was soon replaced by the slow build of another orgasm.

"On one hand, I want this to last. On the other hand, bond," Kane muttered.

"We have all the time in the world," I reminded him.

"Good point." He rolled his hips, pushing himself further into me, then began to thrust with deliberate speed. "Under the circumstances, I'm not sure I could hold it for long anyway."

He nodded toward where Leo was massaging Dyson's balls and sucking him hard. Dyson sat with his head back, ecstasy written all over his face. Through the bond, I felt both of their arousals and every drop of pleasure they were milking from each other. They were as much a part of this as the other guys.

I sought out Nash, who sat away from demons, hungry eyes on me. I knew he also wanted to bond, but he would wait for the other guys. While he seemed to enjoy watching, he had yet to take part in our group adventures.

"Peyton." Kane's voice drew my eyes back to him. "I'm close."

"Let it loose, dude," I said teasingly. I was close again myself.

Kane thrust with frantic speed, then threw his head back. His cry echoed through the night air while his seed rushed into me. This time, I came in perfect unison with him.

The bond took longer to form this time, but when it did, it was as solid as the rest. Maybe the magic was wearing off a little.

"Well, this is cool." Kane cocked his head, as though conducting a scientific examination or something. "I can sense your thoughts and everything."

"Hopefully not everything." I grimaced.

He grinned. "Okay, not everything. Close enough though. Interesting."

I snorted. "You're such a geek."

"Thanks, love you too." He kissed me before he rolled off me.

I turned my attention to Nash and Blake.

"It seems to be getting harder with each bond," I said. "It might wear off before—"

I hadn't finished my sentence before Nash rose. He rolled me onto my stomach and slammed his cock into me.

I let out a cry of surprise. "Oh gods…sir."

He leaned down to chuckle in my ear and give it a nip. "You make the best noises."

"Of course I do." I cried out again when he drew out, then slammed back in harder than before. Caught between pleasure and pain, my eyes watered, but my arousal rose yet again. With no mercy, not even a little bit, he pounded into me, each thrust firmer and more forceful than before.

He pinned my wrists to the sand and rammed me over and over until I was ready to scream for him to either stop, or hurt me even more.

His fingers dug into my skin when he came with a ferocious growl and a thrust so hard I thought he might spilt me in two.

Rather than scream in pain, I cried out in pleasure, caught in another orgasm, doubled in pleasure by feeling Dyson come in Leo's willing mouth.

The world disappeared, replaced by pure sensation. No words, only feeling. Only pleasure. Pain. Love. Bond. Relief. Understanding.

Completeness.

I sagged onto the sand and Nash collapsed on top of me, panting and trying to catch his breath.

"That was worth the wait," Nash whispered. "We're one. All of us."

My eyes went to Blake, who sat looking dejected.

"I trust you," I told him.

He blinked and frowned. "What if there's some plan?" he asked, obviously caught between hope and fear.

"We'll overcome it, like we always do."

Nash slid off me and I reached my hand out to Blake.

His gaze went to Nash. "Do you think this is a good idea?"

"You may never get another chance to bond," Nash replied. "But if you endanger her, I will kill you."

"Get in line," Matt growled.

"Behind me," Kane added.

Blake licked his lips. "I want you," he said finally.

"Then take me," I whispered in reply.

He hesitated a moment longer, then pushed his shorts off his hips and drew me up until I was on all fours in front of him. He pressed his heated cock against my entrance.

"Are you sure?" he asked.

"Positive," I replied. I should be exhausted after fucking three guys, but I wanted more, especially seeing Leo and Dyson had swapped places and Dyson was now sucking hard on Leo's cock.

"I brought lube," Leo said softly. He reached for his jeans and pulled out a tube. "It always pays to be ready."

I swallowed as Dyson let Leo ready him. My mouth went as dry as the nearest desert when Leo lay over Dyson and pushed himself into the dog shifter's puckered hole.

Dyson's eyes widened, but he soon relaxed and Leo started to thrust into him.

The position Blake put me in let me watch everything while the bond let me feel it. When Blake slid his cock inside me, I was almost washed away again with arousal.

"I've wanted to do this since the moment I met you," Blake said.

"For me it was when I found out you weren't a baddie," I said over my shoulder.

He chuckled and started to move inside me. Unlike Nash, he was slow and gentle, as if he was scared of hurting me. He didn't seem to be in a rush, even though the magic might wear off. I suspected Sawyer wouldn't let me near the bonding stone again, so if this didn't work...

I glanced over to the demon, to find him locked in the embrace of a woman I hadn't seen arrive. Whatever, as long as he wasn't bothering us.

Blake slid his arms up my stomach and massaged my nipples in time with his thrusts.

"You feel so amazing," he said softly. "Better than I could have imagined."

"You feel pretty good yourself," I told him.

As if that was a cue, he stilled and then came. He gave a few frantic pumps, drawing out his orgasm before he sagged, breathing heavily.

I came once more, rocking my body against him to increase my pleasure.

It wasn't until I came down I realised the bond hadn't formed between us.

"What—"

With a slow build, like a dam wearing down its banks, the bond slowly inched into existence. It crawled as if it was reluctant to exist. As if the magic was all but sucked dry.

It finally became fully formed as Leo let out a cry that let us all know he, too, was coming. I felt his heat flood Dyson's ass. A moment later I sensed Leo's disappointment. No bond formed between them. I hadn't expected it would unless they exchanged places, but I felt bad for breaking the last piece of faith Leo had in the idea of fated mates.

I sagged on the sand, taking Blake with me. I curled us into a ball of arms and legs and contentment.

Still, at the back of my mind I wondered if bonding Blake might be a bad idea.

1 8

IF I THOUGHT BONDING one or two guys was intense, it was nothing to bonding six. I know, it's my own fault for taking them all on at once, but I couldn't really bring myself to regret it. Sure, it was overwhelming having so many thoughts and feelings in the back of my mind. On the other hand, that was where they stayed. It took no time at all to push them to the back and tuck them away in a little box. It was like shutting out certain sounds. If I let myself become aware, I could tune into one guy over the others, or all of them at once. I hadn't expected to have that kind of control, but I thanked the gods for it.

The guys, however, seemed determined to stay switched on to me and my emotions and needs. I only had to think about tea before someone would bring me a cup. That was cute until three of them had the same idea.

Fortunately when I was in class, they had to focus on their own studies or work.

The CAME campus was totally opposite to the UA or even original AMM campus. Classrooms nestled amongst native trees and bushes. The ground underfoot was as much sand as it was grass and dirt. Most students wore shorts and t-shirts or singlets. Some even wore shoes.

Personally, I was happy in shorts and flat sandals. No tie, no repressed schoolgirl skirts and certainly no jackets. The streak of green in my hair was plain in comparison to many other students. Rainbow or dreadlocks were more common, sometimes both. Yes, rainbow dreads look just as awesome as they sound.

For the most part, the other students gave us a warm welcome. Sawyer and I gave each other the side eye whenever we saw each other, and I avoided his friends and Cordelia. Everyone else was chill though, and free with their offers to share dope.

"No thanks," I said for about the fifth time that day. Even if I was interested in smoking it, I didn't want to put Nash in the position of having to tell me off for it. I had other positions I much preferred to put him in.

"Okay, if you're sure." I didn't know the guy's name, but he gave me a shrug and a smile and went back to sit under a tree with some other students.

I sighed softly.

"You too, huh?" Kane slipped his hand into mine a moment after I became aware of his presence.

"You shouldn't be able to sneak up on me like that," I scolded lightly.

He grinned. "I've been working on my stealth skills. And keeping my thoughts to myself."

I frowned at that. "Should I be worried about you keeping things from me?"

"Only on your birthday." He leaned in to kiss my mouth. "And any time you're with my brother." He grimaced. "Somethings are better not shared, even amongst twins." After all our group intimacy, he was still twitchy about Dyson having any kind of sex life. It was adorably endearing.

"I don't know, you don't seem to mind sharing most other things," I pointed out. "All of you guys are becoming like brothers, in a way."

He swung our hands between us. "Just one big happy family."

"Exactly." It was certainly warmer than the home life I grew up with. And with a lot more sex and tea. What more could a girl want?

"Luckily you guys don't fight like brothers. Not too much, anyway." Once in a while they'd growl over someone having eaten their yoghurt, or drank the last beer, or wanting to watch a particular movie. Mostly it was in fun, with no hurt feelings.

"Not that you can see," he replied, giving me a half smile.

"Ah, but you forget, I would feel it if you argued," I returned his smile.

"That's true, you would. Fine, we'll behave. Although, if we don't, will you spank us?"

My smile widened. "I'm happy to spank you, argument or not. You only have to ask." I squeezed his firm ass cheek, then smacked my hand lightly across it.

"Remind me to order a paddle next time I'm online." I wasn't sure if he was joking or not.

"Don't forget the blindfolds," I added.

"Of course, we can't forget those. And one of those feather ticklers."

I wrinkled my nose. "If you love me, you won't tickle me."

"I love you very much, but do you know how hard it is not to tickle you immediately after you say that?" He wiggled his fingers in front of my belly.

I squirmed. "Don't even joke. I hate being tickled. I would literally let my tiger loose on you if you do it."

Kane lowered his hand, but his eyes shone. "Noted. No tickling. We'll stick to spanking then."

"Agreed." I chuckled and walked with him, approximately in the direction of the beach. The campus was nestled amongst the trees, but the walk to the sand was short. With windows open, the sound of pounding surf contributed to the serenity of the place.

The dope probably helped.

"I've never been anywhere so chill," Kane remarked. "I mean it's warm, but it's…" He flushed.

"I know what chill means, " I said gently, "but were you reading my mind?" I smiled teasingly.

"Just your mood." He ran his thumb over the back of my hand, back and forth and then in slow circles. "You seem so relaxed here."

I hesitated for a moment. "I am. I think this might be the kind of place I'd like to teach. Everyone is just so laid back, even for Aussies. It's as though no one has a care in the world, even when getting assignments done, or sitting exams. Take the one yesterday for example, no one freaked out. We just went in, did the test and left. Even me. Not one word of complaint, no groaning about being sure they failed." Not that I could see anyway. Even the teachers seemed to enjoy being here.

"I think it's the sea," he said at the same time as I said, "I think it's the marijuana."

I fell against him, laughing.

"It could be both," he conceded. "Or just good teaching. That should help. You knew your stuff, though."

"I felt as though I did. I suppose I should by now, it is third year." Grass changed to sand under my feet. I leaned on Kane while I slipped off my sandals and let the grains fill the gaps between my toes.

I stared out at the wide expanse of ocean spread out in front of us. The sea air ruffled my hair and filled my senses with salt and freedom.

"This is—"

I turned toward Kane as a jolt of pain entered our bond.

"What—" I grabbed at him as he crumbled to the sand. "Kane! *Kane!*"

I felt a surge of concern from the other guys and sent back thoughts of extreme worry and fear.

"He'll be fine."

I recognised the voice behind me, but for a long time, I couldn't bring myself to look behind me. I didn't want to confirm what I had suspected for so long.

"What did you do to him?" I fell to my knees in the sand beside Kane. He lay still, eyes half open, but glazed. I put a finger to his neck. His pulse still beat, but slower than normal.

"He's just out cold. What happens to him next depends on you."
I sucked in a breath and looked up slowly.
"What are you doing here, Mother?"

19

I HOPED she might at least try to tell me she was there to make sure I was okay. That someone else hurt Kane, but she'd help him. Deep down I hoped she'd pull me into her arms, rub my back, and soothe me like a mother should.

Instead, she looked at me with cold eyes, like she barely recognised me. Like I was some kind of laboratory experiment and she was curious about the result. There was no hint of warmth, nothing. She was never loving, but I never saw this clinical side of her before.

"What do you want from me?" I felt vulnerable looking up at her, but I was far from that. I could shift and rip her apart in a heartbeat. She knew that, I saw it in the twitch at the side of her mouth. She also knew I wouldn't. In spite of never having been close, she was still my mother.

"I want you to come with me. We have much to learn about the bond." She nodded to someone behind me.

I turned my head just enough to see Corinne. She wasn't what took my breath away. That honour went to Blake, who walked beside her.

"I'm sorry," he mouthed.

What the fuck?

I probed the bond to gauge his mood, but somehow he blocked me out. All I could feel was that he was alive. That wouldn't last long if he really betrayed me.

"This works best if you don't fight us." Lucinda—I couldn't think of her as my mother right now—was all business.

"Did it cross your mind we might have come willingly, without you harming Kane?" I asked coolly. "We'd also like to learn about the bond."

Surprise was the first hint of emotion to cross her features. Of course it didn't occur to her. Ruthless people assumed ruthless tactics were needed for everything. Gods forbid they'd resort to not being assholes once in a while.

The look was gone before I could blink and her mask of ice was back.

"Then we won't have any trouble. Bring the shifter." She turned away and started toward the carpark.

For a moment I thought about setting my tiger or gargoyle loose from my tattoos and letting them rip her to pieces. I curled my hands into fists, but uncurled them. I wasn't lying when I said I wanted to understand the bond better. If I had to play along for a while, then so be it.

Between them, Corinne and Blake supported Kane and carried him toward a white SUV. White, as if somehow my mother was totally innocent.

I trotted to catch up with her.

"Are you really working with Zeta?"

She pulled a key out of her pocket and pressed the button to unlock the SUV.

"Zeta aren't the enemy," she said as she pulled the back door open and gestured for me to climb inside.

"Like hells they aren't," I growled. "Have you got any idea what they've done to me?" My eyes narrowed. "Of course you do, you know all about the attack on the AMM campus in Sydney. I told you. But you knew before that, didn't you?"

She hesitated. "That was an unfortunate misunderstanding—"

"*Misunderstanding?* Fucking hells, people *died!*" I gaped at her. Who was this woman? Had someone stolen my mother's face? "Paranormals died. I almost died! I had to kill to save myself and people I loved!" I was almost shouting now. Tears streamed down my face at the memory of the attack. I wasn't proud of anything I had done, but I had no choice.

"Did you know they put me in a lab and wanted to use me for breeding?" I planted my hands on my hips to keep from wrapping them around her throat.

"That was my fault." Her voice lacked any emotion.

"Your fault?" My stomach lurched. "You arranged to have that happen to me?"

"No," she replied. "I should have explained the purpose you were made for."

What the absolute stone cold fuck?

"Made for?" I echoed. "I'm a person. I decide what happens to my life. I'm not a piece of technology, to be tweaked and thrown around."

She sighed. "Get in the car. I'll explain everything when we get there. You will understand fully and when you do, you'll happily cooperate."

"Doubtful," I retorted. "Right now I trust you as far as I can throw you." I frowned. "Actually if I use magic, that would be pretty far. Forget throwing, I don't trust you as far as I can spit you." I was babbling, but mostly because the rug had been yanked out from under me, yet again. This, though, this was different. I both had no choice, but also a bad feeling that if I got into the car, my life would never be the same. Whatever happened now, there would be no coming back from.

Lucinda shrugged. "That's up to you, but if you won't trust me, then trust your father. He adores you. Do you think he'd let you come to any harm?"

The mention of him left me breathless. "What has he got to do with this?"

Lucinda quirked an eyebrow. She actually seemed amused at the question. "Why everything, of course. You didn't think I was doing all of this behind his back, did you?"

I shook my head slowly. "I have no idea." Honestly I couldn't be sure if she was lying right now or not. My father and I were close. If he was involved then maybe she really wasn't so bad. The idea burned inside my head, but I came to no conclusions. I needed to see him, to speak to him, for myself.

"I didn't," she said firmly. She moved aside to let Corinne and Blake heft Kane into the car.

I shot them both a dirty look. Corinne looked as cool and calm as ever, but Blake at least looked uncomfortable.

"He did well, wouldn't you say?" Lucinda nodded toward Blake. "Your bond will be very helpful."

I shot her a scowl, then turned it on Blake. "If you fucked me over, I'll never forgive you."

"You should get in the car," he said without meeting my gaze.

Yeah, fuck you too, I thought. Tears prickled at my eyes again. I climbed into the car and scooted over closer to Kane.

"Did you get it?" Lucinda asked as she climbed into the front passenger seat.

Corinne held out her hand, palm up. She uncurled her fingers and I gasped. On her palm, she held the stone Leo stole from Zeta, the stone which sucked magic from witches and wizards.

"How did you—"

"He should have kept it in a better place than his pants pocket," Corinne said.

I looked into her eyes, but saw no sign of regret. She played me and felt no remorse whatsoever. Had she played Blake as well, though? I still didn't want to believe he would betray me. Especially choosing to bond me when he knew this would happen. Had he known? Was he as complicit as Corinne and Lucinda? If he was, I was taken in, hook, line, and sinker by that curly hair and those dimples.

My heart ached.

"It's good to have Zeta property back in our possession." Lucinda took the stone from Corinne and tucked it away in her pocket.

I consoled myself with the knowledge that at least it wasn't a bonding stone. That only made me feel better until I realised Lucinda probably knew about those already.

"You arranged it so I'd bond Leo," I said, directing the question at either of them.

"The demon wasn't part of the plan," Lucinda said. "You weren't supposed to miss your train."

I frowned. "But I was with—"

Blake slid into the seat on the other side of Kane.

"You," I finished. "That was meant for you."

He flushed slightly. "I didn't…it wasn't…" he stammered.

"Of course it was," Corinne said sharply. "You were away from Matt, Nash, and Kane. The timing was perfect, until you missed the train." She sounded as if she blamed me for that.

"Well, lucky for you we bonded anyway," I snapped. "You must be delighted I fit into your plans after all." I directed my icy gaze to Blake.

"It's not that simple," he muttered.

"Why don't you enlighten me then?" I suggested.

"When we get there," Lucinda said.

Corinne started the car and we pulled out of the carpark. In the back of my mind, I felt the guys looking for me. I assured them I was okay, but then pushed them aside. As much as I wanted them to come after me and Kane, I didn't want them to get hurt, or worse.

I took hold of Kane's hand and held it loosely in my lap. At any other time, he'd have his fingers between my thighs in moments. Now, he just lay still, face pale, breathing slowly.

"It is just tranquilliser?" I asked. "If you've done him any lasting damage, I'll be much less cooperative."

"He'll be fine," Lucinda said dismissively. "He'll stay that way if you don't do anything stupid."

"When have I ever done anything stupid?" I asked ironically. "Surely I was raised better than that." Putting the blame on her if I did anything rash might be childish, but it felt good. That was until she responded.

"I would have thought so too, but it seems we have some gaps to fill."

"Are you regretting not having me raised in a lab?" I asked. I meant it as a joke of sorts, but once the words were out, I wanted to know the answer.

"Perhaps that would have been best," she said, as if it would have been the most normal thing in the world. "Your father didn't want that for you. In retrospect, I might have insisted."

"Gee, thanks. Don't do me any favours, will you?" I wanted to curl up in a tiny little ball and cry. Even though she was always distant, both physically and emotionally, she did give birth to me. Surely some part of her cared about me? Loved me even? This woman in the front seat of the car didn't seem to have a drop of feeling for me.

Lucinda let out a frustrated exhale. "It might have been a favour, Peyton. Then you wouldn't be so ignorant about so many things. You wouldn't feel the need to fight me. Don't think I don't know what's going on in your mind. It's written all over your face and I know you better than you know yourself."

"Says you," I muttered. "I don't think you know me at all. It's not like you took the time."

She was unfazed. "That might be right, but your friends here will help to fill in the gaps."

I bared my teeth and Corinne's back, but she was focused on driving. I couldn't bring myself to look at Blake. He could certainly tell Lucinda a lot about me.

I gritted my teeth and forced a breath in and out. "So where are we going?"

"You'll see."

"When do we get there?"

"If you start asking 'are we there yet,' it won't end well for your shifter friend," Lucinda growled.

"I wouldn't dream of it." I slumped down in my seat and held Kane's hand tighter. I planned to do just that, if only to get under her skin. I wouldn't risk Kane's hide just for my own amusement. That would take petty a step too far and achieve nothing.

"Good. Now you can be quiet and wait patiently while we travel."

"I thought you knew me," I muttered. If she really did, she would know I didn't do patience well. For Kane, I would keep the peace. For now.

Deep down, in the very back of my mind was the all too real fear we might not get out of this alive.

2 0

We pulled up an hour later. I might have expected an abandoned warehouse, or some sort of industrial looking complex. Instead, we drew through the gates of a huge beachside mansion. I wouldn't be surprised to see a Hemsworth jogging around the grounds, or swimming in one of the enormous swimming pools. My inner kid delighted at the sight of not one but two waterslides which spiralled down toward one of the pools. Real ones, not created by magic.

"Do we get a cocktail upon entry?" I tried to keep my awe out of my voice, but I was pretty sure I failed.

"Once you've heard what I have to say, you can have whatever you want," Lucinda replied.

"Freedom?" I asked.

Her hesitation was all the answer I needed. The gate clanged shut behind us with a finality that made my heart sink. Realistically, I could shift and leave at any time, but my relationship with my mother would be over. Was it already? I could be wrong, but I'm pretty sure her behaviour wasn't normal for a parent. Not a loving one anyway.

I willed Kane to wake up, but he was blissfully asleep, even as a giant descended the front steps of the house and hefted him over his shoulder. Okay, I don't mean a literal giant, but he was at least seven feet tall and almost as wide. I might have been impressed, except the whole working-for-my-potentially-evil-mother thing. All right, maybe I was a little bit impressed anyway. He'd probably be able to walk around with a Hemsworth under each arm.

"It'll be okay." Blake went to touch my arm, but I jerked away. The look I gave him should have melted stone, but probably looked like I needed to use the toilet.

"None of this is okay," I snapped. "I should have known I couldn't trust you or your cousin."

He looked stung, but nodded. "I understand. So will you. Very soon."

"Sure." I turned my back on him and marched up the steps behind Muscles. He didn't even look like he broke a sweat.

"Put him down on the couch over there," Lucinda instructed.

"Aye." Muscles nodded and did as he was told. Did I catch a hint of a Scottish accent in the single word he'd spoken?

He lowered Kane to the couch and tucked a cushion under his head like the owl shifter was some kind of doll.

"So what are you?" I asked. Muscles or no muscles, I still had sufficient power to hurt him. I craned my neck to look up at him and arched an eyebrow. "Demon? Blue whale shifter? Oh wait, let me guess, cyclops?"

Muscles smiled in response. "Name's Macintosh." Yes, that was a Scottish accent, but from the way he turned and walked away, all the answer I would get.

"Well, he's a friendly fellow," I said sarcastically.

"I apologise for not rolling out the red carpet," Lucinda said dryly. "I'll be sure to be more hospitable next time."

"Skip it," I replied. "There won't be a next time." I glanced around and tried not to be impressed by the opulent surroundings. "This doesn't look much like a laboratory."

"No," she agreed. "That's downstairs. If you're cooperative, we won't have to take you down there." The look she gave me convinced me she meant every word.

I flopped down beside Kane and winced when he bounced slightly.

"Sorry, babe," I muttered. Louder, I said, "If he doesn't wake up soon, it's going to put a dent in my goodwill." That was already pushed to the very edge.

"It won't be much longer," Lucinda sat in a chair opposite me, looking like a cat curling themselves, waiting to pounce on unsuspecting prey. "We have time to talk."

I glanced toward Corinne and Blake, who both hovered near the door. Corinne's face was unreadable, but Blake seemed anxious. So he should.

I looked back toward Lucinda and crossed my arms. "I'm listening. You have until he wakes to convince me. Otherwise I'm taking Kane and getting the hells out of here."

Lucinda rolled her eyes as if I was a stubborn three year old who stomped her foot to get her way.

"By now, you've learnt of the existence of hybrids," she stated.

"Yeah. Thanks for the warning I might shift someday." I wasn't going to tell her what I could shift into. If she didn't already know, she wasn't going to find out from me.

"It wasn't assured. You're one of the first ever second-generation hybrids. For all we knew, you'd lack magic, much less the ability to shift. You could have been a mule, magically speaking."

I blinked. "I beg your pardon?"

"A mule," she repeated. "A species, when bred back onto itself, can become sterile. At some point the tinkering might produce—" she grimaced with distaste, "—regular humans."

I snorted. "That would have been ironic." Of all the witches in the world, Lucinda was one of the most powerful. For her child to be lacking in magic would have been a huge slap in the face for her.

"Indeed. Your friend Jess is a good example. Very embarrassing for her family." Lucinda clicked her tongue. "Still, she'll be taken care of."

My jaw dropped. "You can't mean…"

Lucinda gave me a dry look. "We don't condone murder. Besides, her children may be a throwback. We'll be watching carefully. Our little lesson last year will have ensured she keep her mouth shut. She knows our reach is long."

"You had her kidnapped?" I asked, horrified.

"Not me, personally. The decision was made by someone else in the organisation. I was only aware of it after the fact. Still, it served its purpose."

"To catch me. Why didn't you just *talk* to me?" I asked.

Lucinda sighed. "I would have preferred that. Others in the organisation tend to get overly dramatic about certain things. I'm also aware some individuals might have convinced you Zeta meant you harm."

I lowered my arms and sat forward. "An agent named Fitz tried to *rape* me. What conclusion would *you* draw from that?"

Lucinda flinched. "There are bad apples in every bunch. That particular one was taken care of—"

"Yeah, I killed him. I also met a girl there who said forced impregnation like that was normal."

"Some girls don't understand what Zeta is trying to achieve." Lucinda's tone was as stiff as her back.

"That includes me. Why don't you enlighten me?"

Lucinda sighed and waved toward Corinne. "Get us some tea."

Corinne hurried away to do as she was told, like a good little lackey.

Bitch.

"As you know, paranormals are superior to normals," Lucinda declared.

My eyebrows shot up. "Do I know that? I don't recall being tranquilised, kidnapped, assaulted, attacked, or threatened by any normals recently. Paranormals—sure. I'm really starting to think paranormals suck."

"Some paranormals—"

"Oh please," I interrupted. "Don't start with hashtag not-all-paranormals. They were acting for you, with your blessing. I only have your word for it they acted without your full knowledge. Maybe you wanted Fitz to rape me. To *break* me."

Lucinda shifted in her chair. Blake made a choking sound. I didn't even glance at him.

"Was that the plan?" I asked insistently. "To break me down until I had no fight left? To drive all of the spirit out of me so I'd go along like the dutiful broodmare you seem to think I was born to be." I bit back a sob.

"If that was what it took," Lucinda said softly.

I gaped at her. "Why? Because you knew I'd never go along with any of this?"

"You always were a stubborn brat."

Her words left me breathless for a long moment.

"Just like you," I said finally. I remembered something else then. "You took part in the breeding program. Did they *make* you take part?"

She averted her eyes. "I was young. I didn't understand the significance."

"And so you decided it was fine to put me through that?" That revelation cut me through and through, more than anything she could ever have said. She experienced the nightmare, but threw me in anyway. What sort of mother does that?

"Paranormals are dying out," she said finally. "We need to increase our numbers. In a generation, there will be only a few thousand left. Normals outnumber us terribly already."

"I wonder why," I said sarcastically. "Maybe we should stop killing each other."

She hesitated. "The Academy of Modern Magic was an unfortunate casualty in the power struggle between Zeta and the Paranormal Council. The council doesn't agree with our methods."

"Neither do I," I replied stiffly.

"The council would prefer we all die out," Lucinda said as if I hadn't spoken.

"I'm with them." In the corner of my eye, I caught Kane twitch.

"Nevertheless, you were born to help grow the population of paranormals. Now we understand more about the bond, we can extend that to all of our breeders. Running away, for example, will be more difficult."

I glanced toward Blake. He was listening as intently as I was.

"Is that why you wanted me to bond him?" I jerked a thumb toward Blake. "So he could keep track of me?"

"Exactly. In addition, when you two breed, he'll be in tune with your cycles. All the better to impregnate you at the right time."

"What makes you think I'll let him lay a hand on me again?" I asked. I swallowed to keep from throwing up on the expensive-looking carpet.

Lucinda sighed. "You can't really want paranormals to go extinct?"

"That was all you wanted me to understand, wasn't it?" I asked. "That and you think I have no choice in the matter. You'd let him force himself on me."

"There's always a choice," she said. "You bonded several other paranormal men. Any of those would be suitable." She waved toward Kane. "Him, if you must. If you can't choose, we'll choose for you."

"As long as I have a pile of babies, you don't care who fathers them."

"Precisely." She looked relieved, as if she was finally getting through to me. "I blame myself for not explaining this to you sooner. You've wasted a good few years. No matter, you can catch up." She waved a hand as if it was all that simple.

"You're sick," I stated. "Fucked up in the head. If I didn't know better, I'd think you believed all of this shit."

Anger flashed in her eyes. "Don't take that tone with me, or I'll knock you flat myself." She drew magic from the environment around us and held a glowing ball on her hand.

I drew magic of my own, but she reached into her pocket with her spare hand and pulled out the black stone.

"Try it. I'll suck you dry before you take another breath," she hissed. "Then I'll throw you into a cell and leave you to the mercy of the worst of Zeta. By the time they've done with you, you'll beg to be allowed to do your duty." Her eyes were filled with cold fury. I never saw this side of her and it terrified me.

I believed everything she said. Any hope I had that she might care about me deep down fled. She was nothing but a block of ice. Ruined and determined to let me suffer the same fate as she had. Twisted and fucked up didn't come close to covering it.

"Peyton?"

I jerked my head to the side at the sound of a new voice.

"Dad?" I let the magic go and reluctantly looked away from Lucinda. It wasn't the sight of my father that left me gasping for breath. It was the young woman beside him.

She looked a lot like me.

2 1

SHE DIDN'T HAVE the green streak, but the rest of her hair was the same colour as mine. Her face was the same shape and her eyes—

Her eyes were the same shade, but they were so full of loathing. I would have taken a step back if I was standing.

"So this is my sister." She walked toward me, hips swinging with each slow step. She was the big cat, I was the tiny mouse.

I held back a squeak.

"Peyton, this is Rebecca." My father's voice was filled with regret, but I hardly dared to take my eyes off her to look at him.

"Hey." I smiled as warmly as I could manage. "It's nice to meet you. I heard a rumour you existed, but I wasn't sure if it was true or not."

Rebecca bared her teeth, but the growl was aimed at Lucinda.

"I'm the family secret," she hissed. "The disgrace."

"Really?" I asked lightly. "I could have sworn that was me." I gave my mother a sweet smile. I wasn't sure if Rebecca was my ally or not, but she seemed to loathe our mother as much as I had come to in the last couple of hours.

Rebecca laughed, a bitter, cold sound. "You're the one they kept. They left me to be raised by Zeta doctors."

I nodded. "I thought I recognised that bitter expression." I had seen it on Nash and Matt. Whatever childhood they had was tainted by the sick idea that paranormals were superior and needed to be preserved at all costs. I would never understand how my parents didn't think the price was far too high.

For the first time since he'd entered the room, I looked at my father. He seemed to have aged since I saw him last. He looked tired, his face lined and pale.

"So, you knew about all of this Zeta stuff too?" I asked.

He flinched. "In the early days, yes I did. I left. We left. Or I thought we did." His gaze settled on my mother. "I was told Rebecca was dead and they'd never touch you."

Lucinda met his gaze, unwavering. "I did what I had to do."

"You're fucked up!" Rebecca shouted, all but drowning out Lucinda's last couple of words. She lunged at her.

My father was quicker. He grabbed Rebecca's wrist and pulled her back.

She hissed and growled like a cat with its claws caught in a trap, but she only struggled against him for a few moments. Then she sagged.

"She deserves to die," Rebecca said, her chin tucked into her chest.

For a moment I thought my father might agree. Instead, he said, "She did what she thought was best."

I blinked. "Do you know what happened to me?" I gestured toward Kane. "To him? To everyone else I care about?"

Kane's legs moved, but his eyes stayed closed. I felt around in the bond. He wasn't entirely out now, but he was going to keep pretending he was. I sent thoughts of approval. For his own safety, he should keep still for as long as he could.

"I know," my father said softly. "I didn't know until a few days ago. Any of it." He looked at Rebecca with cautious affection. I suspected only his innocence kept her from ripping off his head. What had the doctors at Zeta said she was? Oh yes, a chimera. A dangerous one at that.

"Well, aren't we a dysfunctional family," I said ironically. "How many babies has she had?" I nodded toward Rebecca.

Lucinda snorted. "None, she's too unstable."

"Unbroken too," I observed. Damaged by her upbringing, yes, but she obviously still had her will intact.

"Stubborn," Lucinda said. "The bond will help with that."

Rebecca made to attack her, but again our father held her back.

"You really mean to do that?" he asked. He looked disgusted, but like a man who knew better than to argue. Lucinda would do as she pleased. If not her, then someone else from Zeta.

"Now we know exactly how to do it, and have one who can spell the stones." For a moment I thought Lucinda meant me, but she nodded toward Corinne, who reentered the room carrying a tray.

"I would hazard a bet your young lover could do it too." Lucinda waved toward Blake. "Perhaps I'll have him bond Rebecca."

Blake's eyes widened. An hour ago, I would have defended him, but now I had no idea what he might be capable of.

"I'll tear off his head if he comes near me," Rebecca said, her voice low and dangerous. "Both of his heads."

Lucinda clicked her tongue. "It's past time you learnt obedience." She raised her hand and drew in magic. Before anyone could move, she wrapped a thick tendril around my father's throat.

"Don't!" I was out of my seat before I could stop myself. "Leave him alone!"

His face turned pink and he put his hands up to his neck.

"You both need to learn what happens if you don't behave," Lucinda said coldly.

My father dropped Rebecca's wrist and fell to his knees. Only when they touched the floor did Lucinda release the magic. He slumped forward, coughing and gasping for breath.

"You're not going to win wife or mother of the year," I told her. "In fact, I think that's very good grounds for divorce."

"Perhaps you need another lesson." Lucinda raised her hand again.

"No! No, leave him alone." I stepped between them as Rebecca helped him to his feet. "This is all about you and me. Let them both leave and I'll do whatever you want." Gods, what was I saying? It didn't matter, I meant it. If I had to go along with her disgusting plans to give my sister and father a life, then so be it. They both deserved to be free of Lucinda.

Lucinda regarded me coldly, as though deciding whether or not she believed me. Finally, she nodded.

"Very well. Corinne, see them out. Peyton, I need to be certain you'll do as you say you will."

"I said I would, didn't I?"

"People say many things they don't mean," she replied coolly. "Hold out your hand."

I hesitated, then slowly did as she asked. I thought I heard a choked protest, but I couldn't be sure who it was from. Maybe my father had regrets, maybe Kane was worried, maybe Blake still cared about me on some level.

Lucinda pulled out the black stone from her pocket. Without a second's pause, she touched it to my palm.

A heartbeat, two, three and all the magic inside me slithered up into my hand and into the stone. Not a drop remained. I tried to draw, but couldn't even feel the magic I knew was around me. I immediately felt bereft, empty. I wasn't a witch anymore. I swallowed back a sob.

A flash of triumph crossed her features.

"Peyton—"

I glanced at my father as Corinne herded him and Rebecca toward the door. His expression made my heart skip. It wasn't one of a man whose daughter gave everything to keep him safe. Oh, there was regret, but he looked like a man who didn't like the plan, but was glad it worked. He set me up. Lucinda had never had any intention of killing him.

"I can still shift," I reminded them all.

"But you won't," Lucinda said. "Your sister and your shifter lover's lives depend on you doing as you're told." She nodded toward my father who took Rebecca's wrist again, but this time as a prison guard, not a caring father or husband trying to protect his wife.

"Divorce is still an option," I called out to him before the door closed on them.

I didn't see the slap until the side of my face stung. My head snapped back on my neck and I almost fell on my ass. Only by wind-milling my arms did I keep my feet.

"Have some respect," Lucinda hissed.

I cupped the side of my face with my hand. "Respect is *earned*. You've done nothing to earn it. Quite the opposite."

Lucinda raised her hand, but that was the only indication I had that she was doing magic until Kane started to thrash on the couch. His hands curled like claws and scratched at his neck. His eyes popped open and his face turned red.

"Paranormal shortage," I reminded her. "And if you kill him, our deal is off."

Kane gasped for air and Lucinda lowered her hand.

"Macintosh, take the shifter to one of our *rooms*."

I hadn't seen the man enter the room, but he swung Kane over his shoulder like he had earlier and carried him toward the door.

"Don't worry, you'll be right beside him," Lucinda told me. "The bond will ensure you feel everything he does, or which is done to him. When you step out of line..."

Even without magic, the bond still held. She was right, I would know if she hurt him. Gods, how had I done this to us?

"If you behave, he'll be allowed to visit you. I hear he quite enjoys having an audience."

I flushed. "The others will come after me," I told her.

"It's up to you to keep them away. Otherwise—" She waved a hand in the direction Macintosh had taken Kane.

I licked my lips. "They're pretty stubborn."

"Then your shifter better enjoy pain, because he'll be getting used to it." She took a step toward me. "It doesn't have to be that way. This could be an enjoyable experience for all of us." She moved away from me and toward Blake. She ran a hand down his cheek, over his chest and down toward his groin. "I might even have more children myself."

Blake's eyes widened. He let his control slip for long enough for me to feel him through the bond. He was trying hard not to flinch away from her.

I might have laughed, or felt sorry for him, but he made his bed.

He could lie in it, even if that meant lying with her, too. The idea was revolting, but it still wasn't the worst thing I heard all day.

"I'm sure Blake would enjoy that," I said. Why not twist the knife a little? "He seems to like fucking for the sake of Zeta." I curled my lip at him. "Like a dutiful breeding bull."

He looked away, so I couldn't see his response.

Lucinda chuckled and patted his groin. "That's what I like to hear. Now, Blake, take her up to the rooms. She'll need her birth control implant removed. Again. That can't be done until morning. Make sure she has food and doesn't shift. I would tell you what would happen if you don't, but you know if she does, she'll kill you first."

He swallowed and nodded. "Yes, ma'am, I know she will," he agreed.

"Darn right I will, but it's nothing he doesn't deserve." I gave him an ice cold look, but my heart ached. I had cared about him as deeply as the rest of the guys. His betrayal cut me deeper than if he'd shoved a sword between my ribs.

"Yes, yes, enough of that." Lucinda waved us away. "Just see she's comfortable and behaves until she's ready to breed. That's our top priority here. I will be checking up."

"Yes, ma'am." Blake gripped my arm tight and pulled me toward the door.

"I know how to walk," I growled. "I don't need you to touch me."

"I'm just doing what I'm told," he replied.

"Yeah, that's what I don't get. Why you're on her side."

"I'm on the side of paranormals surviving." He opened the door and pushed me through.

"Me too," I agreed. "Me, Kane, and my sister. You, your cousin, and my parents can go to hells."

22

I FLOPPED down on the bed in the corner the moment Blake shut the door behind us.

"Okay, what the fuck is going on?" I fixed him with a steely gaze.

He looked around the room, ran a hand along a wall. "Kane is in the room beside this?"

I felt for him through the bond and nodded. "He is, but he's pissed off. I can't guarantee he won't peck your eyes out the next time he sees you. And Corinne."

Blake pulled a chair away from the table on the other side of the room. "I'm going to assume we're being watched and listened to."

"Whatever." I grabbed up a pillow and hugged it to myself. "I don't care if they hear. What could you say that would make any of this better? Or worse?" I shouldn't suggest the latter. I'm sure my mother could think up a few ways.

"I didn't mean to hurt you," he said softly. He glanced around again, then let a hint of his feelings filter through the bond. Regret, anxiety, love, fear.

I turned my face away. "You shouldn't have lied to me." The words were harsh, but they had a new meaning now. I understood. At least, I hoped I did.

"I had no choice." He sat forward, hands on his knees. "I had to do what was right for all paranormals."

"Corinne too?"

His lips drew tight. "She believes in Zeta's cause."

I exhaled through pursed lips. I hoped she really was on our side. I genuinely liked her, or I did. Now, she was as bad as my mother. I felt for Blake. He was walking on a tightrope between two sides. One he believed to be right, the other that would kill him if he didn't toe the line. At least for now.

That didn't mean I wasn't still mad at him. He scared me. I honestly thought he went over to the evil side. I couldn't think of it as anything else. Not even the extinction of all paranormals justified forcing young women to have children.

"What about my father and Rebecca?"

"Today was the first time I've seen either," Blake replied. "Your father seems conflicted. I'm sure your mother will keep him and Rebecca in line."

"That's what I'm afraid of." I wasn't sure how conflicted he was. He seemed as deep in this as Lucinda. Rebecca, on the other hand, was as much a victim in this as I was. More so. I could just as easily have lived the same life she had.

I rested my chin on the top of the pillow. "You know I've going to have to escape, right? I know what I promised my mother, but I can't stay here and pop out babies. Even if they have cute, curly hair."

He smiled out the side of his mouth. "I wouldn't expect anything less, but it'll be harder without your magic."

Tears prickled my eyes again. "I'll find a way to get it back."

"And if you don't?"

I paused. "I can be badass without it. They can't take away my ability to shift."

"Not yet," he agreed. "I'm sure they're working on it."

My lips trembled. The idea I could be stripped of every ability that made me paranormal was enough to make me weep or scream. Maybe both.

"I might have babies without abilities if they do," I said finally.

"That would be ironic," he agreed. "After all the trouble they've gone through to convince you to stay."

"That would be so fucked up I could almost laugh at the idea." Almost. Mostly I just wanted to burn the whole house to the ground.

"Yeah, but they're working hard on doing the opposite. I suspect that's what your mother took all that magic for."

I frowned until I understood his meaning.

"You think Zeta wants to make normals into paranormals?"

"It certainly seems like something to try," he replied carefully.

"Then they wouldn't need to breed us." They'd create a shit ton of other problems instead. A normal who woke up one day with the ability to shift or do magic, could cause havoc while trying to figure out what was going on.

"No, but they might start with children too young to understand."

I shuddered. "I thought my mother's job was to stop normals from finding out about paranormals. This would have the opposite effect."

"Only if the children were raised amongst normals," Blake said softly.

My mouth dropped open and I gaped for a solid minute.

"She would do that, wouldn't she?" And Corinne and my father would help her. "I need to get my magic back before she gives it to some unsuspecting normal."

"How are you going to do that?" he asked.

I slumped and held the pillow tighter. "I don't know." I scanned the room. If a camera was tucked away in a corner, I couldn't see it. Or a microphone. Maybe the wall was a one-way window and Kane was watching our every move. And maybe no one was watching, they just wanted me to think they were.

"Is there any chance you could get me some chocolate?" I asked after a few moments.

Blake smiled. "Probably. This place seems to have everything."

"Yeah. Pool, spa, resident evil witch," I said bitterly. "You know, you should probably leave, before you end up dead." I made it sound like a threat, but it was a warning. If Lucinda or even Corinne decided he couldn't be trusted, he'd lose his magic and then his life. Once his usefulness was done, so was he.

"I won't leave until my job is done," he replied. "And right now that means watching over you. What kind of guard would I be if I left?"

We'd long since established that he wasn't cut out to be any kind of guard, so I had to bite back a smile.

"Suit yourself." I shrugged.

"I'm sure you'd prefer not to have a replacement," he said, his voice low. "Macintosh, for example."

I shuddered. "He'd tear me in two. Don't even say things like that."

The hint of a smile on his face faded. "Yeah, sorry. Nothing about this is funny. I just…I'm not good at knowing what to say at times like this."

"Yeah, me either. Except maybe, 'I'm a hybrid, get me out of here!' I suspect Lucinda wouldn't be swayed by that."

"Probably not," he agreed. "Maybe you should get some sleep. I'll keep watch."

I nodded and lay back on the bed. "No taking advantage of me while I sleep." I shook a finger at him.

"I wouldn't dream of it," he replied. A smile tugged at the corners of his mouth. "Actually I would and I have, but I won't."

"Until you have to." I pulled a blanket up to my chin.

"Yeah, until then." He crossed his arms over his chest and exhaled out his nose.

I felt his conflict through his bond. On one hand, he didn't want to be part of Lucinda's plans. On the other, we loved each other. None of us had ever really talked about children, but the possibility for them in the future had always been in the back of my mind. Any child I had would be loved by all the guys. No matter what they went through, they'd have a father they could go to for advice or permission.

"Whatever happens, you'll have to keep doing what you're told," I said, my eyes peeking over the top of the blanket. "Like a dutiful lackey."

"I don't want to—"

He was interrupted by the door opening so hard it slammed against the opposite wall. Corinne stood in the doorway with a specimen jar in one hand.

I sat up and shuffled back against the wall.

"What do you want?" I asked, when Blake apparently had no words to greet her with.

"You might think I betrayed you—" She started.

"That's exactly what I think," I snapped. "Have you told them every detail about us and our lives?"

She shrugged unapologetically. "What was necessary for them to know."

"You arranged for me to bond." I fixed her with a steady look.

"Yes. I told them where I was dropping you off and they arranged the rest." Her expression was so cold I almost couldn't recognise her.

"Why?" I asked. "Can't you have all the little babies for them?"

She flinched. Apparently I hit a nerve.

"I can't have children, or I would. Paranormals don't deserve to die out. We can't afford to be selfish right now. The future of—"

"Fuck the future." I flung off the blanket and got to my feet. "You can't possibly think this is okay?"

She stuck out her chin and thrust the specimen jar toward Blake. "Someday you'll understand."

"What is this for?" Blake took the jar and peered at it as though it might explode in his face. After what we'd seen, it wouldn't have surprised me if it had.

"Lucinda wants you to bond Rebecca," Corinne said coolly. "I convinced her you wouldn't force yourself on her, so she relented and gave me that. I'm sure you won't have any trouble filling it." She shot me a sarcastic smile.

"How do you propose to get his cum inside my sister?" I asked. Even if Blake wouldn't force her, others might.

"You let us worry about that," Corinne told me. "Your mother can be very persuasive. Failing that..." She shrugged.

"This has nothing to do with Rebecca, or breeding paranormals," I said sharply. "You want to punish my sister because of me. Because of things you think I've done."

"Your sister is wild and out of control. Bonding is a last resort. If she lashes out at anyone after that, she will have to be taken care of."

"She's not an animal," I growled.

"She's a shifter," Corinne replied. "A hybrid. You've seen first hand how some of them are little more than beasts. Your sister is one of the worst. A failure."

"I've also killed," I pointed out.

"But you're able to keep yourself under control," Corinne pointed out. "Blake and I both witnessed that."

My mouth twisted. "And if you hadn't?"

She didn't reply.

"The day we met. You knew I was coming, didn't you? You and Blake were placed there to pretend to help me escape?"

"It wasn't entirely coincidence," she agreed. "But Fitz was out of control. We were sent to take charge in case he decided to kill you before you could shift. Or worse."

"Gods forbid he managed to get me pregnant and spoil your plans," I said bitterly.

"Believe it or not, we don't want you broken. We'd prefer your complete cooperation. That would be best for all concerned. You could get a great deal of pleasure out of it."

"Believe it or not, I do realise there's more to life than sex." No, really, it's true.

"There doesn't have to be," she said in a tone that would have sounded reasonable had she been talking about anything else. "Lie back and enjoy the ride." She actually looked wistful.

"Because you wish you could do that?" I frowned. That didn't jive with the kickass woman I knew. Or—thought I knew. Hells, she could be the kind of woman who wanted to be barefoot and pregnant, fawning over some guy who went to work in a bank every day. There's nothing wrong with that, of course, but it wasn't what I wanted for myself.

Her expression tightened. "Just use the jar. I'll be back in half an hour to collect it." She turned on her booted heel and slammed the door shut behind her.

"We really need to get out of here," I said. And get Rebecca and Kane out with us, before it was all too late.

Blake sighed and turned the jar over in his fingers. "Yeah. Yeah we do."

23

"COME ON." Blake waved me over to the bed.

I eyed him, but took the few steps closer. He lifted up the blanket and climbed inside before moving over to make room for me. Something in his eyes made me slip in beside him. He tugged the blanket over us, but left a big enough gap to let in some light.

Tongue between his lips, he unscrewed the lid of the specimen jar.

"You can't really mean to—" I stopped short when he peeled back the lid. There, taped underneath was a small, black stone. "That can't be..."

"It's not the same one your mother took," he whispered. "It looks like a piece of it, or a smaller version."

I leaned back. "If that's the case, whose magic is in there? Or is Corinne up to something else?" I wouldn't rule out my mother's involvement either. Or my father for that matter.

"I don't know. The question is, do we try to use it to give you your power back?" He picked at a corner of the tape with his fingernail.

"The bigger question is, can we trust Corinne or not? One minute we can, then we can't. I don't know what to think now." I liked roller coasters as much as the next person, but not like this.

Blake scratched his head. "She's risked a lot to get this stone to us."

"She said to use the jar," I murmured. "Anyone listening would think..." I might have been clutching at straws here. I wanted to believe she was on our side, if only for Blake's sake.

"She was still in on the bonding," I said finally.

Blake's teeth flashed white in the under-blanket gloom. "She might not have had a choice, but she would have known it was something we wanted."

"That's true." I sighed softly. "There was no reason for her to reveal herself to Zeta when we would have chosen that for ourselves. We *did* choose that." I placed a hand on his rear and gave it a playful squeeze.

"Yes, we did. Now, are we going to try this?" He pulled away one side of the tape and left the stone to dangle.

"Maybe you shouldn't touch that," I advised. "It might suck away your magic instead." I wished I could assume that wasn't the intention. Why suck Blake's magic away though? Unless they knew which side he was on.

I shook my head slightly and reached for the stone. Whatever the intent was, I wouldn't let him risk himself for me.

Tentatively, I placed the tip of my little finger on the stone. For a breath or two, nothing happened. Then, with a rush of heat, a trickle of magic surged into my finger. It travelled into my palm and up my arm. From there, it spread around my body like a familiar warmth I hadn't known I'd missed until now.

I could feel it calling out to all the natural elements in the environment around me. I felt Kane in the room beside us. The bond with Blake strengthened, when I hadn't even noticed it having been weaker.

The stone went cold.

"I have my magic back," I said in wonder. "The amount I had before I was ever near the bigger stone." Maybe Corinne sucked it from the other stone somehow. I hoped so, that would mean it was mine to begin with.

Blake grinned. "She should be back soon. Then we can get out of here." He screwed the lid back on the jar and tucked it under the pillow. "No offence to your sister, but my cum is all for you."

I laughed softly. "Just as well." My laughter faded and I snuggled into his arms. "Should we just try to get out now? No offence to your cousin, but I'd prefer to be long gone from here. If she's going to keep pretending she's on their side, it's better if we don't involve her any further."

"Yeah, that's true." Blake looked thoughtful. "Maybe you should hit me over the head and run."

I frowned. "You want to stay?"

"No, but I want you to be safe." He pressed a soft kiss to my lips.

"I'm not leaving without you," I said firmly. "All for one and one for all, or whatever the musketeers said."

"Okay, you win." He sounded relieved. "Is Kane ready?"

I felt through the bond. Kane was sleepy, but trying to stay alert.

"He'll have to be. Let's hope we can leave without having to kill anyone." As long as we snuck, we might just manage it. If not…

We'd cross that bridge when we got to it.

"All right." Blake took my hand and helped me back out of bed.

His hair was messy in the most adorable way. Mine was probably messy like I'd spent the last decade without a hairbrush. This was no time for vanity, I reminded myself, while I patted it back into place. What? A girl has to have some pride, even if she looks like she went backward through a bush.

Blake unlocked the door and eased it open. Lucinda must have assumed it was enough to keep me in. If Blake was on her side and I had no magic, she might be right. With magic, I could pick that bitch in a heartbeat. The lock, I mean, although let's face it, "bitch" applied to Lucinda as well.

The corridor outside our room was dark. No one stood outside Kane's room. In theory, it was easier to lock a shifter in, but that depended on the shifter. Nash would have clawed the door out of the way without a thought.

I felt through the bond for him and the others. They were getting closer, but were more anxious with each passing minute. I sent thoughts of being fine and Blake being fine, too, but it did nothing to assuage their fears.

Men.

Blake put a hand on the lock to Kane's room. The click as it unlocked echoed through the corridor. It couldn't have been that loud, but it seemed deafening.

I flinched and pressed myself against the wall while Blake eased the door open.

Kane leapt out and swung a fist at Blake's face. He connected hard enough to knock Blake back a few steps.

"You fucker," Kane growled. "We should have known you're on Zeta's side. I'm going to knock your fucking block off." Before he could advance on Blake, I grabbed his arm and held him back.

"It's okay, he's with me," I whispered as loud as I dared.

Kane froze. "I heard him downstairs. Him and his cousin."

"They were pretending," I said quickly. "Like you were pretending to sleep."

Kane frowned, but his body relaxed slightly. "Are you sure?"

"I'm sure of Blake," I said firmly. "The jury is still out on Corinne. Come on, we need to get out of here before anyone comes."

Kane nodded. "Sorry, mate. I just assumed…"

Blake rubbed his jaw. "Yeah, it's okay, mate."

"You two are starting to sound like Leo," I joked.

"I'm not sure if that's a good thing or not." Kane took my hand and we walked silently toward the stairs.

"Better than getting all bossy like Nash." I smiled.

Kane snorted softly. "Nah, I'll leave all the leader-ish things to him and you."

"Me?" I started to say something else but stopped to listen. "I think I hear someone." Considering the amount of noise we had made already, that likely went both ways.

"It might be Corinne," Blake whispered.

It might, but it might also be someone else. I doubted my parents, sister, and Macintosh were the only people in the building. Just because I hadn't seen or heard anyone, didn't mean they weren't here. Gods, there could be rooms of witches locked away.

"They're getting closer," Kane said.

"Can you shift? You could get out of here now. Or at least check the coast is clear."

"I can try." He let my hand go and without a sound, shifted into his adorable—I mean kickass—owl form. His clothes fell to the floor. I grabbed up a shirt and his underpants, while Blake tossed his pants, socks and shoes back into his room. We couldn't very well leave them lying around to be found.

He flapped through the darkened corridor and landed on the top of the bannister leading downstairs. If he was an actual owl, he would have had my blessing to leave a big poop on the fancy timber railing.

Hells, as a shifter, he had my blessing, but he didn't do it. Of course not, he had more class than the people holding us here.

He shuffled his wings and sent a warning through the bond. Whoever was coming, it wasn't Corinne.

Shit.

"Time to go invisible." I grabbed Blake's hand and formed a bubble around us. He could do that for himself, but I might lose him in the darkness.

"I know you're here, Peyton." Lucinda's voice drifted up the stairs just before she appeared. "I'm disappointed your guard turned out to be such a failure, but I anticipated that. He can't keep you both invisible for long, you know."

I let out a soft breath. So she had no idea I had my magic back. I could just reach out with a tendril and give her a shove...

She moved away from the stairs.

Bugger.

"It's unfortunate you chose to break the promise to stay and do your duty," she went on. "I should have raised you better." She stopped and seemed to sniff the air. Was it possible she was also a hybrid of some kind? The thought didn't occur to me before, but I was almost certain she wasn't.

"You don't need to respond, I can hear you thinking."

I was very certain no paranormal had that kind of ability, outside a bond, and we definitely weren't bonded. Well, outside the parent slash child bond, but that was diminishing by the moment.

I tugged on Blake's hand and pulled him closer to the stairs.

"You failed to make your owl invisible," Lucinda pointed out.

I hoped she missed him in the dark, but evidently I was wrong.

She drew in magic and threw a ball of it toward Kane. It struck him and knocked him backward in a shower of feathers.

"Kane!" I shouted before I could stop myself.

Lucinda spun and aimed the magic right at me.

I dropped into a crouch and the magic sailed over my head.

"That was too close," Blake said in my ear. Before I could stop him, he rose out of the bubble, fully visible for anyone to see.

"Leave her alone," he growled. He drew his own magic and went to throw it at Lucinda. Before it even left his hand, she blasted him square in the centre of his chest. He was knocked back off his feet. He hit the wall hard and slid to the floor with a thud.

"You bitch!" I cried out.

"Well, well, well." Lucinda circled slowly. "You have your magic back. It seems I have more than one traitor in my midst. No matter, she'll end up like her precious cousin."

I glanced toward Blake and bit back a sob. He lay still.

I rose and let the magic go. "The only other one who is going to die here is you," I said, my tone dangerously cold. I forced back tears. I couldn't lose focus now. Blake might be dead, Kane too, but I had to deal with Lucinda.

"You can't kill her," a new voice spoke from the top of the stairs. I hadn't heard Rebecca approach, but she was here now.

"Says who?" I asked icily.

"Says me," Rebecca replied. "I won't let you." She curled her hands into claws and started forward.

2 4

I TOOK A STEP BACK. It was a lucky thing I did, or I might have been stepped on by Rebecca's enormous feet.

No, I'm not big-feet shaming my sister, she shifted into what I assumed was her chimera form. Her head was now that of a lioness. Another head that looked like a goat stuck out her back. Her tail looked like a series of snakes, whipping back and forth.

She looked pissed. No, that was an understatement, she looked like fury itself. And every drop was directed at Lucinda.

"Let me guess, you didn't want me to kill her because you want the honour?" I asked. "I'm not sure that's the answer. We could take her back to the Paranormal Council and they could—"

Rebecca swiped a clawed foot at Lucinda's midsection.

Lucinda ducked away and threw a ball of magic at her elder child.

"Or not." Now I *wanted* to be seen, in case Rebecca accidentally clawed me. I sensed she didn't mean me any harm, but she almost hit me with her swaying tails once or twice. All of her attention, however, was on Lucinda.

I considered helping her, but at that moment Blake groaned. That was followed immediately by a heavy thud right above my head.

"Looks like the cavalry has arrived."

The thud was followed by a scraping and tearing on the roof. The ceiling started to break apart and rain down plaster on our heads.

Half a breath later, a dragon nose poked through a hole in the ceiling.

"Oh, hey Nash," I said lightly. "You're just in time."

He snorted softly and ripped the hole wide enough to let Dyson and Leo drop down beside me.

"Peyton, darlin', I was wondering where you got to. Remind me never to ride on the back of a dragon again." Leo gave me a quick hug and Dyson did the same a moment later.

"Where's Matt?" I asked at the same time Dyson asked, "Where's Kane?"

"Matt is alerting the council," Leo said.

"Kane was near the stairs." Torn between looking for the owl shifter and checking on Blake, I settled for the latter when the guys ducked past Rebecca's tails and hurried to search.

By now, Lucinda was backed up against a wall. I guessed I was right, she wasn't a hybrid. Right now, she just looked like a scared woman. I almost felt sorry for her. Almost.

"Rebecca, listen to reason," she called out in a thin voice. "What would your father think?"

"He seemed to think the same as you did," I said. I kept my distance from Rebecca, but stepped closer to Lucinda while inching toward Blake. I poked around in the bond in the hope of rousing him a little more. "Why should we give either of you mercy?"

Blake's eyelids flickered.

"We are your parents," she insisted. She tried a different tack. "Your father wanted the best for you. He spoilt you, I suppose, but you know he adores you."

"He has a shit way of showing it," I replied. I flinched as the ceiling behind me collapsed a little further and Nash dropped to the carpeted floor.

Lucinda's eyes flicked between the hybrids.

"This is Nash," I said conversationally. "He's not happy about your behaviour either. He'd prefer not to bite your head off, but he will if he has to. Right, honey?"

Nash bobbed his head.

"I…" Lucinda swallowed. "Nash is not his real name—"

"I don't care what his real name is," I said firmly. "He can call himself Bob Down if he wants to." I understood then. Lucinda was one of the people who arranged for hybrids like Nash and Matt to be raised the way they were. They ran from her and others like her. It must be taking everything inside Nash not to shred her like cooked chicken. He wouldn't though, unless it was a last resort. He was better than that. Better than her.

Rebecca, apparently tired of all the chatting, let out a growl and resumed closing in on Lucinda. She moved up the corridor enough to let me get to Blake.

"Blake?" I put a hand on his shoulder. I didn't dare to shake him, in case I hurt him worse.

He groaned and opened his eyes a crack. "I'm all right. I think." He winced as he raised one arm, then the other and wriggled his fingers. "Nothing's broken except my pride."

"Can you move? We should give these guys some space." I helped him to his feet. He staggered the few steps to the top of the stairs and sat down out of sight.

Just as he did, Leo and Dyson appeared from the corridor on the other side of the stairs.

"We found Kane." Dyson's voice broke on as he spoke his brother's name. "He's…"

My heart sank. The words choked my throat. "He can't be."

Dyson blinked. "Oh no, he's not dead. He has a broken arm and probably leg. We'll need some help to get him out of here."

I stared. "Later, remind me to sock you for scaring me like that."

Dyson gave me a half smile, half grimace. "Yeah, sorry."

"Mate, don't fuck with a lady's… Don't fuck with a lady." Leo clapped him on the back. "Or a chimera. Bloody hells, she's impressive. It must run in the family."

I smiled. "Probably."

My smile faded when I turned to see Lucinda pinned between two huge talons. Her face was pale, eyes wide with terror.

I felt nothing, not even a hint of sympathy for my egg donor.

"She's not a good person," Blake said.

"No, she's really not, but—" I winced and turned my face as Rebecca drove a talon right through one of Lucinda's eyes. Blood squirted out all over my sister and the carpet. In moments, the expensive pile was slick and red.

"Yuck," Leo groaned. "Have I mentioned I'm really not good with gore?"

"Yeah." I leaned away from Blake so I didn't get him when I vomited all over the floor. "Neither am I."

Rebecca shifted back into human form and fell to the ground, sobbing and rocking back and forth.

I hesitated for a moment, then wiped my mouth and went to crouch beside her. Slowly and tentatively, I put an arm around her. She was covered in blood, slick with it. I had to remind myself not to think too hard about whose it was.

"I'm sorry she did all of that to you." Truthfully, I suspected I hadn't scratched the surface of whatever "all of that" might entail. Maybe I never would.

"I've been wanting to do that for a long time," Rebecca whispered. Her face was so pale I thought she might be in shock. I couldn't blame her for that. I was pretty shocked myself.

"Yeah, I don't think you're alone in that."

"No, she's not." Nash was back in human form and wrapped in someone's jacket. I thought it might be Leo's. "The council is coming. They'll search the place and figure out what else was going on here." His expression was just this side of a thundercloud ready to burst.

"They're here," Matt's voice came from the stairs. He appeared with a grim look on his face to match Nash's. "They've been trying to find this place for some time." He took one look at Rebecca and pulled off his shirt to offer it to her.

I took it with a nod and wrapped the fabric around her shoulders.

After a moment, she tugged it the rest of the way on. Blood soaked into the fabric, but at least she had some modesty.

I rose and moved closer to Matt so I could speak without Rebecca hearing. "My father is here somewhere too. He knew."

Matt gave a curt nod. "I'll let them know."

"Corinne is on our side," Blake said from his spot against the wall.

"We think," I said with a nod.

"She's been keeping the council apprised as best she could," Matt assured us. To me, he said, "There's someone downstairs to see you."

I nodded. "I think we'll need some help to get down. Some more than others."

Dyson and Leo carried Kane between them. His arm and leg were both at odd angles and I felt his pain through the bond now he was closer, but he was alive, thank the gods.

Nash and Matt helped Blake and Rebecca. I walked behind them, not touching, but near enough to know the other was there. We missed so much already. I hoped some day she'd be ready to handle having a crazy sister who had so many guys in her life. One day at a time on that score.

We passed a handful of what I assumed were representatives of the council. They were talking in low voices, several to women in various stages of pregnancy. Each woman had that haunted look in their eyes, but at least now they were free to raise their children without Zeta taking them and experimenting on them. That so easily could have been me. My heart went out to each of them. Doing their so-called duty took its toll. They would need a lot of support in the coming years.

"Peyton!" Another familiar voice greeted me when we stepped out the front door and Ariana threw herself into my arms.

"Ariana, why are you here?" I hugged her tightly.

"Hamish and I were on our way to school when we heard what your mother did. We might have followed Nash." She shot him a sweet smile.

He responded with a frown, but said nothing. What could he say? We all got out alive and more or less in one piece. Without my mother and with the help of the Paranormal Council, hopefully Zeta's breeding program was at an end.

I had a suspicion Zeta itself would go on in one evil form or another, but if they stopped trying to impregnate me against my will, I would appreciate it. I'd quite like a quiet life for a while. I had studies to finish, a job to find, and a life to make with my guys.

"I have great news, too," Ariana said. "Guess what?"

"You're crazy and I'm not?" I replied automatically. "Wait, we all know that isn't true."

Ariana grinned. "No, you're just as crazy as I am. But it's better than that. The Academy of Modern Magic has a new campus! It's up in the—"

I only half listened while we walked out to waiting cars. With any luck, the new campus would be safe for the rest of the school year and the years to come. Maybe I would teach there some day.

Nash slipped a hand in mine and drew me to him as we walked.

Matt took my other hand in his.

I sent them both thoughts of love through the bond. They sent it back. My heart was so full I thought it might burst. This was the best part about the future. The bit I was looking forward to the most. Spending time getting to know and love all my guys.

I don't know how I got so lucky, but I was going to spend the rest of my life enjoying every single second of it.

EPILOGUE

"You look hot, sir." Nash in a suit was enough to make my mouth dry. The sight was almost as good as Nash *out* of a suit.

"I hate this shit," Nash grumbled. He sighed out his nose and cupped my cheek. He ran his thumb over my lips. "I know it's your graduation rehearsal, but this formal crap sucks. I'd rather be alone with you somewhere."

Before I could respond, his phone rang. He looked at the number and scowled before he put the phone to his ear.

"What?"

No one could ever accuse Nash of wasting words.

His scowl deepend.

"What is it?" I whispered.

Nash shook his head. "You already owe me about four favours, Evans," he growled.

He listened for a moment.

I strained to hear, but couldn't catch more than a word or two. Something about car full of paranormals, and Zeta. I grimaced.

"Fuck." Nash sighed. "Where?" A moment later, he added, "Yep."

He ended the call. He was almost smiling. "How would you like to skip the rehearsal and tear off some Zeta heads?"

I grinned. "Let's do it."

THANKS FOR READING.

Come back to the Zetaverse for a whole new adventure in Summoned by Fire, book 1 of Harmony's Magic.

Yes, I know the epilogue is intended to draw you into the new series, but if you liked this one, then you'll LOVE Harmony.

Try it. I dare you.

ABOUT THE AUTHOR

Maggie Alabaster is the pen name of Australian author Mirren Hogan. Mirren lives in NSW, Australia with one spouse, two daughters, dog, cat, and countless birds.

Sign up for my newsletter! Sign Up!
Join my reader group! Join here!
Follow me on Bookbub! Click here to follow me!

Jingle All the Way

Also by Maggie Alabaster and Erin Yoshikawa

Caught by the Tide

Book 1–Pursued by Shadows

Book 2 Pursued by Darkness

Book 3 Pursued by Monsters